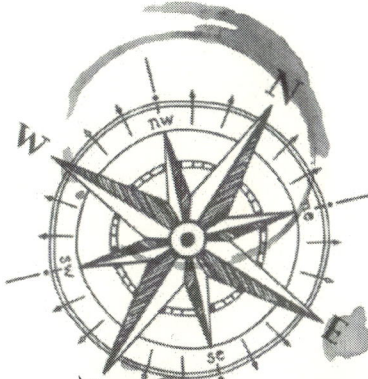

The Gift of the Sea

of the Sea

Book 1 of the Harmony Series

by

T. BISHOP

Cover image – Carlos Eduardo Du, via Pixabay

Cover font – Booter Zero Zero

Internal font - Garamond

Internal Illustrations use vintage vector created by freepik - freepik.com

First Printing, 2020

ISBN 9798553827359

For more, see @t_bishop_writes

To the ones who believed in my dreams before I was brave enough to do so on my own. And to my guardian angel, well... guardian Alice. Without her, this book wouldn't have been possible.

"He felt that there is a loose balance of good and evil, and that the art of living consists in getting the greatest good out of the greatest evil."

~ Machado de Assis, Iaiá Garcia

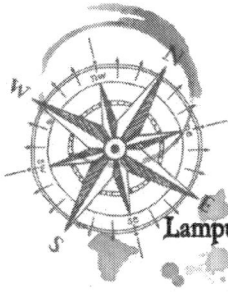

Chapter 1: Hanna

13 April 1691
Lampung Bay, Sumatera, Dutch East Indies

Pain, strong and sharp up my nostrils wakes me up from a dreamless sleep. My eyes fly open and the iron-ish scent moves to envelop my tongue, covering every taste bud, until my mouth is just as polluted as my sense of smell. The sheer strength of the aroma pulls me into a sitting position; it's nauseating. I fling off my thin sheet and throw my legs over the side of the mattress, over the side of comfort, warmth, and safety, onto the night-chilled wooden floor of the early-morning cabin.

I run through the cottage, not stopping for my or Demetrius's boots sitting neatly by the front door. My heart pounds as I yank the door open and take my first step onto the chilly sands. I don't bother being careful with the door; it slams closed behind me as I put on a burst of speed towards the thrashing sea.

I scan the now gray-ish water, dirtied by debris and soot. It twists and folds into itself unnaturally as a huge ship bobs out there like an apple in a bucket. It's nearly twenty-five feet in length, it's probably once-shiny chestnut wood mangled and penetrated by many great, gaping holes. The white sails, still smoking in places, are just as riddled with blackened holes. The flag is decimated into unrecognizable tatters. Its hull is completely submerged and waves push at the objects cluttering the ocean. The still-cloying smell and faint trails of smoke billowing from the wreck are the only evidence of the fire that must have played a part in the ship's final moments.

I sweep the horizon, biting the inside of my cheek, frantically searching the waters. Different sized wooden crates, bits of plank, barrels, bits of ship, spools of unbound ropes, all bob around the tremulous crests. Bodies. All unmoving, only given life from the rocking of the ocean.

I dodge a sand dune and am almost to the shoreline when I see a scrap of black fabric dragged onto the sands by the upset waves. It catches on a stone as the water recedes.

Deme… where are you?!

Seeing no sign of my guardian, I stoop down to pick it up and unfurl the water-logged fabric, seeing no visible marking or symbol. Then I turn it over and almost drop the cursed object back where it came from.

Looking back at me is a face I'd hoped – prayed – I'd never see again. Its white dye beginning to bleed and crack from the water, a hollowed, eyeless skull. Its toothless mouth hangs wide in an almost sinister greeting. Two bones crossed below it. Everyone knows this symbol, even the poorest villager.

Pirates. This is a pirate ship.

This time I really do drop the piece of cloth, stepping away from the shore and the sinful piece of fabric with its devil's mark. My heart pounding in my ears is now a terrible storm, so strong my entire body is shaking.

Rough hands grab too hard at my arms, pushing me down a dimly candle lit corridor…

The sudden remembered smell of mold, rot and too much brine eclipses the smell of smoke, as the monsters of my past threaten to crack away at my carefully crafted armor.

"No…" My voice is weak, even to my own ears.

I take another step back, legs trembling hard, then turn to bolt from my worst nightmare brought to life, back to the safety and comfort of my home… when a flash of white hair against the thrashing sea freezes my steps.

A survivor? An old man…?

The urge to jump into the unknown nearly drowns me, and only magnifies as I watch the helpless, motionless pirate cling to a plank of wood barely staying afloat. My indecision cripples me, a vice squeezing the air from my lungs. I can't breathe. I can't think. Everything's moving too fast around me, quicker than I can keep up with, quicker than I think I can handle.

Just as I feel like I'm about to be swept off my feet completely, the small flash of white dips out of my view as a wave crests and knocks the small plank around like a tree in a windstorm. My heart leaps and I find myself re-taking the steps I previously retracted. I add one more, then another, then I'm running as fast as I can toward the ocean. My mind barely has time to question what my body is doing before I'm shedding my slip and tossing it onto the sand. I spare a quick glance about as I run into the surf, then raise my hands high above my head and dive into the cold, unsettled waters.

The moment I'm completely submerged, a pleasant burn begins in the soles of my feet then expands, ropes of warm flame coursing up my legs, altering them. I fall in the comforting arms of the sea, letting it cool me as the rush of my transformation spreads into my hips. There's a soft tugging, then a sudden shift. It doesn't hurt anymore. It used to, in the beginning, but now I relish it, crave the sensations of what two things becoming one feels like, what feeling complete feels like. I keep my clasped hands high above my head as I push forward toward the surface, gliding easily as I beat my tail fin behind me, hardly even a thought anymore.

I break the surface, my dark purple tail fin following after. The tips of my fluke ripple the surface and the small scales of my lower half catch the sun, reflecting it back into my eyes. I release a slow breath, stretch out in the water, and give a hard beat of my fin, energy flowing into my arms as I propel myself toward the wreck of the ship and its seemingly sole survivor. Even if they are pirates, I feel pity for the fallen squirming its way into my heart… But I clamp down on that and sidle up to the half-submerged plank the old man is clinging to, face down, hands dirty and bloody.

I maneuver to his side and rest a soft hand on his back, immediately feeling the gentle rise and fall under my palm, the steady pounding of a heartbeat. Thank the stars, just unconscious. Let's hope he didn't cave his head in…

I turn to survey my surroundings and my stomach immediately gives a dangerous roll as I see the multiple bodies floating around me. I give the closest ones a look over to make sure no one else has managed to make it through the sinking of the ship and what must have been a most bloody battle. I bounce around the sooty waters, vehemently hoping to see a twitch of life, a splash of distress, anything. But, as I see no motion besides that caused by the rocking waves, my spark of pity flares into grief for the lives wastefully lost today, even ones as unsavory as these.

I shake my head sadly, turning my full attention to the living human next to me, grabbing his shoulder as gently as possible and tugging. I'm surprised how light he is and how easily I roll him onto the trunk of my tail, using myself as a makeshift table. He's obviously malnourished. I twist my torso to better tend to his possible injuries. First, I'll check the head for any lumps or gashes. I use one hand to steady the human and use the other to lift his chin to better look into his face. I gasp out loud. The jawline is soft, hairless, and the mop of white hair I'd seen from the shore isn't white from age, but pale blonde bleached from its time under the sun's harsh rays.

And it isn't a man. It's a young woman!

Her eyes, almost hidden behind waterlogged hair, flutter before slowly opening at the sound of my gasp. They are the color of foggy, stormy skies and they meet mine for only a moment before closing again.

I suck my cheek into my back teeth and try to make my heart slow as I hold the once again unconscious woman to my chest. What have I gotten myself and Demetrius involved in?

I sigh, then lower my upper body more fully into the water. The woman lifts from my tail, buoyed by the water for a moment, until I flip her onto her back and catch her beneath her armpits, keeping her above the water with my right arm. Her head lolls against my shoulder. Then, clearing a path through the debris and swollen bodies with my other arm, I beat my tail fin and propel us swiftly back towards the shore, retracing the path I'd taken to reach her. I don't take my eyes off the fair corn-silk crown of her head, carefully ensuring her pale face remains free of the muck of the ocean. Is she a pirate? *Could* she be one? Deme's never mentioned female pirates, and I've certainly never seen any.

I slide the unconscious woman onto the beach, the froth of the surf lapping at her dripping body, tugging at her bare feet, and look around furtively, checking no one's been drawn by the commotion. Our quiet piece of paradise is still clear of prying eyes, so I turn into a sitting position and carefully slide onto the sand. Then, with a deep breath, I heft my entire tail out of the shallows, holding it in the air. The moment the air hits it, the transformation back to my human form begins. It's much quicker than the transformation to mermaid, but not as painless. The pleasurable burn I felt on entering the water is now a sharp tearing, like parchment being suddenly ripped in two. I close my eyes and remember to breathe as the intense pain becomes almost unbearable. I slowly come back to myself and thank the gods I no longer go utterly mad and sob every time I revert, thinking my legs broken and incapable of working correctly again. Grand days *those* were…

I wait for the pinpricks to fully fade from the pads of my feet before rotating on my bum away from the water, and gently drop my legs onto the sand. I exhale, peek at the woman, and send a silent prayer to whatever god was responsible for keeping her unconscious through all of this.

I climb to my feet, scoop up my slip I'd carelessly tossed aside earlier, give it a shake, pull it back over my head, and tug it down over my body. Then I pull my heavy, dark waist length hair free from the collar and throw it over my shoulder. I hesitate only a moment before scooping the female into my arms, one hand under her knees, the other under the hair at the nape of her neck.

I'm at a slight loss as to what to do now I have this assumed pirate actually *on* land. So, I do the only thing I can think of; what I always do. Go to the cabin and heal, the rest can wait. I nod to reinforce the confident, commanding voice in my head and trudge through the sand, focusing on my path to the door instead of what my next steps should be when I get inside.

At least there's a safe, solid 'inside' for me to get us into, and for that, I'm grateful. Demetrius had built the cabin himself long before the land was known as the Dutch East Indies. He *still* calls this place the Netherlands East Indies. He hadn't wanted to be stifled by the town's colonizing, or the restrictions of being indoors, but still wanted to experience what it meant to be 'human'.

He'd made it medium sized; three rooms with a small flume through the roof for our cooking range. He'd told me he'd only used logs from trees that had met their end naturally to build it, all laid horizontally on top of one another, interlocked and notched together at the corners to create the walls. I'd asked him how he managed it all by himself, when I was old enough to string together the question; a question to which he'd simply replied: 'very carefully.' All the joints and gaps left after construction were packed tight with moss he'd gathered, sealing out the brisk winds that sometimes whip up during the rainy season.

The roof had been wooden too, until five years ago when the town started building their homes out of brick or stone. Two of the inland villagers made the half-day trek to our cabin to offer their building services, for a fee of course, and now our roof is triangular and ridged to let the rain run off and keep the doorway and windows dry. It offsets the natural elements of the cabin - the moss-covered walls and wooden beams – with a pale, washed out sandstone. It's simple; Demetrius wouldn't allow much else. The builders had come back later to try and convince him to bring the whole cabin down and rebuild entirely in stone or brick; they said it would be better insulated – cooler in the scorching summers, dry and warm during the cold nights. Deme had not-so-kindly yelled a Finnish word at them, one I still don't know the meaning of, then slammed the door in their faces. Though they had never returned, Deme had gathered more moss and covered the entire roof with it, just to spite them. So now our cabin, with its rugged wooden base, mossy joints, pale sandstone edges peeking through the green roof, and casement windows that still open on rusty, slightly noisy hinges, reminds me of something from the fairy stories Demetrius read to me as a child. It's odd, cozy, and warm, cradled by the sounds of the ocean and the wide skies. It's home. Safe.

And now, benevolent Poseidon watch over me, I'm mere steps from bringing an outsider, a stranger, a possible pirate, in.

I'm about to shift the arm supporting her neck to try and open the door when I catch movement from the corner of my eye. It stills my hand, though I already know who it is, even before fully turning my head.

6

Demetrius, both hands full with woven baskets nearly overflowing with items from the market, his tall, lean torso clothed in a billowy, white cotton shirt beneath his heavy dark gray cloak that hangs to his shins. Those plain gray trousers and black square-toed shoes he always wears to market. A look of worry causes his usual easy smile to be wiped clean, his thin lips tightly puckered, and his almost luminescent emerald eyes darkened with concern. "You risked your life for that human? How unlike you, Hanna."

His expression quickly shifts to one of great curiosity, though, as he closes the space between us. The worry in my chest dissolves immediately at the accusation in his words, contorting into annoyance at him not being around when I needed him.

I shift the woman in my arms, hardening my gaze as I stare up at him. "How nice of you to finally join us, Demetrius. I could have used your assistance ten minutes ago."

He flashes me all his teeth as he grins, holding up both his baskets, almost like a peace offering. "I was in town picking up supplies when I heard whispers from the villages of a pirate ship and smoke on the southern horizon. I came as soon as I was able to. I was worried for your safety…"

He eyes the human still cradled in my arms, suspicion and curiosity vying for control. "It seems I was correct. What do you plan on doing with… *her*?"

The way he says '*her*' has an odd chill lancing up my spine; I have the sudden urge to shield the unconscious woman from his impenetrable gaze. I sigh, pulling his attention back to my face. He cocks his head, raising one arched brow. I feel like he can see the thought that's just raced through my head.

I pull myself to my full height, which sadly isn't much. "I plan on taking her inside and healing her, if you can manage to open the door for me without one of your games."

He blinks a few times, taken aback, then bursts into his deep rumbling laughter. He shifts both baskets into his right hand before grasping the door handle, an exaggerated pout curling his lips. "Is that any way to speak to the one who raised you these last twelve years? The one that *still* watches over you, even now? I'm

7

certain I did not teach you to address your elders that way." He brings his hand to his chest, feigning distraught pain, fluttering his long, dark eyelashes dramatically as he pushes open our front door.

I roll my eyes and move past him into the cool half-light inside. "Are all water nymphs dramatic babes? Or is it another one of your special attributes?"

His outraged squawk sounds behind me as he follows me inside, closing the door behind us. "You wound me deeply, child," is his only reply.

I sigh for what feels like the dozenth time since Deme returned; he's always been very capable of doing this to me. "And you are avoiding my question." I cross the small communal living area and head into the biggest room in our cabin, my bedchamber, not bothering to wait for a response.

Uncaring of the state of her dress, I lay her carefully onto the goose feather mattress. She doesn't so much as twitch a finger at being moved. I feel Deme at my shoulder but ignore him in favor of getting my first good look at the lone survivor of the wreck.

Her clothes are odd. Her dirty white shirt is noticeably oversized despite still clinging wetly to her small body. Her trousers are like Demetrius's, hugging her lower half, tears in the fabric at her thighs and ankles. An odd assortment of straps, buckles and trinkets hang around her hips. A thin bangle around her slim wrist has miraculously survived the wreck and the sea, even when her boots did not. Her sun-lightened hair splays about her head in a stringy, pale halo. She has an oval face, a softer jawline than Deme's, but more angular than mine. Her cheeks are void of any baby fat, brows thin and pulled downward as if contemplating something very deeply, despite being unconscious. The left brow has a small but deep-looking gash through it.

"Deme, could you please get me the –"

"The vari-essence?" He's already holding out a strip of fabric and the small vial of clear liquid.

It'll help the wound heal quicker and lessen the chance of infection. I give him a small smile as I take the offered items. I uncork the vial, dump a small amount of the bitter-smelling liquid onto the cloth and gently dab at the cut. As I dab, I look over the rest of her face, using my free hand to push gently on her head, feeling for any more cuts, bumps or worrying soft spots. To my surprise, despite the ruined clothes and gash on her brow, she seems otherwise unharmed. She's been extremely fortunate. Someone was watching over her. I guess we'll find out soon if that fortune is a blessing or a curse.

As I pull my hand away, I catch sight of a faint silver scar marring her top lip; it loops down from the left before disappearing between the seam of her lips. I'm leaning forward suddenly, toward the scar, like an insect drawn towards a lantern. Just before I touch it with the tip of my finger, Demetrius lays a hand on my shoulder. I look up into his face, a question on mine. He only smiles and ruffles my hair, something he hasn't done since I was a child.

"Come, let our guest rest. I am certain the Peranakan Cina will have quite the tale to tell us when she rises."

I frown. "*What* did you call her?"

"She's a Peranakan Cina…" Deme gazes thoughtfully at the woman. "Chinese, in modern tongue, and…" he absently touches her white-blonde hair, "somewhere else." He glances at me again and smirks. "She cannot get her proper rest if you are hovering at her elbow."

His grin turns more teasing as heat rises to my face. I straighten and shove the vial and now-soiled cloth towards the infuriating nymph. He chuckles and accepts them, then jerks his pointed chin toward the door, signaling me to follow. I do, begrudgingly, closing the door behind us softly.

He goes into our small kitchen to dispose of the medical herbs as I sit on the bench in our living area with yet another sigh. I've been doing that far too much lately. I cup my chin in my palm and prop my elbow on my thigh. This entire day has been confounding since I opened my eyes. Deme hovers by my side a moment before joining me on the bench, taking my free hand and gently lacing our fingers, pressing our palms tightly together.

9

He looks at me, his bright smile wilting slightly around the edges. "You remind me of your mother when you wear that puzzled look."

I resist the immediate urge to pull my hand from his at the mention of my mother. "Don't compare me to that... *woman.* That fool and I have nothing in common."

He squeezes my fingers, his jaw flexing as he swallows. "Do not speak ill of the dead, Hanna. Your mother was a dear friend to me, and a good spirit."

Tears sting my eyes, and a lump fills my throat as I remember the day of my tenth year. "She got herself slain... left me with him, then after *hell,* he sold me off to the highest bidder..." I sniffle, gripping his fingers like they alone have the power to hold me together. "If you hadn't found me on land two years later, I would be dead, or worse..."

My tears flow freely now, and when Demetrius moves to wrap his long arm around my shoulders, I let him; he pulls me against him.

"Han, your mother loved you. She tried her best to do right by you. You know the Gift's magic... I'm not trying to make excuses for her, but even I could not foresee Kai's betrayal... he could be quite charming when he was not –"

A growl slips from between my lips before I can stop it. "Wasn't being *what,* Deme? A no good, dirty rotten pirate?!"

Now it's his turn to sigh. "Pirates cannot *all be* rotten, Han. You just rescued one, unprompted. Now why is that?"

I jerk my head to look at him, anger momentarily cooled by curiosity. I blame Demetrius for this particular character flaw of mine. "So, she *is* a pirate? You never told me about female pirates. Can a woman truly be one?"

His lips twist, before he quirks his head to the side, pondering. "People can be anything they wish to be, if only they know the proper way to do so." He prods my cheek with a finger. "Now who is avoiding answering questions?"

Not knowing and not answering are two very different things, but I have no energy to try and out-wordsmith him right now. I stand abruptly and he doesn't try to stop me.

"I'm going for a swim."

I turn my back on him and cross the drawing room in three long strides.

"Swim safe, Han." His voice is a soft, even tenor.

I nod in response, open the door and exit, leaving my guardian sitting on the bench and the strange, unconscious pirate in my bed.

***

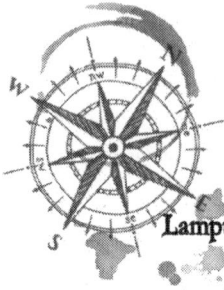

Chapter 2: Una
15 April 1691
Lampung Bay, Sumatera, Dutch East Indies

I blink slowly, terror twisting my guts. The pounding in my head is unbearable, like the time the grog turned sour and turned the entire crew's stomachs, mine included. I smell bitter medicinal herbs as my mind focuses. The fear I'd immediately felt upon waking dims slightly. A healer means I'm not about to become shark bait. I sit up gingerly, bringing my hand to my temple, feeling a split in my eyebrow. What the hell?! The vague memory of concerned lilac eyes suddenly flashes through my head. That's right… a lass rescued me, pulled me from the ocean's death grip. I flex my hands and notice my knuckles are swollen and scabbed. The glint of the brass bangle snaring my wrist has me glancing away, an uncomfortable knot in my gut. I'm glad it's still there but it angers me. So, I take quick stock of the rest of me instead. Everything is moving. Nothing seems to be missing. Other than my head and the scrapes on my hands, I'm all in one piece. By all accounts, that's a bloody miracle.

I breathe through my confused thoughts, focusing on taking in my surroundings instead. I'm in a bed chamber. Some would probably say it's a modest size, but it's a whole-arse castle to me. The bed coverings are cotton. The walls are soft blue, reminding me of the sea, and lining those walls, shiny oak bookshelves lined with leather-bound books, so many they outnumber everything else in the chamber. On the opposite wall, hung on display - weapons. Muskets, a flintlock blunderbuss, even a cutlass. All old, but well cared-for. Who in three hells is this rapscallion? But the unease is short lived as I realize I can hear waves, out there, beyond the walls. And there's a fine sheen of sand dusting the floor, piled into corners and edges. I must be close to the shore!

Next to those shelves is a waist-height chest of drawers made of deep, dark mahogany, inlaid with even darker walnut veneer. It has four horizontal inlaid panels, one on top the other, and it easily costs more than everything I currently have to my name. Perched on top, a rectangular draughts board, some sort of faded yellow curling map, and a towering, almost toppling pile of thick-spined tomes. *Who in three hells is this rapscallion?!*

I carefully toss the blanket aside. A cold chill runs up my spine as my bare feet meet a smooth, cool wooden floor. With a tentative wince, I stand, and again, am amazed at the lack of pain or injury as I walk quietly across the room, peering at the odd books on the bookshelf that's taller than me. I can read some of the titles. *Atlas* – that means maps! But the lettering on some of them is beyond my understanding.

I turn to the opposite wall with the weapons. These are all well within my understanding. I finger the handle of the ancient-looking but well-kept cutlass and I'm just about to pull from its hook when a wave of dizziness has me nearly falling as my vision spins. I lean against the nearest wall, gripping my pounding head. I need to get a blasted grip on myself. I don't have time for this… every moment wasted here is another moment Elyse gets further and further from my grasp.

My vision clears. I grip the gleaming cutlass hilt and pull it from the wall, testing its weight, getting used to the feel of it in my palm. I'm not in full condition to fight, but just in case I can't slip out unnoticed, better to have some form of weapon. Don't need to use it well to threaten someone.

I turn, slower than the last time in case the dizziness returns, and edge towards the door, pressing my ear against it, listening for any signs of life. I don't hear anyone. No movement except the familiar roll and crash of waves out there somewhere. Getting out of here before someone does return is more important than pillaging further, though my inner scallywag wilts as I turn from what's surely a goldmine right here in this room and grip the door handle. With a tentative push of my shoulder, it opens.

I tiptoe through what's clearly a living area, barely sparing the rest of the home a second glance as I edge closer to the front door, closer to my freedom. The knob suddenly begins turning from the other side, my fingers inches from grasping it. I take a wobbly step back, gripping the cutlass tightly. Shite… I'm in no condition to fight… but – I rotate the shoulder holding my only line of defense against whoever's coming through that door – that's never stopped me before.

Before I can fully decide on my plan of attack, the door opens and in walks the lilac-eyed stranger that plucked me from the sea, a basket of fruits in her arms. She's haloed by sunshine. I see sand and the silver, glittering band of ocean behind her. Our eyes meet. I remain silent, cutlass raised, holding my ground and her gaze.

Her mouth drops open to speak but I lunge forward, the butt of my blade already aimed for her temple. I tower over the lass by a solid four inches, it'd be an easy line up, a 'one hit and out cold' situation.

Except that's not how it plays out.

Her eyes widen as she steps sideways, dodging my strike completely, bringing her basket up as a shield between us, before shoving it into my face and kicking out one of her bare feet. On a good day I'd dodge the half-hearted kick but leaping back so quickly has the room spinning again and I'm suddenly flat on my arse, the cutlass clattering loudly onto the wooden floor.

The lass leaps after me, grasping the pommel and bringing the point of the weapon inches from my nose. It's such a fluid motion, I'm momentarily startled. Her waist-length midnight-dark hair flicks about her unfitted dress

A look of shock flashes across her face as if she's surprised by her own speed and actions, the tip of the sword dropping a moment before she steels her nerves and straightens her pale arm.

A tight-lipped, almost forced, smile comes to her lips. "You're finally awake. You were unconscious for two whole days. How are you feeling?"

I focus on the glimmering point between my eyes. "That's an odd question to ask someone you have a weapon pointed at." My voice is raspy, my throat aching from the strain of not using it since the fire.

Her forced smile turns into a sneer, transforming her almost angelic features into a monstrous grimace. "Attacking someone who just saved your life seems a far stranger thing to do, if you want my input on the subject."

Her voice, which I'd expected to be as soft and bell-like as she looks, has a rough edge to it, like she's had little practice using it.

"If I lower my weapon, will you allow me to pick up my fruit?" She gestures with a tilt of her head to the spilt basket.

I eye the front door warily a moment, before looking at her beyond the weapon she still points at my face. The cards are really all in her hand.

I nod. "You're in charge, *boss*."

She rolls her eyes as she lowers the sword, stepping from me. "Envious much? Green really isn't a flattering color on you, Pirate." She squats, balancing on the balls of her feet, and flips the basket upright, sword still gripped in her left hand.

I scramble back from her and rise unsteadily to my feet, face burning with heat at her condescending tone. "You're lucky I'm still not at my best. You wouldn't have gotten off so lightly had I been fully able and ready for your attack. I would have laid you on your arse, that's a fact."

She snorts as she picks up the scattered fruit one piece at a time, the tip of her sword still pointed toward me. "Well, thank the gods that you're still too weak to properly attack me. Small miracles, I'm sure." She lays the last orange in the basket and whips the sword away from my face, before rising and turning her back to me, making her way to the small kitchen.

She lays the basket on the center island separating the kitchen from the living area, placing the cutlass right next to it. A strange feeling bubbles in the pit of my stomach at her unforeseen snark, and the utter distaste she seems to have for me. Just me, or for buccaneers in general? Why had she saved me then? It's that curiosity, as well as the realization that I don't have a scrap to my name, not even my God-be-damned boots, and no idea where in the three hells I am, that keeps me from turning the door handle and leaving immediately.

I take a hesitant step towards the strange lass, but her next question shocks me further.

"Are you hungry?" The woman stares at me, her head tilted slightly.

My stomach answers for me, growling suddenly, the sound echoing through the silent space. The woman bursts into loud laughter that reminds me of gull's cries. For some reason, the sound causes my cheeks to heat.

"What's so damn funny?" I fold my arms over my chest, frowning deeply to hide my embarrassment.

The woman shakes her head weakly as she tries to compose herself, wiping tears from the corner of her eyes, a large, slightly crooked smile on her face.

"It's nothing… forgive me. I just expected a pirate to be more…" She gestures at me like that explains it all, but then she's lost to her laughter once again.

Embarrassment prickles deeper, causing my anger to spike. "And what do you know about buccaneers anyway?" I scowl at her. "You're just some weak, defenseless wench, living alone in a cottage. You don't know a *damn* thing about me, or what it takes to be a buccaneer, so don't stand there acting all high and mighty, pretending you do. You can take your fancy footwork, and your expensive clothes and weapons, and shove off!"

The anger pulls the words out of me, so fast I'm left breathless, panting. I brace myself for her angered or upset response, but instead, she offers me a soft smile, this one not forced or filled with undisguised disgust.

"Why don't you rest some more? I'll come wake you when the meal is ready?"

I open my mouth, intent on saying something further to the lass who grows stranger by the moment but find for the first time in my entire life, I'm at an utter loss for words. I sigh loudly and do the only thing I can do – I head back toward the bed chamber.

***

18 April 1691
Lampung Bay, Sumatera, Dutch East Indies

A prodding in my cheek pulls me from my sleep. I blink rapidly, trying to erase the fog from my eyes and the haze from my brain. I'm met with deep green eyes instead

16

of the soft lilac I was expecting. I bolt upright, instantly on the defense. Demetrius… I let my body droop back onto the mattress.

"This is starting to become a habit. Do you *have* to be so damn annoying when you wake me up?"

Hanna's guardian, if you can call him that, laughs – no, *giggles,* bastard that he is – and stands. He turns, his tall, lean silhouette clothed in dark breeches, an emerald brocade waistcoat, and that bothersome gray cloak he likes to flap around in, and moves to one of the stuffed bookshelves.

"What you see as annoying, I see as merrymaking." He runs a finger along the spines. "If you always take life so seriously, you will always be lost to the bigger way of things. Plus, you will get wrinkles."

His laugh is joyful, very childlike despite him apparently caring for Hanna for the last twelve years. He's older than he looks, though, so maybe his foolish words about wrinkles and merrymaking hold some merit… Or maybe I've been here too long and I'm finally going loony…

I pull myself into a sitting position as he pulls out a thick, leather-bound book. It's heavy and old, but the man holds it easily to his chest with one arm. He spins in a half-circle before plopping down in the sand-dusted space between the bookshelf and the chest of drawers, folding his long legs.

He opens the book, doesn't look up at me. "I came to tell you that supper is ready and that you should wash up." He props his elbow on his thigh and rests his chin in his large palm, turning a page slowly.

I eye the strange man. I still don't know what to make of him. He'd greeted me in such a friendly manner when I'd woken for supper three nights ago, had given me new clothes, some of his since I refused one of Hanna's shapeless dresses, and allowed me to stay in Hanna's room. She's been taking the settee, while Demetrius seems content on the floor. Strange. Everything about their set up here is strange. And even stranger is the way he speaks – like nothing I've heard before. Like a preacher or schoolmaster who's somehow missed the last fifty years of the world. And she speaks like the mainlanders, but has adopted some of his manner of talk, after being around him for so long, I suppose. They are strange, and infuriating, and I still have no real information on where I am, so I've no choice but to put up with it all.

I rise from the bed, keeping an eye on my oddly hospitable host. "And you're not going to eat?"

"I'm not famished just yet. I will read, then join you both in a while." He doesn't bother to look up from the page he's reading.

I can't stop my eyes from rolling. He either doesn't stop talking or you can't get him to talk at all, annoying bastard.

I crane my neck slightly, trying to peer at the book in his lap, and adjust the white cotton shirt around my hips, unused to the fine texture of it against my skin. "What's more interesting than food?"

He snorts a half-amused, half-annoyed laugh, lifting his eyes from the page. "Are you insinuating *you* are interested in something other than weaponry and Hanna's cooking? What an improvement."

I immediately regret showing any interest in the book. I'll find information on the island without his help, one way or the other.

I head for the still-open door. "Washing up for supper. Got it."

I slam the door behind me to another burst of his annoyingly carefree laugh. It echoes in my ears long after he's stopped.

I wander outside onto the hot sand and into the intense heat. The glittering ocean stretches before me, no sign of the massacre from days prior, and that drags another heavy sigh from me. Demetrius had lied, the food isn't ready, not even simmering yet, and Hanna is nowhere in sight. I suspect Demetrius just wanted the bedchamber to himself to read his unnecessarily large books.

I breathe in deeply, the familiar scent of ocean air calming my frayed nerves. It's been almost six days since *The Protector of the Sea* was sunk, and the loss of my crew weighs heavily on my mind. You will pay, Elyse. You will pay with your life. I swear on my own. I grit my teeth.

A sudden flash of color and movement against the blue of the surf catches my eye. I blink against the sunlight and… my heart leaps into my throat, nearly choking me. It's Hanna. And she has… a tail!

I scurry behind a sand dune and peek around the hillock, careful not to be seen. It's definitely Hanna and that's definitely a tail. It's deep purple; the scales scatter rainbows across the rocks in the midday sun as she flips and slides beneath the surface for a moment. Then she re-emerges, and hauls herself up onto the rocky outcrop, her dark raven hair cascading down her thin, naked shoulders. I watch, amazed, as she pulls her tail completely from the waters and it begins to morph, the glittering purple scales receding, smooth human skin taking their place. She's already yanked her damp slip over her body before her legs have fully finished doing… whatever the hell it is they're doing.

I quickly draw back behind the bank, panicked. She's a… a mermaid?!

I've heard tales of beautiful women luring sailors to their deaths, sinking their ships, but I've never heard of them taking on human form.

With my heart pounding in my ears, I watch as Hanna picks up her small basket from the rocks, straightens her slip, and heads back towards the cottage. Puzzle pieces are falling into place. This explains how she managed to save me when I was so far out in the ocean, and why she and her guardian apparently live half a day's walk from the town, why they're both so… odd and well read. Best way to stay ahead of stupid humans is to stay better informed.

I swallow the panic. I know what I need to do. I'll stay here until I've gathered information on the land, the wildlife, the people, figured out where in three hells I am, and where I can commandeer a ship from. I need to round up a crew and set sail. I need to get out of here. I'll stay no longer than I absolutely must. I glance at the cottage, cool and dark and full of secrets. I don't think it's safe here. I steel my gaze, looking again out into the tumbling waves.

I'm coming for you Elyse. You too, Kai.

***

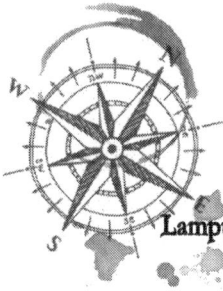

Chapter 3: Hanna
18 April 1691
Lampung Bay, Sumatera, Dutch East Indies

I straighten my gown, body buzzing with renewed energy. My swims are always rejuvenating and invigorating. My half-ling status allows me to live on land, but every now and again, I must return to the sea; a compulsion, drawn almost as if by some unknown song. I'm jarring some of the eel grass I collected from the coves and tide pools, laying the rest out to dry on a rock in the sun. The dried sea grass is ideal for bandaging wounds. The work lets me refocus my attention from being annoyed at Demetrius – he'd not come to get me when the food was ready. We're having soto and I'd found it almost bubbling over when I'd returned. I'm just stacking the last jar when the door opens. My annoyance flares once more; Demetrius was supposed to wake the pirate before coming to find me for dinner. He'd clearly been out wandering the beach instead of doing either.

"Where have you been, you useless excuse for a nymph? You were supposed to come find me when she woke up…"

My rant is cut short as I turn and meet two curious dark cerulean eyes.

Her lips quirk into an easy, arrogant smirk. "Nymph, you say? That explains a few more things. How about that?"

My stomach clenches as the pirate saunters in, closing the door behind her. She looks waifish despite her cocky expression; her small female form is draped in Demetrius's cast-offs. She's wearing an old velvet waistcoat and satin sash of his, both a rich, deep blue. The sash is tied diagonally around her waist, no doubt helping to keep the oversized clothes in place. She stands a good four or five inches taller than I, her skin tan, her time in the sun obvious and a marked contrast to the paleness of her hair. That hair's cut short, ends barely grazing her chin. Her boots Deme procured from some lad in town, since his own would be much too large.

These suit her very well. Soft leather, almost to her knees. Her posture is straight, shoulders squared, head high, jaw set. An obvious leader, natural born or otherwise.

"Like what you see, Fishy?" Her expression is still cocky, her tone daring me.

And I do. I can't help it. Seeing me riled up only seems to make her shine brighter. Heat rushes to my cheeks even as my anger flares, her arrogant smile slowly growing and causing my blush to deepen.

"How could I possibly like someone I know *nothing* about?" I turn from her, my skirts flowing around my ankles in quick currents. And then I stop. *Fishy*?! I fold my arms tightly over my chest, like that alone will contain my heart threatening to beat itself out of my chest. She knows! What will she do now that she knows?

The tension in the room is palpable, so thick it's clawing its way down my throat, catching any further words I might want to say. My fear is so stifling I feel lightheaded. I'm unable to pull in a full, clear breath. Right before I think it's going to smother me, she speaks:

"The name's Una."

I whip around to gape at her, scarcely able to believe what I'm hearing.

"What?" My voice is a breathy whisper.

She steps closer, closing the distance between us. With a genuine smile I didn't know she possessed until now, filled with unexpected kindness rather than snark, she holds out her hand.

"Una. Buccaneer."

My hand visibly trembles as I awkwardly take her hand. Her grip is callused, her handshake firm and strong. "Hanna…" I force myself to meet her straightforward gaze. "Mermaid…"

The handshake is brief, but the warmth of her hand lingers.

"Hanna, then." She nods. "You have my thanks for saving me and for letting me stay here until I'm recovered. I owe you a life debt."

I cross my arms back over my chest, suddenly very aware of her unflinching gaze. "That won't be necessary. All I ask is that you keep my secret... and Demetrius's. They'll hunt us, kill us if they find out." Visions of the townsfolk descending on us with their fire and their blades makes me shudder.

Una nods again, her stormy eyes drawing me in, drowning me, dousing my fear. "You got yourself a deal, Fishy."

***

"Una, take a seat around the bench." I'm stirring the food in the pot. "We use it to put the food on."

From the corner of my eye I see the fair-haired pirate, *buccaneer*, hesitate a moment before dropping to her knees and slowly folding them underneath her body. She scratches her cheek before folding her hands self-consciously in her lap, focusing on the far wall. I inwardly smirk at her awkwardness, all traces of her seemingly inexhaustible arrogance gone.

"I shall put the tableware on the bench!" Demetrius skips from the kitchen with the wooden bowls, plates and spoons. "You gather the cabya and the kuluban!"

I shake my head at his capering. Una watches him with one fine, blonde eyebrow raised so high it almost disappears into her hairline.

"Is that even real food?" Una asks. "It sounds like you made it up." Her lip curls. "It wouldn't surprise me if you did."

I snort a laugh at how easily she's already learned to take Demetrius's tales with a grain of salt, and at the dismayed look pitching Demetrius's face into a sour twist.

"You are in for a treat, child." Demetrius lays out the tableware. "This area's cuisine is some of the most flavorful and luxurious you will ever try. I hope you like spice, or the cabya will go to waste. There's no way I can eat it all alone. Hanna does not favor such spiced dishes, but I find it pairs quite heavenly with the soto."

He begins to hum a merry tune, drawing Una's attention downward when he lays a bowl and spoon in front of her. She stares at the wooden tableware as if it's an oddity, a curiosity.

I smile slightly as I lift the large serving tray fashioned from a slab of bark onto my palm. It's piled with a collection of raw sliced cucumber, carrots, cabbage and celery. I place the ceramic bowl of cabya — a spicy pepper, garlic, lime juice and ginger paste crushed together using a pestle — in the center of the tray. Demetrius loves the stuff, and though he *says* he can't eat all of it, he could. Easily. He could eat more than the both of us combined in a three-day period, in one sitting, if he really wanted to. I've seen it. He's a bottomless pit.

As I set the tray on the bench, Una frowns at Deme. "Do you even *need* to eat? You aren't even human. Hanna, I get, being half human. But you?" She shrugs her slim shoulders.

Demetrius laughs, doubling back to the kitchen to grab three pewter drinking beakers. "While I am in this form, I do. Hanna, do we need anything else?"

He changes the topic so easily. Una huffs out a sigh and reaches for a slice of cucumber, scooping up a huge mound of cabya before popping the entire disk into her mouth.

I wince as I head back to the kitchen to collect the pot of soto. Though it's usually a combination of meat, vegetables and broth, Demetrius doesn't eat meat of any kind, so I make it with extra vegetables and milk to thicken the liquid.

"I'd be careful if I were you Una, that stuff's hotter than it looks!" I call.

When I turn back, Una's face is twisted into an expression close to bliss; eyes closed, cheeks moving quickly as she chews and swallows, followed by a rapturous grin.

"Never... mind?" I raise an eyebrow at her.

This Una is an odd one. Half the time she's every inch the arrogant, cocky pirate I grew up hating, and the other times? She's actually... enjoyable to be around. She's almost as curious as Demetrius, and it's fascinating to see her slowly opening up bit by bit. Now here she is, enjoying my cooking. I can't stop the flush of pride that swells in my chest.

Demetrius passes behind her, then drops to the floor on the opposite side of the bench, his familiar smile playing around the corner of his lips. "You had nothing to fear, Hanna. Seems the pirate has some good taste in her after all."

"*Buccaneer*," Una mutters around her mouthful of food, rolling her eyes and grabbing another slice of cucumber to pop into her mouth.

I set the pot down, laughing softly, and sit between them, a warm feeling entering my chest at the companionable energy that seems to thrum around us.

An energy that's shattered as Una squawks out a half-yell, half-choke. She swallows her food hard, left hand grasping her bare right wrist, her eyes bulging.

"My bangle?!" she splutters. "Where's my bangle?! It was just here!" She looks around frantically, searches the floor, going as far to lift her legs up and feel beneath her rump.

"You mean *this* bangle?" Demetrius spins the thin brass bracelet on one of his long fingers.

Una and I snap our heads towards him simultaneously. He grins.

Una's eyes bulge wider as she looks from her naked wrist to the bracelet, and back to her wrist. "How did you –? I didn't even feel you take it."

Demetrius laughs, sliding the bracelet across the bench toward Una, who snatches it up and slides it back over her slim wrist.

I sigh, pouring soto into each of our bowls. "Deme, not even the adult townsfolk enjoy those… *tricks*. No-one above the age of ten does, so I'm fairly sure Una won't enjoy them either."

He grins. "Simple pickpocketing skills, my girl. That and," he waggles his fingers in a flourish, "a bit of *magic*." He winks roguishly before picking up his bowl and taking a long drink from it.

Una catches my gaze and rolls her eyes, though a playful smirk curls her lips before she picks up her own bowl and takes an equally long pull from it. I can't help the laugh pulled from my chest at their oddness, but this is nice. We never have guests, so I never get to cook for anyone other than Demetrius.

He leans back on his palms and gives Una a cool smile. "So, I have been curious. How did you and that ship end up in our lovely bay? I sense a long and interesting tale."

That carefree energy that had been illuminating her as she ate begins to fizzle; that soft smile slips from her lips and her sun-tanned face hardens into an unreadable mask. I glare at Demetrius; he responds by raising his shoulders nonchalantly and mouthing *what?*

Una sets down her bowl and looks deeply into it, like the contents somehow hold all the answers. The air becomes heavy, thick with Una's anger, rage, grief at whatever had happened to put her into that situation. She's not spoken about it since I rescued her and I've not pressed her, too afraid to spook her and make her leave before she's healthy.

She grasps the bowl in both hands, thumbs the rim of it as she continues to peer into the soup. Then she speaks, her voice so low, so whispered, I'm unsure at first if she's speaking at all.

"Kai and Elyse…"

My heart stutters in my chest. I hadn't expected an answer from her, or for it to be a name I recognize. There's no way it can be the same Kai, right? It's a common name. There's a lot of Kai's, aren't there? I need more information before jumping to conclusions.

"Kai and Elyse, you say?" Demetrius leans forward. "Were they your comrades?" His eyes swirl with curiosity. It seems the same thoughts have occurred to him. That isn't good. Once he's set his mind to something, there's almost nothing that'll shake him off, once it's piqued his interest. And his particular style of questioning would definitely spook her off! Time to engage the 'Distracting Demetrius Defensive Maneuver' tactic.

"Didn't you want to teach Una to play draughts?" I blurt. "You'll finally have someone to beat other than me."

His head swivels in my direction so fast I'm surprised he doesn't break his neck, but his eyes sparkle with new excitement. Excitement is better than interrogation, though Una's looking more and more uncomfortable.

He jumps to his feet. "What a superb idea, Hanna! Una, do you play?"

He doesn't wait for her answer as he disappears into the bedchamber to retrieve the board and pieces, a spring to his already light steps. I laugh and look at Una. She's smiling that soft, genuine, open smile again, but when she catches me looking, it shifts into a decidedly more pirate-like smirk.

"Is he always so…" She gestures vaguely.

"Upbeat?" I take a bite of my carrot.

This elicits a laugh from Una, softening the hard edge to her face. "That's certainly a more polite word for it… So, draughts?"

I grin, with a lightness in my chest I never thought I'd feel in a pirate's presence ever again, as she grins back. Maybe this mundane life has finally broken its routine. I shall just have to wait and see.

***

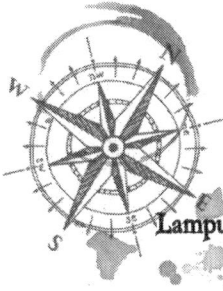

Chapter 4: Una
20 April 1691
Lampung Bay, Sumatera, Dutch East Indies

What in damnation is *Ja-kar-ta*?!? I huff and throw another useless scroll over my shoulder onto the bedchamber floor. Just like all the others I've found, it covers too large an area to identify any of the coastline I've walked around the cabin, or anything I saw back on the ship. All these maps, with their incomprehensible words, are too big, or languages too foreign. I need something local, not Finnish, or whatever fancy-arse tongue the nymph knows, damn it. I need to know where I am to figure out where I need to go. I'm sitting on the floor surrounded by all the discarded scrolls, and I kick the chest of drawers in frustration, sending all the objects balanced on its top clattering to the floor around me. I turn and lean back against it, thumping my head against its solid drawers. Once again, my efforts to peep through their books to get my bearings, in one of these stolen moments while they go for one of their swims, has proven pointless. My discoveries have left me with even more questions than answers.

Of course, I've thought about just asking Hanna about it. I'm not a captive here. I can leave whenever I'm well and able enough to. And I'm quite well now, definitely the most fed I think I've ever been in my entire life, but not quite able. All their maps, tomes, scrolls, are filled with lines of script I can't dream of ever being able to read for myself. Some of it doesn't even look like words, more like small individual inky pictures in rows. I know I could ask; it'd be such a simple thing. But the fact is, I'll float belly up in the sea before I ask for help from most people, and I don't trust these people fully. Especially not that *water nymph,* or whatever creature he claims to be. He is by far the most bizarre thing in this entire situation and, damn it to all hell, if he doesn't like to ask personal questions every chance he can. 'Getting to know my house guest' he calls it. Whatever it is driving his questioning, I'm not going to risk my revenge, or the look on Elyse's face when I punch that smug-arse smile off her face; the fear I'm going to instill. I want, no, *need* it. My fallen crew earned it; they deserve to see me put that backstabbing scourge at the very bottom of the ocean.

I bang my head against the drawers again as my anger rushes through me, its heat warming me. I *could* ask Hanna for help... No. Asking her is the same as asking Demetrius. He's always hanging around her like a bloody shadow. At best, I'd get a few moments alone with the mermaid... half-ling, I mentally correct myself, then wonder why it matters to me whether I call her the right thing. I'll eat their grub, sleep in her warm bed, and lay low until I can get my hands on information to lead me out of here.

Feeling cheered, I stand up. I've been sitting so long, my legs have gone numb and I have to lean on the edge of the chest of drawers. I need to keep looking. There must be something here that I can actually read that isn't all this prim and proper shite.

The drawers. I haven't opened them at all since I've been using the room. Looked through the endless tomes, gandered at the wall of weapons, picked through all the trinkets, yes, absolutely. But the drawers are heavy, noisy. I'd never had time to try without someone being in the cabin to hear me delving into a closed place, with things they obviously didn't want on display. Until now.

My fingers tingle as I heave open the top drawer by its brass knob, the compartment opening with a *thunk* that makes me wince and glance to the door... but when no one comes bursting in, I exhale and look inside. *More* maps. I paw through the papers that range from splotched, brown parchment, to faintly yellowed, to some that look relatively new.

I pull out one that looks newer, parchment still pale and unstained, and unroll it across the draught board, excitement already swirling in my gut. It's much more localized; I can see individual bays and coves, rocky outcrops. A thrill of recognition as I spot the headland I'd seen from the ship before the fighting had started. I purse my lips against the unwelcome memory and keep scanning, using my finger to follow the curves and juts of the shore. There. That outcrop, the rocks I'd seen Hanna climb onto with her mermaid tail a few days back. I peer closely at the inked words scrawled over the bay, mouthing the shapes of the letters silently – *Lam-pung*

Bay. Yes! Lampung Bay! I know that name! It had been on the charts in Pa's cabin; he and the navigators had spoken it. We'd seen it from the deck, before the shouting and the sound of steel and the blood and the fire and…. I clamp down on that. I can't open that memory yet. I stab my finger on the bay. That's where I am. I'm chewing my lip, tracing a finger further down the rugged hand-drawn line of coast – I bet Demetrius drew this, seems the sort of prissy, precise sort of thing he'd enjoy doing – and I'm looking, hoping…

I hear something. My hands freeze. I look towards the door, barely breathing, barely blinking. They can't be back already! No, I'm so damn close! The front door bangs against the wall. Hanna's voice echoing in the living area has my heart leaping into my throat. I roll the map as quickly as I can and shove it back in the drawer, closing it softly, wincing at its inevitable *thunk*, trying to not make too much noise. Then I scoop up all the discarded maps, placing them back where I think I found them… I pause, eyes darting between the map of the entire Dutch East Indies I've just placed on top of the drawers and the one of the Indian Ocean I've just laid back along a shelf edge. Is that right? I swap them over frantically. Boots head toward the bedchamber. A bead of sweat drips down my neck as I dive not-so-gracefully onto the mattress. I don't even bother to pull the thin sheet out of the way, simply flinging myself onto my side, facing the wall, faking sleep. I try to slow my breathing, unclench my muscles, as the door opens, and I feel someone staring at me.

A moment passes before the door softly clicks closed again and I heave in a shaky breath. I hear Hanna's voice through the wood as she walks away.

"She's already asleep. You'll have to teach her how to play pall-mall tomorrow."

I roll onto my back and unwrap my arms from around myself, a giddy grin nearly spitting my face in two. *Port*. I'd managed to see the word on that map, south along the coast from here. I know where I am, and I know where I need to go. A small lead, but a lead, nonetheless. I'll take it.

***

22 April 1691
Lampung Bay, Sumatera, Dutch East Indies

I stretch out in the warm, soft sand, the slight wind coming off the water cooling me, soothing the last of my aches from my narrow escape from Davy Jones' Locker. I survey the waves every few moments. The wreck from days past isn't even a spec of ash in the great, deep blue. Demetrius said he'd taken care of the bodies and the rest of the debris. In a few days no one will even remember what happened out there, except for me. It's that yawning emptiness and loneliness that keeps me from asking how he'd managed to do it all by himself, and he's made no move to tell me.

I stare into the dipping sunset, lost in its fire, its large sphere holding my attention as easily as any shiny trinket or pretty wench. I'm waiting for Hanna to resurface; she's gone down to collect more seaweed. She uses it in her medicinal ointments, like the one she used to heal the cut above my eye that's now only a thin barely visible pink line. Her cool hands tending it, hair tucked behind her ear, eyes intent...

I shake the thought of the half-ling from my head and close my eyes, sucking in a deep breath, wriggling deeper into the warmed sands. I'll be out of here soon. I'll grab that map, some food, and I'll be gone.

The sound of Hanna breaking the surface of the water has me reopening my eyes, raising to my elbows. She swims leisurely, arms stretched ahead, her large deep purple tail thrashing a sure beat behind her. As she nears the shore, she curves slightly, heading for the small cluster of rocks I'd recognized on the map. The water barely laps at the rocks. I try not to notice how the setting sun makes her almost porcelain skin glow as she places the satchel full of her harvested plants on the rocks and begins laying the glistening strips of sea grass out to dry with care. Heat fills my cheeks and I advert my gaze as Hanna hoists herself out of the water. I hurriedly focus my attention on the sands instead of the lass as she transforms back to her human shape. I want to watch – it's remarkable how she does it without so much as a broken bone – but I can't watch. It's... it's not decent.

I risk a glance after a moment and, once sure she's clothed, see she's dutifully tending the newly harvested seaweed, a huge smile on her face. I'll be out of here soon… and no half-ling is going to change that. Once satisfied with her work, she wanders over to me, her bare feet silent against the sand. Her short body is clothed in an odd combination of clothes; her damp under-slip and a billowy white cotton shirt several sizes too large, the kind of clothing I use to hide my female appearance. She casts me a smile that's been slowly edging its way around my barriers as the days pass, and sits cross-legged in front of me, her back to the waters. I try not to dwell on the way her smile has the cursed lump of meat in my chest twitching.

"What's wrong, Una? It looks like you tasted something most foul." Her brow creases as she tilts her head, those lilac eyes looking at me, *through* me.

She knows so little about me, has known me such an insignificant amount of time, and yet she can read me so well… I throw a quick smirk her way, hoping it's enough to mask my thoughts. "Everything's fine. How'd yer harvestin' go, Fishy?" I raise my brow, flash my grin, knowing I'm probably overdoing the pirate's drawl that flows so easily when I'm trying to seem more intimidating, or less unsettled. But it works and my smile grows as I watch a pale flush spread over her cheeks and work its way down the curve of her neck. Guess I can still turn on the charm when I need to.

"I really wish you would stop calling me that, it's quite unsightly." She sniffs, turns her eyes to the beach, avoiding mine.

That has a laugh springing from my chest. "Unsightly? That's –"

Her pale hand rising sharply silences me. Her head tilts to the side. She's listening for something and it has my grin slipping. Her carefree face clouds like a bad storm brewing, darkening her illuminating glow.

That tilted head then whips toward the ocean as she turns onto all fours. "We must go. We must go now! Away from the water!"

She's on her feet so smoothly, I almost miss the movement, her waist length hair like a swinging cloak as she spins slowly, looking between me and the waves. What's crawled up her arse?

"Hanna…" I scramble to my feet. "Away from the water? Why?"

Her alertness, her panic, infects me. Gooseflesh rushes up my spine and along my bare arms. "Other creatures reside in the seas besides Demetrius." She's scanning the water, eyes intent and bright with fear, clumsily trying to pick up my boots from where I'd tossed them earlier. "Terrible, deadly, monstrous ones. Creatures from nightmares…" She's halfway to retrieving my second boot when she pivots to me. For a moment, I think she's going to tackle me, but she sidesteps me and rams her hip into mine, knocking me off balance, off my feet and to the sand a good distance away from her.

I land hard on my arse, the air rushing out of my lungs. I push the hair from my face, about to ask the half-ling what came loose in that thick skull of hers, when I see the color drain from her face. The pupils of her eyes are blown so wide that just a thin band of color remains, and there's a thick green thing that looks at first like a corded vine wrapped tightly around her torso. It shudders, alive, and I realize it's a tentacle belonging to something unseen beneath the surface. It glistens wetly, pinning her arms uselessly to her sides, then ripples, yanking her backwards towards the water a few paces, but she digs her heels into the sand. I'm still on my arse, staring wide-eyed, mouth hanging open, no sound escaping. I can't… I don't know what…

Hanna grits her teeth and, with an impressive show of strength, takes a step toward me, fighting against the tentacle. Her determined gaze focusses on me. "Una." Her voice holds a command to it that I've not heard from her before. "I'm almost certain this is a scylla. It's got six heads and a venomous bite…" The tentacle surges then seizes her backwards. Her heels are grazing the water, her chest heaving, her cheeks flushed with the effort of trying to breathe as the tentacle tightens around her. I'm on my feet and running to her, but she shakes her head violently, calling out: "NO! Una, no! Even one drop could kill you, as a human, so you mustn't try to help, no matter what!"

I slide to a stop, balling my fists in frustration as she grunts and fights against the force pulling at her.

A large disturbance beneath the water twists and heaves the waves as whatever it is begins to rise. The creature finally breaks the surface, and my knees go slack.

Just like she said, the monster has six huge snake-like heads and they're towering so high I have to lean back to take in all their reptilian features, their gaping mouths full of razor-sharp teeth. So many writhing, flailing, plant-like tentacles sprouting from the center of its bulky body. Its scales are mottled grays and greens, darkening as they near and dip below the water. Even in my terror, I know it's the perfect disguise for this underwater predator. I stare from the towering heights of its heads to Hanna struggling in front of me, feeling a useless anger welling in me.

"What about your human half?!" I yell. "Will your mermaid blood protect you?!"

She lifts her chin, fixes me with a strained smile. It's the only answer she's going to offer. Damn it. The blood in my veins turns to icy slush and my mind whirls as I look around for a viable weapon. I've become sloppy. Lazy. Before the wreck, I'd have never been unarmed, not even when relaxing. I growl. Other tentacles snake around Hanna and yank her from her feet. She flies, like a flag on a stiff breeze, through the air and into the ocean with a loud splash. The repulsive being, all six heads and thrashing tentacles, all its yellow eyes full of unholy evil, and all its gnashing teeth, begin to descend around the spot where Hanna went under.

A frustrated, pained yell escapes my throat. I won't fail her, too… The cabin. The wall of weapons. I tear my gaze away from the ocean, sand wedging between my toes as I push against it and run as quickly as I can get my legs to go back to the cabin. My mind goes to the water nymph who'd gone for a swim earlier in the day. As much as he pisses me off, I wish he were here now to help. But he's not, and I am alone. It's up to me to help Hanna. She's not going to lose her life. Not today.

I fling open the door and run to the bedroom, my eyes going to the walls of weapons. The guns are useless. Broadswords and cutlasses are too heavy. Just as my overwhelmed brain is about to combust, I see the medium-sized short, curved blade as long as my forearm. I'd seen the nymph shining the bird-head-shaped pommel days ago. It would do well enough. I grab it, and sprint back out across the sand. I can see the beast still thrashing about in the water, but no sign, nor fin, of Hanna. I hurtle into the shallows, silently cursing the nymph for still not showing his ugly face. She's his responsibility, not mine. His. I don't care if she lives or dies. I don't. I don't care and I can't see her anywhere, though the monster is towering above me, body the size of a galleon, jaws and pointed teeth slathered in frothing, repulsive, dark green spittle, my heart threatening to pound itself right the hell out of my chest.

"Blast it!" I shout. "BLAST it, Fishy, don't do this to me…"

Movement to the right of the creature has my head jerking, arm instinctively raising. A flash of midnight, a bit of purple.

Hanna heads inland at an inhumane speed, tail a rapid blur of motion behind her, pale arms cutting through the waves like they're nothing. The beast spots her and roars thunderously, shaking the ground, shoots off another tentacle, too fast for Hanna to dodge.

And yet she does.

Without so much as looking over her shoulder, she changes course by just a breath, causing the tentacle to soar harmlessly past her, sending sea-spray into her face. Unafraid, she continues her race towards shore, as the beast lets out another guttural roar, all its eyes full of mindless fury. The giant mass of its body begins to move. It's going after her. But it's slow, cumbersome above water. It's churning the waves until the ripples lap against my toes. My arm is still raised, and I wave the blade gripped in it, pumping it in the air, adrenaline and relief surging through me. She's going to make it!

"ALMOST THERE, HANNA," I'm screaming, so loud my throat feels raw, like I've torn it, "JUST A BIT MORE!"

Two of the heads turn at my voice and spy me. My stomach sinks with a nauseating plummet as it throws out two more tentacles, one successfully wrapping around my raised arm, the other around my ankle. A yelp is forced from my lungs as I'm hoisted upwards. I'm airborne in one fluid, harsh yank, sailing through the air, heading right towards the thrashing waters of the Indian Ocean.

***

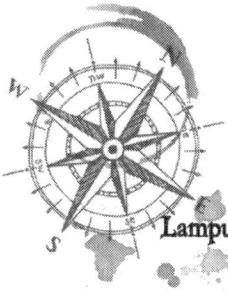

Chapter 5: Hanna
22 April 1691
Lampung Bay, Sumatera, Dutch East Indies

Fear claws up my throat as Una sails through the sky and into the frigid waters without having a chance to fight against the scylla. I change course back towards the terror of a beast; back toward something I'd always thought would be interesting to meet, in theory, but I'd never truly considered the reality of it occurring. Back towards Una.

The blade she'd managed to keep hold of as she was flung through the air now sinks, free from her grip.

I dive after it, knowing if I'm not quick enough, this sharp gift from Una will be lost forever. With a surge, I grasp its hilt, the deep grooves of the bird head pommel biting into my palm. It feels heavy but familiar in my hand.

When I breach the surface, I see the monster is no longer swimming slowly but staying eerily still, all six of its head focused and trained on a viciously thrashing Una. It holds her by an opposite ankle and wrist so all she can do is flail uselessly in the air.

The center head, obviously the dominant one, roars before tightening its vine-like tentacles around her, successfully stopping her thrashing. Then, without any hesitation, the scylla slams Una against the surface of the water with such force, the sound her body makes connecting with the water makes me queasy. Almost like snapping a twig beneath your foot. The tentacles raise her high again but she's not moving now, I clench my jaw.

Satisfied with its dirty work, the scylla loosens its hold, pulling the green tentacles back beneath the waters, as Una's unconscious body drops into the water. Is she dead?! But the scylla swivels all its heads towards me before I can confirm. The noxious, green froth drips from its teeth into the waters, staining the ocean. I grit my teeth, letting the bite of the blade hilt in my palm calm my frayed nerves. It's now or never…

I swim in ever-tightening circles, round and round, each revolution faster than before, until I'm whipping around fast enough that the scylla's heads are weaving to keep up with me. I flick out of the spin, the speed shooting me through the water towards the beast, then at the last possible moment, I use my tail fin to launch myself, tail and all, out of the waters, my heartbeat the only sound I can hear.

My lower half is already transforming, the searing pain splitting my tail into legs fueling me forward with a grunt. Once within range, I throw the blade with all the strength I can muster in my tired limbs. For a moment, I worry the heavy pommel will pull it out of its arc too soon, but it slices through the air with a high pitched *zing*, and embeds itself into one yellow, snake-like eye on the beast's dominant head..

It lets out an enraged howl before heaving its massive tail from the depths and, with alarming speed, whips around, colliding its fin with my still-airborne body. It hurts, the way being slammed against a rock hurts, and sends me sailing a good fifty yards, before I splash back into the water, the force of the strike still reverberating through my entire body and rattling my teeth.

I right myself as quickly as possible; my vision is spotty, my head filling with dense fog, making it hard to concentrate as I swim. That blade went deep, it should hold the beast up… at least for the moment…

I search the depths until a flash of white catches my attention. I twist, whipping my hair from my face, and see Una's motionless form, floating down into the unforgiving waters. I dive, reaching out, and grab one of her arms, pulling her to me. My tail does most of the work as I focus on holding onto the limp body, the dread in my belly swirling faster.

I work quickly but carefully, swimming towards the rays of dull sunlight still managing to permeate the darkness, and break the surface, making straight for the sandy shores, away from the scylla still writing and thrashing out there somewhere behind us, making low gargled wails of pain. I don't risk a backwards glance, instead careful to keep Una's drooping head above the waves. The fact that this is how I first met her, doing almost the same thing for her, isn't lost on me.

36

The waves caused by the scylla help us coast onto the beach and I slide Una onto the sand, onto her side, before finally sneaking a peek over my shoulder. The scylla is nowhere in sight. I scan the horizon, my chest heaving, my breaths short, quick puffs. The giant disturbance from moments ago, the terrible, destructive force from bedtime tales, gone like it was never here in the first place.

I relax onto my back, next to Una's still form, staring up into the sky for a moment, trying to slow my breathing, then heave my tail from the water with my hands, holding it aloft with shaking arms. I shut my eyes tight and breathe through the transformation. I'm exhausted. Afraid. Angry. My heart is pumping my emotions so strongly, I barely feel the pain of transforming. But, once I'm done, I raise shakily onto my knees, my body still trembling. I'm cold, naked, hair dripping and hanging over my chest. I hope to Poseidon there's no one else on the beach right now as I lean over Una. Her clothes are as ruined as my slip.

My stomach rolls as I press my ear carefully to her chest and then it's *my* heart that's stuttering a moment. There's a pulse but it's weak, fluttering. She isn't going to make it…

I know I can change that. I also suspect that what I'm considering would horrify Demetrius. Is that enough to stop me? I look at Una's pale body, her chest barely moving with the weakness of her breaths. The last nine days with the surprisingly pleasant buccaneer have been… enlivening. Her constant curiosity about Demetrius and me, our home, our lives. Her odd fondness for sunrises and sunsets; the way she'd stop whatever she was doing, sometimes even mid-sentence, to take in the too-brief flash of fiery sky, savoring it with a softness in her eyes. Her rakish smirk. The surprising honesty in her laugh. I would have never thought it possible of a pirate getting to know her. I can't let her fire fizzle out.

I won't.

I lean down, sealing my lips over her cold ones. Burning heat unlike any I've ever felt immediately fills my chest, like I've swallowed the sun. Wave after wave of power flows into her from me. Her body pulses and twitches as she reacts to the sudden healing magic.

The heat fades. I hold my lips against hers a moment longer before pulling back, my pulse roaring, my lips tingling like they've been struck by lightning. I watch color slowly return to her ashen cheeks and, beneath my palm, her barely-there heartbeat begins to pound steady and strong.

I release my held breath in one hard whoosh, my head coming down, my forehead almost touching hers. Thank the gods… all of them.

"Are you content with what you have just done, Hanna?" Demetrius's voice is so deep and low, so sudden, so unusually serious, that it makes me jump.

He stands beside us, chestnut curls half-mutated into the writhing dark water-like mass his hair becomes whenever water touches him. His chest is bare, toned, and tanned. His hands sit on his hips as he looks down at me, his knee length woolen breeches still dripping with sea water.

I don't know how to answer him, staring up at him. Shame and fear pricks at me.

His jaw clenches as he steps closer. "You saved her life, but in so doing, you've forced her into a life of servitude." His expression softens, as if his disappointment and anger is suddenly sucked out of him in a rip tide, replaced with a thoughtful look that glimmers in the ocean of his emerald eyes. "There was already a natural bond forming between you, this just made it more… permanent."

I refocus on Una's face; the sun-darkened skin, that blonde hair cut short to better blend in as a boy in a world that would condemn her for being exactly who she is. My heart gives a strange leap as I trace every dip of her face, every shadow that darkens the corners of it, the steady rise and fall of her chest.

"You gave her *The Gift of The Sea*, but once the strings of fate are tangled, child, there is no undoing it, not completely. You have sealed her fate. And your own."

His words echo one of the few things I do know of my mermaid half. In bestowing the Gift to her, it saves her life, heals all the trauma the scylla and her time underwater has caused. It'll also give her the ability to breathe underwater. But, whether she asked for it or not, magic of any kind comes with a cost. I've given her something, the Gift, only able to be given once in a mermaid's lifetime, so she must

38

give something in return. Her servitude. In the old days, the Gift was how mermaids found viable and loyal mates. They'd lure men who worked the sea with their otherworldly beauty, always the downfall of a weak-willed man; all just a camouflage of sorts, another branch of their magic. Mermaids become whatever the unsuspecting man wants them to be. Once the Gift was bestowed, the human would be powerless to refuse the mermaid's whim, no matter what they may ask. The mermaid would then hope to fall pregnant with male offspring. All full-blooded mermaids were female, though their preference for male half-lings is unclear – the male half-lings stayed in the ocean, always. At least that's what Deme told me; for what reason, or why, is as unknown to him as it is to me.

But my mother's tale is one of caution; the risks of carelessly giving away such a precious gift, or *curse* depending on how you look at it, are high. If the will of the bonded human is strong enough, they can battle against the bond, the call, the instinct to obey the mermaid who bestowed the Gift. In those instances, the bond's magic will weaken, fade, and if the human is of exceptional strength, the magic will shatter altogether. It's rare but a human who can break a bond will be fine after the exhaustion of breaking it wears off.

And the fate of a mermaid whose human has broken the bond of the Gift of the Sea?

Death. Always death.

I trace the rosy glow spreading across Una's cheeks that shows me she's alive and strong. She's still unconscious. Not a drop of regret wells up inside me. I'd never regret saving her life, and I'd do it again. A hundred times over I'd do it again.

***

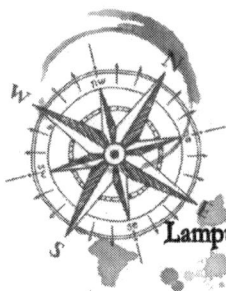

Chapter 6: Una

24 April 1691

Lampung Bay, Sumatera, Dutch East Indies

I sit up slowly, careful to keep my eyes closed against the dizziness. My sleep was pleasant; surprisingly so, considering. I'd been relaxing on a beach, warm rays of sun caressing and tanning my skin… But I'd awoken with a start, thought I might've been at the bottom of the ocean, or worse, in the belly of some mythical beast that no one would ever know had eaten me, waiting to be shat out like just another meal, like I was nothing. Then I'd opened my eyes and found myself once again in Hanna's darkened, quiet, bedchamber, and my fears were quickly snuffed out. She'd somehow saved both of our hides from a creature I don't even think a full ship of able men could kill.

I'd inspected my body and found nothing alarming, no broken bones, cuts, not even any bruises. The second time in less than a month. The only thing that remained was a deep ache I can still feel now, in every part of my body, my soul. It's not wound pain or even muscle pain, it's somehow deeper than that. It's kept me lying on the mattress for who knows how long. Not sleeping, not thinking. Just simply lying here, *being*. It's a strange feeling, not having to look over my shoulder, or try to sleep that strange half-sleep I'd adopted over the years; the not-quite sleep, where your body is too prepared for sudden attack to ever fully relax and fall into a deep sleep. I've probably never slept so much in my damn life, or ever will again once I leave this place. But I ache.

And then there's the buzzing. It's not quite a physical buzzing in my ears, but it's damn annoying. Like a concussion without the headache; of being out of kilter somehow. It began like an itch in my brain. Persistent, but the barest trickle. A mild inconvenience, but enough to stop me returning to that pleasant slumber. Now it's a roaring that has every nerve in my body coiled tight and alert. Maybe it *is* a concussion? I open my eyes slowly and pray to whatever watches over us that the room doesn't shift in front of my face. It doesn't. Success. A small one, but I'll take it.

I swing my legs to the floor and take a slow breath, willing that blasted buzzing to stop. I tear my hands through my hair, like I could reach inside and scratch the maddening itch. As I'm rubbing at my scalp, I spy my leather boots sitting by the slightly open door and get the sudden urge to walk through it. Almost as if I'm being led by an invisible tether, I cross to the door, peer out into the darkened living room and see Hanna sleeping on the settee. The water nymph is nowhere in sight.

That bothersome itching in my brain suddenly grows louder, turns my stomach, fills my ears with a loud, overwhelming rushing that threatens to consume all my senses the longer I stare at the sleeping lass. I'm taking a step forward and crossing the room, kneeling next to her, before it's even completely registered in my mind that I've moved. Before I can be too surprised with my own body, the roaring recedes to that manageable trickle. Being close to her makes the rushing, roaring, buzzing grow quiet.

I can't find the energy to figure out why, as I choke down a sigh of relief, and lean in a breath closer, studying and memorizing every detail of the half-ling's face. I ignore the logical voice in the back of my mind that says I'm being a swine, being so close to a lass while she's unconscious and in nothing but a slip. The other half, the buccaneer part, the *curious* part, the part that doesn't seem to think at all, is so taken by the soft, delicate slope of her neck, the slight roundness of her cheek, the flawless skin, that I don't seem to care if Hanna wakes up right now and finds us in such a compromising position, though logical-me knows she'd surely punch my head clean off my shoulders.

I lean closer still and see a dusting of faint freckles across her cheeks, a thin sliver of scar along her cheek marring the perfection. The tips of my fingers tingle like they do when I'm about to find something really worth finding, usually precious, always priceless, definitely getting me a good coin or two. Every instinct tells me to abandon ship as my fingers raise, almost as if they have a will of their own, toward those barely-there freckles. Logical-me is livid, in a far-off, back-of-my brain way. What in three hells am I going to do?! Am I going to touch her face?!

41

That thought cripples my stomach in knots. Even so, my fingers don't stop in their seemingly determined movement.

That's when I notice the sleepy, lavender eyes staring right into mine, her hands still folded on her stomach.

Over a dozen endings to this play out in my head, all ending with me in pain or losing a limb if she tells her overbearing guardian about this. I can't decide whether to jerk my hand away or slowly lower it and play it off as nothing at all, unsure which will seem more suspicious, and so I do neither. My hand just hovers in the space between us, inches from her face. She doesn't move either, her bizarre-colored eyes tracing my features, memorizing them like I'd done to her just moments before.

She breaks the heavy silence first. "You sure do like to go down for two days and worry the hell out of me, Una."

Her wide, searching eyes narrow in annoyance and the folded hands move to cross over her chest like a physical barrier between us.

My hand drops on its own and I put some distance between us by tipping back from my knees onto the balls of my feet. Did she just…

"Did you just curse?" I ask.

Her top lip twitches like she's going to smile, before she stops herself, face deepening into a scowl. "You aren't the only one who can have a foul mouth when the time calls for it."

Is that a blush blooming on her cheeks?

"And *does* the time call for it, Hanna?"

The head that had begun to turn from me jerks to focus on me again, annoyance replaced by shock. I know why she's looking at me like I've done something worth getting worked up over – I used her name. I hardly ever use her name. It's always 'Fishy', 'Half-ling', 'Lass' or some form of the three.

The shock levels out all the hard, angry lines of her face, softening them with one of defeat. She sighs and those tightly folded arms droop. "No, I was just concerned I'd been too late to help you. You're well...?" She drops her head, peeking at me from under the hair that falls into her eyes.

My heart throbs like someone's gripping it in their fist for a moment, and I almost wobble backwards. I swallow awkwardly, giving a short nod. "My head hurts a bit..."

She's suddenly leaning close, her face a mere wisp away, the back of one of her hands pressing against my forehead gently. "You don't feel warm. Most likely just some residual effects from the scylla dropping you into the water so hard. A few more days taking it slow and you'll be back to your usual spunk."

I can't jerk back, and my words are stuck in my throat, wadded into a tight ball. I can't find the words to tell her I've already stayed too long, regardless of what I want; that I need to head out as soon as I can. Instead of telling her that's what I plan to do, I just stare into her face, and my hand is doing what it wants to, tracing those damn freckles over the soft curve of her cheek. I let her hand stay where it is against my forehead, not trying to shake her off.

"You'll stay then? A few more days until you're feeling completely well?"

My head is nodding despite that distant voice in my head desperate to tell her no, that I can't, that every moment here is a moment my revenge slips further away from me... but as a huge, radiant smile cracks her face open like a sunrise, I lean forward on my toes, invading her space again, our foreheads nearly touching.

"I could arrange for that to happen," I mutter.

Her lips curve into an amused grin and she tilts her head, fully connecting our foreheads. I feel that blasted organ in my chest give another harsh jerk. *She'd been worried about me.* The fact I'd been on her mind, and the way she's looking at me now, makes my stomach clench. Even though my instincts are telling me to run out that door this minute, I can't. I feel myself leaning closer. I have no control over what my body is doing. Her breath fans across my lips.

She seems frozen to the spot, her fingers still at my brow, but they tremble slightly. It vibrates through my body, has my heart taking on a strange, off-beat rhythm. She glances down to my lips and back into my eyes. I swallow hard, involuntarily doing the same to her.

I want to kiss her. I want her to kiss me.

The pounding in my ears is a loud rushing again as I hold her gaze, unsure of what's going on, or what's about to happen, if I want it, if she wants it, or even if I care to stop it at all.

Just when I think the tension is going to strangle me alive, the front door flings open, banging against the wall and Hanna and I spring apart like two children caught doing something naughty. I fall onto my arse with an *oomph* as Hanna scrambles into a proper sitting position on the settee, smoothing her hair as her pale cheeks blaze crimson.

"The scylla does not seem to be anywhere in the area," Demetrius announces as he strolls in. "Surprising, considering how territorial those beasts are, especially once they get a taste of something that they like." The nymph's favorite gray cloak whirls about around him; he's seemingly unaware of what he'd almost walked in on.

I exploit his lack of attention, and haul myself to my feet, straightening my shirt, tugging at the high collar that tries to choke me. "What are ya getting at, nymph?"

Demetrius doesn't seem to notice how tense I am as he crosses to sink onto the settee, somehow folding his long limbs beneath him without getting tangled in his cloak. A puzzled look draws his brown eyebrows down. "Scylla are notoriously known for keeping to certain territorial patches of sea their entire lives, picking an area to call their own once they reach maturity."

Hanna grins crookedly, eyes glittering with a childish curiosity I've grown used to seeing when Demetrius mentions something particularly to her liking. Apparently great beasts who almost snap me in half then drown me are on that list. "You said it's gone, but will it return if our bay is its home? What did you mean by 'it's got a taste for something that it liked'?"

The aloof nymph turns an affectionate half-smile at her. "It usually feeds on the flesh of other unfortunate creatures that wander into its territory; sea animals, humans that stumble into trouble… but, strong magical beings like you or I would give it a boost beyond that of just a meal. It would absorb our essence, gaining the rest of our years and taking them for itself. I was not aware one had come into maturity and wandered into this area. I will keep an eye out, but you landed a blow to it, both physically and to its ego. It will think twice before showing its heads around here again."

Hanna blinks, almost unbelieving, at him, her pouty lips dropping open.

I snort, folding my arms over my chest. "Just how many of these creatures have you met in your time to know them so *intimately*, Demetrius?"

His smile melts like the first frost to dissolve after the winter, his mouth jerking into a sneer. "If you could read tomes that were beyond that of a ten-year old's comprehension, maybe you would know of them as well, Urchin."

My eyebrow twitches at the careless words he spews from his foolish mouth, and my anger rises as he smirks, infuriatingly. I want to punch it off his face. I'm going to.

Hanna abruptly stands and raises her hands, putting a barrier between him and I.

"Una's decided to spend a few more days here with us while she fully recovers from the attack, isn't that lovely?" She's not smiling at him. She's using that commanding voice she keeps buried. It does something strange to my stomach. "You'll have a chance to teach her how to play pall-mall after all."

Demetrius leans to the side, looking around Hanna with a grin as large as the thorn he's become in my side, looking every inch the child he acts like at times. "That is quite lovely, Hanna. *Quite* lovely indeed."

As Demetrius grins like a predator finally catching its prey, anxiety ripples through me. Is it too late to go back on my word? Shite.

***

28 April 1691
Lampung Bay, Sumatera, Dutch East Indies

"It's not a sword, Una. Hold it more gently, like this!" Demetrius tells me. The cheery nymph turns his heavy mallet, as long as my arm, downward and mimes swinging it underarm gently. *That* wouldn't be very useful in a fight. I stare at the apparent not-weapon in my hand and attempt to mimic him. What in God's name have I let them talk me into? I feel like a buffoon…

"Lovely form, Una, you learn quickly." I'm not looking at him but can hear the smug smile in his voice as he continues, "As I was saying, usually in pall-mall we would hit this ball through metal hoops embedded in the ground, attempting to do so in the fewest strokes in order to win."

I slowly swing my mallet back and forth, scuffing my toes into the sand, but still he goes on, wittering away like a seagull.

"The way I taught Hanna to play is a touch different. We simply push a stake into the sand and whoever gets the ball closest, in the fewest strokes without sending the ball past it, is the victor! Understand?" He flourishes his words by holding up the palm-sized leather ball in one hand and pointing, with the mallet in his other hand, at a thin wooden stake three paces away.

I try not to glare at the grinning nymph. I'd agreed yesterday to join whatever game he wanted to play, thinking it would be some sparring or training activity, only to find an odd parlor game. I know he's reveling in this. He loves seeing me the fish out of water. Delights in it. I feel so foolish. What am I doing? But I nod dutifully, noting the excitable fire dances brightly in Demetrius's emerald eyes; one I've seen countless times since being here. One that means I'm not getting out of this game, no matter how foolish or useless it is.

"Delightful. I shall go first and show you how it's done. Come, follow me a distance!"

Before I can give my answer, he dances up the beach, swinging his mallet in front of him like a pendulum as he hums to himself. What a loon.

46

"Is Hanna going to be joining our little game, or do you have her reading another useless book?" I call after him.

He stops his odd gallivanting, whirling around to throw me an appalled look dropping the ball onto the sand. "No book is useless, Una. A different world resides in each one, and in the maps I keep. But she will indeed be joining us! She's gathering some milk and sugar cakes for afterwards! You'll adore them, they are so sweet and fluffy!"

Once again, before I can voice any retort, he turns, flips his mallet the 'correct' way up and hits the ball across the sands. It skitters along the beach, stopping two feet from the stake. He lets out a whoop of excitement and strides toward the ball. "You are going to have your work cut out for you, child. I feel the gods on my side today!"

I roll my eyes at the strange man. It's at his and Hanna's persistent pestering that I'm still here four days after that scylla attack. I'm fully recovered to how I was before the mutiny on the ship, *better,* if I'm being honest. I can't remember ever feeling this full or relaxed, which is barmy considering I've been snooping through every corner of their cabin anytime they're off somewhere, looking for more information on the island. I've been eating all the food they offer, still taking the only real bed in the place, and I've come to appreciate the oddly enjoyable company of and conversation with Hanna. It's all too peculiar. But if I'm not careful, I could get lost here.

The thought jars me, has me gripping the handle of my mallet tighter, as I watch the chestnut-haired young man - *nymph* I remind myself - take his second swing. They aren't even human. Lord help us all if I can't get a hold of myself. Elyse must die, there's no two ways around it. Not only because she abused and dishonored the most important code to us buccaneers, not only because she's betrayed every spit of trust and love I put into her, but because she's far too dangerous to leave slithering about. If she can slight her own sibling as thoughtlessly as she has, she'll do much worse to strangers.

"Your turn! That was two!"

47

I'm jolted from my thoughts as the ball rolls to the stop at the tip of my boot. I blink at Demetrius standing on the far side of the stake rammed into the ground, a huge grin splitting his face in half.

I sigh, shaking my head and line up the circular part of the mallet with the grayish black ball, and draw my arm back. Well, here goes… *something*. I swing the mallet down to connect. The ball sails into the air, much higher than I intended it to. It cuts through the sky, and Demetrius and I both crane our heads back to follow it. I know it's going to plop into the ocean behind him. I'm already wincing…

But it doesn't happen.

In one fluid motion, the nymph drops his mallet at his feet, then leaps like a cat and catches the incoming ball, the sound of it slapping into the center of his hand loud in the quiet cove.

He sends me an annoyed look. "That was *not* 'gently'."

Heat fills my cheeks at my total failure to be gentle at anything, including a children's game, even though seeing the nymph leap so gracefully and impossibly high into the air was quite impressive. He rarely shows these otherworldly abilities. Not like I'd ever admit I'm impressed out loud, or that I wouldn't mind seeing more of his abilities. It's clear from the look on his face that we can both agree on one thing: I'm a clod.

I toss the offending mallet down and cross my arms. "This is by far the most useless thing you've asked me to do since being here. What's the *point* of this?"

Demetrius looks at me like I've sprouted another head. He tilts his, studying me like he can't quite understand my question.

"Have you never participated in merrymaking?" He rolls the ball back towards me and I stop it with the side of my boot. He smiles, softer this time, bracing his mallet across his lean shoulders and hooking his wrists over either end. "This is another form of it. Taking a moment to just stop, breathe, and *exist*. Feel the air rushing through your lungs? The energy flooding your limbs as your heart beats. Be thankful for those small things, for they're what truly matter at the end of the day.

48

And be thankful for pall-mall, because once you get the hang of it, it too is one of those small joys."

His words have an unfamiliar feeling swirling in my gut, one I don't know if I fully like. It makes me tighten my arms around myself. I'm about to open my mouth when movement in my peripheral has me turning. I swallow. Hanna.

She strides toward us, small woven basket in her hands, her dark blue skirts flaring about her ankles, white cotton waistcoat fitting to her body almost too perfectly. Her grin is almost as blinding as Demetrius's had been when I agreed to be a part of his foolishness. So easily pleased. So pure it almost makes me want to vomit.

Her smile dims as her large expressive gaze takes in the scene. She twists her lips to the side, holding the basket closer to her chest. "Did you lose? He really is a sore winner. I can't remember a time he's ever let me win anything. Even when I was a child and inexperienced. Don't concern yourself with him. Will you play a round with me? I'll even give you a chance, unlike this half-wit." She jerks her head at Demetrius.

He squawks out a strangled noise of indignance, putting his hands on his hips, pouting. "I take offense to that, Guppy! I've let you win a bounty of times. Your memory must be failing you in your old age." He grins at Hanna as she drops her basket and stomps over to him, her pretty face morphed into one of displeasure. I'm honestly not sure if she's going to punch him or shove that mallet she's currently picking up into his mouth. I'd pay to see her do either.

But, alas, seems like there's not going to be a fight, since she points a finger toward the cabin, scowling at him. "Go have a sugar cake and cool down, *Father*. I think you've had enough sun for now. It must be going to your head in *your* old age."

He only grins, unafraid of and unbothered by her anger. He drops a quick kiss onto her temple and does that odd little dance of his as he dodges her swat. His joyful laugh echoes as he heads away from us. "Be inside before the sun sets, Hanna. Nefarious things happen when the shadows come out to play."

She and I both scoff out loud before our eyes meet, and her lips turn into a slow smile. I can't help grinning either, and then we both break into laughter. The action lights her face, making it more ethereal. She's unlike any woman I've ever met, in every meaning of the word.

"Ready to play?" she asks.

Although her request comes out in an unserious laugh, I find myself leaning down to pick up the dropped mallet as if she's ordered me at gunpoint. I didn't even stop to think before I moved. I nod even as my stomach squirms with the knowledge of what I'm going to do tonight, what I *must* do. I'm healed, I have what I finally need, and my lingering here is starting to mess with my brain. I can't lose myself here. I can't waste another day. So, I'll let myself have this moment with her. This last moment. It has to be the last.

***

I lie in Hanna's bed until I'm sure the pair must be far enough out on their nightly swim to not sense the misdeeds I'm about to commit. No. Not misdeeds. Necessities to survive, to get what I need to get. Hanna will understand.

Focus, Una. Get the knapsack, grab the map, the weapon, rations, water, and MOVE. They could return at any moment. I growl at my pushy inner voice, though it aids me. I let the prospect of being caught quicken my movements as I stand and push my feet into the boots I'd left here for quicker access earlier.

That energy flows into my limbs, forcing out the heaviness threatening to slow my movements, the sudden knot of ill feeling curling deep in my gut. *Guilt.* It's an uncommon feeling for me. I've only felt guilt twice before in my life, and feeling it now for something as trivial as this? I've been here too long. It's making me soft.

I gather the knapsack I've had hidden for three days from behind the chest of drawers. I've filled it with some of Hanna's ointment for small injuries, a couple of the sugar cakes (I'll have to eat those first so they don't go bad), some bread rations, the calabashes filled with water that I'd taken from their kitchen earlier today, and the map that would lead me to the first steps in gathering another crew, a boat, tracking down that blasted sibling of mine, and putting her head on a spike. The map I'd unearthed shows the nearest port as the *Port of Bakauheni,* south of here, and by my reckoning at least a two day's walk if I can't find a horse to steal or a merchant to bribe a lift from.

I hook the small sack over my shoulder and pull the shiniest, sharpest cutlass they have on display from the wall, that flame of guilt burning hotter as I loop it through the sash wrapped around my waist. For you, Pa.

I head for the open door, only stopping to take Demetrius's cloak, the one he always flaps around in like it's made of spun gold instead of thick gray wool. It'll serve me well on my journey and serve him right for all his teasing and games. I fasten it over my shoulders as I continue through the quiet cabin, the only sounds my footsteps and the rapid beat of my heart in my ears.

I fling open the front door to the darkness of the vast night sky and rolling waves, and step into the cool night air. I breathe it in deeply and close the door behind me, peering out one last time toward the sea.

"God be with ye, Hanna," I mutter to the darkness.

***

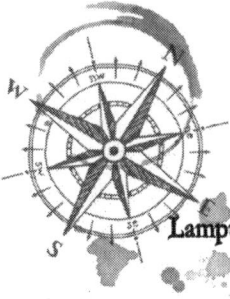

Chapter 7: Hanna
29 April 1691
Lampung Bay, Sumatera, Dutch East Indies

I flop on to my mattress, still drained of energy even after the extra long swim today. The strain the distance between Una and I is putting on the bond is already painfully evident. It's been one whole day since Una's sudden and silent departure in the dead of night, while Deme and I were out recharging ourselves on our nightly swim. No note or thought to find to say farewell. Only the thought to steal from us and take almost our entire supply of fresh water.

Once the anger and foolish disappointment had passed, I'd quickly concluded that this was for the best. Slinking away in the shadows like the buccaneer she is. The better to keep me from saying or doing something completely foolish… this is for the best, for everyone.

Another wave of mind-numbing exhaustion ripples through me. My eyes are heavy and gritty, like they're full of sand. A mere day and my body is already starting to shut down. Extreme fatigue, the first sign of a rejected bond.

My aching body forces me to shift onto my side. At this rate, I won't last very long. I suppose I'll find out soon enough. My vision blurs around the edges. The sweet lull of sleep tugs me towards blissful oblivion, as I struggle to keep my eyes open. Then nothing at all. Sleep's dark and endless abyss finally pulls me under.

***

Persistent shaking on my shoulder. My eyes fly open to meet Demetrius's worried cut-jade eyes. I inhale deeply, trying to center myself and clear the dense fog from my sleep-impaired brain. But the unshakable fatigue persists; the sleep hasn't dented it at all. I try, and fail, to smother a yawn forcing its way past my lips against my fist.

"What is it?" I mumble around the yawn.

He lays his pale hands on his hips and puffs out his lean chest, attempting to look bigger and more imposing, his expression one I immediately know means he's about to offer some grand tale.

"We have to bring the pirate urchin back here. You will perish if we do not."

I blink up at him, confused. His roundabout, fluid thinking has always been mystifying and puzzling since I was young. His words are often a game I can never seem to win, a riddle I can never seem to solve, frustrating beyond measure, even now.

My body aches and groans with the effort of sitting up. "She's made her decision, Demetrius. I'm not going to force her into servitude, or command absolute obedience from her, just so I can live. Bond or no bond, I'm not afraid to die. It's okay."

He sighs, his shoulders tense as he slides himself onto the bed beside me, the mattress dipping under his extra weight, his lips curling into that familiar pout. "If you were just to tell her of the Gift... As I said earlier, a natural bond was already forming between the two of you, I saw it with my own eyes. Is it such a stretch that she –"

"That she would what?" I interject. "She would give up on her plans and life for a person, a *woman* she knew only a short while? On the off chance she possibly *could* care for something like me... I won't steal that choice from her. I won't steal her life."

Demetrius's normally carefree demeanor crumbles and I'm left staring into the face of a familiar stranger. The seriousness that permeates his every pore has my heart stuttering. His whole being commands that I pay attention, that I listen, that I understand him. "If we do not go after the pirate child, she will not get a choice. She will die, most definitely, sooner or later, and your noble sacrifice will be in vain."

I'm puzzled by his behavior. "With her lifestyle, there's always a risk of death... but don't you think you're being a touch dramatic? I thank you for caring so much, but *what* in all the ocean's waters *are* you going on about?" I inwardly pray he isn't headed in the direction I'm worried he is.

He sighs loudly, his shoulders slumping, all that intensity zapping him of his strength, and he looks at me with tired eyes. "You heard the same words I did during our meal all those nights ago, do not bury your head in the sands."

My vision blurs again so I lean against the pillows and exhale carefully, the deep exhaustion settling into my bones, but not snuffing out the growing pit of dread in my stomach. I beg him with my eyes to continue his explanation, to soothe my thoughts.

"I have many abilities as a water nymph. One is that I can sense the shadows, the *essence,* of people who linger in the water too long. It leaves an imprint. There was a shadow in the Bay almost identical to Una's, and another remarkably similar to yours. That generally only occurs amongst family members. Siblings, children, a parent. Sometimes cousins. I kept thinking I must be wrong, that I was just picking up on the trails of you and Una in the water… but no. Subtly different enough. I am sorry, my darling, I don't think I am mistaken. I believe Una has a sibling and that sibling is with Kai. Yes, *your* Kai. And Una is sailing right back into his clutches if he remains anywhere near her sibling. He is a vicious smog that will poison and darken Una's soul. Will you stay here and let her meet her end? Or do we go, and stop Kai from killing Una?"

The fatigue in my body is nothing compared to the bone-chilling feeling lacing through my blood now. The pounding in my head makes it hard for me to pull in a steady breath. "She's going to try and get revenge on Kai… and her sibling? Elyse… a sister? *Gods,* Deme. Kai'll more than kill her, he'll wipe her out of existence. We have to stop her, we have to…" My body trembles as I suck in breath after shuddering breath. All I can think about is Kai inflicting all he had done to me onto others, onto Una. Her life ending, and me staying here, knowing what she's going to attempt, and not lifting a finger to help. She may have stolen from me, but it's not like I hadn't been expecting something like that, and it's not reason enough to condemn her. I swallow harshly past the lump in my throat. "I have to try and stop this… stop her…"

Demetrius's firm, familiar grip on my shaking shoulder pulls me back from a dangerous cliff. "Han, take a breath and think, here. You know as well as I that she will not stop, even if we tell her Kai is your birth father... she is a pirate after all."

Grief unlike any I've ever known fills me; stronger even than when I realized Mother would never come for me, or when Kai sold me on land. Hot tears stream down my face as a hollowness twists under my ribs. I'm losing a part of myself, the most sacred, precious, irreplaceable part. The part of myself I haven't even gotten a chance to explore fully yet, hadn't realized I'd had. Mermaids only have one bonded, one mate. The Gift of the Sea makes certain of that. The magic used when giving it is so interwoven through us, so ancient, so powerful. Deme's always said he's sure that's why a rejected bond always ends with the death of the unfortunate mermaid. He's always comforted me. Whenever I grew tired of always hiding, whenever the loneliness almost drowned me, whenever I thought life would be better if he just left me on land to die, he always cared for me. To cheer me, he'd tell me of fate, destiny and how one day, my mate – a person specially made for me – would find me and accept and love me for all of me, that they'd cast away my loneliness. That when the time came, I'd know it, sense it. And I do know it now. I feel it with every part of my being. It screams it at me. Una is mine. Una is meant to be mine.

I look at the one who saved my life – my guardian, best friend, father. "I can't let her die... not like this, not to him. What are we going to do?"

A sudden grin lights his face, his emerald eyes once again glee-filled and mischievous. "We're going to join her crew, and then we shall aid her in bringing Kai down."

***

Chapter 8: Demetrius
29 April 1691
Lampung Bay, Sumatera, Dutch East Indies

The corners of my lips twitch upwards. The look of complete confusion souring Hanna's face is utterly laughable and completely precious. I've often, over the last twelve years, tested Hanna's intelligence and, often enough, her patience with games. When she could not decipher my riddles or puzzles, she'd turn tyrant, ranting and raving sometimes for days about how I just did foolish things to get an outlandish reaction out of her.

Only partly true.

There's an unhealthy sallow tint to her normally porcelain skin, her cheeks hollow, dark bruises beneath her lilac eyes.

"And how do you intend to get on her ship? Or even in her crew for that matter? Just traipse forward and just ask nicely? You can't so much as look at the ocean without going all…" She wiggles her fingers around her head, which I'm assuming is supposed to describe the way my hair changes form and colors around water.

I chuckle and gently stroke the hair from her sweaty forehead, something I've done since I first found her on land. And she calls me naive. "She's not going to know it's us, obviously. Observe." I close my eyes and concentrate on my magical core, focusing the power always gently swirling close to the surface, rippling just below my skin, waiting for me to call on it. It rushes forward eagerly, the feeling of coming home filling me as I let the magic wash over me.

I breathe out slowly, allowing that magic to spread outward, completely covering me from head to toe like a second skin, like a wave. I feel my stature shorten, muscle packing onto my usually lithe body, hair lengthening to hang over my forehead and brush just below my eyebrows. Then the powerful swell of magic that was so eager to help recedes to a pleasant, hypnotic humming melody just below my skin, coiled and waiting.

I spin in a slow circle, opening my eyes, showing off the completed transformation. Those eyes that remind me so much of her late mother stare wide, her mouth open in a little 'o' of surprise. The laugh that had been building in my chest finally bubbles over. I lightly press on her chin, tilting it upwards. "Hanna, close your mouth. It is quite unladylike."

She scowls and weakly pushes my fingers from her face. "And you can do that to me as well?"

I nod and let the magic encasing my skin shatter. It coils back towards the center of my magical core; that warm, comforting feeling goes with it, leaving me almost cold. I look like myself once more. Or at least, the me that walks the land amongst humans.

"I don't know a lot about the Gift," Hanna is rubbing at her tired temples, trying to think, "but I know what the distance is doing to the bond. And when she was here, close, I was drawn to her. It wasn't particularly strong, but it made me want to check where she was every so often. Won't it work the same for her? You said when I'm near, the natural allure of it will gnaw at her. She'll eventually piece things together. She isn't a fool, despite what you may think of her being so unread…"

I hold up a hand to stop her. She's a clever girl, but does she think so little of me that I won't have considered this? I dig into my trouser pocket and pull out a cork-stoppered vial filled with murky, green liquid. "I finished this elixir this morn. It will transfer *all* the bond's effects onto you temporarily. For Una, it will mask the allure and need to obey you. But, unfortunately, you will still feel the effects of a rejected bond, and without her acknowledgment and acceptance of it, you will still be slowly dying."

She looks from my face to the vial tube in my hand, then back to my face, a kaleidoscope of emotions flickering across her face. "How did you learn to brew that? More mementos from Mother?"

That little vexed crease appears between her eyes that always rises to the surface at the mention of her mother. I nod curtly and shrug, curling my fingers around the corked tube, pulling it away from Hanna. "If you do not want to partake, we will most certainly find another way to suppress the side effects, or perhaps another plan entirely, but if we wait, it may be far too late to track her down. It will be another half a day before we can set out as it is…" I let my words hang in the air like a cloud heavy with rain.

Hanna bites her lip, a nervous habit she's had since childhood, one she would not be happy to know she picked up from her mother, Ondine.

She sighs after a pause and holds out her slightly trembling hand. "Let me have the elixir. Save your dramatics for another day. We have ourselves a pirate to save. Where is it exactly we need to head? Do you even have a clue?"

I grin at her. My Guppy, my pride, my *daughter*, and toss my arm over her shoulders, hugging her tight to my side. "Put on your best riding boots, sweet one. We are taking a journey sixty miles south, to the Port of Bakauheni."

***

Chapter 9: Una
1 May 1691
Port of Bakauheni, Sumatera, Dutch East Indies

I'm going to gut that gill-fish wide open, skin him and use his bones to pick my damn teeth. This place is *not* what the map led me to believe it'd be. I clench the useless map in my hands, tempted to toss it away. I don't; that will just draw more attention. Instead, I pull the odd-smelling hood higher over my head, covering my face even more, despite the darkness of the night.

That odd smell lingering in the nymph's hood is almost peppery, becoming more apparent the longer I walk through the disappointing port. The buildings here are not much like the cabin, with its odd wooden base and stone top all covered in moss. The islanders' houses are wooden, painted a clean, bright white, all raised on wooden stilts to keep them safe from flooding rains. Most have stairs looping around the entire home up to the front doors. They sprung up alongside the road, a few here and there at first, but I'm surrounded now, dozens of them, all spread out in a little town, before I've actually reached the port.

My feet ache, my back is tight, but I keep walking, past the homes into what looks like a marketplace. I haven't seen this many humans in a good while. It puts me on edge, but it's also exciting. The market stalls are uniform wooden huts, all with huge painted signs, presumably describing their various wares. 'Presumably', because, as I peer from the shadows of my hood, keeping my feminine form as concealed as possible, it's like being at Hanna and Demetrius's again. I can't read a damn word.

My anger flares intensely for a moment, threatening to take any good sense from me, but I force myself to focus instead on the smells wafting around me. Besides these market stalls, with their unreadable signs, are huge barrels filled with different kinds of spices, the combined aromas in such a small area making for an interesting, heady scent in the air. But there's definitely that warm peppery smell weaving

59

through the others. It's the smell trapped in the wool of the cloak, a smell that reminds me immediately of the nymph, Hanna, their home. The recognition, the strange ache and comfort that brings me, the automatic urge to nuzzle into the cloak, disturbs me and I clench my fists against it. No time for softness. No place for it… but I know the smell will linger long after I make my way to the port, where I need to scout out my next step in getting off this godforsaken rock. I ignore the comfort that scent brings me for all I'm worth.

The night market is bustling, alive, people pushing in around me. It's hot. So bloody hot. Too many bloody people, dammit. As I walk, the stolen cloak begins to feel like a choking vice, the heat of the hood pulled so fully over my head beginning to seep into my bones. This place is like being pushed into a fire. Sweat slides from the nape of my neck down the curve of my spine. I hadn't realized how hot this country is; being near the ocean since my rescue spoiled me.

I scan more of the stalls, partly intrigued by these new and unfamiliar wares, partly wondering what this all might be worth, when I notice the lad purveying the stall to my right. I pause to watch him. Even if I hadn't been trained from a young age to notice things that don't quite belong, he'd stick out. He doesn't seem to realize I've got my eye on him.

The people of this island, even more passive and boring than the two supernatural creatures living almost under their noses, wear clothes of so many different colors, fabrics that my head spins the longer I look at them all. But this man's clothes are different.

He's far taller than me, I can tell even from a few feet away. I have a side view of him, his stature is thickly built with broad shoulders that make his dark waistcoat look like it's going to burst its stitches. He's wearing a white, ruffled cotton shirt tucked into equally dark knee length breeches. No cloak. Stockings as brilliantly white as his shirt cover his calves below the short breeches, feet are adorned with dark shoes with a high heel, but no sign of the frilly ribbons that usually come with them.

As he reaches for something on the stall, I see a flash of steel, a sword belt hanging diagonally around his waist, and spot a flash of the insignia around his upper arm. Pa had shown Elyse and I this insignia in some of our earliest lessons with him. The band on his arm is white with a large black V in the middle, a smaller O and C looping between it, the three letters becoming one symbol. *Vereenigde Oost-Indische Companie*… the Dutch East-India Company. Oh, Demetrius's bones will be used to pick my teeth *and* to kindle my fire.

Men without honor sold their souls to do the Crown's bidding to line their pockets with easy coin. People that think they can own the ocean and everything that happens in it, control who can trade and barter. If anyone's caught not following their up-their-own-arse rules on 'moral conduct' they'll take everything you're trying to trade, and everything else you're not trying to trade, and throw you in the cells to rot, or until they decide to take you to see good ol' Jack Ketch. The Dutch East India Company are worse than those damn British 'Jack Tars', the lot of 'em.

I force my legs to move, quickening my steps past him, keeping my head low, purposely melding into the edge of a group laughing and talking loudly as they pass through the market, heading right where I want to go. The group passes the dock entrance and I slip in, keeping my steps light as I make my way down to the strangely quiet docks.

Keeping my head low, the nervous knot in my gut begins to churn like the waters lapping at the small ships here, all at least half the size of Pa's ship. There's fishing and merchant vessels too, dotting the inky waters like the last leaves holding onto a branch before a gust of wind forces them to the ground. Slim pickings.

Damn it all to three hells, I'm back where I started, with nothing. It's like waking up inside Hanna and Demetrius's cabin all over again, confused and not knowing a damn thing. I don't even have anything that I can sell for coin. All that wasted effort spent sneaking around, eating their food, playing their odd games, masquerading around like I actually enjoyed their company, Hanna's…

You did. You do.

I clamp down on that annoying voice that's slowly been growing louder and more persistent since I left the cabin. The goading voice overlaps with my rant, over the lies I've been carefully pretending I believe. It has my head spinning and I head toward the closest darkened alleyway. I need a few moments to settle the dangerous storm threatening to spill up out of me that's daring my fingers to clench into tight fists, itching to punch the first lad who dares even gaze in my direction.

I duck, unseen, into the alleyway. There's nothing here save two crates at the opposite end, and I head for them, leaning against one, allowing my eyes to close for one blessed moment. This is bad. I've no idea where to go, and I can't go back to the cabin, to Hanna. I stole from them, took probably the most important thing to them, their water, without a thought, even after she aided me, despite her reservations and without much contempt for who I was.

But you have thought about her, haven't you?

I jerk into a standing position, fists raised like I can physically fight that mocking voice of my twisting, turbulent thoughts. Before my fist can connect with anything a disembodied voice – a real one, not the one plaguing my mind – permeates the cool shadows of the alley.

"What's a lass doing paradin' around the streets at night? And dressed as a lad no less. How scandalous."

 The sing-song sound of it tells me it's a female, but that knowledge does nothing to calm the fear, sudden and sharp, in my stomach.

I whip around, my small hidden blade already in my grasp.

Odd golden eyes regard me from under a black hood, the moonlight casting an almost inhuman glow to them though they're mostly hidden. She's a head taller than me and all hidden under the ankle-length black hooded cloak.

As I stare into her eyes that seem to be staring *into* me, I step back slowly until my back is firmly pressed against the wall, the rough brick of it biting into my shoulder. "Identify yourself," I demand, glad my voice is strong.

She lowers the hood at my words, revealing a pale heart-shaped face with sharp cheekbones and a strong jaw, unusual on a lass. Small, upturned nose, full rose-colored lips, a dimpled chin, and thin unruly eyebrows. She wears her hair sitting just on her shoulders, kissing the hood with dark, coal colored ringlets. It's not a style I've seen any women sporting. Not boyish, like mine. Not long like Hanna's. Not pinned up in combs like a lot of the women in ports I've stopped in. This lass is… different. In every meaning of the word.

She raises her hands, palms up. I see the glint of a weapon on her hip, a sword so old, so unlike any sword I've seen before, it looks unkempt. It's only on my second glance that I realize it is taken care of, not rusted, it's just that ancient.

"Peace, bucko," she says, "You're in no danger from me. I'm a lass, too."

I flash my teeth as I sneer, raising my weapon, challenging her. "I've met many a lass worse than any *lad* I've come across." My eyes dart to her arms as I notice the odd black tattoos twining round them both, like curling ivy.

The lass snorts a laugh, though she still frowns at me. "Touché. The name's Selina. You're the first female I've seen since arriving in this land. I figured I could commission you to be my muscle."

I blink at her. Does she think I'm a local here? I don't look anything like these people. How does she know I'm a lass? Does she suspect I'm a buccaneer? No longer under the protective coziness of the cabin, my body is back to being tense, on guard.

"How did you know I'm a lass?" I decide to ask her the easier question first to buy time to concoct a story on why I can't aid her in anything.

Her lower lip twitches, those pools of honey twinkling with something close to amusement. "Your gait."

I wait for her to go on, but she doesn't. My *gait*?! This lass is as loony as the last one I met. I scan her from head to toe quickly. This one does seem to be as human as I am, thankfully. I run through all the possible outcomes in my head. Staying here isn't an option, and going back isn't, either. Maybe this lass could be the foothold I need to make it to the nearest trade route or a port with a wider selection of actual ships to work with. I'll have to be careful, though. I lower my weapon. "And what if I can't help ya *now?* What if *you* help *me* first? Get me to an actual port with more to offer than this pathetic slop bucket, or point me in the direction of something can, and I'm sure we can come to an agreeable deal where we both get what we want."

Her top lip twitches again, another snort slipping through her nose. "Now there's no doubt, you *are* a buccaneer. No one else could come up with such terms on such short notice."

I blink again, completely taken off guard, but quickly cover it with my usual snark. "And what of you, lass? Traveling alone? That's even stranger than me hiding and paradin' around as a lad. Either you're a buccaneer yourself, or a daring lass looking for adventure?"

I know I've said the correct thing when her eyes sparkle with unhidden excitement, a corner of her mouth daring to lift upward a moment.

"A bit of both perhaps? Seeing what else these vast oceans have to offer me," she quips.

I know now she's not about to attack me, since she's folded her arms over her chest, so I loop my weapon through my sash under my cloak. "You navigate yourself?"

That slight upturn of her lips turns into a full smirk, her arrogance coming off her in thick, heavy waves. "One of the finest on the waters, if not the finest."

Bold words. But it gives me an idea. "How about this." I brace a hand on my hip. "You get us to the nearest more populated area, and a spot on my crew is yours. Guaranteed."

Her smirk deepens and she holds out a hand. "Make me a quartermaster and I'll take ya to a lad named Atropous who can get us to Banten. Heavy trade route runs through those parts, you'll find everything you'll need there."

I stare at her offered palm, excitement curling under my ribs. What do I have to lose? I grip her hand in a firm grasp. "You've got yourself a deal. You can call me Captain Una."

***

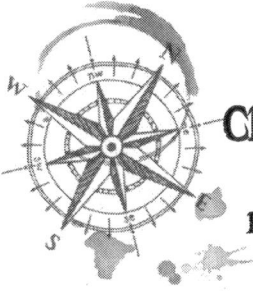

Chapter 10: Demetrius
17 May 1691
Banten, Java, Dutch East Indies

"I've never seen such a place in my entire life, *Aurelius!*"

I watch Hanna, entirely transformed by my magic, twirl around in a hazardous circle as she struggles to take in all the new sights, sounds, and structures she has never encountered before. Her cotton breeches, a size larger than she is, billow on her slight frame. My magic makes her taller than her original form, but still shorter than me. Her bright blue silken waistcoat gleams beautifully in the slowly setting sun, her annoyance at high collars and restrictive wear melting away the moment her excitement and curiosity overwhelmed her. It was either this garb or one of the frilly layered dresses women in these parts favor. Unsurprisingly, she'd refused the dress. She spins again, the tip of her rapier almost knocking into a fabric stall. The knot of her now shoulder-length light brown hair, that I'd painstakingly tucked under her matching bright blue bandanna, begins to slip. My jaw clenches as she flashes the annoyed merchant an apologetic smile and needlessly adjusts the cloth hanging off the side of his stall.

She turns back to me, her now small almond-shaped nut-brown eyes glittering with the most mirth I've seen since the urchin left and made a bigger mess of things. Her smile, now slightly crooked on sun-blasted lips, is blinding, as she dances upon her toes, a habit she's somehow picked up from a mother she never had the opportunity to really know.

"These buildings are so different from our cabin, and any building at home that I've ever seen. The tops really wouldn't do any good to stop the intense rainfall from our side of the island," she's telling me, as if I don't already entirely understand this. "It's made of straw. It looks like hay. Do you suppose they'll change it soon? You saw how easy it was for me to almost knock something off it, it's the most curious thing." She darts away toward another stall selling fishing and netting supplies.

"Octavia…" Her new incognito name still feels strange to say. "No, pause a moment." I grasp her wrist, gently tugging the now deeply frowning child back to my side. I guide us out of the flowing stream of island humans, wedging us between two oaken barrels, one half full of rice, the other holding sticky cut stems of sugarcane. Her tanned hand pokes at the sticky sweet sugarcane, an awed child-like look permeating her face. 'Tis like she did not even hear me at all! I once again gently grab her wandering hand and pull her distracted gaze finally to me. I lower my voice, so that only she can hear me. "Look at me, Hanna. I know you are excited, but things have not gotten any better since I found you on land twelve years ago. If possible, it has gotten worse. I raised you to be able to read, write, to protect yourself, but most women have not been given the same opportunities as you. You must be careful."

That fickle gaze dances from me again, going back to the sugar at her hip. "I will, I will. We must get going, right? The longer we dally the farther Una gets from us."

She half hardheartedly pulls at my grip on her wrists as her head turns, already locked onto something else that's piqued her interest. I sigh. It's like dealing with twelve-year-old Hanna all over again. Ancestors, watch over me. I drop her wrists and ruffle the fringe of her hair, purposely sliding the bandanna down over her eyes, forcing her focus back onto me.

She growls as she adjusts the headscarf back into place, her thin lips curled into a decidedly unamused frown. "And what was the purpose of that?"

I link our arms together, flashing her a wide grin to melt her defenses. She never could stay upset with me for long, not when she knows I only do my best to take care of her. Not when she knows how much I adore her.

"It got your attention, no? I could tell you heard me, but you weren't listening. I want to help you, very much so, but your safety is my top priority." I turn us back into the crowd, keeping Hanna close to me. "The dangers of this world are very real. I know you understand that. Better than most people your age, far better than you probably should. But I know you can persevere and get through this because not only is that who I raised you to be, but because it was you before I ever found you. When you focus on something, you produce results that are astounding. We can have merrymaking, but we must always keep our wits about us."

She nods, and this time, she leans into me for comfort. "I trust you, I believe in our combined abilities, but how in Poseidon's name are we ever going to track down Una in a place so big? Let alone before she manages to put a crew together and leave. She's had days on us."

The energy of the crowd pulsates around me like a large stone cast into the middle of a still pond. It swirls through me, causing a chill to race up my spine. My belly tingles with excitement. It has been some time since I've been in a crowd so large myself. I indicate with a jerk of my chin and a squeeze of her elbow, towards the street in our left. I lay my free hand on the hilt of my rapier. "Obtaining a crew is only half the battle. Getting a *ship* for her crew? Even with her spirit, that will be even more of a task for her. Unless she is a very skilled haggler, good at threats, or willing to have loose morals, it will take her time, and that is the disadvantage we will take advantage of."

I gleefully watch Hanna's new tanned, more-chiseled cheeks flush with embarrassment at my choice of wording, I suspect, about loose morals. "Or," she huffs, "she could find allies… that's also something she could do."

I chuckle and continue to lead my charge, my *daughter,* further inland, away from the many stalls and at times overwhelming scents, toward the heavier stone buildings, though their roofs still look like furry pointed hats, and towards the inn I know will have the twenty-four-year-old woman at my side turning once again into her youthful self. Instead of irritation, anticipation wells up in the center of my being at the thought of another grand adventure. "Oh, Guppy. I still have so much to teach you."

***

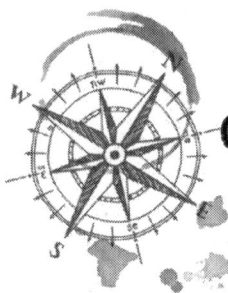

Chapter 11: Atropous
20 May 1691
Banten, Java, Dutch East Indies

"Forgive me! I'm late for an engagement!" I hoist the supplies I'd gotten at the marketplace, hugging them against my chest as I catch the falling broom with the tip of my raised boot. I hover my foot in midair a moment before flicking it and catching the handle in my free hand. I flash the startled-looking elderly man a smile that hopefully tells him how sorry I am for running him down in the middle of the road during the wee hours of the morning, then push the broom into his still-flailing hands, before continuing my sprint to the tavern where Una had told me to meet them once my tasks were complete.

I inhale deeply, trying to fill my lungs as I run, taking in the unique smell of salt and sweetness, of spices and heat, trying to not stumble as I dodge and weave the early morning townsfolk. Some are getting ready to start their day, others well into theirs and sporting tired frowns that erase all joy they might feel about this astonishing island. It's quite sad, but I can have enough joy and excitement for all of them.

Pausing to aid a struggling Selina with her cloak was the best choice I ever made for myself. Simple merchant, navigator… now pirate! If only you could see me now, Father! I accidentally cut through a group of people, shout an apology at their disgruntled cries, my attention consumed by the unknown. So close, yet so far away, from my home.

I turn down the road I *think* is the right direction to find the two females who're sure to be waiting impatiently. Despite the proficient tongue-lashing Captain is sure to give me at being late, again, I feel a smile tugging my mouth upwards. I'm certain I look like a loon, smiling in my own company, but Una is both everything and nothing I thought a buccaneer would be. Granted, she's the first one I've met, male or female, but she's proven to be all the bite, all the rough edges, every inch the gooseflesh-inducing buccaneer Father always warned me to be mindful of. But she's also nothing like the tales, the severe warnings. She has this *softness* that reminds me of an older sibling. A vexed and annoyed older sibling not shy in letting me know I've done wrong. Or, what I assume older siblings to be like, since I've no blood ones of my own. But the heat that floods my chest at the thought of Una's squawks when I don't meet one of her obscenely high pirate standards isn't caused by fear but happiness that she's noticed me at all.

I pause outside the biggest tavern I've ever seen in my entire life. I haven't been alive that long, a mere nineteen years, but my statement still stands. It's unlike the other buildings, stalls or small homes nestled away from the loud busy port with its shouting merchants, the constant movement. This building definitely has a foreign influence. Dutch, if I'm correctly remembering Selina's lesson on the layout of the island. The heavy nature of the almost entirely stone building looks out of place amongst the other soft-angled buildings with their high, swooping ledges. The tavern is kind of an eye sore compared to the rest of the port town. *Most* of the port town, I correct myself, remembering the ugly huge walls that cut Banten into inner and outer sections. I'd never put up an ugly wall like that. I'd want everyone to live together, with easy access to see their friends and loved ones.

I let out a breath that is all exhilaration, none of the hesitation I should probably feel, as I grasp the cold metal door handle, ready to meet my Captain, and Selina, the first Quartermaster of her crew, head on, I had leapt at the chance to leave my ordinary, mundane day-in-and-day-out life almost before Una had finished laying out her terms of what was to be expected of me.

A cool, thrilling rush flutters in my chest, close to my heart. I wonder what adventures await. Here's to finding out, and having a damn good time while doing so. I open the door and the warm, heady glow within, the rush of voices and music, washes over me.

***

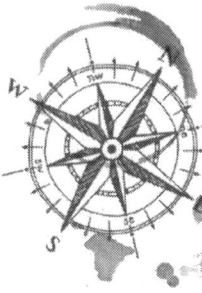

Chapter 12: Hanna

22 May 1691
Banten, Java, Dutch East Indies

I didn't know it was possible for one's head to hurt so badly... I groan into my flattened pillow, uncaring how loud or far it echoes. With each beat of my heart, the one in my skull matches it in intensity. My punishment for Una straying so far from me for too long. I'd gotten used to the constant exhaustion, the heavy limbs I could handle, especially when something piqued my interest, but what I can't stand is the headache. It's crippling and leaves me unable to do much of anything until the throbbing stops.

And I really need it to stop; Demetrius will be returning soon from scouting for information on Una. I groan again at a particularly strong throb and the wave of nausea that twists my stomach. Must be grand not needing to sleep. How convenient staying in his original water state must be, and for that to be enough to stave off sleep.

Before my thoughts slip into deeper, darker self-pity, a warmth that's slowly becoming familiar sparks in the center of my chest and flutters under my ribs. I pull my face from the safety of the pillow and prop myself up on my elbows, the fluttering blotting out some of the pain in my head.

I'm not sure what it is, but it started after I'd saved Una's life and given her the Gift of the Sea. I assume it's just another effect that will keep coming with this bond. Which are my own personal effects and which I'm taking on for Una, I've no idea. I highly doubt Demetrius knows either. He's told me all he knows about mermaid culture, which isn't very much. My mother was apparently tight-lipped about a lot of things. Even with my mother's journal, his last reminder of her besides myself, he's still no closer to understanding the limitations and risks that come with the Gift; *curse* is what it feels like more often than not. A curse that will either steal my life or grant me a new one I never thought I'd have.

70

I consider telling Demetrius about this new development – the fluttering in my stomach – but quickly decide against it; he doesn't need something else to worry over. It isn't causing me any harm; it isn't even as uncomfortable as the pain that comes with my tail transformation. Quite the opposite actually; it's almost… comforting in a way. I can almost pretend the energy in my stomach is Una lending me her endless supply of strength, fortifying my own. A small smile curls my lips.

And then Demetrius storms into the room, a ball of energy, enough for the both of us, slamming the door too loudly and rattling my brain. The sharp sound causes me to wince and the room to spin for a moment as my head throbs. He's still disguised as his alter-ego Aurelius but holding himself in a noticeably confident Demetrius-like manner, his posture almost too straight, his hands folded behind his thicker, steadier-looking frame. His usually unruly locks are wheat-colored now and slicked back rakishly, dripping like he's come from a swim in the ocean. A pulse of longing ripples through me; it's been so long since I've gone in the water.

His almost overbearing energy dims as he sees me sprawled on the mattress, and he tilts his head, those defined brows pitching upwards in another look that can't be snuffed out by his magic. He crosses the small space between us and perches on the edge of the bed, laying a hand on my shoulder, the action immediately comforting me. "Are you okay? Did something occur while I was out? Did you get ill again? Do you need me to get some more black coffee? It eased your belly last time." He's already standing, no doubt intent on fetching me something to aid me.

"I'm okay. Really, Father." My words halt him mid-stand and he hovers, concern scribbled over every dip and curve of his new, rounder face.

But then the concern lifts into a hesitant smile and he settles back beside me. "You feel well then? That is marvelous to hear. Better news than I have to report. My night was as uneventful as all the others. Still no sign of Una. She is being very discrete with her movements."

I can't help but shoot him a teasing smile. "Did you expect any less from her? She is quite resilient, and clever."

His smile grows into a grin, even as he rolls his eyes and casts me an unimpressed look. "Cleverness, spunk, I suppose they can mean the same thing if you really wish them to."

He holds my gaze a moment before we break into undiluted laughter, the kind that leaves me breathless and shaking with tears. My headache has eased, thankfully, and I'm grateful for this moment – something Demetrius and I haven't had the chance to do in a long while, to just converse and enjoy each other's company. It's a breath of fresh air among the smog of worry. I push myself up slowly into a sitting position, my legs crossed under myself, my chest and head feeling a bit lighter.

He brushes a stray hair from my eyes. "Do you feel up for some exploring? The air's still filled with early morning dew, and the town is still mostly asleep. It will be the perfect chance for us to try the local cuisine."

My stomach lets out a loud rumble and Demetrius smiles, placing his hand on top of my head. "I'll take that as your final answer. I know just where to take you. The spice combo of this stall far beats anything back home."

As he speaks, the warmth in his palm fades, replaced with a coolness that slowly seeps into my scalp. Once an alarming phenomenon, it's now a curious and exciting moment that, in my opinion, is over far too quickly. His bottomless eyes flare with green fire as he calls on and channels his magic into me, cloaking me in my disguise. It's a process that makes me feel oddly connected to him, like maybe my magic senses and is responding to his.

With a smile and a quick tousle of my hair, he stands. "Päättynyt!" he declares, in Finnish, giving an overdramatic spin before dipping into a bow.

I shake my head at his quirkiness, but can't help smiling; he's always been able to make me feel better when I've just wanted to wallow in my own doubt and self-pity "Am I finished yet?"

He grins, pride shining at his eyes, and pulls the black cotton cloak from his shoulders, draping it over me. This cloak is longer than the one Una stole. "Now you are." He steps back to appraise me, nods. "Let us be off. There are many stalls to visit, and so little daylight!"

***

"Try this one next, *minun maailmani*!" Demetrius tries to shove something wrapped in a large, wilted leaf at me, but I already have a mouthful of a flavorful sweet-spicy roasted corn served in what looks like a drinking beaker. He's used that expression enough times that I know it essentially means 'my world'. It's sweet.

Despite the crumbs flung from his still-full mouth, I smile at his excitement and reach for the still-warmed leaf husk. "And you call me the child."

We head for a quiet corner of the market, both of us laughing at his childish antics and I'm about to take a large bite of this mouth-watering food, when Demetrius collides with a large man. Deme drops his food. The hulking man drops his drink. Suddenly I'm looking into the angry mud-colored eyes of this huge man. I notice, in my peripheral, a smaller hooded figure standing aside, watching. I assume this hooded figure is with the man? Are we in danger? Alarm rises with indignation that this man is glaring so fiercely at us and that his companion is standing by so silently.

The barrel-chested man, clothed in brown woolen breeches, black stockings and black boots with small golden buckles and gray cloak, is smooth-shaven, bald. I'm shocked I can't see myself in his shiny head though there's stubble on his scarred, pointed chin and gaunt cheeks.

He shoves a meaty finger into Demetrius's chest, his eyes promising more than just a talk. "You made me spill me peach juice, runt…"

His hooded companion remains silent, crossing their strangely tattooed arms over their chest.

Demetrius glances at me then flashes the livid man a large smile. "Many apologies, chum. You know how the hard cider can hit you if you don't eat before! Let me buy ya another."

The stranger merely growls, taking a wobbly step towards my guardian. "You made me spill my peach juice… the peach juice I bought with my last pistole…"

The angry man's friend doesn't move to stop his stumbling advance, only snorts a displeased noise, though in a higher-pitched voice than I'd expected. I wonder...

I fumble my coin pouch from my belt, the string getting caught on the guard of my sword. "Aurelius, the picaroon is obviously unable to understand reason, let's just go." I thrust the pouch at the drunk man. "Here, this should cover your beverage."

The brute seems to fully notice my presence for the first time as he sneers down at me with crooked yellow teeth. "A lass... what kind of lubber lets a woman speak for him?" He squints at me with a slightly unfocused gaze. Scars of varying degrees of age, size and healing decorate his olive complexion. "Maybe I'll take the li'l strumpet and yer weapons as a fee for wastin' my time."

In one fluid motion, he pushes Demetrius to the dusty earth and forces me against the wall by my throat. It doesn't hurt; he's too drunk to put much force into it. I look from his grubby hand, to his twisted angry face, to the still silent hooded person, then to Demetrius. I bite down on my anger, because Demetrius has told me often enough to watch myself out here, but his small, approving smile steels my resolve. I'm curling my hands into fists as Demetrius casually climbs to his feet, dusting off his trousers and cloak, and says, "I really wouldn't do that if I were you."

Those mud colored eyes flash angrily, the large man's grip tightening around my neck. "And what yer gonna do about it, chum?"

His words spark anger in the pit of my stomach, sharp and hot as the hand continues to squeeze. Memories of Kai and the way he always grabbed me spring forth in my mind, blotting out my caution and steeling my resolve further. I grip the pommel of my weapon, letting the steel fill my limbs with strength. "Well, then it looks like you'll be the one dancing with Jack Ketch, *chum*."

I surprise the grotesque man, pulling the weapon from my holder and striking him with the pommel to the center of his stomach before he can even think enough to blink. I move with more strength than he probably thought I was capable of, more strength than a human female should be capable of. His surprise is glorious. I smirk as he stumbles, eyes wide as he almost trips over his fallen beaker and our wasted food.

I straighten, fueled with rage and the courage Demetrius has always said I possess but I've hardly believed in myself 'til now, and step forward. I'm intent on teaching this vile man some decent etiquette, something whoever had the displeasure of raising him failed to do, but the cloaked human finally moves, taking up a defensive position between us.

They hold up their pale, bizarrely marked arms, palms out. "Peace all. Stand down, Caleb." The hood twitches as the figure glances down at the sprawled man. "As the newest among us, I'd watch your step. You've already messed up and gotten on the Captain's bad side. Let's not add to your list of sins."

I blink, my weapon lowering slightly at the lightness of her voice. So, I had been right. A female. The man, Caleb, struggles to pull his obese body to his feet, his left leg trembling as he stands fully to his boots again, a loud snort exploding from him. I'm sure he's about to let the hooded woman know just where she could put those words, but he surprises me and falls silent, and now it's his turn to fold his arms over his chest.

She lowers her arms, but leaves her hood up, revealing only a slither of cheek, the rest shrouded in shadow. I can't make out any more of her features as she bows oddly, stiffly, from her waist. "I'm Selina, this clod over here is Caleb. With your show of weaponry," she nods to me, "and your dignity at letting him shove you down," she gestures to Deme, "I'm interested in talking with you both about a job opportunity. One with quite a large payout."

I meet Demetrius's even gaze with a frazzled one of my own, slowly looping my rapier back through my sash Could we finally have a lead? I'm still livid at Caleb, and swallow hard.

Thankfully, Deme seems more in control of his voice and emotions, flashing them his easy, charming smile. "Let me buy you a beverage, Selina. The way you put the wee one in his place so gracefully, we can spare a few moments of our day with you. After you."

Selina chuckles beneath her hood, as Caleb throws my guardian a look which suggests, if it were possible to set things ablaze with your eyes alone, that Demetrius might need a water pail.

Demetrius gestures at our new… companions? – I throw a wary glance at Caleb – with a leading sweep of his arm and we wander away from the unwanted eyes that had begun to settle on us the longer we stood in one spot so in the open. Instead of heading to another stall, the woman leads us towards an even more deserted part of town.

Demetrius nonchalantly hooks his elbow through mine again, tugging my body close. "Are you leading us to a stand we haven't been to yet? That's so exciting!" He makes a show of bumping his shoulder with mine, diffusing his unease with a carefree attitude.

Selina stops and turns toward us, Caleb staying right at her left, his beady little eyes never once leaving me, and I'm certain they're about to jump us. I feel Deme tense beside me. "As much as I would love a drink, we have a meeting to get to." She braces her hands on her hips, and I breathe out a small laugh, relieved. Surprised, pleased this mysterious woman isn't about to rob us, as she seems the more dangerous opponent of these two, but relieved, nonetheless. "But," she continues, "meet us at the tavern just north of the fishing and tackle stall thirty paces from here, three days from now. Just before the sun dips below the horizon, if you're interested in meeting with my Captain and hearing about our little… venture."

Caleb snorts beside her, and the sound has a chill lancing up my spine.

"I'll be with our Captain, that's how you'll know you've arrived at the right spot. Until then." Without waiting for a response, the strange woman turns her back on us and strides away, the larger man lingering a breath longer before following.

I stare at their backs until Demetrius's gleeful laugh has me jerking my head to look at him. The victory burning in his face has a flicker of hope flaring to life in me.

He drops our twined arms, laces his fingers with mine. "The person who waits patiently will always obtain the largest reward, remember that."

***

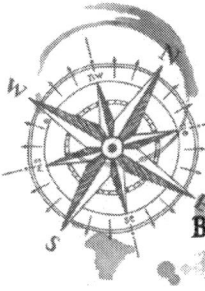

Chapter 13: Una
25 May 1691
Banten, Java, Dutch East Indies

"Bar keep! Another round over here!" Jonah's heavy, bright emerald doublet sleeve almost knocks over the half-full one still in front of him, as he grins a slightly lopsided smile my way, his teeth far too shiny for my liking.

I'm not sure I like the vibrant spark of mischief glittering dangerously in his deep, dark brown eyes. It makes me momentarily wonder if the water nymph has other brethren out on land, parading around like they were human. The moment the thought crosses my mind, my stomach falls out of my arse, the tidal wave of guilt threatens to pull me down to the bottom of the ocean, and a pair of oddly charming lilac eyes flash through my mind again.

I swallow hard before taking a deep drink from my tankard, letting the sharp tang of brandy dance a trail of fire down my throat and into my belly, burning out the pesky emotion that keeps trying to rear its ugly head, trying to force me to feel things I haven't had the need for in a very long time, see things that I've never thought I would allow myself to want.

As the half-ling's smile tries to take over my brain, I cough, setting my tankard back on the table that Selina, Jonah, Atropous and myself currently occupy, waiting for the two land-lubbers that had made an impression on my at-times-sullen first mate.

"I'm *trying* to stay off the grid, Jonah." I pinch the bridge of my nose. "If you could lower your voice? I know all that cannon fire with the Royal Jollies wrecked your ears, but the rest of us still have full use of our hearing."

Atropous snorts into his tankard, bubbling up liquid all over his thin scruff of brown beard, and the tabletop, and his lap. His heavy-lidded eyes, the color of sage, are wide at my words to Jonah before he erupts into laughter.

I nurse the slowly growing pounding in my head with my open palm. My damn crew… If Elyse could see me now, she'd laugh herself into her grave before I'd get the chance to put my blade in her neck.

"Oh Cap, you're perfectly safe in here," Jonah grins. "Plus, even if we did get into a touch of a scuffle, we'd make it out just fine. You have Selina, Atropous and I to guard your back."

Selina nods silently and Atropous's laughter dies to a soft snigger, his large tan hand absentmindedly clawing through his dark shoulder length curls. He looks just as serious as the equally dark-haired Jonah sitting at his side.

I sigh, as I try to fight the smile threatening to curve my lips. "As exciting as a brawl sounds, let's not have a fight right now. We are *so* close in achieving our goal. If Selina's hunch is correct, we'll have our last two crew mates."

Atropous looks past my shoulder just as the bar wench returns with a tray of ales. I turn in my high-backed chair, and barely catch the gasp that tries to weasel out of my suddenly parched throat. Among the dull sounds of the dark musky tavern, among the otherwise dull-looking patrons, two brightly dressed people stand side by side, three steps from us. My eyes are immediately drawn to the lass first. She's one of those natives from the Americas, an Indian. Her dusky-skinned body is clothed in sand-colored trousers and an expensive-looking waistcoat the color of the ocean. Her feet are clad in knee-high boots that look to be on the pricey side as well. But the most interesting thing is the weapons on her hip; not a normal cutlass that you'd see on your average buccaneer, and not the heavy, steel, dangerous-looking swords any common folk could use. *Definitely* the priciest weapon I've seen since leaving the cushy cabin. The tingle in my fingertips is all the info I need to confirm the shiny weapon's price. The slender, blue gem encrusted guard and pommel just begs me to steal it. An espada. Not just anyone would have one of these, let alone use it for defense. Espadas are sharp as anything, sell for a hell of a lot given their rarity. In the wrong hands, you'd end up doing more damage to yourself. Only skilled duelists use these. Usually ex-militia, a seaman, possibly the odd pirate, but a female carrying one? Even rarer.

Her dark, almond shaped eyes focus on me with such intensity. These must be the two that had made such a huge impression on Selina and Caleb. She's a pleasure to look at, with that defiant stare, impressive weaponry, and her ocean colors. Her features are much sharper and angular compared to Hanna's softer, rounder ones, but still – a comely lass.

The stout lad at her side is a head taller than she, with hair almost as light as mine, but slicked back and almost as meticulously kept as Jonah and Ambrose like to keep theirs. Is this lad an ex-Jolly too? His eyes, unlike hers, are empty, dark holes. His tanned, muscular arm is linked through the crook of the young lass's and he's clothed much the same as she. Except his waistcoat is a fantastically bright green that rivals even the squint-inducing one Jonah likes to wear on 'special occasions.' A heavy, thick-looking cloak is layered over his wide shoulders like a cape.

He casts our group a wide smile, his thin chapped lips almost cracking around the edges. "Selina, sorry to be late. There was a brawl in the middle of the road and it took a moment to get past. I hope that doesn't mean we've missed our shot?" He cocks a head at me in a way that reminds me of the water nymph… gah! I need to get my head out of my arse. There'll be time to think of them, of her, later. Right now, there's work to be done. There's blood that needs spilling.

I smirk at the pair and gesture to the open chairs we'd saved for them. "If you're as worthy as Selina says you are, your lateness isn't an issue."

Jonah hoots out a trill of laughter as the duo take their seats.

"I do quite like them both already, Captain, their clothes are the best I've seen on the island. Is that Duroy cloth, Miss…?" Jonah blinks long-lashed eyes at the lass, who's slowly looking more uncomfortable as all at the table turn to her.

Her dark eyes dart to her companion before she nods awkwardly. "I… suppose so? It was a trade and I'm no expert on clothes." Her voice is low, almost hoarse sounding, like she's nervous to have so many people looking at her.

I take a quick sip of my brandy. "Jonah, leave her be. She ain't even part of the crew yet and yer already busting her arse. Let me at least tell them what they're to be a part of. The many positives and the just-as-many negatives."

The new lad straightens at my words, a twinkle in the abyss of his eyes. His female companion doesn't so much as twitch a lip at my gag. Her thin shoulders are stiff; the candlelight casts shadows over her cheeks, making them look hollow for a moment.

She straightens when our eyes connect. "Your proposal then?"

"Right to the point, I like that. In three days, my gathered hands and I will be leaving this blasted rock. Our next port will be Île Sainte-Marie, a twenty-five-day sail, port to port. There's some... *associates* of mine that I'm looking for. It's possible they could be there. I'm lookin' for two more hands to assist me."

The lad leans his elbows on the table, holding his pointed chin in his hands. It's obvious he's enjoying this. "Associates, you say? And what kind of associates could those be, chum?"

Anger kindles hot in my chest at his tone, his smugness. I lean forward. "Associates perhaps you're already familiar with... *chum*."

The woman, sensing the rising tension, finally speaks, her voice tight and forced. "What do you plan to do once you find these associates of yours?"

I glare at the slightly smiling lad and feel the eyes of my crew boring holes into me, wondering why their Captain is letting two no-ones get under my skin. And hells if I know. I ignore the unknown, rolling it into a tight ball and shoving it into my back pocket for later inspection, and focus on the things I do know. "When I find my fellow *buccaneers*, I'll completely wipe their existence from the books. No-one'll remember their names when I'm done with those scourges of the Seven Seas."

A tense silence settles over the table, the only noise coming from the other chatting patrons. After a few heavy moments, the thick air is finally cleared by Jonah.

"Did anyone else get a rush of gooseflesh down their neck as she spoke? That was a brilliant speech, Captain."

Atropous laughs and slides a new tankard to Selina, who dips her head appreciatively before picking it up, and Jonah grins cheekily at our table mates. I reign in my sparked anger and end up shaking my head at Jonah's idiocy. I stare down the new duo, trying to regain the control Jonah's comment had untethered. "Ask yourself these two questions: One, are you willing to join my crew, knowing my goals? And two, are you willing to risk your life to make sure it comes to pass?" The lass's unwavering steely gaze is disconcerting, so I opt to look at her still-annoyingly-smiling companion. "When my goal is obtained, you'll get whatever reward you wish. Agree to my conditions and meet at Banten's port two days from now, just before the sun peeks over the horizon. Don't be late this time. The dawn high tide and the winds won't wait." I look at the lass, "Yer in," then at her grinning companion. "You, though, Smiles, have still got to prove yourself."

The pair lock gazes a moment, before the lad nods and stands. The still-unnamed Indian follows, staying right at his elbow, even as he circles the table, returning to the position they'd been standing in when I first spotted them. I turn in my seat to keep them in my sights.

"You propose a very interesting deal, Captain," Smiley Boy says. "Until the port, then. Octavia, come along."

The lad turns on his heels and heads toward the tavern's double doors. The lass hesitates, dancing on her toes beside us, then ducks her head, bowing a little like Selina had the first time I'd met her. Then she turns and almost runs to catch her friend, and just as I'm about to turn back to my crew and my brandy, the female's voice drifts towards me:

"Until then, Una."

I almost get up. I heard that voice, Octavia's voice, say my name. My hand claws itself impulsively on the tabletop. *My* name. A name I never gave tonight, and none of my crew mates would have used either. Before I can begin accusing those at the table of having loose lips, Atropous speaks up, taking the words right from my mouth.

"Did you introduce the Captain with her real name when you met those two?"

Selina scoffs, her hood still pulled up over her head, the noise sounding a lot like the sound Caleb makes when he can't fathom your stupidity. "I didn't forget the rules. As far as the rest of the world is concerned, she doesn't have a name. She doesn't exist."

Jonah chuckles around the rim of his tankard, though his face doesn't hold his usual joyful expression. Instead, his face is hard, potently serious, making his features sharp. He's usually so... silly, boyish, but right now, he looks just as dangerous as any buccaneer I've ever stared down in my life, maybe more so. "You suppose your sibling somehow knows you're out scouting for her? Would you like Ambrose and I to... dispose of them for you?"

The blood lust that fills his normally carefree, brown eyes momentarily has me blinking. His swift change in demeanor, his alertness, is all ex-Naval officer. I take a sip of my brandy to hide how off-guard he's made me. I swallow and shake my head. "No, we don't know if it's my sister's dealings, or if I've just become that fabulous a buccaneer that my name precedes me these days. But whoever sent them, they've been sent to slay me, and now the idiot's given us a warning, that's a reason to keep an eye on them."

Jonah's smirk deepens and he rubs the knuckles of his free hand along the sharp, scruffy curve of his jaw. "Your leadership skills and the way you deduce things never cease to amaze me, Captain."

Now it's my turn to snort out an amused laugh. "I'll take that as high praise coming from the likes of you, First Gunner."

Jonah's smirk cracks, returning to its impish jovial one as he raises his near empty tankard in my direction in a salute. "As very well you should."

The table collapses into peals of laughter as that pommy, fruity accent of his swirls his words and cracks the buccaneer facade he tries so hard to put on. One thing Jonah isn't very good at is hiding his status and heritage, and he gets more shite at it the more ale he drinks. I don't try to hold them back this time, I join in, letting the rush of getting a step closer to my end goal burn away the lingering darkness of my guilt, and my suspicion of the newcomers.

If all goes as planned, in two days I'll have my full crew, have the water under my new ship, wind at my sails, and be on course to give Elyse and Kai exactly what they deserve. I smirk over the lip of my mug. Enjoy your final days dear sister, they'll be coming to an end soon. Very soon.

***

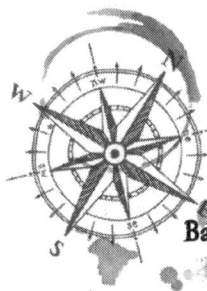

Chapter 14: Hanna

27 May 1691
Banten [Port], Java, Dutch East Indies

"One step, two step, three step, four step! Come on, Octavia! We're almost to the port, is this not the most exciting thing that has happened in *years*?" He twirls around me, as light as ever on his feet, as we make our way to the agreed meeting place. We're just forty short paces from the port, and the trek here was almost *too* quiet. There hasn't been this still-a night since the first eve we arrived. It has that almost unbearable knot in my stomach twisting tighter; it makes my limbs heavier, like there's bricks tied to my wrists and ankles.

"How can you be so calm? Who knows what foolish task Una's going to make you do in order to get onto her crew? What if I get in and you don't? I can't do this without you."

His inky black eyes narrow in mock-seriousness as he pulls his espada free from his sash, making a show of slashing random patterns into the sky, he steps complicated zig zags around me. "I will conquer whatever challenge your bonded can throw at me, Guppy. No need to fret."

I grip the pommel of my weapon harder, trying my best to rein in the urge to punch the idiot out of him. At least the swim got him back to his usual, exasperating self. Small miracles. When I'd slipped up at the tavern, I'd hoped he hadn't heard me, but one look at his expression told me he had, absolutely. After that, he'd turned icy toward me, spending most of that eve in the ocean.

His chuckle draws me back to the present, and I watch him, my worry trying to crawl up my throat as he stores his espada back in his sea-blue sash. His laughter softens as we enter the port. I try to sponge up some of my guardian's limitless reserves of strength. The smell of ocean air and brine is strong, and it permeates the pre-dawn air. I spare a quick glance at Deme, his magical transformation holding strong despite him staying up half the night. The thought had momentarily struck

84

me on the way here, and concerned me – would Demetrius be able to hold up his magic for twenty-five days in a row? Me not dipping a toe into the ocean as a half-ling will prove difficult enough, but him? I try to sense some sort of hesitation or weakness in him. Before I find any, we come to the northernmost corner of the port, and the bond's effects sizzle along my flesh as we near Una and the seventeen other figures flanking her on the wooden dock. Poseidon preserve me…

Una and six others pull away from the group. Of the seven pirates approaching, I recognize most of them from the tavern: Selina. Jonah, the man with the strangest accent I've never heard before. Caleb. The bearded young man with the long wavy brown hair, his name still unknown to me. Even during that tense meeting, the kindness in his eyes, that were almost as green as Demetrius's, was evident, and he hadn't tried to hide it like Una, or the soft-spoken Selina had. But the young Black man with fear-filled hazel eyes and the most beautifully crafted figure, in pale tan trousers and a shirt of rough-looking cloth is a total mystery. I'm quite intrigued, my world knowledge being limited to only what I learnt with Kai and from living with Demetrius. I've never come face to face with one like him. I wonder what his voice sounds like.

The second stranger is another young lad wearing much the same outfit as Demetrius, but a duller, faded blue, like he's owned his brocade a long while. His hair is just as short as Deme's in his Aurelius disguise, but as bright as a fox's pelt, a dazzling copper I've never seen in hair before. Where was he born to have hair like that?! He's as tall as Jonah, on his right, but not nearly as packed with muscle. From this distance I can't see much else of him, but I do see him wave at me in a strange greeting. Before my thoughts can wander too far, Una is close enough to extend her hand to me, grasping my forearm. I mirror her, trying to move as quickly and as gracefully as possible to not seem like I've no idea what I'm doing.

"Good Eve, Octavia. I realize I failed to formally introduce myself at our little meeting." Her pink lips quirk up as she unsubtly taunts me "Una. Buccaneer."

She did hear me that night. My stupid bond-ravaged brain. I'd been so tired, and she'd been right there, and it had slipped out and she'd heard me. We're booked. We're done for. I suppress a shudder at the familiar greeting as her voice washes over me, the bond at near combustible levels at such closeness. All I can do is nod my greeting and quickly release her, my palm still tingling as I bring it back to my side. I wait to see how this will play out. Will she call me out? Will she attack? What does she think of me? Who does she think I am? Deme hasn't reacted at all, his expression open and curious. He's better at this than me. I've always been a horrible liar. This is going to be a disaster.

Una shrugs. "You already know Caleb he's one of my quartermasters. Think of them as my eyes and ears. The best of my best." She barely looks over her shoulder at the bald pirate.

What? That's it? She clearly knows I messed up. But… she's not acting on that? Caleb nods curtly at Una's words, his muddy eyes downcast. The right side of his face is puffy, his eye is swollen, eyelids touching in an unwanted kiss. His olive skin is blotted with an array of blues, black and reds. Did Una do that to him? Is that violence to come my way as well? Una continues the introduction completely undeterred. "This is Atropous, my lookout." She cocks her head at the giant man with all the hair, finally named.

Up close, I really get a good look at him. He's lean and tall, his skin tanned by obvious time in the sun. Despite the scruff on his jaw and chin he looks barely out of boyhood. His mass of brown ringlets cascade down his doublet-covered shoulders, the brocaded vest stopping at his elbows. His gem-like eyes shimmer a green that nearly rivals Demetrius in his true form. At his waist is a curved cutlass, the silver blade glittering dangerously in the grey pre-dawn light. An odd contrast to the friendly smile curving his wind chapped lips. At my side, Demetrius stirs. I spare him a quick glance and find him tensing his jaw as he grinds his teeth.

Atropous dips his head in a quick bob of greeting. "I'm also the navigator."

Selina, tall and cloaked, hidden within her hood and, so far, silent, clears her throat loudly.

Atropous rolls his eyes in a very Demetrius-like manner. "Excuse me, one of the *two* navigators of this ship. It's nice to meet ya, officially!"

Una pinches the bridge of her nose. "And our co-navigator, as you know, is Selina."

Selina's wearing black woolen trousers and leather boots that stop mid-calf. A glint of steel peeks from beneath her billowing cloak. "Salutations." Her disembodied voice is modulated and low.

"And the fourth and final Quartermaster; Solomon my strategist."

The tall, thin Black man smiles brightly. He bows his head, rubbing a hand through his black, tightly-coiled hair. "Thank ya Captain. It's nice to meet you both."

Caleb scoffs, folding his arms. "Kissin' arse blue-skin half-caste mongrel… *strategist*! Hogwash is what it is."

Una and Selina turn sharply to the muttering buffoon, quickly silencing him with their glares. He holds up his hands in surrender, taking a step back.

I intervene by dipping my head. "I'm Octavia and my companion is Aurelius."

I'm still waiting for Una to do something, say anything, about my mistake at the tavern, to challenge me, but she doesn't say a word. I look at Demetrius, expecting a flamboyant grand display of a greeting. Instead, he merely nods, holding his mouth in a tight line.

Una finally turns her stormy eyes to my guardian, acknowledging him for the first time since we arrived. "You ready to prove yourself?"

Demetrius inflates before my eyes, his chest puffing out. "Aye. Name the challenge."

Una laughs softly with a cruel smirk. She turns, addressing the entire crew, arms held high. One balls into a tight fist and she punches the air excitedly. "Were going to have ourselves a li'l brawl. Yer opponent; Atropous."

Mutters break out among the crew, fueling the dangerous excitement flickering bright in Una's eyes. "The rules? Win at any cost. The brawl is over when one of you concedes, renders the other unconscious, or one of you dies."

A gasp sticks in my throat. A fight possibly to the death? What is she thinking? Is this her retribution for thinking us traitors or spies or whatever she believes the reason I accidentally used her name to be? So many things could go horribly wrong if Demetrius participates in this.

Bloodlust swirls dangerously around the crew of buccaneers. Una, too, given her menacing sneer.

She turns back to us, arms still held out wide. "Don't worry about getting caught, dock workers have been paid off, or otherwise held up." Her eyes slide from me and back to Demetrius, who's still eerily silent. "Are you in or out, Aurelius?"

"In, obviously." Demetrius makes a show of stroking the blade of his weapon slowly, an equally nerve-inducing snarl on his disguised face.

She lowers her arms, still smirking. "You have five minutes to steady your wills. Use it well, lads."

Deme's already removing his thick black cloak. There's a gnawing pit already beginning to consume my stomach. I accept the cloak from him, though he's lost in thought, the deep crease furrowing his brow a dead giveaway. Something about Atropous has thrown my guardian off since the evening we met him.

"I'm worried…"

Demetrius ruffles my hair in that familiar, affectionate gesture, and it immediately eases my worry. "All will be well. Trust in me." He squeezes my hand once before turning to his opponent, who's already making his way off the wooden dock onto the solid earth.

I sigh, holding the cloak close to my chest, taking a spot next to Selina, the only other lass in the crew. When I get too close, she folds her arms over her chest. The pre-dawn light brings the pinkish undertones of her skin to the surface, the color reminding me of the inside of a seashell. And marring that skin, as far as my eye can see, are those black ivy-like tattoos. She looks at me and I get a glimpse of a pointed chin and strong jaw, full lips. "How good is this swab of yours?"

I clutch the cloak tighter as Demetrius and Atropous stand across from one another. "He taught me everything I know. He can't lose." I sneak a peek at the hooded woman. "How good is Atropous?"

A cool smirk curves those thick lips. "Hopefully as good as your bucko, or this is going to be a complete bore."

Una stands a little way from the pair, a fierce glimmer I've not seen before in my bonded's eyes. "The brawl begins... NOW!"

I can't help gasping loudly as Atropous leaps, unarmed, at my guardian. My hand immediately sneaks out to grip the closest form of comfort. It meets skin as warm as a campfire, and just as comforting. I look up and meet Selina's odd amber eyes for a moment before she looks away and gives my fingers a gentle squeeze. "It'll be fine, no one will be dying today."

I follow her gaze back to the ensuing fight and my heart leaps again as Atropous aims a series of complicated, unfamiliar strikes at Demetrius, who narrowly dodges each one, his hand gripping the pommel of his weapon.

Demetrius continues to dodge and weave around his opponent's blows and kicks but makes no attempt at returning any strikes. What are you doing?! Stop fooling around... end this now!

As if hearing my inner plea, Demetrius drops low and kicks out one leg, aiming a strong-booted foot at Atropous's shin. With almost feline-like reflexes that shock me, Atropous jumps straight up into the air, completely dodging the kick all together – a kick Demetrius had truly been trying to land to end the match. Aurelius lands, his boots hardly making a sound, his hand already balling into a fist, then rears back to strike. That's when my guardian makes his move.

Like a serpent, Demetrius lashes out with a fist of his own and lands a staggering punch to the lad's jaw, the resounding impact sounding meaty, but there's a crack of bone in there too. Atropous stumbles and my mentor uses that opening to land two more strikes, the second one to the temple knocks the wide-eyed young man to the earth. Demetrius draws his espada with the fluid grace most only get to

89

witness once in their lifetime. The blade shimmers dangerously as he presses the weapon's sharp steel into the tender flesh of the pirate's neck. They lock eyes.

Then Demetrius begins to laugh.

Atropous soon joins in. "Okay… I concede, you win. This time."

I exhale. Beside me, Selina lets out an amused chuckle. She gives my hand one final squeeze before releasing it, folding her marked arms over her chest.

Demetrius pulls back his weapon, wiping it on his thigh and looping it through his sash, eyes still trained on the fallen lad.

"Gonna help me up or what, comrade?" Atropous smirks as he holds up a hand to Deme.

Demetrius looks at it for a second before taking it and pulling his new crew mate to his feet.

"And that makes twenty." Una's commanding voice pulls everyone's attention, her gaze as hard as any steel, as stormy as any ocean during a typhoon, and as hypnotic and dangerous as any whirlpool.

I can't quite believe it. This match seems to have proven our combined worth to Una regardless of who she thinks we might be, despite any suspicions she might have. She's letting us both join. My relief is palpable.

"Hope you lubbers have yer sea legs ready. *The Revenge of the Sea* awaits."

***

I trail closely behind a re-cloaked Demetrius, his hand already clutching tightly at the pommel of his weapon. His eyes, two pools of swirling ink, are focused ahead. We follow at the very back of the pack of buccaneers, our backs safe from attack if everyone else is in front.

We follow Solomon until we're all standing on the dock, which shifts and rolls with the water. The mast of *The Revenge of the Sea* gleams like a beacon as its unfurled sail reflects the slowly rising sun. The ship must be at least sixty feet long and over a hundred tons. Its single mast is nearly as tall as the hull is long and it's got to be at least twice as big as the wreckage of the one I pulled Una from over a month ago. The wood is a deep cherry brown that looks freshly buffed even in the dim light. The hulking beast of a ship creaks and groans as the rising tide laps at its bottom, shifting from side to side, eager to set sail on its own, if not for the anchor keeping it firmly in place. Across from the flag's post is an equally tall crow's nest, the perfectly round circle sitting high above to let a look-out to see oncoming dangers, storms, or other ships.

My chest constricts as we begin walking again. Una leads us onto the ship and up onto the wooden main deck that stretches from one side of the *Revenge* to the other. I can do this. This isn't like the last time I was on a ship… Great Poseidon's arse, who am I trying to fool? This is exactly like last time! Tack on a Gifted bond, and a mischievous magical tag-along pal who might well get me into even more trouble, and this just keeps getting better and better.

Solomon's strikingly intelligent hazel eyes are suddenly before me, the wide smile on his handsome face thankfully putting my spiraling thoughts to rest. "A sloop like this one would usually have no trouble supporting a crew of this size, but Captain has ordered us to bunk up in pairs, in the forecastle. The other section of living quarter space has been rearranged to better fit our needs." He eyes the espada at my waist for a moment before continuing, "It was a splendid call on Una's part to let you join, considering the kinds of weapons you two are carrying."

Dozens of suddenly-overly-interested eyes zero in on mine and Demetrius's weapons.

Demetrius moves closer and boldly laces our fingers together. Lifting our joined hands to his chest, he throws the strategist a cheeky grin. "Sorry lad, this one's already spoken for. You'll have to ask another one of the fine lasses on this ship to be your bunkmate. Selina, perhaps."

The mischievous gleam I'd gotten so used to seeing in my guardian's eyes comes blazing to life in his disguised face as we watch Solomon flush crimson from nearly head to toe. All the onlookers erupt into loud, callous laughter.

Solomon raises both his hands and furiously shakes his head. "I– I didn't mean it in that way, sir. I assure you, my intentions were only to relay the Captain's orders.

I –" He looks to Selina, his blush burning even hotter. "I didn't mean to – to think myself fit to share a bunk with you, when we haven't even begun to properly court!" He coughs. "I'll share a bunk with another hand, as is proper."

My last meal, which had threatened to breach the seam of my lips the moment my guardian had laced his hand with mine, tries for it a second time. I swallow it down. The soft-spoken and hooded navigator scoffs loudly, folding her marked arms. She lowers her head, obscuring her face further, but though I can't see her eyes, I feel like I'm locked in a heated gaze with her, the intensity of it like a flame against my skin.

"AHOY!"

Una's shout pulls every eye to her. She stands tall, hands on her hips, the broad brim of her tricorn hat angled down just above her left eyebrow. The soft edges I'd seen begin to take root in her eyes, her face and her heart back at the cabin, are gone now, her gaze hardened sapphires. "Solomon, Selina, Atropous, join me in my quarters. Ambrose, Jonah, see to it that the cannons are swabbed and ready in case of attack at sea. The rest of you lot, claim yer bunks, get to know *The Revenge*, gain yer bearings. Be ready to sail in one hour before the tide wains."

With those words she turns her back on us and heads below deck, Selina and a bright-eyed Atropous going quickly after her. Solomon casts an apologetic smile our way before he follows. Jonah, ever-grinning, and the redheaded Ambrose send us quick parting waves before they too dive below deck.

Given our orders, Demetrius and I follow the rest of the crew down those same steps and toward the forecastle. I'm acutely aware of how close Caleb is following behind us. We're engulfed by the ship, it's dark hulking walls curving round us, groaning and shifting on the water. Some of the picaroons pull ahead, running, shoving and cursing, trying to claim the best bunks for themselves. Soon the only ones left in the narrow hallway are Caleb, Demetrius, and me.

The gentle grip on my hand turns crushing as Deme glares at Caleb, who's gawking back at us. The shadows from the small, brass gimballed oil lamps bracketed to the walls makes his mottled collection of bruises even more gruesome.

"Can we help you?" Demetrius snarls, barely above a whisper.

Caleb takes a small step back, holding up both hands, placating. "I mean no harm. I thought, since we're the muscle, that it'd be smart to stick together."

I bark out a laugh before I can fully tamper it. "Muscle? Us? Band together with *you?*"

He nods, running one meaty palm against the scruff on his jaw. "Yuh. You got pretty boy, the blue-skin, and the hooded wench kissin' elbows with the Captain. Then there's the other hands, and finally us. I might not be smart like the rest of ya, but I know what my eyes see. And what they see are duelists. Trained fighters. Hired blades." He shoves the sleeves of his cotton shirt up past his elbows, then holds both arms out to show us the scars crisscrossing his skin. All different depths and at various stages of healing. "I ain't gonna judge yer for it."

Deme looks venomous and yet he still manages to plaster on a convincing smile. "Empty words, coming from someone like you."

Caleb clicks his tongue, seemingly exasperated by the entire conversation, though he'd initiated it. "Is this about the whole 'me pushin' you down' thing? If you can look past my misdeeds, I'll look past you siccing yer wench on me to handle yer fights."

Demetrius pulls me deeper into the passage and further from this utter buffoon. A sickeningly sweet smile still blooms over Deme's face, even though his eyes promise certain death. "How gracious of you. We'll talk over your little alliance proposal, then get back to you. Thank you, Caleb."

I glance at Caleb over my shoulder just before I'm pulled into an empty berth, the dumbfounded look on his face almost worth all the embarrassment and anguish I've been submitted to thus far.

Almost.

The thin tarp parading as a door flaps closed behind us, sealing us in what is to be our home for the next twenty-five days. I look around, scrunching my nose. How... *lovely.*

The bunk would be fitting if it were housing just one body. But two? One cot meant someone would be sleeping on the floor. A thin grimy sheet is laid haphazardly on the bed. Surprisingly, Demetrius doesn't inspect the room. Instead he stares blankly at nothing, toying with the knot on his sash.

I drop onto the stiff cot, the mattress as thin and about as soft as a plank of wood. My body melts into it, nonetheless. Now that the excitement and adrenaline has worn off, the full toll of the rejected, or rather in-stasis bond, really becomes apparent. The ever-present headache blooms full force, now a loud heartbeat in my ears. My arms hurt, the wrist that Caleb had grabbed hurts, even my hair aches.

"Are you okay?" The hard edge to my mentor's voice is gone, and when I look at him, I see his eyes are once again gleaming emerald. He's already back to his most familiar form.

"I could ask you the same question. You've been acting odd…"

For a moment I think he's going to avoid explaining his odd behavior, but he turns, sighs, and drops gracefully to the ground beside the cot. He crosses his once-again lithe limbs over themselves, opens his mouth, then closes it again, his voice failing him. For the first time in my life with him, my guardian doesn't know what to say. It's equal parts fascinating and terrifying.

He glances over his shoulder as if checking to make sure we are truly alone before leaning close. "Atropous is not human. Well… not fully human. He's a half-ling, like you, but of my race."

"*What?!*"

Demetrius raises a finger to his lips, glaring at me, and I immediately clamp my hands over my mouth, darting my eyes towards the clothed door. After several long tense breaths, I dare to utter, in a whisper, "Are you certain? How do you know?"

"Nymphs, be they of water, earth, air or even flame, share a connection. Not in the way your kind has bonds but more of…" He sighs like he's unsure how to continue, unsure of himself. "Nymphs, sprites and sylphs… we are all spirits of nature. We inhabit all corners of the earth, protecting its forests, rivers, oceans. Even the smallest streams are worthy." His eyes flash back to life, glistening jewels in his face once more, as he proudly talks about his origins. "We are created and birthed from nature herself; to protect it, nurture it, help give it life. We are all naturally in tune with others of our kind. I knew he was of my race the moment I saw him."

The realization of this new discovery, while curious, adds even more troubles. For many reasons. Was this the sole reason he'd been acting so odd since that first meeting, and why hadn't he told me that he knew? I don't ask; there are more important things, more damning things I need to know. "Do you know if he... sensed you back?"

He gives a weak shrug. "I am not certain. If he did, he's very good at concealing it. But to be honest, half-lings of my kind are a rarity, a myth in the eyes of some. I've never met a half-ling of my kind, and do not know of anyone who has. His abilities could be the same as mine, or something completely different."

I curl my pulsing, aching body into a fetal position. "Your race doesn't mingle with humans? I would think, with how intertwined you are with humanity, you'd mix the most."

Demetrius shakes his head, his chestnut locks spilling from under his bandanna and into his eyes. "We are created from the earth, for the earth. We are protectors, we keep balance in our own way, and do not meddle with human dealings."

I smirk. "You *usually* don't meddle."

His lips quirk into an affectionate smile as he looks at me. "Some occasions cause for a bit of... intervention." His eyes stray from my face as the ship groans to life beneath us, the waters already gently swaying *The Revenge of the Sea* as we begin to move away from the dock.

"Should we be concerned about Una's unwillingness to share her plans with us? We're her crew, shouldn't we be up there tending to the ship? Or swabbing the deck?"

Demetrius's shoulders begin to tremble, then a moment later he crows out a laugh, the sound so loud it fills the small room. "You know about as much of boats and ships as I do. As much as it pains me to say this, Caleb may be right. And since your error at the tavern, I'm certain all eyes will be on us any chance they get. We'll have to be even more careful."

I scoff, flopping onto my back in a huff, angry that he had just uttered those words, even after my abject fear of being called out, up there on the dock. "I'll have to stick extra close to you, seeing as you are my *beloved*, after all." He grins and goes to grab my hand in a comforting gesture, but I slap it away before he can grasp my fingers. The anger is blazing, in comparison to all the other emotions I currently feel. Anger is better than the other emotions. Anger, I can deal with. "That joke has gone on long enough. I can't believe you said you were… you couldn't say you were my sibling or friend? Uncle, perhaps? *'She's spoken for'*? You made me sound like a damsel in distress. I don't need you hovering at my elbow all the time. I can do this."

"I'm well aware of your capabilities, but also your limitations. This bond does not have you thinking the clearest. You have already slipped up once. You both had a natural attraction building before. You bestowing the Gift upon her just sped up the process. The closeness should take some of the edge off, the more you two are exposed to one another, but soon the bond will have to be made known; she will have to accept it, and a physical exchange will have to be made to solidify it. If not, you'll continue to wither until you perish. I being your pseudo-lover will explain why I am watching you so intently and it will also keep those unwanted, pesky suitors at bay." He grins again, completely satisfied with his plan. "Two birds with one stone, if you will."

I groan, pressing my palms into my eyes. "Please never ever say *pseudo-lover* again."

He chuckles and gently lays his palm on my forehead; the action instantly has my hands falling from my face. His jade eyes swirl with his hidden magic, hypnotic. "*Sleep.* The journey ahead will only prove more strenuous, we will need to be at full strength for the trials ahead."

His words wash over me like sunshine, the warmth amplifying the exhaustion I already feel. I blink rapidly, the feeling of sand and grit seeming to get stronger, until I give in and keep them closed. "Hey, Deme…" I force my heavy lids open once more to ask a question I've always wanted to ask but never had the nerve to. "How old are you?"

His cool hand smooths my hair from my forehead. "I stopped counting after seven-hundred years…"

Wow.

Demetrius's strained smile is the last thing I see before the siren song of lady darkness finally pulls my eyes closed for good.

***

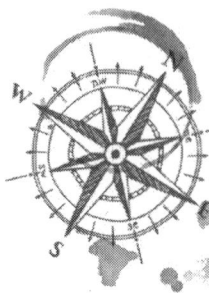

Chapter 15: Elyse
1 June 1691
Île Sainte-Marie, Dauphin

"Asa, you worthless bilge rat! You tryin' to set this ship sailing away on its own?!" The last word is barely out of my mouth before the back of my hand connects with the scrap-of-a-lad's face, sending him sprawling hard to the deck. Not hard enough to break any bones, no, that would be too much trouble. But enough to cause the whelp to sit there a moment before he stirs, pulling himself onto hands and knees.

My anger boils as I take a step toward the shaking lad. "Clove hitches are weak for holding the anchor. It'll come loose as the waves rock the ship in the port. FIX IT!"

I draw my fist back, and Asa jerks his head up to look at me, his large brown eyes full of fear. He then drops into a small ball, skinny, dirty arms covering his face. "I remember now! I swear, don't hit me again, I remember!"

"I remember now! I swear, don't hit me again, I remember!"

"No Pa, leave Elyse alone. I'll take the punishment for her!"

My hand drops, instead seizing the useless bangle around my right wrist, the only piece of jewelry I wear. A vice squeezes my heart hard and I sigh. "Get your arse up and start on your task. No meals for two days."

Without so much as a word of protest, the child pulls his body off the ground and scuttles toward the aft of the ship, his small hands tugging up the long ends of his patchy trousers to avoid tripping and falling over them.

I let go of the piece of garbage jewelry I should probably just toss overboard, and pinch the bridge of my nose, trying to quell my anger. It wouldn't do any good killing the lad now.

"Maybe your sister isn't the only one who be soft, girl."

98

Even before I face Kai, my lips are curling into a sneer. He ain't even supposed to be up here… Standing in front of me is my dual Captain, dressed in gaudy knee-length breeches the same shade as the waves kicking against the hull. His top half, burly with sloping shoulders and arms packed with muscle from years on harsh seas, is covered in an equally flashy deep blue brocade coat. It's detailed with expensive braiding along the trims. Underneath is a new, puffy white cotton shirt, and so many golden trinkets around his neck that I'm surprised he can even keep his head up.

A smirk full of amusement curls his sun-weathered lips, his dark eyes full of their usual malice and darkness. The lines creasing around his mouth and eyes, and the slight silver streaking his dark hair, are the only real show of the nineteen-year age difference between us. He can still raid with the best, most youthful of our crew. His eyes flick over me and the longer I glare right back at him silently, the bigger his smirk grows.

"I left you at the tavern. What are you doing here? Think I can't manage the crew on my own, old man?"

He only laughs, taking my words as an invitation to step closer. "And here I was at the understandin' that we were in a partnership, Captain. Is it so out of my station to come check on the hands of my ship?"

I want to bury my fist down his throat until he's choking on it, begging me to stop. I want to rip his tongue out. I want to hurt him. "No, guess not." I fold my arms to stop from grabbing his throat. "Well, good luck with that." I don't wait for a response, turn on my heel and head down the three small steps that lead into the forecastle of the ship, no goal in mind other than putting some distance between us. If he weren't seasoned and vicious, I wouldn't even bother still trying to maintain this troublesome partnership.

He doesn't try to stop me, but I feel his eyes on me as I duck below deck into the cooler underbelly of the ship, his deep chuckle the only thing that follows me. He's a nightmare, even more so than Una was.

The thought of my sibling, dead by my own deeds, causes my steps to stall. My hand almost grabs for the metal loop around my wrist of its own accord. We'd each had one, a matching set. Una had sported hers until her demise. My chest squeezes again at what her actions had forced me to do in retaliation. My own sister's betrayal burns like fire in my blood, fresh still as the day it happened. Una… I hope your soul rests in the deepest, quietest pits of the sea where you can be at peace, free. Hopefully. If shite like that really happens…

I walk, trying to clear my mind, taking a turn about the orlop before heading back to the top deck, foot on the bottom step, when the nasal, heavily-laced voice of Gaspar stops me in my tracks.

"Have you thought about what we talked about earlier, Captain? About the *mujer joven*?"

My teeth clench at the sound of his voice. He's hidden from my sight by a pile of sacking and crates. I don't even need to lay eyes on the eccentric Spaniard, I can picture him in my head. Barely older than me but parading around like a peacock in that ghastly ruffled, white cotton shirt that always threatens to strangle him without ever, unfortunately, managing it. With his slicked black-as-night hair, swarthy skin, small brown eyes, always dressed in padded crimson breeches and matching jerkin over his doublet, he always looks like a bird with its feathers all fluffed. Trying to seem bigger, *more* than he is. I know enough Spanish to know the words he used means 'young lady'. He sure as sin better not be talking about me. I move closer, slowly, careful to not let my boots make any sounds on the steps. I hover just below the uppermost deck, ear trained on their conversation. What could Gaspar possibly have to say?

Kai surprises me by speaking instead. "I have, but ye haven't told me *why* you want Elyse out of the crew. She was here before the lot of you. Code states the entire crew must vote, including her. Why should I change that for you?"

Gaspar wants to go against the code to get me out of my own crew? Knave… I resist the immediate urge to cover the remaining distance between us and tell him just where I think he can shove whatever foolish thing is about to come out of his mouth. But my more sensible self tells me I should wait and listen. I focus on the treachery occurring just above me, on my own damn ship. Blood will spill, but for now…

"The girl herself goes against the very code you try to uphold… *Captain*." I hear Gaspar clear his throat loudly, and the deck above my head creaks as he moves. "Word will get around, a *mujer* on board a splendid vessel. No one will take us seriously. We will lose coin."

I barely stop the snort that tries to explode out of me. Preaching about keeping hold of coin, after his homeland declared sovereign default nine times. Utterly laughable. Did he even think before he opened that greasy mouth of his?

As Kai snorts out the sound I hold back, I know Gaspar hasn't thought at all. And that's something my fellow Captain dislikes more than hands being disobedient or breaking the code. Idiot lads who lead more with their gut, their emotions, than with the thing between their ears. Like Una always had done.

I've heard enough.

I take the last step, not caring about being quiet anymore, my hand going around the hilt of my cutlass, my body burning with anger. How dare he try and turn Kai on me, *my* ally. I found him. He's going to learn just what I'm capable of; what I will bring him. As I step onto the upper deck, I see Gaspar a few paces from Kai, who still stands with his arms crossed over his chest, his face split with dark, amused mirth.

Gaspar spies me before Kai does, his round eyes widening as I pull my blade free of my sash. His tanned skin pales as he takes in the death-glare in my eyes, *his* death. "Hello, Elyse…"

I don't hesitate. Never hesitant; that's when you die.

I reach up, gripping his shoulder tightly and feel his body tense under my touch. "It's *Captain*, Gaspar. How many times do I have to tell you?"

Then I'm burying the sharp end of my cutlass through his gut.

He gurgles through his shock, as I twist the sword in his stomach, his hand grabbing at the front of my shirt, trying to knock me away. I smirk and chuckle, twisting the weapon the other direction, pressing harder under I feel something give. My blade passes through his body. It's a death sentence he brought upon himself.

I finally look him in the eye just as he coughs a mouthful of blood it drips down his dark stubble, along his sharp, pronounced jawline. Just as that annoying spark begins to fade. "C–captain…"

I nod, bringing my boot up. "Very good, now… get off my sword. Yer getting it dirty." I shove against his hip as hard as I can, pushing him off my precious weapon, the sound sloppy and wet as his body connects with the wooden deck at my feet. I throw a steely look at a still-smirking Kai, as Gaspar twitches and gurgles. "Who's become soft?"

Kai's only response is a deep chuckle, and an appreciative nod in my direction. I return the nod, not bothering to give Gaspar another thought. "Get someone to clean that up. I'm going to the tavern, I've earned one."

***

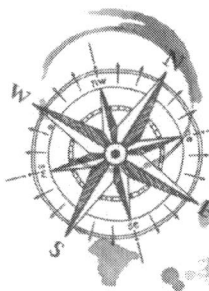

Chapter 16: Hanna
4 June 1691
Somewhere in the Indian Ocean

Rough shaking has me smacking blindly at the source and rolling away from it, groaning loudly into my arms

"Aurelius said you'd be a terror to wake. Pity he was right."

Panic has me reaching for the weapon at my waist. My fingers clench at nothing but fabric. My espada is gone, placed on the small stool beside the bed before I'd gone to sleep last night.

I tear my eyes up to an unfamiliar face. Amber eyes gleaming at me, unwavering and intense, framed by dark lashes. Then she blinks, they kiss the angular cheeks, her shoulder length black ringlets touching a heavy, familiar-looking dark gray cloak. Selina. I've not yet seen her without her hood drawn up. She is quite striking.

"Looking for this?" She holds out my espada with a tattoo-twined pale arm. "He also said you're a bit touched in the head when you first wake up. Sad to see he was right about that as well."

My cheeks burn as I grab the espada and clutch it to my chest. It's then that I see the small wooden tray balanced on her palm. The contents are still unknown but the smells wafting toward me make my belly growl, nonetheless. "Is that for me?"

Selina's cheeks flush slightly and she averts her gaze as she shoves the tray into my arms, before promptly folding her arms back over her chest. "You slept through breakfast. Captain would skin my hide if I didn't make sure everyone on her crew was fed and ready to port."

I look down at the tray's contents: a ceramic bowl of clear broth with a small bland-looking piece of bread no bigger than the palm of my hand. My chest warms and the tight knot that had formed the moment I stepped onto the ship loosens slightly at her kind gesture. No matter how snarkily she might have delivered it.

I kick the sheets from my legs and set the espada down before picking up the hard bread. I take a bite – it's as tasteless as it looks. After a few sips of the salty, watery broth and stale bread, I look up to see Selina staring awkwardly around the bunk.

"So where has that giant pain in my side run off to this time?" I ask.

The sullen woman croaks out a laugh, the first I've heard since boarding *The Revenge*, her shoulders relaxing. "Last I saw your perkier half, he was engaged in an intense conversation with Atropous."

I take another bite of the hard-as-rocks bread, using the time to chew to simmer my anger. I'm seriously going to kill Demetrius this time... "And Una and Solomon? Are they manning the ship?" Since arriving, I've only seen Una at evening meals, but we all eat as a unit, so our conversations have been limited. Both a blessing and a curse, really. A curse, because I ache to talk to her again; bring back the warm energy that had begun to grow around us at the cabin. But also, a blessing, because I honestly don't know what I would do if we were alone together. The bond is ever a growing presence in my mind, body, and soul. It permeates every corner of me.

Selina's lips twitch like she's trying to keep herself from smiling or laughing. "Yes, if you call what those two do 'manning the ship'."

Self-conscious under her gaze, I quickly polish off the rest of the food. "Did Aurelius ask you to come here? Don't take this the wrong way but it doesn't seem like something you'd just... do."

This time she lets the cackle tumbles through her lips. "He seems to think you need looking after."

Now finished with my meal, if you can call it that, and thoroughly embarrassed, I lay the tray on the cot and stand slowly. The sway of the boat momentarily causes my vision to dance with spots. When it clears, I grab my boots, using the wall to balance myself as I tug them on as quickly as I can, highly aware of the eyes closely watching my every move. Once booted, I turn back to Selina. "I assure you, it's he who needs looking after."

Selina caws out another laugh as I reach across the small cot and grab my espada, looping it through the sash at my waist. "Don't lads always, though?"

My laughter joins hers, lightening the weight in me. I quickly regret it, though, as it leaves my head swimming. With great effort, I try to casually lean against the doorframe. "So, eighteen more days?"

Selina nods and briefly unfolds her arms to push her unruly hair from her eyes. "Don't worry. Caleb and the Captain gathered enough rations, sheets and light beer for the voyage."

Living with Demetrius the last twelve years has had its advantages and disadvantages. While educated, I have no experience beyond the cove and our cabin. The only things I know of the world are what I read in books, and even then, it has always been limited to what Demetrius had available around the cabin. "Have you been there before? What's it like?"

Her gaze softens into warm honey as a smile curls her lips. "It's a haven of sorts, for pirates and buccaneers alike. A large trade circuit flows that way, can't go six paces without seeing a trade or haggle happening. You can get some exotic goods there, way easier in that part of the world. Loads of ships carry expensive goods from India ripe for the taking." Her eyes sparkle with emotion I've not seen in my usually taciturn crew mate before. "You haven't truly lived until you've experienced a raid. The salty air in your lungs, the smell of gunpowder in your nose…" She clears her throat, her cheeks darkening with embarrassment. "I'm sure you'll see the differences when we arrive."

I cover my laugh with a cough and a curt nod. "And do you know what my function will be?"

Since I've been on the ship, I've learned the ropes from Felix, a ten year old wisp of a lad so skinny I'm always afraid, when he's in the rigging, that the wind is going to blow him away.

Now it's her turn to hide her smile. The corners of her lips turn upwards as she fakes a disinterested yawn. "Once we port, you, Caleb and Aurelius will head into the ugly pirate under belly and sniff us out some viable information. I'm sort of jealous. You get the fun job. I'll be lucky to see one tavern brawl that actually ends in bloodshed."

Gather information on my father and Una's wayward sibling… no problem. Simple, really. I nod to myself as Selina rotates her head on her neck, yawns widely, a real one this time. "Now the pleasantries are over with, Una's next orders are for you and your good bucko Caleb to bury the hatchet. I'm to lead you to the converted orlop."

I sneer without meaning to at the mention of the dense-headed muscle man who doesn't seem to understand when someone is purposelessly trying to avoid them at all costs. I'd made part of my daily task list to talk to the meathead as little as possible. Without waiting for an answer from me, Selina lifts the flap of cloth at the door and ducks under it, leaving me to scramble dejectedly after her. Seems like I won't be able to finish my task list fully today. What a shame.

This orlop ends up being the lowest deck on the ship, the temperature drastically cooler down here, and gooseflesh instantly covers every part of my body. The dark hallway is only dimly lit by six of those small flickering brass oil lamps.

As we head further down the confined hallway, the distant sound of something hitting against something else echoes down to us. Ten more paces and the mystery is solved; toward the back of the opened-up space, Caleb stands with his back to us, throwing knives at a hay bale marked to resemble a target from an archery range. All his focus is on that small stack of hay as he casually tosses a small silver dirk and, surprisingly, hits the bullseye dead on.

"Listen up," Selina's voice booms, holding almost as much command as Una herself. "You two have until supper to resolve your differences. Failure to do so will result in no food rations until we port, and then the Captain will sort this out for you, if you're somehow still alive at that point." With one last bone chilling stare at me, Selina heads back the way we came, her footfalls eventually fading away, leaving Caleb and I completely alone together. Oh, joy.

For several heartbeats, the only sound is Caleb's loud breathing and the repetitive sound of his knife hitting the target. He hasn't turned once to look or acknowledge me. I sigh heavily and take a few hesitant steps towards the bald pirate. "You're very skilled with that dirk."

At my voice, Caleb's hand pauses mid-throw, before he lowers it to his side, and turns to me, all traces of fire gone from his brown eyes. "I meant what I said the day we boarded. You and yer partner are strong allies to have. Three swords are better than one, and all that nonsense."

I stare into his scarred, bruised face and sigh, holding out my hand to him. What the hell. Seeing as I've already ruined my list for the day. He looks at me, brown eyes huge and disbelieving, before quickly covering it by puffing up his already large chest and clasping my forearm in a now-familiar handshake.

As we release forearms, I throw him a playful smirk. "Ya know… I'd be an even stronger ally if I knew how to throw knives like you."

His wind-chapped lips mirror my smirk with a playfulness that rivals even Demetrius. He extends the gleaming hilt of his dirk to me, two of his fingers delicately holding the tip of the sharp blade. "Well, do I have a teacher for you. Octavia, meet Marigold. Marigold, Octavia."

***

Chapter 17: Una
4 June 1691
Somewhere in the Indian Ocean

Solomon bows a final time before I leave him alone at the wheel, his hazel eyes already focused on the vast expanse of thrashing waters. That won't ever stop being strange… wonder if I can break him of that bowin' shite?

Atropous will soon be returning from his little chat with Aurelius to relieve Solomon, a light storm has started to brew, it's half 'til supper, and I've yet to hear any word from Octavia or Caleb. I duck below the deck, my boots heavy on the wooden steps as I make my way down the narrow hallway towards the close-set living quarters.

My world suddenly spins, everything blurring harshly as I take the last few stairs. Octavia's face flashes through my thoughts, but instead of her intense brown eyes, familiar lilac ones now take their place… As quick as the phantom thought enters my brain, it leaves, taking the dizzy spell with it.

I brace myself against one of the oak walls of the hull, pulling in a slow, steadying breath. What in Davy Jones's locker was that?! I wipe away the beads of sweat that had burst onto my brow. I truly let that half-ling get into my head. I scoff at my own silliness, pulling in one more centering breath before I pull myself up to my full height. I wipe all emotions from my mind and force my frantic thoughts to be still. Then I pull my shoulders back and hold my head high, putting on an air of confidence I currently don't feel. All I feel is exhaustion and a sense of being off kilter.

I continue along the forecastle, dipping my head in greeting as I pass the hands of my ship. They instantly stop to acknowledge and greet their Captain. A swell of pride fills my chest, warmth pushing away the cold weight that had begun to roost beneath my breast. My ship. My crew. My weapons… and soon, it'll be Kai and Elyse's heads on my pikes.

I turn into the lightly lit orlop, the chill of the lower decks bringing gooseflesh to the exposed parts of my arms. A couple more paces and the sound of steel on steel reaches my ears, echoing from further down the vessel. What in the Seven Seas are they doing? My heartbeat and my steps quicken as I hear Caleb's gruff and foreign laughter. Blimey! I might be out of a crew mate already! Two more paces and my legs are locking at the scene in front of me. Rapier and cutlass crossed in battle, their gazes locked, twin smirks of amusement on their faces. Caleb and Octavia stand off against each other, frozen like two statues, their arms not even swaying. Even Caleb's gimp leg holds itself strong. Suddenly Octavia drops low, mimicking the move Aurelius had tried on Atropous during their match before we set sail, but instead of missing, like he had, her boot connects with Caleb's left shin, dropping him to his knees instantly.

His brown eyes widen for a second before he breaks out into loud, unrestrained laughter that crinkles his eyes. "You clever minx. When did ya notice my left leg is bum?"

Octavia's smirk melts into a smile as she extends her free hand down to a still laughing Caleb. "You favor your right leg and refuse to put your full weight on your left. Dead giveaway. May want to work on that, bucko."

Instead of his usual angry or violent response, he just grasps her offered hand, his gruff laughter getting louder. As she pulls his beefy body to his feet, with surprising ease I might add, Caleb finally notices me.

"Captain! Normally I charge ten doubloons for the show you just got, but since you let me join this merry band of outcasts, I'll let this one be on the house!" He loops his silver cutlass through the thin gray sash around his hips and cuts a small smile Octavia's way.

Her smile's been replaced with a neutral look of indifference, her brown eyes guarded once more. "Captain."

My head spins and my vision blurs again until there's four people in front of me instead of two. I blink quickly and grip the hilt of my own weapon, allowing the cool metal to steady the slight tremor in my fingers. "I see the issue has been dealt with. Caleb, go eat supper and pass along a message to that swinging-the-lead navigator of mine. It's Solomon's turn for a meal and Atropous's turn to arm the ship."

Caleb casts a glance at the now stone-faced Octavia before he nods, saluting lazily. He quickly gathers his dirk and boots before taking his leave, leaving Octavia and I alone in the Orlop.

She seems on edge, holding her shoulders tense and so high they're almost bunching up by her ears. Her rapier is now stored back in the brilliant blue sash around her waist, a sash that has to cost more than all the clothes currently on my body. Her almond shaped eyes dart around me, never lingering on my face for too long. "Do I need to fetch Aurelius? You're here to explain our part in your plan once we port, yes?"

I'm momentarily taken aback by how easily she's figured out what I'm thinking and planning. How unsettling. "No. I'm sure you're quite capable of relaying the information I'm about to tell you back to him."

She nods, her left hand fidgeting with the handle or her weapon. I'm drawn to the action, those tan fingers tracing over the decorative engravings again and again. I clear my throat, tearing my eyes from the hypnotic dance and back up into her serious brown gaze. "Our main targets are Elyse and Kai, true scourges of the Seven Seas. They won't be easy to track down. That's where you, your partner and Caleb come in. We'll dismantle their little crew from the bottom up."

Octavia adjusts her hold on the hilt of her weapon, tightening then losing her grip like she's nervous. "Meaning we're going to go after their quartermasters?"

I can't help the impressed smile that quirks my lips upwards, and I nod. "They're a pair of brothers; Ezekiel and Elisha, the younger goes by Eli. I hear they're nearly as bad as their masters, and ugly to match. The eldest has a deep scar over his right eye and wears a patch most of the time. His brother won't be far from his side, and they're good shots with their guns. They'll be hell to break, but that's why I'm hoping to find their cabin boys first."

She tilts her head to the side, some of her light chestnut hair spilling from the bandanna and into her eyes. "Cabin boys?"

I blink. Just who in three hells does she think the lad she'd been getting her own lessons from is? "They're ship hands; young lads that usually help the cook, delivering missives and, in some cases, like on my ship, they know the ins and outs of it. Elyse and Kai have three cabin boys. Unfortunately, information on that trio is scarce. Atropous was the only one that saw the lads. But they'll bear the mark of their masters."

"Which is?"

I reach into my trouser pocket and grab a rolled-up piece of parchment that Atropous had hastily inked his sketch upon. I unroll it and show the instantly enraptured woman; she leans in close, taking in the standard skull and cross bones that our brethren always bear, but with one difference: a huge, jagged vertical slice starting above the eye and straight down through the cheek, stopping at the jaw.

"Commit this symbol and their names to memory, find them and break them. They have information that'll lead me to either the quartermaster brothers, or to Kai and Elyse themselves. Get it by any means. That's your task. We're going to stay on Sainte Marie until we have a lead that leads us elsewhere."

Octavia nods once, no emotion in her eyes. Only cold, detached acknowledgment of her duty "Anything else, Captain? Or am I free to go?"

Don't let her go.

The alarming thought in my mind blazes to life as I struggle to think of something that would keep the confusing woman around longer. "Um… want to have supper together? I mean, I can show you to the kitchens…? If you're up to it?"

You idiotic arse, what was that?!

She surprises me by throwing me a wide smile that nearly splits her face in two. Those empty, cold eyes are now golden honeysuckle, like the first rays of a sunset, so full of life and honesty that it has my heart skipping a beat, then making up for that by picking up its pace.

"After you, Captain," she tells me.

The galley is nearly deserted as Octavia and I enter. Only Selina and my red-headed master gunner, Ambrose, are here He notices me first, his pale green eyes lighting up. He's a good two feet taller than me, lanky but packed with lean muscle. He leads a small team of six men – his 'second' being Jonah – that help him aim, fire, reset, swab and reload the cannons in the event of an attack.

He waves a scarred, pale hand at me, his perpetually rosy-cheeked face flushing even more when he notices who's at my side. "Captain! Aye! A good eve, is it not? Who's your new bucko?"

Selina sighs and turns, pulling down her hood and balancing a tray of food on her other hand. "Don't be an idiot, Ambrose. We all met for supper last eve. I think the gunpowder dust has finally gone to yer brain."

His smile widens, green eyes focused on Octavia, who's starring equally as intently back at him. "Was it only that short a-time? Hmm, she and I never really get the chance to chat formally. Captain always has me tending to the cannons and cleaning the cannonballs when I could be bonding with my new crew mates." His eyes flick from Octavia to me. "It's almost like she's keeping me away from you for a reason."

Octavia's cheeks darken, made worse as Selina barks a laugh and almost drops her tray of food. Dropping her dinner would be too light a punishment for that one…

As Ambrose's attention focuses back on Octavia, I leave the trio, the sounds of Selina and Ambrose's playful bickering following me into the galley. An odd bubbling under my ribs causes my anger to flare at the overly interested look Ambrose had been giving Octavia, and how she'd returned it. Preposterous.

I head to the caboose of the kitchen and wait at the entrance for one of the cabin boys to deliver a tray of food. I tap my foot, impatiently, simmering in my thoughts, before Felix delivers the small wooden tray. He adds an extra serving of rum when he notices who he's serving, which makes me smile slightly. We're still early enough in the voyage that our food rations are at their best, and my stomach growls loudly as I gaze at the feast of cured meats, fermented vegetables, slightly stale bread and even some thimbles of milk. Good to see the cow has settled to sea life well. We'll have milk until we have to slaughter it! I grin at the tray as I make my way back to the galley. Only Octavia remains, leaning silently against a pillar, so deep in thought that she doesn't hear me approach. I use her dropped guard to take in her sharp, exotic features, so different from Hanna's. Yet there's something so annoyingly similar between them; I'm grasping at straws trying to pin it down. But her sparkling brown eyes, filled with mirth, are suddenly dangerously close; so close I can feel the heat rolling off of her.

"I hope you got enough for me too, I'm starving."

I step back, startled, before trying to wipe the surprise off my face at her flip-flopping mood. One minute she's as cold as the first frosts of winter, the next it's like the sun itself is shining on me. Which way is the wind blowing here? And why do I care?

Octavia thankfully interrupts my inner turmoil by gently taking the tray from my suddenly unresponsive fingers. "Want to have supper on the main deck?"

I blink a few times to erase the fog from my brain. "Sure… I know the best spot on the ship."

She smiles at me and my heart does an odd little leap. "Lead the way, Una."

It's the second time today that she's invited me to lead her. First time today she's used my name. I don't want to think about why it makes me blush.

I lead us onto the main deck. The moment we emerge, I inhale deeply, the strong smell of brine filling my nose, and I'm instantly calmed. We settle cross legged on the deck, the lone tray the only thing separating us. My eyes are drawn to the sky above the turbulent ocean. We've come above deck just in time to indulge in my favorite part of the day. The usual pale blues and grays of the sky are now muddled with shameless red, ethereal pinks, golden yellows, and endless oranges. The achingly wonderful sight momentarily steals my breath. How can something so beautiful exist in this shite world? As the colors blur and the last ray of light dips below the horizon, I turn to Octavia and another gasp threatens to spill from my lips. Her hand hovers above the tray, but those almond-shaped eyes are trained on me. Slightly unfocused, the warmth there darkening them.

I clear my throat and try to push down the traitorous blush I already feel staining my cheeks. "How's the food? Silas didn't muck it up too badly?"

She blinks and focuses, blindly grabs at something on the tray and brings cured beef to her lips. The moment it touches her tongue, she inhales it, quickly finishing off the ration, a grin lighting her entire face up. "Oh! It's very good! I've never had this kind of meat before!"

I grab my ration and take a bite, smothering my laughter. A lightness that I haven't felt since before I left Hanna and Demetrius consumes me. I swallow. "Enjoy it. The longer we're at sea, the harder it is to hold things like this."

She smiles faintly and we fall into companionable silence long after the last bite of food has been eaten.

***

I watch Octavia duck back below deck as she turns in for the night. Then I sigh loudly and lean heavily on a spar, looking over into the now-still, slate-colored waters.

"So, having last meal together tomorrow eve as well? Sure that's wise, Captain?"

I start, whirling to face a cheekily grinning Atropous. His ringlets are held from his face at the base of his neck. I eye him suspiciously as he joins me. "You're supposed to be at the wheel, relieving Solomon."

He props his bearded chin in one of his large palms, his emerald eyes like two glittering jewels. "Selina was there when I came up to relieve him. She'd brought enough food to feed the four of us. He was much more willing to stay after that wee hooded one offered to stay with him."

I roll my eyes, but the action has no true bite behind it. "Ever the matchmaker, Art."

"Speaking of matchmaking…" he straightens and turns the full power of his gaze on me, "You and that little vixen are getting pretty chummy. Remember she's a taken woman. What would the other members of the crew think?"

114

Heat and anger rush to my cheeks at his words. "That's enough, Atropous. You know I…" The near euphoric look in his eyes makes me pause as he once again puts his thumb into another pie that's absolutely none of his business. I grind my teeth. "Not another word about her. Captain's orders."

Atropous wilts and, for a moment, I feel guilty about enforcing my rank to shut him up. "Okay, okay. My real business is to tell you that Aurelius and I worked things out." He fishes in his pocket a moment before pulling out a silver flask and uncorking it. Without hesitation, he takes a long, slow drink.

"What was the lubber's problem with ya?"

He laughs loudly and passes me the flask. I accept and take a well-needed sip. I revel in the burn as the spicy liquid trails down my throat.

"He thought he lost a fight to me once years back. Seems his ego was still badly bruised from it." He cuts me a sideways, knowing look.

I pass the flask back and he takes another swig, his shoulders bouncing with laughter. I suppose a case of mistaken identity is a possible reason behind Aurelius's discomfort around Atropous.

Or not.

That initial feeling of doubt and suspicion around them both comes surging back to the front of my mind; Octavia knowing my name before I gave it, their odd choice in weapons, Aurelius's obvious mistrust of Atropous. Sure… a lost fight. Or my sister really does have moles in my crew somehow.

"You got yourself one hell of a crew, Captain… it's definitely something I've never seen before."

I gaze into Atropous's excited eyes and sigh. "Let's just hope it's enough."

It *has* to be enough.

***

115

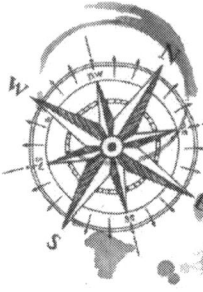

Chapter 18: Hanna
8 June 1691
Somewhere in the Indian Ocean

And Demetrius said the closeness would 'take some of the edge off'... Lying nymph! My head spins again and my vision momentarily goes black, causing me to nearly miss the last step back beneath deck. I pause in my unsteady steps and feign adjusting my espada strap, using the nearest wall to lean my back against. Another crew member casts me a curious glance before he continues down the hall to the forecastle. My stomach gives another lurch and I purse my lips, trying to hold down the food Una and I had just enjoyed together. Again. We're making a habit of eating together, it seems.

Una.

I'm suddenly remembering the way the setting sun had intertwined its soft oranges and bloody reds together four evenings back, a sight I'd only had a moment to enjoy until, in true pirate fashion, she'd completely stolen my attention. The hardness to her gaze, that makes her eyes like slate, had completely melted into two shimmering aquamarine oceans. The tightness around her mouth had softened, her lips even turning up into a smile. Not the cocky smirk she uses to feign bravado, or the flirtatious one she uses to put on an air of indifference, but a genuine one. The one she'd started to show more freely the longer she'd spent on the island with Demetrius and me. The sight of her unburdened had taken my breath for a moment. Then the sunset's spell had broken, and she'd looked at me and had the nerve to blush and ask how I enjoyed the food, like she does every day we eat together. Our picnics on deck are the only thing that gets me through my tasks, the strain of the bond sending me into a deep sleep almost as soon as I touch my bunk. It's the reason Demetrius and I have yet to discuss what Una had gone over with me days prior. I follow the path the other pirate had taken, but at a much slower pace, each step sending another shock of pain up my weary legs and into my upper body. I think of my mother; how she must have felt much the same when my father refused their bond. I let my mind wander as I take the narrow hallway. I only have one foggy memory left of my mother.

She was holding me amongst the swelling waves of the ocean. I remember the smell of the water and familiar lilac eyes looking down at me as she crooned out a song I only remember the faint melody to now.

The nine years after that are memories of Kai, my father, the pirate.

When I was seven, finally old enough to ask where my mother was, *who* she was, all I'd received was a laugh in my face, and a tale that she had been a bar wench he'd bought when he'd been ported, and that a year later I'd shown up in a basket at the inn he was living in. Then he'd promptly told me never to bring it up again and took my food rations for three days. I knew something had been off about his story, even then, but my age and fear of more punishment kept me from ever asking again. Three years later I would find out just how right that feeling had been.

A hypnotic melody had woken me from my sleep, the beautiful tune sounding like a lute, viola, and harp combined. I don't remember climbing the stairs from my bunk, and I definitely don't remember leaping overboard into the sea. I'd come back to my senses in the middle of the ocean, with a tail fin, and Father's look-out screaming bloody murder. The entire crew, plus my father, had gathered on the main deck in seconds and, even from my position in the thrashing waters, I could tell how livid Father was. Perfect time for my enhanced vision to kick in.

He'd lowered the Jacob's ladder and I'd climbed it, scared, bare, and completely confused. I'd been hauled to his quarters and locked inside for what I later found out had been seven days. Kai had brought water and food rations once a day and never looked at, touched, or talked to me. Another seven days after that, we'd ported and I found out just what 'trouble' my little stunt had cost him. His crew had to be silenced; only the bare minimum had been spared, only enough men to help Kai tend the ship until they could port, then they, too, had been killed.

The next thing I knew I was being auctioned off to the highest bidder. Paraded around like livestock, like vermin, until Kai got the coin he was looking for. He left, and the next two years my life were nothing but mind-numbing, soul-altering darkness. Every night I prayed to whatever higher power may be listening that they might end it, to send someone to save me from the nightmare of my life, to end my suffering. Then one day my prayers were answered.

My master and I quickly learned that every few weeks I'd need to be exposed to the ocean. If not, I'd become inconsolable and even the threat of physical harm couldn't stop my desperate attempts to get to the sea. It was during one of those outings that Demetrius had appeared, rolling onto the beach like a wave. That turbulent twisting of water had quickly taken human shape, and the longer I'd looked, the more details had filled in, until Demetrius, not much different than he is today, stood in front of us, his algae green hair morphing into the mousy brown I'd grow familiar with.

He'd asked if my name was Hanna, said he was a friend of my mother's, and that he'd come looking for me, as that had been her dying wish. He had been looking for me for nearly thirteen years. My Master had been frightened, to say the very least, and had fled with no regard or concern to take me with him. That was the day I was granted my freedom. And learned the truth.

My mother had been a mermaid, and she had fallen in love with Kai, fallen with a child, and bestowed on him the Gift of the Sea. In exchange, a year later, he stole me and fled across the oceans. My mother, heartbroken, betrayed, and suffering from a rejected bond, died.

Demetrius, for all intents and purposes, is my father. He saved me, then raised me for twelve years. He did his best to prepare and educate me, but nothing could've prepared me for the weight, strain and drain a bond that has yet to be neither accepted nor rejected would have on me.

Another wave of pain flares in my chest as I take the last turn that leads to the forecastle. That ugly, brown sack of false door has never looked so heavenly. I push it aside and all but fall over the threshold. Deme looks up from his perch on the edge of the cot, his eyes jerking to my face, startled, then concerned. His gaze softens as he stands, waving his hand in a wiping motion as he moves. I feel his cool magic slip from my body as he dispels his transformation spell with practiced ease.

"Hells… you look even worse than yesterday. The effects do not seem to be slowing from the exposure to her. I was afraid of that."

I sloppily step around him and pick up the still-full tray of food from the cot, gently pushing it into his waiting hands. He looks exhausted. "I could say the same about you." I slip the heavy boots from my aching feet, unwind the sash that suddenly weighs a thousand pound from my waist and lay my weapon next to Demetrius's, before I sink into the cot's embrace. I trace the dark shadow-like bruises beneath his green eyes. "Is holding the transformation in place nearly all the time difficult for you?"

He smiles tightly. "Don't fret. I'm used to it after so long."

A pang of guilt flickers through me. I'm causing him so much trouble. "You know, you can't nag me like a proper father if you wither away to nothing. You should eat, it's actually not that bad."

His eyes widen slightly, and his mouth drops open like he's going to say something, then closes it and smiles instead. He lowers himself, cross legged, next to the cot and lays the tray on his lap. With a glance over the contents, he swipes the still-soft slice of bread and digs in with gusto, seemingly finding his appetite.

"I see your talk with Atropous the other day went well." I finally delve into the conversations we should have had days ago.

He swallows his food with a deep drink of rum. "Seamlessly. I told him I mistook him for a lad I lost a brawl to. These espada are proving their worth time and time again." He takes a bite of the smoky cured beef and nearly blanches before setting the food back on the tray. "It helps that the lad seems to have led a fisherman's life; he's far too trusting." He takes another long sip from his clay cup, eyes slowly slipping closed. As he pulls it from his lips, one of those green eyes opens, full of all too familiar mischief. "And how about your chat with our new good bucko, Caleb?"

I scoff as he chuckles. "We seem to have an alliance. How long that'll last is up to him."

Demetrius beams. "That's my guppy."

119

I roll my eyes at the nickname. He said when I was young, I swam like I didn't know how to use my tail correctly, like it was too big for my body. All awkward and endearing like a guppy. "On to more important bits of information. As you suspected, we'll be doing the dirty work while Una leads all of us from the shadows."

Demetrius sets the mostly empty tray to the side and stretches out his long legs. "A good decision on her part really, considering she's supposed to be dead twice over at this point."

I chew my lip a moment before I nod. "She wants us to find Kai and her sister's quartermasters, a pair of brothers named Ezekiel and Elisha. But she'd prefer us to get our hands on their cabin boys, Seraphim, Asa, and Josiah. A trio of hands I really hope aren't as young as Felix. Una says they'll be easier to 'break'. We're going to stay on this Sainte Marie until we acquire new information leading elsewhere, or to our intended targets."

Deme nurses his cup as he thinks; I can practically see the wheels turning as he digests the information I'd just given him. He sets the cup beside him before finally speaking. "And how are you feeling about our task, about Una?"

The answer comes to me without any hesitation or question. Demetrius and I have always been that way. No secrets, always so easy to talk to him about my feelings. "Do I like the idea of harming and possibly torturing other people? No. Do I like being on a ship again, where every shadow cast by those lamps reminds me of the worst days of my life? No. Do I look forward to coming face to face with Kai again, with the chance that I'll have to slay him with my own hand? No." I swallow and feel traitorous tears begin to prickle behind my eyes again. "But I can live with all of that. What I can't live with is a world without Una."

Deme's face remains passive, giving nothing away. "Do you think it is the bond forcing you to say and think that?" He gazes at me, unreadable, but there's not a shred of judgment in his voice.

"I knew what she was the moment I saved her. Both times. I've thought about what her life must have been like that led her to that point. That still didn't stop me from being relieved she didn't leave the moment I gave her the chance. Bond or no bond, I'd choose Una. Of that I'm certain."

He flashes me a teasing smile, with that mischievous glint in his eye again, but it turns impossibly warm and faraway, like he's somewhere else entirely. "You are just like Ondine. Your hearts are far too big for this harsh, dangerous world."

I ignore the comment and the way it doesn't stir up the fire in me that usually accompanies any mention of my mother. "Do you really think Atropous believed the whole 'mistaken identity' lie?"

He shrugs. "He seemed to. He also seemed to be none the wiser about mine and his... condition."

"Perhaps he's just a human after all? Maybe when those two species mingle and bear a child, it's just a normal, mortal human? No nymph abilities? Could you just be sensing his parentage?"

Deme sighs. "When I said 'myth' earlier, it was not in jest. He could have all my abilities or none of them at all."

"And that frightens you?"

His soft gaze instantly freezes over, and his relaxed, slouched posture draws tight like a bow. "Not frightened. Just wary. As you should be. You're getting far too chummy with the hooded woman. And be careful being above deck for so long. I do not need you going green around the gills on me."

My laugh bubbles over before I can stop it. "I'm certain you're the one who goes all gill-fish if you get splashed. Oh! Have you tried splashing Atropous? See if he turns all watery?"

He rolls his eyes, but his shoulders slacken as he raises an eyebrow at me, amused. "How many cups of rum did you have at supper? Yes, Han. As I was trying to make peace with the boy, I *also* convinced him to let me fling water all over him."

His sarcasm makes me grin. "If you've taught me anything, it's that anything is possible when it comes to you."

Our laughter dies after a few blissfully normal moments, and we lapse into a comfortable, companionable silence. The comfortable feeling soon gets eclipsed as that exhaustion washes over me and my mind begins to wander. What if the surf splashes Deme while he's out on the main deck? What if he falls overboard? Oh shite… what if it rains?!

Demetrius suddenly stands, dusting his hands on his pants and casting a smile down at me. It's as if he can sense my inner turmoil. He lays a cool palm on my forehead, smoothing my hair from my eyes. "Don't fret, Guppy, everything will work out as is intended. You'll see."

***

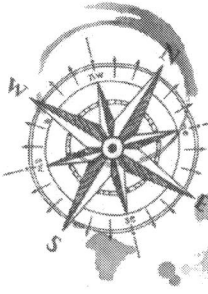

Chapter 19: Solomon
11 June 1691
Somewhere in the Indian Ocean

"And to untie a bowline, simply flip it over, and break its back by bending it downward, like so." I demonstrate the correct way, before looking up at Octavia and Aurelius. Today is my day to teach them something useful. The duo is skilled in many things but being useful on a pirate ship does not seem to be one of those skills. On the uppermost deck, we enjoy the cool breeze as we glide across the seas, and I'm trying my best to teach them the seven most important knots any buccaneer or sailor should know.

Octavia catches on faster than her partner and holds up her undone knot, a small smile curving her thin, chapped lips. Aurelius, on the other hand, glares down at the still-knotted rope in his lap, his arms folded just as tightly over his body, lip lifted in pure disgust, like the rope has somehow offended him.

I stifle my laugh. "Excellent, both of you! You've both come a long way since this morn!"

My smile is joined by Jonah's deep melodic laugh. "The lad may need just a touch more tutelage, Solomon. Brilliant go at showing them the way of the knots."

Collectively, we turn to see him. His eyes sparkle a deep brown, filled with playfulness. First mate to Ambrose, the master gunner of our ship. His clothes, usually brightly colored for all to see when on land, are muted now that we're back on the waters. He's tucked his tan breeches into his plain leather boots. A white, ruff-less shirt stretches tight over his chest, with the long sleeves rolled to his elbows. His tanned forearms ripple with trained muscle as he places both hands on his hips. Even in clothes similar to the rest of us, he still looks the most well-put-together of us all. I'd heard from Caleb on many occasions that it's because both Jonah and Ambrose were once in the Royal Navy. Though, I highly doubt that our master gunner, with his even stranger accent, hails from the same home place as Jonah.

I smile at the man. "Greetings, Jonah! I'm sure if you were to join us and impart some of your knowledge, they'd learn much faster! Don't you think so, you two?"

Octavia's staring warily, but Aurelius is grinning widely and seems to have gotten over his unhappiness about his lack of knot work skills.

"Yes, please, Jonah, join us." Aurelius beams. "I'm sure you have many things you could teach all of us."

"I want to join too! I know lots about knots! Captain taught me herself!" Before Jonah can answer, Felix bounds into the center of the group, his hair and clothes a dripping mess, like he's taken a dip in the ocean. Where has his footwear gone? Maybe he really did fall overboard. He *has* been on rigging duty today…

Before anyone can speak, or stop him for that matter, the full-of-energy child snatches the rope held loosely in my grip and twists it quite quickly into a perfect bowline. He presents it to Jonah, who's trying to suppress a large smile. "How was that?"

Felix lets loose a high peel of laughter as Jonah takes the offered knot, his other hand clutching the front of his shirt, his eyes wide. "You are a little bugger, Felix. I am stunned, honestly. Well done!" He holds out the perfect example knot to Aurelius, warm grin turning roguish. "For you, mate. I think you'll need it more than I."

Aurelius's smile slips slightly before he catches himself, pulling it back into place. He takes the knot and sets it next to the horribly tangled one still sitting in his lap. "You're too kind, *mate.*"

"This doesn't look much like work to me, crew."

We all turn at the sound of Caleb's voice, and find the man with a medium sized oak barrel lifted onto one of his beefy shoulders, his signature scowl on his round face. His beady eyes cut to Felix, who had frozen at the sound of Caleb's raised voice. "You! I didn't know the riggin' moved over here by the main mast!"

"Quartermaster Caleb?! Yes sir, right away!" The still-damp ten-year-old scrambles backward. His bare feet are loud on the deck as he runs up the two small steps to the quarterdeck and makes a beeline for the ladder that'll lead him up onto the yardarm and into the rigging. His job today is making sure the system of interwoven ropes, chains and tackle are free of snares and knots, so when the time comes to change directions and unfurl the sails to catch wind and pick up speed, it can be done in an orderly fashion.

Jonah cups his hands around his mouth. "Watch the lee, lad! Wouldn't want you to take another tumble into the sea. Might not be able to catch up to the ship next time!"

Jonah breaks into loud laughter as Aurelius and Octavia share a worried look, a feeling I share deep in my chest, for the small boy. Enthusiasm doesn't take the place of skill; if he doesn't have it, his life will be snuffed out like a candle's flame.

"And you!" Caleb rounds on the dark-haired gunner. "Aren't you supposed to be with Ambrose? I heard somethin' about him moving some cannonballs to the other side of the hold."

Jonah's eyes go wide. "NOT MY CANNONBALLS, HE DOESN'T!"

With more speed than I thought even possible for him, Jonah throws his hands in the air, turns on a pin and darts down the steps. The only thing we can hear are his heavy foot falls as he makes a mad dash down to the bottom of the ship.

Octavia tilts her head, a slow rarely seen smile blooming on her face, like a flower opening its first petals during the spring. "Was Ambrose really going to move the cannonballs, or were you just running a rig on him?"

Caleb gives us a wicked grin before covering it with a cough, hoisting the barrel higher up on his shoulder. "You, Solomon. Have them experts by supper. I get them tomorrow. I'd rather not want to throw myself overboard at their lack of useful skill." He turns from us and heads toward the quarterdeck, not bothering to look over his shoulder at us again.

I nod quickly "R— right! I won't let you down!" Nervousness fills my chest as I eye the perfect bowline knot, done by someone an entire ten years younger than me.

Seeming to read my very thoughts, Octavia gives me a bright smile. "You are quite good with your hands, Solomon. For one so young, and to be so well versed, and spoken. How did you come about knowing so much?"

Aurelius's ink-pot eyes are back on me, his head cocked to the side curiously, like he's trying to forcibly see inside my heart and down to the feelings that I do not want to think about.

I chew on my lip and pull at a loose thread on my trousers. "I was raised in the kitchens with my mama… after she left, I had to pick up where she left off. Before she went, she taught me a lot of things." The pain of thinking about her burns like a fireplace poker against my skin.

Now it's Octavia tilting her head, looking a lot like her male companion. "Where did you live before coming here?"

I hesitate a moment, consider lying to them, but I immediately feel guilt in the pit of my stomach and decide the truth is for the best. Always the truth. As much as I can give, anyway. "A tobacco plantation. When it was my time to go away, like Mama did, a group of buccaneers raided the ship before it could leave port, slaughtering all the masters and sailors. I, never seeing anything like that before, ran." I mess with the thread, tugging it until it pops loose, as the memories of that day washes over me. "Let's just say, once I got over the shock of Una being the very thing that frightened me, I realized the ones that raided the slave ship weren't the only kind of pirate there is… Joining her crew, I finally gained my freedom."

They watch me, odd looks eclipsing both their faces. Heat enters my cheeks and I move my hands to my lap, lacing them together, smiling at them timidly. "Like I told Captain, I don't want no one feelin' sorry for me. My past made me who I am at this moment, and I happen to like this 'me'."

Aurelius speaks first, the thin line of his frown lifting as he speaks. "That's very noble of you Solomon."

Octavia nods, beside him. "Yes, your bravery is noteworthy Solomon!"

That heat in my cheeks feels like a campfire that spreads to my entire face, as I widen my eyes. "I didn't tell you to try and seem braver than I am, but in hopes that we could be… friends?"

I wring my hands together, feeling even more the fool than I had before. *Be friends?* How pathetic can you sound, Solomon? I'm a grown adult, not a child like Felix! I spare a sideways glance at a tight-lipped Aurelius, his inky eyes void and unreadable once again, and that knot in my naval turns into a bottomless pit. Does he not want another male being friends with his wife? Or is it because of *who* I am? I suppose I could understand that, if that's the case.

But then Octavia smiles, probably the biggest smile since she joined the crew. "I'd to be friends." She looks out of the corner of her eye, like she's nervous her companion is going to lash out at her, or the both of us.

Is he violent towards her? Or maybe it's Elyse's influence? Maybe they *were* sent here to harm the Captain? I truly hope not, despite the constant warnings from Una, and my own senses. Something just feels off with the pair. Whether it's good, or bad, I'm still uncertain. There's just something more about them, something… charming, an underlying kindness that rivals only Atropous. It's had the urge to befriend them consuming my thoughts as often as gentle Selina dances through them. So, of course the question eventually just came out of me, I couldn't help it.

My stomach churns the longer Octavia's husband stays silent. But then Aurelius's lips also turn upwards, though it's not nearly as blinding a smile as Octavia's had been. "Friends. That sounds like a grand idea, Solomon."

My heart swells with such a rush of happiness, that tears almost come to my eyes. I stare at my two crew mates, my friends. *My friends.* For the first time in my entire life, I have friends.

"Good to see my crew looking so chummy. I hope just as much work got done as bonding. Anyone hungry?"

The Captain.

At her voice, Octavia whips her head around so fast, I'm afraid for the safety of her neck, the ends of her hair smacking her close-sitting companion right in his face.

The man blinks back the strike and sighs, shaking his head slightly. "Good eve, Captain. I hope you brought enough food for the four of us. Your quartermaster worked us hard today. I can barely move my fingers." He makes a show of weakly curling his fingers toward himself. It has me laughing and Octavia rolling her eyes toward the sky.

"Captain, I'll serve the food rations!" I go to stand when her sudden hand on the top of my head causes me to tense under her surprisingly light touch.

"Sit, Solomon. I'll serve us. Don't get your trousers in a knot, save that for the rope."

My lips raise as the others laugh. They're not laughing to be cruel, or to make me feel worse about myself, but because they care enough about me to involve me in their teasing, and a meal. And as the Captain herself begins to portion out our meal, beginning with *me* of all people, I now understand why. *Because they're my friends.*

***

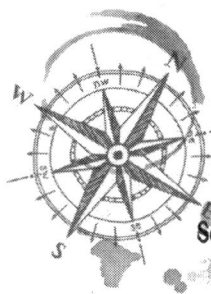

Chapter 20: Una
14 June 1691
Somewhere in the Indian Ocean

I smother a yawn against my fist, then wipe the grit from my still-heavy eyes. I love the high seas as much as the next buccaneer, but longer than three days and those stiff-as-tits cots and hammocks will have you walking funny. I bring the last roll to my mouth and tear into it with gusto, even the stale bread tasting like a meal fit for kings. Bone soup and hard tack for all… fantastic.

I grimace slightly and shudder, as I head above deck to inspect how that godforsaken crew of mine is tending to my *Revenge*. Save for Caleb, Aurelius, and Octavia of course. Especially *Octavia*. Just two days ago I'd found the usually stoic Selina doubled over, tears spilling down her cheeks from her laughter. Apparently, Octavia had come and asked, very seriously to 'aid in steering the wheel.' I chuckle despite the absolute horror I'd felt at the time. Yeah… definitely better if she keeps her paws off my ship.

I squint into the morning sun as I come up onto the main deck, the scent of brine filling my nose. The first thing that catches my attention is Solomon; he stands at the stern, one hand desperately trying to hold her steady and the other clamped over his eyes. Every so often, he spreads his fingers, peaking through the gaps to make sure he maintains his course, before dutifully closing them again.

Selina's near the mast, her hands clenched tightly around one of the thick ropes that make up the central rigging system. Despite her hood shielding her face, her tension is plain as day; her shoulders are nearly bunched up behind her ears. That's when you know she's really on edge.

Laughter draws my gaze upwards to the crow's nest where Atropous stands, leaning way over so he can throw a shite-eating grin my way.

129

I do a quick sweep of my crew and find them all mostly frozen to the spot, hands fumbling with their jobs, their minds and attention clearly elsewhere. "Are you lot three sheets to the wind? I don't pay you to stand there catching flies!"

No one so much as bats an eyelash at my raised tone; my lip twitches as my anger spikes. Then I follow their gazes. Holy shite! What in God's name is going on?!

On the starboard side of the ship, towards the rudder, lies Octavia. She's lying on one of the starchy white sheets we used on the cots; somehow, they looked even duller compared to her perfectly sun-tanned skin. Of which there is certainly a lot currently on show. Is she just in a slip?! I'm immediately transported back to that godforsaken bay and am almost unbearably full of warmth as the memory of lilac eyes flood my thoughts again.

And then I blink, and Hanna is gone, replaced with Octavia, her somehow still silky chestnut locks blowing gently away from her face, those sometimes too intense eyes closed. Her expression is completely serene. Her expensive blue waistcoat lays folded, along with her breeches, beside her, long forgotten, boots and espada not far away. Is this some kind of run-a-rig? I'm torn between gaping like the rest of my crew, stabbing every eyeball currently gawking at her out, or hurling myself overboard into the sea. All three are very tempting choices at the moment.

"That slip certainly leaves nothing to the imagination, eh Captain?!" Atropous's loud voice is a pistol shot in my ears, echoing high above the rest of us.

The crew dissolves into laughter, breaking whatever spell had been cast over them. No words come to me and all I can muster is a loud smattering of gibberish. Port-side, Selina seethes and poor Solomon has turned an impressive shade of red.

The loud laughter finally seems to rouse Octavia. She yawns before propping herself on her elbows. She gazes at the crew almost lazily, then her smoldering gaze finds mine and it takes everything in me to not immediately look away. Before I can say anything, Aurelius strides above the deck, his blonde hair shimmering like spun corn silk in the sun. His eyes widen the moment they spy Octavia. He whips off his cloak and hurries to her side, his gaze hardening with each step. He wraps the cloak around her, looks over his shoulder, and that almost neutral look in his eye that I've gotten used to is completely shattered. He's livid.

"Care to contain your crew, Captain?" His words come out condescending and barbed, sharper than any weapon I've ever owned. As he shakes his head, his attention returning to Octavia, I feel like a punished child. Heat slowly fills my cheeks.

Feeling sheepish, I stand as tall as I can. "You heard him. Get back to work!"

Whether they listen because they respect me, or out of fear for their lives, all still casting nervous glances at the obviously angry man, I'm not sure. But they obey. I watch Aurelius fuss over Octavia, her previously relaxed brow pitched together in annoyance as she re-clothes behind the curtain of cloak her man has held up.

An old pang of loneliness punches me in the gut and my mind wanders yet again. I wonder what Hanna's doing right now...

"AVAST, YE! Abaft the stern, white sails on the horizon!"

Another boom of Atropous's voice above has me moving into action, thankfully stopping my thoughts, which were heading toward dangerous waters.

"Atropous, lower the jolly roger! Selina, help him!"

I pull the small spyglass from my pocket and extend it, peering through the eyepiece. A flat-bottomed ship – wide, strong and three masted – greets me. It's no good as a vessel for me, its speed too slow, but the possibility of what goods the cargo ship could carry is almost too good an opportunity to pass up. Almost. My only goal is getting to Sainte Marie and getting a head start on gathering information on Elyse and Kai. Pillaging right now will only slow us down. It'll have to wait. What a damn pity.

"Come *on* Captain, just one ship. It won't put us that much behind."

I lower my spyglass, close and pocket it, as I take in the disgusting slop of a pirate in front of me. Enoch. Rolls of fat hang over the sloppily tied sash around his waist, a rusty cutlass on his hip. A filibuster, one I'd only hired because he'd been ridiculously cheap help.

His outburst ripples through my crew like a stone skipped across the ocean's surface. Murmurs of boredom, restlessness at the lack of excitement and any action all blend into a pounding in my skull. I grip the already loaded pistol at my waist and point it at the nearest hand. Felix the cabin boy yelps, dropping the bucket of water he'd been carrying. "We all came to an agreement before any of us stepped boot on *The Revenge*. I am the Captain, and my word is law as long as you are in my crew." I cast one more hardened gaze over my slack-jawed crew, before lowering my gun and turning my back on them. "Now get back to it. Or I'll let Felix do your job, and you can swab the deck."

***

"So that's about half our hundred-and-six miles traveled, and about the same amount to go." Solomon traces the dotted line across the lightly blue shaded stretch labeled Indian Ocean, toward Sainte Marie.

Selina leans forward, brushing her curls from her face and points to a spot on the waggoner. Her fingers are whisper-close to a now straightened, blushing Solomon. "And you're certain our rations will hold us until we make it there? We won't have to cut down to one meal?"

I watch them, smirking. Your hand needed to be that close to his when you said that because *why*, Selina?

Solomon swallows and spares a warm, quick glance at her, before turning eyes to me. Ohhh, Atropous is going to love this!

"It should, yes. If I were you Mas– Captain Una, I would slaughter the cow. You got that salt I asked for. I'll teach the kitchens to salt the meat for consumption and storing."

I can't help smiling as I nod along with the ever-surprising lad. A loud knock on my quarters stops the words on the tip of my tongue.

"Captain? It's Caleb! You and me need to have a li'l chat!"

Selina snaps upright, her almost-smile melting into a snarl. I turn and take the one step between my desk and the door, and open it. Caleb stands there, his fist still raised to the door, his brown eyes widened in shock.

He takes a hesitant step back. "Look... we need to talk... er... it's important..." The odd seriousness to the loud-mouth ex-sailor has me very curious.

I step aside, allowing Caleb to squeeze past into the now severely cramped room, before closing the door behind us. Selina folds her tattooed arms over her chest and leans as far away from Caleb as possible, Solomon mirroring her as his honeyed-colored eyes hold Caleb's, unafraid.

Solomon's meekness is a mask now. "Make it quick. The air in here is suddenly too smoggy for my liking."

Caleb shifts uncomfortably from boot to boot, then he finally looks at me. "Enoch came to me after you left. He ain't happy playing second rate to wenches and blue-skins. He's talkin' mutiny."

Mutiny.

The word is poison in my veins. Bile rises in the back of my throat.

Mutiny.

Selina snorts, throwing Caleb a sour look. "And why should we believe you? You could really be the one trying to usurp Una."

Solomon cups his chin in his hands, a pensive look pinching his face. "We're nearly eight full days from any possible port. No one gains anything from a mutiny. Caleb's not stupid enough to have not thought that through. Maybe Enoch really is the wrongdoer."

I look to Solomon, to a still-fuming Selina, then to Caleb. "Give me one good reason I should believe a word that crosses your foul lips."

Caleb holds my gaze, his eyes vulnerable, no spark or usual malice. "Octavia trusts me enough to form an alliance and forgive me. Being my Captain, you should too, and trust me."

I had heard of the tentative alliance from Octavia a few nights ago during one of our suppers out on the main deck. It's becoming an odd ritual, so much so that even other crew members have started making themselves at home between us some nights. Caleb has been one of them.

I sigh, making my decision.

"I believe you. Gather everyone above deck. I do believe you just saved me some meal rations."

***

I hear loud talking as I ascend the stairs and know Caleb has completed his task. As I emerge onto the deck, the chatter stops and all nineteen pairs of eyes, minus Solomon who's holding the helm, turn to me. I sweep my gaze slowly over them as I make my way to the transom. I've tried so hard to keep this crew from ending like the last, and I'm already failing.

I grip the hilt of my cutlass, and revel in the pain of metal biting into my palm. I then draw it, turning it slowly until it catches the sun. I smile in the direction I know Enoch is standing. "Li'l birdie told me mutiny has been whispered inside the hulls of my ship. Enoch, you wouldn't have heard anything about that would you... bucko?"

He purses his thin lips as his body tense in place, locking, his eyes widening in panic and terror. Good. Be afraid. There's no going back now, not after what you've done.

"I... You..."

I tut as he fails to defend himself, but I now know Caleb can be trusted. Not liked, barely tolerated really, but he *is* loyal – to his coin, and where it flows from, at the very least. "Selina, Atropous, if you would be so kind as to lessen Enoch's load, looks a li'l heavy from here. He won't be needing those weapons."

They move with efficiency, both well worth the coin. I'll no doubt end up owing them; Atropous pins the struggling man's arms behind his back while Selina strips him of his weapons. His cutlass is taken from him first. She then rummages through his pockets and finds a dagger and a gun. He's been holding out on me? Now I'm really wounded.

"You can't do this to me, you filthy wench! You belong in the nearest tavern, not leading a bloody crew!"

Selina delivers his weapons to me with an amused smirk, while Atropous silently restrains him. No other member of the crew so much as move a finger to help him or stop me.

"It's too bad you feel that way. But actually, I can do this, and I will."

I inspect the rusted, ugly blade, its worn handguard not even worth the effort I'm spending looking at it. I buff the neglected blade on my thigh before inspecting it closer. "You accepted the job, took my coin, stepped boot on my ship, ate my food and slept in my cots. And this is how you show your thanks? Polluting my ship and crew with your filth and lies?"

I walk to the side of the ship and throw the useless heap of metal overboard. I slip the acceptable dagger into my boot and check over the ancient gun. I don't even know what kind this is. I run a finger around the smooth, ornate handle and barrel, then I wiggle it at Octavia before tossing it her way. Her eyes widen in surprise, but she easily catches it, turning it over in her hands delicately.

"So… what do we think? A little visit to Hempen Halter? You look like you're just itchin' to dance the Hempen Jig… or maybe just a quick slice." I make a show of slowly drawing my cutlass across my throat, the blade just a breath from my skin. I chuckle darkly. "No… too easy. Too quick. I think a good keelhauling is what you need. A good ol' proper pirate send off, since you seem to be the only true buccaneer here." Enoch begins to fight in earnest against Atropous's iron hold. Uselessly, of course, but it sure is entertaining to watch him squirm. "Atropous, strip the filth. Felix, bring me a long sturdy rope."

The young dark-haired cabin boy dashes off to do my bidding as Atropous wordlessly strips the still-shouting buccaneer. "T– This is crazy! You can't do this! It's torture!"

135

I slip my cutlass through my sash and turn to look out across the glittering water. It always seems to fill me with peace and helps me find my strength. He's not wrong, but I must crush any ideas that I'm soft, that I can be overruled. "Give no quarter."

Felix staggers under the weight of the rope spool he's carrying but kneels in front of me the moment he's close enough, dropping the bundle and presenting one loose end to me. I take it and shoo him back toward the crew. Some of the buccaneers begin to cheer and it swells, encompassing everyone, save for Octavia, Aurelius and Atropous.

"Shark bait!"

"Shark bait!"

"Give no quarter! Give no quarter! GIVE NO QUARTER!"

I allow their voices to fuel my anger and to steel my resolve for what I must do. I toss one end of the rope to Caleb, standing on the far side of the deck. He plucks it from the air, nods his understanding, and with a handful of crew, they unwind enough rope to cover the width of the ship. Then they take it to the stern and toss the length over, keeping the end of the rope in their grasp. As Caleb makes his way back to stand opposite me, the rope is now looped beneath the ship, one end in my hand on the portside, the other in Caleb's on the starboard side. A stone-faced Atropous helps me tie Enoch's fat arms tight to his side with my end of the rope.

I drag a resisting Enoch to the portside edge of the ship. "Selina, want to give me a hand?"

A sinister grin splits her lips. "With pleasure."

Together, we heft a still-fighting Enoch up onto the rail – no easy feat given the weight of him and his struggling legs. Atropous has to help us. He's teetering halfway off of the ship. We're the only thing holding him there. Shite, he weighs as much as a beached whale and smells twice as bad. And then we give him one hard shove and his body falls out of view, down, until he splashes into the water. Caleb and the men with him give their end of the rope a tug, and then begin to haul Enoch's body beneath us. Gulls screech overhead. The wind whips my hair. His last moments will be spent dragging the width of the boat as barnacles as sharp as steel slice him to pieces.

I hear Caleb and the men helping him grunting as they haul as I wipe my hands off on my brocade. I turn back toward my crew. I catch Octavia's face among them. Are those tears in her eyes?

I swallow down that treacherous, useless guilt, hardening my gaze and my heart. "Looks like I really can do it. You all know the code, agreed to my terms, were all paid the same coin to make sure what I want comes to pass. Until that day arrives, or you die trying, your lives belong to me." The sweet silence is all the answer I need. "Now, get back to your posts. Everyone loses meal rations until tomorrow's supper."

I turn away.

I peek over my shoulder, when one of my boots is on the top step. Caleb is leaning over the side of the ship, peering down into the waters. He seeks me out, gives a small nod. It's done, then.

"And be ready to draw straws upon port. One of you sods will be responsible for scraping that useless carcass off the side of *The Revenge.*"

With that, I head below deck, unable to stomach looking into Octavia's haunted, brown eyes a moment longer.

***

Chapter 21: Hanna
14 June 1691
Somewhere in the Indian Ocean

I exhale the breath I've been holding the entire walk back to our bunk, afraid that someone would say something about the tears that pooled in my eyes during Enoch's punishment.

No one does.

And finally, when that blessed faux door flaps closed, I allow the tears to fall. I'm not allowed to cry alone for long. Demetrius's arms come around me, already transformed back to his usual self.

He hugs me tight to his chest, his warmth seeping into my back, calming my ragged breathing. He gently lays his cheek against the top of my head. "It's okay, Han… you can let it out. None of my teachings could have prepared you to witness something of that nature."

I close my eyes and let myself bask in his always-comforting embrace. Ever since first finding me, he's always been able to soothe me. It often had me wondering if he'd ever cared for children before, maybe even had some of his own. I revel in the familiar comfort a moment longer before turning in his arms and looking up into his curious jade eyes.

He lets his arms fall to his sides. "I sense you have something to say. Do not be afraid. No matter what it is, you will always be my daughter. I love you."

A flood of affection thumps through my chest. I smile through my tears at my forever-accepting guardian. "I'm not crying for Enoch… or for his death. But for Una. Twice now, she's placed trust in others and twice they've betrayed her." The sharp sting of tears prick my eyes again as I remember the angry grief darkening her face, as she'd turned and tossed me the flintlock pistol. I yearned to ease that pain.

"I couldn't imagine dealing with that mistrust. That doubt would root itself inside me. With Enoch gone, maybe that seed won't fester within her."

"You shed the tears that the urchin cannot." Demetrius looks at me oddly, his brows drawn together like he's thinking something over really hard, his head slightly cocked to the side.

Embarrassment burns my cheeks as he continues to stare at me unabashedly. "I haven't seen you look at something so intently since they tried to make you eat bone soup for the first time… it's starting to spook me, could you stop?"

He blinks slowly, then chuckles loudly, waving his hands horizontally between us in the air. I both feel and see the effect dissolving the magic has on him. Deme's eyes sheen with an ethereal glow before returning to their luminescent emerald. "It just amazes me how alike you and your mother are, despite you only getting a year with her. Your mannerisms even mimic hers at times, it is truly baffling."

Curiosity outweighs the usual anger at mentions of my mother. I'm momentarily taken aback. My curiosity trumps my anger. I blame Deme and his riddles.

"How long did you know my mother?"

He tries, and fails, to smother the grin that overtakes his face. "Nearly a century."

Now it's my turn to gawk in awe. "How did you meet? Where did you meet? Were you around when she met Kai?" I suck in a much-needed breath, my exhaustion pushed to the side in favor of learning more about Demetrius and my mother. I've never had the urge to ask him all this before, and I can tell it pleases him that I finally want to know.

He laughs. "Get into bed and I shall tell you."

I make quick work of shedding my espada, sash and boots, and jump onto the cot, laying out on my belly, my folded arms under my face.

Demetrius laughs again and shakes his head at my child-like antics, plopping down cross legged by the cot. "What do you wish to know first?"

"How did you meet?"

His normally alert eyes glaze, as he remembers a time before everyone walking around now was even alive. "I'd been exploring a cluster of reefs when I felt a disturbance in the ocean. Water nymphs are tied to the water. When the balance gets tipped, we feel it."

Balance?

His soft smile is replaced with the hard line of a frown. "I went to see what had the ocean upset, and I found a dolphin trapped in a fishing net. Back then they were even more bizarre than they are now, but with determination and a sharp piece of shell I was able to free the distressed creature."

He met my mother saving a dolphin. A hundred years ago. Wow.

"Unfortunately, when I freed it, the bindings had bitten quite badly into the dolphin's skin. It was weak from hunger and infection, and I was at a loss. But then your mother came from nowhere, seemingly a part of the sea herself, hair as deep and dark as the waters, with scales that shone even below the surface. I'd heard of mermaids but never met one, until that day." His frown melts back into a soft, affectionate smile. "Without a word, her webbed fingers had begun to glow a soft, warm, pale green – a magic I'd yet to see in all my years. Then, to my wonder and marvel, she healed that dolphin." He laughs then, the sound the lightest I've heard from him since we stepped foot on the ship. "I was in awe of her, and she was in awe of me. She'd never met one of my kind either. It was probably that mutual curiosity which sparked our odd friendship."

Correction – my mother helped him save a dolphin, with... healing magic? My head's spinning. "Could I... do that? Do all mermaids have that ability?"

Demetrius scratches his jaw thoughtfully. "Even when I first found you, you seemed well versed in medicinal herbs. It could be possible. We'll have to investigate that at a better time. As to whether all full-blooded mermaids can heal like that? Yes. One of the few things your mother disclosed about her heritage."

Excitement flares hot in my chest at the prospect of a new ability, along with overwhelming curiosity at why my mother didn't seem to like her mermaid upbringing, not even enough to disclose basic information to her closest friend.

"Did you only spend time together in the ocean? Could my mother come on land...? Considering circumstances, she must've –"

His laughter stops my ramblings. "Circumstances, indeed. But yes, she could. For three days at the start of each month, she'd be human enough to explore on land. It's because of her that I grew accustomed to holding my human form so well. We explored every chance we got." He smiles, his eyes losing their focus again as he disappears into another memory. "We did that dance for ninety five years, then bonding season for mermaids came; a once-in-a-hundred-year occurrence, a happening she was forced to participate in, though she never told me who forced her." He sighs. "I didn't see my friend for three years. I built the cabin, our cabin, close to the spot where she and I met, in hopes that one day she would return." Those distant eyes fill with warmth as they slide to me. "Then she did, and she wasn't alone. You were with her, a mere babe, and she no longer the exasperated woman who had left three years prior on her forced obligation." His gaze turns wistful. "Then, just as quickly as she'd come, she left. After but one conversation, one afternoon, after so long apart." His face darkens with sorrow and he does something I've never seen him do.

He cries.

Tears fill those emerald eyes, making them sparkle in the dim candlelight. "A year later she returned to my cabin; ill, dying and without you. She told me of Kai and the rejected bond. And that is when she asked me to find you." He looks down, tears spilling onto the hands clasped in his lap, and my all-knowing, all-seeing guardian has never looked so small, so fragile. His voice cracks. "Then she died..."

Hearing the full story completely wipes the anger that has been fueling me for over a decade. Now all I feel is sadness, guilt, and a longing for the mother I never had the chance to know. "Did you ever think of not fulfilling her last wish?"

He raises teary, red rimmed eyes to me. "No. The moment I pulled myself from my grief, I started my search. I knew I would find you."

"D– do you know why he took me away from her?"

He lifts his lithe shoulders in a shrug. "To sell you, perhaps? But why he kept you for so long is beyond my comprehension."

I try to digest all he's given me, but it's so much. Too much. Add on the crippling exhaustion and pounding in my skull, and the room around us turns in an unfocused tilt. For a moment, I'm afraid I'm going to upturn my stomach, but just like always, when I'm about to spiral out of control, Demetrius leans forward and smooths back my hair. "Enough talk for now. It has been a taxing day. Now, *sleep*."

And again, just like always, I'm lulled into a dreamless sleep by his hypnotic voice.

***

21 June 1691
Île Sainte-Marie, Dauphin

A crushing weight atop my already sore body has me jolting from what had been a restless, fitful sleep. My heart leaps into my throat as my pulse pounds. I wrestle my hands free of the sheet and grab for my espada, or where my espada *should* be. With my eyes still screwed tightly shut, I probe at my hip again, my hand meeting warm flesh, instead of the cool steel I'm expecting.

"It's good to see you too, Han." Demetrius's playful chuckle has me finally opening my eyes. Two eyes like pools of ink greet me and a very Deme-like grin curls '*Aurelius's*' thin lips. He's already apparently transformed for the day.

I thrash, struggling under the weight of his body in my weakened condition. "Why can't you wake me up like a proper person? Must you act like a child all the time?"

His grin widens, until his eyes are wrinkling around the edges. "Una's given the word. We're docking in Île Sainte-Marie as we speak. I was ordered to come fetch you."

The ship *does* feel like it's moving differently beneath me, around me. Shallower waters. It creaks and clunks.

Deme leans closer until the tips of our noses are brushing. "She seemed in grand form this eve, very keen on seeing you. You've not been unfaithful to your dedicated, *loving* spouse, have you?"

I fight against his weight in earnest now, until my arms burn, and my breathing is ragged. Boots on wood outside our bunk has me freezing. *Shite. Shite. Shite!*

"Aurelius? You get lost? Captain already started addressing the crew…"

Ambrose? Sweet Poseidon's trident we're doomed.

I'm about to call out, stop him entering the bunk and catching me out of my Octavia disguise, when Demetrius clamps a hand firmly over my mouth and leans in very close, so close I can feel his breaths over my face. A mix of flushing embarrassment and rage rush through me. And then the cool icy sensation of his magic begins to slide into me, cloaking me in my disguise.

The pounding in my head is nearing unbearable levels, making me want to push him off of me, damn the consequences, when the warning in his eyes tells me to hold still, to go along with it. How can I go along with this, with my father's lips so close?! I feel queasy. The bond can just take me now.

"Ah, I see." Ambrose's laugh is deep and smoky. "It harms me to intrude on such a private moment, and I say this with a very, *very* heavy heart, but this fun'll have to wait."

The heat in my cheeks turns scorching as Deme presses his lips against the back of the hand across my mouth, before casually climbing off me and throwing the grinning Ambrose a grin of his own. "Seems the jig is up and the cavalry has arrived for us, Octavia. We'll follow you up, Ambrose."

The gunner chuckles, his pale green eyes gleaming with mirth as he mock-salutes my guardian, then he about-faces and exits the bunk, leaving Demetrius and I alone once again.

I avoid the nymph's gaze as I rise from the cot, the ache in my body from the bond's burden now a constant presence. Even sleeping at obscure hours and for often long periods of time hasn't lightened the exhaustion. I struggle to pull on my boots, my arms feeling like weights are tied to them. I catch my breath as I loop and tie my sash around my waist.

"Han… it was the only way to shield you and keep up appearances…"

I thrust my espada through the sash then shove the flintlock pistol Una had given me next to it before I turn to glare at him. "If you *ever* pull anything like pretending to kiss me again, keeping up appearances will be the very least of your concerns. Now come, the Captain awaits."

***

The moment we step above the deck, the crisp, air has gooseflesh rising over my body. The air is mixed with the familiar briny scent from the water lapping so close to the dock's legs. Smokey scents, sour ones, sweet ones, there are so many smells I've never smelled before, and it has my head in a dangerous spin. I look across the huge harbor, in awe of all the other ships anchored here. Some are smaller - brigantines and sleek, quick merchant's vessels; some are larger – vast galleons and Man-o-Wars. And just as Selina had said, groups crowd the docks trading, bartering, yelling. Merchants, opportunists, and women for sale – the odd boy too – move through the crowds, touting their wares. This is absolutely astounding! Who knew a place like this even existed outside the cabin?

"Come, Guppy, Ambrose is already off the ship."

I trail closely behind Deme, my eyes unable to stay on one thing for longer than a few breaths. There's *so* much going on. How does one keep it all in order?

Una had explained that there's an underground shipping arrangement; buccaneers residing on this island attack ships carrying exotic goods from India, take those things, then the local traders sell the booty to crooked merchants in places like New Netherlands. Selina said the raids to acquire those goods are exhilarating, life-altering. Part of me wishes I never have to experience one, the other part desperately wants to stop missing out on things, no matter how frightening they might be, and be involved in a raid. I follow Demetrius across the gang plank and onto the pier. Ambrose is already heading toward the crew huddled together down on the docks.

My legs feel like rubber, my first few steps not as steady as I'd like. Once I can walk without fumbling, I'm captivated once more by the bustling crowds, the people, the colors and smells. I've never seen anything like this in my life… I truly have been missing out on life.

As we near the huddled crew, I see that Selina, Solomon and Atropous are missing. I catch the end of Una's address to the intently listening men.

"– into town to find people to trade coin for the booty we looted before the voyage."

Her stormy eyes clear the moment they land on me, the hard lines around her mouth smoothing; the action has my pulse racing – both from excitement and jealousy. Excitement because she's looking at me like that. Jealousy because she thinks she's looking at Octavia like that. Is it possible to be jealous of yourself?

"Did you want to sell the gun? I can send it ahead with Felix," she fires at me, and I find myself shaking my head instantly, moving my head to clutch the butt of the weapon at my waist.

"I'll keep it."

She holds my gaze for another moment, like she's searching for something in mine, before nodding and moving her gaze onto someone else. It makes my chest ache. Will I ever stop responding to her like this? Maybe after she accepts the bond… if she accepts it.

"We'll meet Selina, Solomon and Atropous in the main square where those lubbers should've rounded up enough coin to get rooms, alcohol, grub and entertainment at the nearest inn." Cheers of excitement explode, so loud my ears ring, as the crew shows their Captain just what they think of her plan. Those petal-pink lips twitch into a pleasing half smirk. "Let's have at it, then, lads!"

***

The trio have indeed accomplished their task, and we have enough coin to room us for seven entire days, in pairs of course. All nineteen of us sit at one long wooden bench, worn and faded from who knows how many years of use. The inn isn't huge, but big enough to cater for a pretty large crowd. It's almost filled to capacity with people of all sizes, shapes and colors, in all kinds and styles of clothing, most of which I've never seen in all my life. The air is thick with dense cigar smoke, loud laughter, and even louder conversations in tongues from all reaches of the world.

The moment our arses had touched the wood, Ambrose sweet-talked Una into letting him put in the food and drink order, Jonah not far from his elbow. The pair had apparently been to this island years prior and know the cuisine well. Those poor, unprepared kitchen staff. Ambrose had really let them have it, and pushed Una to near combustible levels in the process, nearly spending all the remaining coin he was given on the biggest bounty of food and drink I've ever seen. I laugh around my pint of brandy as I watch Solomon, usually timid, nearly inhale a wheel of cheese the size of his fist, a euphoric expression on his face.

Salad with cheese (or without, considering Solomon has eaten it all, already), roasted chicken with herbs unfamiliar to me but no less pleasing, veal, scotch collops, trout, and for a treat, gooseberry pie and fruit tarts – something most of us have never had before. It's truly mind boggling. My simple diet of bread, grains, vegetables and occasionally milk the last twelve years, living with a completely meat-free Demetrius, has not prepared me for such exotic new flavors. And, as I should have expected, where there are buccaneers, rum, coin and gambling are going to hold a lot of eyes. Even timid Solomon and usually uncaring Demetrius have been joining in on the odd bet or two.

Felix claps and cheers as Caleb guzzles an entire pint of ale in one go, a task my guardian has bet two doubloons he couldn't do. With a loud smack, he slams the empty mug on the table and wipes a dirty hand across his lips. "Pay up, buttercup."

Una laughs around a mouthful of fruit tart, spilling fruit juices down her chin, as a now deeply frowning Demetrius slaps the owed coin into a grinning Caleb's palm. My heart stutters at her laughter. After her second round of ale she too has begun to let her guard down and have a little fun. I trace the hollows beneath her eyes with my own, wishing I could use my finger instead.

Una had given Octavia the pistol as a gift, not me, but that doesn't stop the blush it brings to my cheeks every time I think back upon it. I am Octavia, just as I am Hanna, but Hanna *can't* be in Una's life. Octavia can. Yet… I am here… but it isn't truly me getting to know her. The whole situation is breaking my brain. I can continue getting to know the woman beneath the buccaneer, as I'd begun to at my cabin, but she can't continue to get to know me as me. And I must keep pretending Demetrius is my *spouse*. Ugh. Even thinking that makes my stomach twist sharply. Everything would be so much simpler if I could just tell her the truth.

'Hello Una, yes. Do you remember the mermaid half-ling you left in the middle of the night? The one you stole from? You *do*? Lovely. Well it's me, I'm Octavia. And I'm Hanna. And I sort of followed you and snuck into your crew. Why? Well you see, the man that helped your sister almost kill you? He's my father – the biological one, not Demetrius. Oh Demetrius? Yes, he's here too. Surprise…'

Like that would go over well. Best case, she'd maroon me on the nearest island and not kill me immediately for lying to her for so long, for betraying her. Like everyone in her life has done to her before.

As if she hears my thoughts, her eyes slide to me, a playful smile tugging at her lips. "How's that brandy treatin' ya?"

I immediately feel my cheeks flush hotter, too hot. "Fine… I mean it's decent… um. What I mean to say is it's… good?"

She smiles more and opens her mouth to reply to my idiotic babbling, but she's cut off by sudden loud, off key, cup-shot singing. If you can call it that. Who knew one day I'd be glad for god-awful singing? Some of the crew stand up from the table, swaying with tankards raised, joining in with the other singing patrons of the inn, and not surprisingly, Jonah and Ambrose are among their ranks. It's a bawdy song about an innkeeper's wife.

Demetrius leans in close to me, whispering so only I can hear him. "I think this is our sign to turn in for the night before things get out of hand."

I wholeheartedly agree. I nod and follow Caleb's earlier lead, tipping my mug back and draining the rest of my beverage in one go, but I splutter slightly as I stand, the spicy liquid causing my eyes to water and my throat to burn. Deme laughs and pats my back gently.

"Before you two bunk up for the eve, I want to go over our targets with you a little more. Caleb, you in?" Una pipes up.

Inwardly, I groan.

Caleb, bent over his mug with eyes half mast, snaps to attention. He stands abruptly and slams both fists on the bench in front of him, making the surrounding cups and discarded plates rattle. "I'll cleave him to the brisket, Captain!"

Una's been careful to stay hidden and obscure her female form, and her identity, in case her sibling or Kai are in the area. Selina and I have been following her lead, Selina keeping her hood pulled high and I wearing my bandanna and Demetrius's cloak. So, I expect her to chastise Caleb for his raucousness and drawing attention to us. Instead, she shocks me, simply laughing at his antics. The ale must be treating her right! She stands and stretches slightly, her gaze moving from Caleb, over to a joyfully clapping Solomon, and a softly smiling Selina who's trying her best to get him to eat more food to soak up all the ale he's been consuming. "Sel, I can count on you to make sure these sons-of-a-biscuit-eater stay in line, eh?"

She looks up from the shadow of her hood, eyes glinting like hard amber. "I'll definitely try my best, but Jonah and Ambrose *really* seem to be letting loose. Worse case, I'll take Atropous and Solomon and make a run for it. Act like we don't know those two fools." She dips her head back down again and angles herself closer to Solomon, who's still merrily clapping along, oblivious.

Una only shakes her head and turns toward me with a hint of a smile, and affection in her eyes. "After ye."

***

Caleb barrels ahead of us, running quite steadily for someone three sheets to the wind, right to Una's chambers. Once we're all safely inside, I close the door. Wow… a real, solid door. Who knew I'd miss something so trivial?

"Shite, lass, your bunk's twice the size of the one the gunner and I got put in."

"Comes with being in charge. Now shut ya trap or I'm revoking your slops chest rights."

148

This instantly stops Caleb's pacing and babbling. He snaps his head in her direction. "Right in the bollocks, Captain. Okay, I fold."

This has her laughing as she tugs off her bandanna, trifold, and kicks off her boots. She sets her weapons on a makeshift table consisting of two heavy oak barrels and a long plank. "Boots off and by the door, then we'll get started."

She drops to the ground in her stockinged feet, and stretches out, eyes glowing like the glittering shells I used to find along the beach. Despite what's sure to be a taxing conversation for her, she's never looked more at ease. We do as instructed and place our boots at the door then join Una on the floor. Caleb fumbles around in one of his trousers pockets a moment before holding up a silver flask victoriously. He unscrews the cap and offers it to Una with a wiggle and a raise of one of his unruly eyebrows. She surprises me again by letting out another loud, musical laugh and accepting the offered flask. She then takes a sip, humming a low sound of approval, before taking another, deeper, drink. She wipes her mouth on the back of her hand before handing the flask back to Caleb, who then in turn offers it to Demetrius. Deme hesitates a breath before he, too, accepts.

Una clears her throat and I'm instantly focusing on her. "As I told you before, the information on the cabin boys is limited. But Selina has proven her worth again and has a contact here who's been searching all day for something to help us in the right direction. He's come up with a name: Asa. He's apparently very loose-lipped. He'll be the thread we need to pull to completely unravel Elyse and Kai."

I accept the flask from Deme and take a sip. I nearly blanch at the taste. Yikes… that is *potent*. I pass it back to Caleb, who grabs for it blindly as he listens, completely enraptured. His focus, despite his drunkenness, is admirable.

"As for their quartermasters, the brothers Ezekiel and Eli, they use pistols like the one you have, Octavia."

"The eldest has a scar, does he not?" Demetrius asks

Una nods as she accepts, and takes another drink from, the flask. "Over his right eye. He'll be the one with the patch."

"And the younger brother?" Caleb accepts and recaps the now empty container.

149

"Unfortunately, no information. Kai and Elyse have the very large advantage of being able to move freely… I don't." Her aura of contentment is shattered as the mirth drains from her eyes.

"And Kai?"

The mention of his name has nausea swirling dangerously in the pit of my stomach.

"He's tall, like Caleb, but not as packed with muscle. He likes his fancy-arse baubles, charms, the real superstitious sort. He'll never be caught without some overly flashy one on him. Dark hair and, last I saw him, a beard, crooked front teeth. I remember his empty black eyes staring down at me, and that twisted smile full of nothing but pure evil."

Gooseflesh rises over my body and it feels like a stone has been dropped into the pit of my stomach. Flashes of uninterested obsidian eyes and uncaring words has me wanting to curl into myself as far as I can, where he can't possibly find me.

A harsh sigh from Una shocks me back from a path I'm not ready to travel just yet. "And then there's Elyse… well, she looks like me."

I wait with bated breath for her to continue. I've been waging an internal war of being completely terrified of finally meeting Una's sibling and of utter curiosity. The chance to learn and know more about Una, even the dark parts, nearly steals my breath away.

But she doesn't continue.

Beside me, Demetrius urges, "Yes… as Eli looks like Elisha. More… *detailed* information would make completing this task much easier."

Even Caleb's steel focus wains and his brows crease with confusion.

Una grinds her jaw, her hand moving to that brass bangle at her wrist. "She looks *exactly* like me… some would say it's like seeing double."

"TWINS?!"

"There's two of ye?!"

I'm speechless. Demetrius once told me of a pair of twin men he saw on land long ago. They'd looked the same, down to the clothes they chose to wear. I never thought I'd ever meet someone who is a twin, let alone see both of them before me. Now I have to survive, at least that long.

Demetrius clears his throat, clearing some of the heavy tension that's begun bleeding into the air. "If we happen to come upon her, how are we to tell her apart from you?"

That tight lipped line of her mouth morphs before my eyes into an unabashed smirk. I can practically *feel* the smugness radiating off her. She traces the tip of her finger from just above her eyebrow, down over her sun-kissed cheek, and stops just at the jaw, indicating that her twin's face is marred by a scar. "I just hope the infection didn't get to her. I want to see her breathe her final breath."

Caleb cheers and pumps his free hand into the air. I laugh; I can't help it. Despite all the talk of what's to come and all the unpleasantness, tonight has been the most enjoyable evening I've ever had, the freest I've ever felt.

Una's loud yawn bounces off the walls and she stands. "You can start gathering information tomorrow afternoon, we all deserve to enjoy a bed every now and again." Her eyes linger on me a moment as she opens the door, and it makes my stomach squirm. "Meet back at the inn for supper and we'll talk about what you learned, if anything."

Demetrius stands and I follow him, with Caleb joining us at the door as we all put our boots back on. We say our farewells and good tidings, then exit her chamber. I cast one more furtive glance over my shoulder and find her clouded-sky eyes holding mine a second longer. If she asks me, I'll... I'll stay... but she closes the door, effectively breaking the spell she cast over me.

Demetrius links our arms together and pulls me down the narrow hallway back to our shared bunk where a gloriously soft bed awaits me.

"Octavia, Aurelius wait for me!" Caleb stumbles towards us, sheepishly grinning. He comes to a halt, casually gripping the hilt of Marigold. "Ye up for gettin' a head start on our mission? I find I'm mighty inspired right now."

151

The eager gleam in his dark eyes is contagious, and an excited thrill lances up my spine. I look to my guardian, who's regarding Caleb with a raised eyebrow and a slight tilt to his head.

"It's midnight," he says.

Caleb's gleeful grin grows. "The witchin' hour. I do some of my best work at this time."

Deme rolls his eyes. "You are so cup-shot you'd only hinder us in a fight."

Caleb scoffs and puffs out his already inflated chest, placing both hands on his hips. "I can knock any bilge rat on his arse, one hand bound behind my back!"

This makes me snort and I cross my arms. "Was *that* the problem when we spared the first time? One arm wasn't bound behind your back?"

Caleb gapes at me and, for a moment, I'm frightened we're going to brawl for real. But then there's a rumble, deep in his chest, and soon he's doubled over, hands on his knees, laughing. "That was a good one, mate. So, we doin' this or are we to bunk up like a bunch of marooned landlubbers?"

I glance to my guardian who, to my surprise, is grinning just as widely as Caleb. "Let us have some merrymaking while we're at it, huh, picaroons? We're in."

***

As Demetrius had predicted, information or leads of any kind are few and far between this late. Our 'great mission' has ended up with us out by the docks. The ocean's still, not a ripple to be seen. The only sound in the windless, silent night is Caleb's laughing as he lists the boats and ships he sees as he passes them, and the sound of Demetrius as he hums a chipper tune to himself, hands in his trouser pockets, his eyes cast ocean-ways.

We're all sober now and toward the back of the harbor, where smaller sloops sit like statues perfectly illuminated in the moonlight. It really is a beautiful sight. The pounding in my head that's near constant surges back to life, ruining the peaceful moment, and I feel a burning in my legs reminiscent of when I transform into my full mermaid form. I breathe slowly through it, knowing it's because of my lack of

152

time in the water. This is the longest I've ever gone since starting the transformations.

Caleb's beefy arm shooting out in front of us has my tingling legs locking and a swirl of dread forming in my stomach.

Demetrius throws him a questioning look. "What's wrong?"

Caleb points to two men huddled together by the cluster of boats. Their clothes are shabby, but the lack of sunlight doesn't dull the glimmer of steel amongst the folds of their clothes.

"Buccaneers out in the crack of night near some undefended ships... pretty suspicious, if you ask me."

"No stranger than us, Caleb, we're here too." Demetrius chuckles. "They do seem to be up to no good, though. Better to check than end up with our own ship looted. The Captain wouldn't like that one bit. It'll be our arses over the side of the boat next."

Caleb echoes Deme's chuckle, then looks at me. "Whaddya say Octavia? Feel like taking the lead in this one?"

I mimic his smirk, understanding where his thoughts are headed. I remove my hat, my bandanna, and Demetrius's cloak, laying them over a thin railing. "After me, then."

I walk towards the men, putting on an air of confidence I often saw Una adopt when addressing the crew or dealing out orders and punishments; a bravado she lowered when we had our suppers together, but the exact bravado I need to seize for myself right now. "You lads lost? The inn's in the other direction."

The men jerk apart and wheel around to face me, their eyes blown wide, their dirt-smeared cheeks flushed from their obvious enjoyment in the surrounding establishments. At first, I wonder if we've miraculously found the brothers Eli and Ezekiel, but neither of these wears a patch, nor do they look like siblings. The larger one, with an unkempt curly black beard and a surprised look, turns predatory in a blink of an eye. A smirk curls his wind chapped lips.

"It seems ye be the one who's lost, traveling these dark, abandoned paths. And so *alone*."

Nervousness momentarily blocks my excitement. Caleb and Deme better not be too far away... His companion looks at me from head to foot, then licks his lips wetly, the grotesque sound permeating the silent night.

"The strumpet does seem to be a bit on the lonely side, don't she?"

I grip the handle of my espada, and the buccaneers laugh, a mocking, loud sound that has my blood simmering.

"Seems the wee lamb picked up more than she can handle. Why don't you let my matey and I show you how proper buccaneers handle their steel?"

"A pity I don't see any proper buccaneers here." Demetrius, his eyes obsidian and deadly in the night, appears over the larger man's shoulder.

Caleb's dark chuckle follows my guardian's hissed words. "That stings, bucko. I'm standing *right* here."

The bearded man is suddenly airborne as Caleb kicks his legs out from beneath him and he falls into a heap upon the wooden pier.

I draw my weapon from my sash and give it a test slash through the sky. "Is that any way to speak to a lady? Your mother must be just turning in her grave right now."

"We'll give ye the count of three to get your arses off our dock." Demetrius hisses. "One..."

"*Your* dock?" the one Demetrius had snuck up on snarls.

"Two."

I disinterestedly inspect the shimmering metal of my blade under the moonlight. "I'd go if I were you, he's such a terror when he gets tired."

The bearded man scrambles to his feet, and before Deme gets the chance to say 'three', the pair are up and running, as fast as they can into the dead of night.

"Well that was a treat. Sainte Marie Island isn't all that bad after all." I put away my blade.

Caleb and Demetrius share a laugh and I spy a scrap of black on the wood where the imbecile had fallen. A scarf? I bend and snatch it up quickly. It's not a scarf at all, but a piece of black fabric. I unfold it, and gasp.

"Octavia? What did you find?" Demetrius peaks over my shoulder and huffs out a surprised laugh. "Well how about that."

On the black fabric is a symbol I've only seen once before in a hastily drawn sketch on a rolled-up piece of parchment. The standard skull and cross bone but with one difference; a jagged slice through the eye of the skull straight down through the cheek and stopping just at the jaw. A wound that is now awfully familiar to me.

"Should we track 'em down?" Caleb's voice booms beside me, as he too looks over my shoulder.

I shake my head. "No... this is enough, for now. We know for certainty that we're on the right path." I grip the jolly roger, crushing it in my fist. Prepare your will, Kai. I'm coming for your head.

***

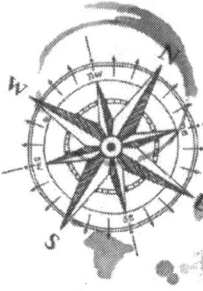

Chapter 22: Kai
26 June 1691
Île Sainte-Marie, Dauphin

"Bar wench! Another three tankards of your best ale. Make it fast!"

I chuckle around the lip of my almost empty cup and pray a word of thanks to God that Richer, with his ever-disgusting unkempt black beard, is feeling very generous with his pockets this eve. Not that I'm going to stop him, or give him more coin, after he foolishly spends his week's pay in a single night. His loss be my gain.

On Richer's right sits Nicklas, a lad over twenty years our junior. Not the sharpest knife in the pouch, but he is daring, willing to do anything and everything I ask of him, in a manner that doesn't waste my time, and he doesn't ask to be coddled. Those aspects help me overlook his dullness as a person and focus on his usefulness as a buccaneer on my crew. *Our* crew, for now, as long as staying together continues to benefit us both.

What the spitfire lass lacks in charm or grace, she makes up for in her combat skill, ruthlessness, and smarts. I can't deny the many times she's blind-sided me and taught *me* something I hadn't known prior to meeting her. Stopping to have a li'l chat with the lass that day truly was the best decision I've made since I chose to sell off that filthy blood of mine.

My eyes are drawn back to my crew hands by a high-pitched female titter, and I find a bar wench with a very ample bosom spilling from her corset leaning toward Richer, giving him an eye-full of her goods, as he, grinning like a dog that's caught his supper, places the coins for our drinks into her cleavage. Lucky bastard.

As she grins and sashays away, he attempts at slapping her arse, missing and only swatting air, his cheeks flushed from the previous four cups of brandy he's had. Nicklas is holding his coin, and beer, better than Richer. That *is* embarrassing.

Richer catches himself on the edge of the bar, blinking back grit, and the duel specters of us, since I suspect he's seeing four of us, instead of two.

Nicklas snickers loudly, wiping his knuckles across his nose and mouth as he inhales deeply, a huge shite-eating smile on his lips. "I haven't seen ya this off your rocker since that woman and her two male chums scared our souls out our arseholes."

He laughs again, as Richer almost spins out of his chair with the strength at which he turns to glare at Nicklas. Though this *lass* and her two male companions does have me painfully curious, I don't want to fuel Elyse's paranoia, that only seems to worsen every damn day… but, you can never cover your arse *too* much. "A lass you say?"

Richer whips back to me, his unfocused eyes huge, and for a moment I'm sure he's going to shout in my face, but for once he surprises me and leans close, looking from side to side a moment. "Don't worry, it wasn't Elyse's sister. Just some Indian and two filibusterers with trousers too big for 'em. I'm sure the island'll cut them down to size. If not, their egos are sure to cross paths with us again."

Just beyond his shoulder Nicklas nods in agreement. "As long as I get the pretty one. I've never had an Indian before."

I scratch a scarred hand through my beard before speaking again. "And… did you tell Elyse about this?"

The carefree air around Richer darkens, and his lips twist into a disgusted sneer. "Don't take offense, I know you two have been together since before I joined, but a woman will *never* be any Captain of mine. You are my Captain, sir. My loyalties will always lie with you." He nervously pulls on the long sleeve of his doublet, his eyes not quite being able to stay on my face. Behind him, Nicklas looks on, the same hesitant air hanging over him.

"And what say you, Nicklas? Do ye feel the same about Elyse?"

The lad gives a careless shrug of his lanky shoulders. "If they aren't making me food, bringing me ale, or there for me to dance the Paphian jig with, I don't care for them. I'm with you, Captain."

I smirk at their spouts of loyalty. Elyse may be cunning, and just as deadly as any lad, but she is still a lass, and that'll always be an obstacle she'll have to climb, no matter how much money, or fear, she's able to gather. A hurdle I'll never have to deal with, but one that will never stop growing taller, or more impossible to climb for her. It's why she needs me. It's why she needed me then, and why she'll continue to need me.

And I need her, in the way that a master needs its slave. She's more than happy to handle the crew, dealing out the daily orders and dishing out rations herself, while I'm only needed during our weekly crew meetings. I'll relax for a while, enjoy myself, tend to the ship, and let the li'l lass think she's in charge. Sounds like a damn good way to live for a bit, until I decide to take back the Captain's hat fully again.

I flash another smile at *my* two crew mates, reaching for my money pouch hanging off the crimson sash wrapped twice around my waist. "Bar wench, another three this way. This one's on me."

***

158

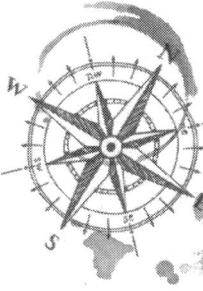

Chapter 23: Una
1 July 1691
Île Sainte-Marie, Dauphin

I stare at the wooden ceiling of the inn, counting each glint of exposed metal I can find. Hope this rust bucket doesn't come crashing down on us… that would be an utterly shite way to go.

Atropous sits opposite me, his back pressed against the closed door of my room. He's currently balancing a draught board on his crossed legs, his hand idly running through his coarse brown beard. Those sharp green eyes are focused on the board, his free hand holding one of the light pieces. He'd gotten the small board and 'men' from Aurelius, apparently to keep his 'mind from waning'. Bizarre lad, that Aurelius.

It's an abstract strategy game that Atropous seems wholly fascinated with. He'd delighted in giving me a long explanation, one I didn't need but feigned interest in, as it had my mind once again returning to that blasted cabin by the sea, and the time Demetrius and Hanna had taught me how to play for the first time.

I sigh, burning with frustration. I'd let myself begin hope when the trio had brought me the jolly roger that first night, and now? Octavia, Aurelius, and Caleb had been all over the island within a five-mile radius of the inn and docks where they encountered two of Elyse's hands and found nothing further. Perhaps I should have them push out even farther…?

I roll onto my side, Atropous glancing at me as another sigh pushes its way through my lips. And the boredom! I'd decided the best plan was for me to stay hidden for as long as possible. The longer my survival is kept a secret from Kai and Elyse, the longer we'll hold our advantage against them. The jolly was proof enough for me that they're here on the island. We need to tear down whatever crew they've put together before we go for the heads. The moment they catch wind of my survival, they'll do one of two things. Either they'll turn tail and run, my *beloved* sibling knowing full well what I'm capable of and how deep my hatred for

159

backstabbing scourges runs, or they'll seek me out to finish what they couldn't do before. If they choose the latter, they won't care who they have to cut down in their path to get to me.

A pair of honeyed brown eyes and Octavia's breathy chuckle flick through my mind. Then, just as quickly, those eyes shift into startling lilac ones. I sigh yet again and grind my teeth. Right now, I'm not sure which one of them it's better to let myself think about.

That arse-numbing boredom is only curbed during supper, when the entire crew comes together to eat and update one another. They tell me what they've learned and how their tasks are going, and in turn I give them new orders to carry out while I'm bunked away like a frilly chambermaid. 'Course, Octavia has a lot to do with quelling that boredom. Now that is a whole other headache. She's equal parts deadly as she is gentle and, dare I say, soft hearted. She can easily bring a grown man to his knees and just as easily wrap his wound. And she's one hell of a storyteller. Bards would be envious.

My favorite tale of hers has been the one about the first time she'd explored the ocean surrounding the place she'd lived before joining my crew. She'd described the cool water and smell so well, I could practically taste the salt and feel the water on my skin. She'd been extremely excited and nervous to explore new territory, and in her overzealous trek, had mistaken a length of kelp to be a sea monster trying to pull her to her watery demise. She said she'd never gotten out of the water so quickly. I'd gotten so lost in her smooth voice and the carefree tale. Free of codes, back stabbings, and soul-altering betrayals. It easily blotted out the darkness of the day and quieted my constantly turbulent thoughts. She was like Hanna in that aspect; they both had a near delirious effect on me. I could easily forget the real reason for coming to this floating hunk of rock.

That thought, so easily flowing, has me sighing loudly *again.* I sit up on the cot and fold my arms over my chest tightly, like somehow this alone will keep the pounding in my chest from beating any harder. Blasted half-ling… what has she done to me?

"You okay over there? I'm starting to think you may not be getting enough air to your brain." Atropous's rumbling question jerks me from my thoughts. Immediately realizing my mistake in letting my guard down around him, I glare at the now cheekily smiling lad. He'd opted to stay here instead of going to haggle in the square with Selina and Solomon, showing up at my door just past daybreak, 'to keep ya from keeling over from boredom' he'd said. A kind gesture that would've been far kinder if I hadn't seen the haunted darkness lurking in those jade eyes of his.

Guilt gnaws at me again, sharp and sudden, for what feels like the hundredth time since I had to enforce the code, *my* law, since he'd seen the example I'd had to make of Enoch. Atropous knew what he signed up for. But he'd led a simple fisherman's life; seeing that happen right before his eyes first-hand is another kind of experience altogether. As I hold his gaze, I feel my well-placed armor begin to rust. He wanted adventure and got more than he was ready to handle, and now it's far too late to turn back.

His eyes soften and he gives me a comforting smile. "Let me in. What's going on in that big-arse head of yours?"

I snort. And there I was, worrying about him. I cock an eyebrow. "Just gettin' jittery from sitting in one spot for too long."

His soft smile cracks into a wide grin, that sparkle of mirth back. "Well lucky you! It's your favorite time of the day!" He scoops the draught pieces and stands nimbly to his feet.

I tilt my head, baffled. "And that would be?"

His grin only grows. "Supper."

I groan. I take it back; I'm not worried about the idiot. Not one bit.

***

When we come downstairs into the oval-shaped inn, the entire crew is already gathered around our usual long wooden bench. The ever loose-pursed Ambrose is already carrying two overflowing pitchers of frothing beer to the chattering group.

I smile as I watch Octavia light up as she holds her mug for Ambrose to fill. As he rotates back to his seat, his eyes catch mine and he raises a hand in greeting. "Well, look what the ocean washed in! Get your arse over here and join us, Cap'n!"

I lower my trifold, shielding my face more as I cross the half-full inn. Aurelius elbows Caleb in the ribs, so the bigger man sighs gruffly and grudgingly stands, moving to the other side of the bench beside Felix. Aurelius and Octavia scoot down the bench to make space for us to sit down. As I slide in beside Octavia, she throws me a casual smile, her usually guarded face light and open. Atropous slides in after me, already reaching for the half-eaten gooseberry pie in the center of the table. Solomon gives me a sloppy salute as he shoves a piece of herbed cheese into his mouth. Selina mimics him, her salute much lazier than her companion's.

I nod my own greetings to everyone and grab some ale for myself. With a relieved sigh, I take a sip, letting the smooth liquid warm a trail down my throat and into my chest.

Caleb lets out a deep rumbling laugh. "Must be pretty tirin' sitting in one spot all day."

I smirk, setting my mug down. "Almost as tiring as it must be to lose to Octavia every time you brawl. How's the arse?"

The table explodes into loud laughter as Caleb's cheeks flush and he mumbles something into his mug.

"Wanna speak up, Caleb?"

Caleb straightens, though his eyes remain lowered, submissive. "I said we should get to work."

I chuckle. "What a grand idea, mate." I take one more long drink before turning my eyes to my awaiting crew. "Any news to start us off with, Caleb? Since you're so chatty right now."

He toys with a piece of bread before stuffing it into his mouth, moving it over into his cheek so he can speak. "Same as yesterday. Seems we might have spooked those lubbers too badly."

Aurelius's snort of laughter surprises me and he raises a glass toward Caleb before he takes a long drink from it.

That frustration that's been festering all day rises another degree, but I pull it back in. "Solomon, I hope you two have better news?"

Selina doesn't pause as she drinks from her mug, reaching under her flowing cloak and producing a green drawstring pouch. With a flick of her wrist, she tosses it across the table into my awaiting palm with a pleasing thud. I test its weight before stashing it away for later. "We'll cut shares tomorrow at supper. Can we all *try* to hold onto it for a fortnight? I'm lookin' at you, Jonah."

Ambrose's first gunner and best bucko casts me a sheepish, crooked smile, his brown eyes sparkling with mischief. He's almost a bigger thorn in my side than Ambrose, and when they're together? They're just two annoying peas in a pod. Should've known better. Pair of Jollies.

"Same tasks as yesterday. Yer all dismissed." I wave a hand absently.

Relieved, some of my crew begin their own conversations. Others disperse around the inn, relaxing while also being my eyes and ears. Atropous nudges me, pulling my attention back to the table and to a grinning Ambrose. "You say something?"

He wiggles a stack of small rectangular playing cards at me; they're faded, obviously well used. "Veintiuna, anyone? We're ported, have coin and drink. It's time we all had a little fun, nay?"

Twenty-one. A pretty self-explanatory and simple game that could get serious far too quickly. I'd won my cutlass in a game of twenty-one many moons ago.

Young Felix runs a grubby hand through his tawny locks and leans forward, cupping both hands around his mouth like he's going to whisper a secret. "I thought gamblin' went against the code?"

163

Caleb ruffles the lad's hair roughly, nearly knocking him off his seat. "You know that only goes for when we're at sea. Get the barnacles outta yer ears, boy."

Jonah swings his arm over Ambrose's broad shoulders, a grin on his rosy lips. "What do you say? You in? We can only bet with what we have on us. Will that work for you lot?"

I smirk. "Only if Octavia and Aurelius play with us."

A touch of pink spreads over Octavia's tanned cheeks as everyone still present at the table looks at her. Beside her, Aurelius throws me a grin that's much too wide for his face. "Well *I'm* in."

Octavia's intelligent brown eyes slide to Selina and Solomon, softly chatting, heads bent close. She clears her throat. "I'll play if Sel and Solomon will."

At his name, Solomon casts us a timid but hopeful smile. "I've never played before… but I'm curious to learn."

Selina sighs gently underneath her hood. "Guess I've been out voted, eh? I'm in."

Ambrose and Jonah let out twin hoots of glee that has me gritting my teeth, resisting the urge to punch them both.

"Felix!" The lad jumps to his feet at the sound of his name. "We'll need more pints." Ambrose presses his small pouch into the boy's hand, and Felix scampers off.

***

We're several hands in, warm from ale and laughter, and Ambrose is winning. The sod. But Caleb's making a good show of it.

"That be sixteen. I'll hold." Caleb settles back, a cocky smirk curling his thin wind-chapped lips.

Aurelius returns from relieving himself and slides back into his seat, eyes sweeping the table. He groans. "Blast. I owe you two pieces, Octavia. I was so sure Caleb would be out with that hand." He raises an eyebrow roguishly at Caleb and presses the coins into her hand. Octavia grins triumphantly as we all roar with laughter, even Caleb

"Am, you're next." Jonah bumps Ambrose's broad shoulder with his own.

"Give me all you got, kid." Ambrose throws the entire group an arrogant grin.

Felix flips the first card, seven of Espadas.

"Again."

Four of Copos.

"Ya lucky bastard!" Caleb slams his hand on the table before pointing a finger at Ambrose.

Ambrose only smirks, folding his arms over his muscled frame. "Card, Felix." Third flip. Nine of Bastos. "And that makes twenty. I think I'll stop here." Ambrose drops several more coins onto the table.

"Cheat!" Caleb points his grubby finger at Ambrose again.

"And pray tell, Caleb, how I managed that?"

Caleb opens his mouth to respond when a bar wench approaches the table, a pint and a rolled-up piece of parchment in her hand. She dips her head and sets the pint and parchment down in front of Selina. "From an admirer." She curtsies low, her frilly pink dress billowing around her ankles before wandering back toward the bar.

Solomon is suddenly on his feet, his head swiveling around the room. "Where?!"

I laugh at my navigator's obvious jealousy, his cheeks burning a bloody crimson as he sits back down, making sure to avoid everyone's eyes.

Ambrose laughs loudly. "Wee hooded one, are ye hidin' a possible suitor in that there cloak of yours?"

Solomon surprises me by jumping in to defend Selina; he's *glaring* at Ambrose, lip curled in absolute disgust. "How dare you speak to a lady in such a way. Apologize now."

I'm mildly concerned this might erupt into something, my beer cup half-way to my mouth, but Ambrose holds up his hands in silent surrender, his pale green eyes widening in shock. "Hey now, I meant nothing by it, a mere joke between comrades."

Selina's head is lowered so I can only see her chin and plump lower lip, but I swear on *The Revenge*, I see a hint of a flush staining her flesh.

Caleb slams his mug on the table, his brows pitched. "I'm obviously out voted here, but the parchment is much more interesting than who's beddin' who."

Selina clears her throat, returning from whatever stupor she'd been lost in, and reaches for her parchment. "For once, the buffoon speaks sense."

I hold up a hand, silencing a red-faced Caleb before he can even start, and wait as patiently as I can for Selena to unroll and read what her 'admirer' has sent her. She raises her head and I see a smirk on her usually neutral face. She slides the note to me, and I read:

Asa sightings:
* Market Square
* Sulter
* Chandler

Hope flares back to life in my chest, brighter than it ever has, my stomach twisting into delighted knots.

"What's it say, Captain?" Felix leans over the table trying to get a better view of the missive.

"It's our next step in taking down Elyse and Kai."

Gleeful chatters break out around the table, our game suddenly forgotten. I smile down at the missive. Better sharpen your steel sister, you're going to need it.

***

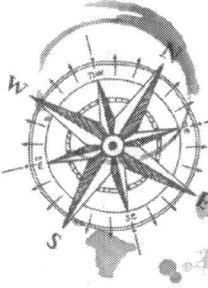

Chapter 24: Hanna

3 July 1691
Île Sainte-Marie, Dauphin

"Quit fluffing around, lad. Some of us here are trying to run a business!" A beefy man sporting a messy white apron and heaving a bag of flour over one shoulder doesn't wait for me to step aside before he's pushing past me. I watch him go, dodging and weaving his way through the early morning crowd of townsfolk.

Caleb is at the Chandler's looking at shipping supplies. He's currently trying to haggle a sharp-looking hatchet from the man by offering up some medicine from the slop's chest. I remember his joyous and slightly unnerving grin when asked why he needed it: *"We be needin' it for the job."* I really didn't want to think about what that could entail. I really hope the Chandler doesn't give in. Let's hope Caleb is in one of his less persuasive moods.

Demetrius is at the sulter's, looking curiously over nets and tackles. It may be only morning but the businesses around this town are already in full swing. We've continued to stake out the square and the other spots mentioned in the secretive missive so frequently now that a more observant eye would know we're up to no good. We haven't had a shred of good fortune.

As I walk casually through the square something unusual, even for all the things I've witnessed thus far, catches my attention on one of the stalls. A single white plate with a beautiful image of a blue bird surrounded by intricate weavings of pink and white flowers. The lone vendor is busy with another customer so I can't ask him about the exotic plate. Maybe Deme will know.

I turn to leave and nearly collide into a boy; he's small and gangly, all arms, legs and head. His dark clothes are dirty and at least a size too large. His dark brown hair is greasy and messy like he's just rolled out of bed. His equally dark eyes are large and rimmed in long, thick lashes. Around one of those doe eyes is a nasty, blotchy bruise; the multicolored pattern telling me it's healing at different stages. He's been struck multiple times.

He throws me a toothy grin and points a small, dirty finger at the plate. "It's called Kraakaware. It's from a place called China."

I tilt my head, looking between the plate and the bizarre lad. He's so tiny; he has to be young. "Kraakaware?"

He nods, his hair flopping against his forehead, with an approving smile. He then leans close, cupping his hands around his mouth. "Yup! And did ya know the stuff they trade around here isn't the really good stuff? It's porcelain, yeah, but the stuff they keep for themselves is the King Die-nasty, way more 'spensive. That's what my Captains say, anyways."

This child is speaking in tongues. What on earth is a king Die-nasty? Does he mean the Qing Dynasty? My thoughts come to an impressive halt as they catch up to the rest of the words the young boy had said. *Captains* as in – more than just one. I quickly scan the boy and see no jolly roger to speak of. "How'd such a tiny kid know all that?"

The lad lays his small hands on his hips and puffs up his chest, reminding me of Caleb. "I'm not just a kid!" He lowers his voice. "I'm a buccaneer."

Could I really be so fortunate? I mimic his pose. "And does this brave buccaneer have a title?"

He deflates, shoulders sagging briefly. "They call me Asa."

My heart skips several beats before picking up its efforts double time. "And would the great Asa like to try a special fairy tart? I was just leaving to go have one myself."

His head tilts, a look of curiosity instantly lighting up his face. "Fairy tart? I've never heard of no fairy tart."

I lean in closer, dropping my voice to a whisper. "Only the strongest and most skilled buccaneers know about this delicious, delectable treat. I could take you to get one."

He purses his lips and looks up at me. "How come my Captains don't know about it?"

I straighten slowly, shrugging one of my shoulders. "They must not be very strong. Are you?"

His puny body goes rigid and he glares at me. My heart skips again as I momentarily panic the young lad is onto me somehow. "I'm stronger. Let me see this fairy tart!"

I motion for him to follow me. "There's a secret entrance. It's this way."

Asa immediately begins to follow me, a slight spring in his step. I purposely pass Demetrius, who's seemingly gazing out to sea, but he glances briefly at me then to Asa. A pleased smirk curls his lips and I refocus on leading the unsuspecting lad into the alley closest to the inn. This is really happening. Holy shite… we've found Asa.

I peek over my shoulder at the none-the-wiser lad. He can't be any older than ten. Such a puny wisp of a lamb, he skips merrily after me, his large expressive eyes cast toward the glittering waters. Each step I take into that alleyway feels like I'm treading water; the exhaustion I'd awoken with feels all consuming. The guilt of leading an innocent child into the middle of this is almost too much for my heart to handle. Pull it together, Guppy! We're doing this to keep Una safe. With a decisive nod of my head, I lead Asa to the spot Caleb and Demetrius had decided on a day prior. When we're midway into the smelly, dank passageway between the buildings, I turn to face the lad. He stops abruptly, his hands folding behind his back as he looks around, inspecting his surroundings. Caleb and Demetrius slip in behind him silently, a cruel smirk already twisting Caleb's lips.

The child looks up at me. "Where's the secret door?"

"Right here."

Before the kid can turn around, Caleb balls up one of his meaty fists and strikes Asa in the back of the skull. His brown eyes widen in shock before they flutter closed, body crumbling in a heap of limbs. Caleb wastes no time in scooping up and cradling the unconscious lad against his chest like a babe and throwing me a satisfied grin. Great Poseidon's arse cheeks, we really just did that!

Demetrius's disgusted scoff pulls me back to him. His stout body is taut with obvious annoyance, his Aurelius-disguise muscled arms folded and inky black eyes trained on Caleb. "Must you always be such a brute?"

Caleb snarls, flashing his teeth menacingly at my guardian. "And must *you* always be a delicate, prissy, holier-than-thou princess?"

Deme's face darkens as he steps toward Caleb. "I'll show you just how delicate I am, you dim witted neanderthal."

Caleb matches his step, so only the unconscious child remains between them. "What'd you call me?!"

I sigh, folding my arms, letting the bite of my nails in the flesh of my forearm steady my rapidly pounding pulse. "Can we save whatever this is for another time? I'd quite like to not meet the hangman's noose anytime soon."

The brewing storm between the two seems to clear slightly, and Demetrius's eyes slide to me. "Right as always, my dear. Let's get to it."

***

I brace myself against a wooden beam, my vision momentarily spotting black. The trek up the stairs to Caleb's quarters almost stole the breath from my lungs, the effects of the bond making even the most trivial task an obstacle. I blot out my pain and focus on Asa; he lies, still unconscious, on the floor, his arms and legs bound by the wrist and ankles with rope.

"Well done on knocking the child into oblivion," Demetrius mutters, shaking his head disapprovingly.

Caleb jerks his gaze to Demetrius as he unsheathes his blade Marigold and raises it threateningly. "I could wake him up, if yer so impatient, yer majesty."

Demetrius rolls his eyes and squats down, brushing the boy's dirty hair from his face before gently cupping a dirty cheek. The moment he does, Asa wakes with a start, jerking away from the foreign touch. He rolls until he bumps into the far wall

170

then wiggles into a sitting position. His gaze flicks from Demetrius to Caleb, then finally to me. Hurt flashes momentarily in those dark eyes before he turns away. Guilt punches a hole through my chest again, leaving me feeling hollow.

Demetrius slowly stands and looks down at the silent lad. "No speaking unless we ask you a question. Nod if you understand and intend to comply."

Before Asa can respond, Caleb turns the ever-sharp Marigold on the lad. "And no screamin'. One peep outta you and your tongue is going to take a li'l trip from yer mouth."

Asa nods quickly, his too-large eyes widening further.

Demetrius sighs loudly. "Let us have a little chat, the three of us." He motions to Caleb and me. I go to him instantly and, after a moment and a growl, Caleb follows. "If we are to get anywhere with him, his tongue *stays* in his mouth."

Caleb's lip twitches with annoyed disgust. "The Captain said at any cost or means. Ye two are too soft for this."

My patience snaps and a feral, unrecognizable growl slips through my lips. My exhaustion blots out my common sense. "Soft? Take a step closer and you'll see soft, you over-muscled, mollusk-brained monkey!"

Caleb's brown eyes become narrowed and deadly, but I can't find it in me to care, his rage and anger only fueling my own.

"Care to say that again? I'm sure your dear Aurelius would hate to see that pretty face of yours all scarred up. Maybe Una wouldn't be too fond, either, hmm?"

My vision swims red at Caleb's obvious taunt, and I reach for my espada. Deme's cool hand covering mine stops me from following through with my plan of detaching Caleb's annoying head from his useless shoulders.

Deme fixes me with one of his 'you've crossed a line' looks before he turns to Caleb. "Think about your next words carefully. You're clearly out-classed here. I will take the lead in this little game. You and Octavia will watch and learn. Now, nod if you understand."

My fire fizzles out; the cool, controlled anger in Deme's swirling eyes leaves no room for arguments. I nod slowly, relieved I won't have to lead in this untasteful affair. Caleb sighs loudly but nods, his shoulders sagging, defeated.

Demetrius gives a curt nod before turning to address the silently watching, wide-eyed boy. "Asa, how old are you?"

The boy just stares up at him, his lips sewn tightly shut.

Beside me, Caleb stirs, his agitation rolling off him in angry waves.

My guardian seems undeterred and reaches into his trouser pocket, pulling out a shining golden coin. He offers the coin to the lad. "Would you tell me for some coin?"

Asa seems to think it over for a moment before taking the coin from Demetrius' open palm. "Seven. I think."

My heart feels like it stops in my chest. He's even younger than Felix. He's just a babe... That hollow feeling moves through my body; my stomach constricts, and I feel like I'm going to be ill.

Demetrius continues, seemingly unbothered by this new discovery. "Wow, a buccaneer at such a young age is quite the feat. Do you want to tell us about your crew?"

Instead of answering, Asa closes his fist around the coin, and abruptly turns away from us. Caleb growls low in his throat, the sound made louder and more threatening by the otherwise silent room.

Demetrius begins to pace back-and-forth in front of the boy, a pensive look on his face. "How about your masters? Who do you serve?"

Asa remains quiet, not so much as twitching a lip in Demetrius's direction. Deme suddenly squats, balancing on his heels, elbows casually propped on his thighs. "Look, we're all chums here, you can tell me."

Asa finally turns his head slightly, casting a positively venomous look at Caleb. "Didn't know chums hit each other over the head." Those wide eyes flick to me and I'm once again overcome with heavy guilt. It coils itself tightly against my chest like steel rope and I feel the dark, cold tendrils of it begin winding dangerously deep into my soul.

Caleb steps toward Demetrius and Asa, a cold sneer on his face. "I'm getting real tired of his lip, Aurelius. It's time we showed him who's in charge around here."

My guardian, my father, stands his endless obsidian gaze void of anything, an equally cold mask over his features. "You may be right." There's a darkness shrouding my usually carefree, cheerful father's disguised face. It feels soul-altering. What is this? Some act to intimidate Asa? Or is Demetrius really going to…?

Asa holds his bound hands protectively against his chest, the coin still gripped tightly in his small fist as Caleb gleefully watches and Demetrius turns to fully face the lad.

"I can't be a part of this," I mutter.

Demetrius shrugs, uncaring, not bothering to look over his shoulder. "You don't have to, just stand over there and don't get in my way."

It feels like I've been struck, the sting of his words bites into my flesh. Never, in all the years under Demetrius's care, has he ever spoken to me like this. He seems twisted in his cold calmness, nearly distorted into a creature I hardly recognize. I shake my head, tears burning my eyes. "No… I can't be here at all. I need to leave."

Demetrius gawks at me, a bewildered look creasing his face. He looks about to refuse when Caleb, surprisingly, steps in. "If the lass wants to leave, let her be. No need to sully her hands when we can handle this."

My guardian's hardened features melt and I'm staring once again into his kind eyes, though he's still disguised as Aurelius. "Take a walk and come back, okay? I can't do this without you."

Reeling from this new facet of my guardian, this hardened and sharp, cold thing, I do all I can – I nod my understanding and leave Caleb and Demetrius to their own devices.

***

My walk brings me to the docks, the salty air giving me gooseflesh. Without a full transformation or dip into the ocean's waters for months now, the closer I get to it, the more my skin burns from the inside. The alluring siren call of the sea tries to lull me into the same trance-like state that had called me overboard when I was ten. I clench my jaw and fight the urge to run to the water, the pull no less consuming in my older age.

A bright flash of scarlet catches my attention at the other end of the dock, a stark difference to the wooden barrel the scarlet-wearing figure is currently trying to crouch and hide behind. I slowly move closer, wondering if some scoundrel is about to try to lift a purse... my hand hovers at my espada's hilt until I finally realize who it is. Atropous? What in the blazes is he doing?

His usually flowing brown hair is hidden under a bright red bandanna and an old trifold hat. It was the end of the bandanna flapping in the sea breeze that I'd seen. When a trio of men pass by his hiding spot, he darts out onto the farthest path from the townsfolk, quite light on his feet despite his tall stature. Atropous is just as mischievous and playful as Demetrius, with an even bigger heart, if that's possible. The humble fisherman is only truly arrogant and cocky about one thing – his hair. He spends more time on it than even I do on my long mane, always tossing it in the face of anyone who would give him a second glance. That's why him hiding it from view is so strange, on top of his odd scuttling. He seems to be heading back to the inn. I quicken my steps but am careful to keep a safe distance from him as I follow him down the dock and around the tavern building.

I finally catch up with the long-legged beast of a man between the inn and the church, and I have to smother my gasp against my fist at the sight that greets me. Atropous stands tall, his hands twisted into his no-longer-brown locks. Turbulent, swirling blue and green hair that isn't really hair at all thrashes around his shoulders in currents, like the ocean itself sits upon his head. Just like Demetrius when he goes into the water... sweet Amphitrite, preserve me. But he's terrified, pale, trembling. Poor lad.

"Atropous..."

He jerks and he whirls around, his distress dissolving into sheer panic. "Shite, Octavia. I– I can explain... well, actually, I can't... I don't know what's going on."

His voice cracks as his words trail off, and that has me crossing the distance between us. I pull the bandanna and trifold from his grip and study his face for a beat. Then I dutifully tie the silken cloth over those cold-to-the-touch swirling strands, stand on my tiptoes, and place the trifold on his head. I nod, satisfied with my work, wrap my hand around his wrist and pull him down the building's edge into the thankfully empty inn. Without a glance back, I quickly drag the lad up the stairs, and to the quarters Demetrius and I have been sharing.

Once safe behind the closed door, I release his arm and turn to face the wide-eyed, slack-jawed navigator. "Okay, now, take a breath, and tell me what happened, slowly this time."

Atropous blinks slowly a few times, staring at me like I've sprung another head. "You aren't going to go tell Cap?"

"I reserve the right to withhold judgment until after I hear the entire tale."

He sighs, relaxing slightly. "What about your task?"

My stomach tosses like a ship caught in a storm and I swallow. "Aurelius and Caleb are handling it. So, what happened to your hair?"

He hangs his head, lowering his eyes to the floor. "I got bored, so I wanted to go to the docks, maybe see a huge ship or something. A gust of wind sent sea spray over me, and it was like my head was plunged into cold water. I touched it and it felt... *feels* like water. It's never happened before, I swear."

The inner war I struggle with daily nearly becomes unbearable. All the secrets and lies It would be easier if everyone could know the truth. For a breath, I toy with the idea of telling him of his nymph heritage. The desperate look in his normally cheerful eyes is a vice around my heart. But then reason reasserts herself and all the repercussions of that action press down heavily on me.

His desperation turns to fear. He clasps his hands together like he's praying. "Please, please don't tell the Captain... I— I don't know what's going on with me, but I'll figure it out. I'll learn to control it, just... please..."

I gently grab his clasped hands and feel a tremor running through them. I hold his pleading emerald gaze. "I won't."

His hands go still at my words. "You... won't?"

I shake my head once. "No."

He looks like he doesn't believe me. "Why not? Not that I'm not eternally in your debt, but —"

I stop his worried ramblings with a gentle squeeze of his hands. "It's not my secret to tell. Besides, you're still the same person you were before. You're still my friend."

Atropous grins, the biggest one I've seen since Una had to slay Enoch. "Thank you... in a world like ours, where being kind is seen as a weakness, people often forget that kindness can get you just as far as someone fearing you."

I squeeze his hands again before dropping them. "I have to get back before one of them comes searching for me. Stay here until your hair reverts back to normal."

Atropous looks doubtful. "You think it will?"

I nod. "Water caused it, so being away from it should make it go back to normal."

"Should?"

I shoot him a small, hopefully comforting, smile. "Make yourself scarce before Aurelius and I return, I'll try to delay us as long as possible."

He grins again. "Thank you."

I mirror his smile and quickly, as quietly as possible, slip out of the room, closing the door gently behind me.

Halfway to Caleb's chamber, an idea strikes me, *'People often forget that kindness can get you just as far as someone fearing you.'* and I change direction heading toward the kitchens. If this works out, I owe you one, Atropous.

***

I push into Caleb's chamber and let the door click closed behind me. The first thing I notice is Caleb and Demetrius chatting softly together in one corner, Asa huddled in another. The boy is angled away from them, his whole body curled in on itself, arms wrapped around his face.

Demetrius looks from the cloth-wrapped bundle in my hand to my face. "Enjoy your walk?"

I nod, glancing at the child. "Can I speak with him?"

Caleb snorts a disgruntled laugh, throwing his hands above his head. "What are you going to do, sweet cheeks? Ask nicely and give him some treat?"

Demetrius holds up a hand, silencing him. "Go ahead, Octavia. There's no harm in letting her have a try."

Caleb grumbles to himself as I walk over and kneel in front of Asa. "Asa, I'm sorry I tricked you into following me. You see, your friends are trying to hurt mine, you're the youngest on their ship and that makes you an easy target. That's why I was in the square today." My soft words seem to reach some part of the boy and he lowers his arms, turning toward me slightly. "If you tell us what we want to know. I'll give you this fairy tart and you never have to go back there ever again."

Asa is quiet for a long while, Caleb's heavy breathing the only audible sound. "You swear it?" His voice is barely a whisper.

My heart goes out to this obviously frightened and hurt child. I untie the knots binding his wrists and ankles, then offer him the linen-wrapped bundle I brought in with me. In it, a spoon and a tower of dense yellow disks of cake. Between those layers are whipped, sweetened cream and fresh berries. It's topped with more fluffy cream and a whole, fresh strawberry. "I swear it."

Asa doesn't hesitate; he accepts the treat and utensil. "What do you want to know?"

I let out a relieved sigh, my chest suddenly feeling a thousand pounds lighter. I look at Demetrius, who's grinning proudly, then settle cross-legged beside Asa as he hesitantly tries a bite of the sugary confection. "What are the names of your Captains?"

Those dim, dark brown eyes light with sheer delight at the taste of the cake, and he exuberantly shovels another large spoonful into his mouth, trying to talk around the bite. "Elyse and Kai. The nastiest baddies I've ever met."

Demetrius, still standing at Caleb's side, speaks up. "And your lodgings? Where are you all staying?"

Asa shrugs his thin shoulders. "All I know is they have three different spots, but they don't let me see…" He pauses to take another bite. "One of the quartermasters gets me at the dock at sunset, covers my eyes and leads me to one of the three places."

Caleb's feral hiss echoes through the room, the sound causing Asa to visibly jump. "Wasted coin, wasted time, and we're no better off than we were before."

"Silence." Demetrius's command draws every eye in the room. He's cupping his square jaw in one hand, blonde brows drawn together as he thinks through all the information he's just received. A slow smile starts to spread on his lips. "Maybe not a total waste."

I cock my head, looking up at my guardian. "What are you thinking?"

Demetrius clasps his hands behind his back, looking like he's the cat that's got his cream. "Asa is going to go meet his quartermasters, as planned," he pauses to chuckle, "but, unlike their original plan, they'll have a surprise waiting for them."

Asa swallows his mouthful of food then looks up at Deme, a bit of cream smeared over his lips and cheek. "What's the surprise?"

Demetrius slowly draws his espada from his sash, his gleeful smirk contorting around the edges. "Us."

***

Demetrius and I pretend to admire the wares of a fisherman's stall, one eye always on Asa, who stands to the side of the Kraakaware stall, his small fists balled behind his back as he fidgets from foot to foot. We wait for his quartermaster to retrieve him. The sun has dipped below the horizon and my body is abuzz with anxious energy. This has to succeed. Just when I think I'm going to combust from all my thoughts and anxieties, a tall, copper-skinned man approaches Asa.

He's taller than Demetrius in his undisguised form but packed with thicker muscles. His long straight-as-a-needle black hair is tied at the nape of his neck. His densely packed torso is clothed in a deep, vividly violet doublet that's trimmed in brilliant braiding. His pantaloons are a deep gray, nearly black. They look pricey. Silken. A pair of leather boots adorn his feet, and a heavy gold chain lays around his neck, a deadly-looking pistol secured on his hip. He speaks unheard words to Asa, then turns and leads the boy out of the square.

Demetrius gives a sharp nod to Caleb, who stands a few stalls away. At this signal, the three of us begin to follow them.

Caleb falls into step on my left. "Remember the plan, Octavia?"

I sigh, rolling my eyes skyward. "I don't see why we have to use this plan, again."

Caleb shrugs one of his large, beefy shoulders. "Why change what works? You up for the challenge or not?"

My decision is made for me as I watch the pair disappear around the side of a Smith's shop. Oh, for blessed Poseidon's mercy… honestly. I sneer at the grinning buffoon as I tear off my bandanna, shoving it into his dirty hands. "You. Owe. Me."

With those words, I turn my back on my crew and shadow the duo as quietly as I can. I rotate my espada slowly in my sash, moving it to a less visible position behind my back. The knot in my belly spurs me on and when I round the corner they've just disappeared around, the buccaneer has just finished tying a thin strip of cloth over Asa's eyes.

He pauses when he notices me; two sharp, uninjured eyes looking at me. This must be Elisha. "Think you've got the wrong building, lass. The sisterhood is two over."

I slowly edge closer to the man; high, distinct cheekbones, full lips and a strong, clean jawline greet me. "I've actually been searching for you…"

As previously discussed, Asa throws himself onto all fours at my words and, as Caleb predicted, Elisha turns his head to reprimand the disobedient lad.

That's when I strike.

I reach behind me and draw my espada. Raising it high, I bring the hilt down as hard as I can, crashing it into Elisha's jaw. Sleep time. The sharp focus in his eyes glaze over and they fall shut as his body wobbles slightly, trying to fight the force of the hit. He fails and comes crashing down in a tangle of limbs and dirt. I let out a shaky breath. Elisha doesn't attempt to rise again.

Asa pops up, tearing the cloth from his eyes. They sparkle with bright triumph. He shoots me a wide, toothy grin. "That was brilliant!" He jumps into the air, before giving the prone body on the ground a sharp kick in the ribs.

I can't stop the laugh that bubbles over at the endearing, if not slightly violent action. "Quiet, Asa. Remember, as quiet as a dormouse."

He claps both hands over his mouth and nods enthusiastically, as Caleb and Demetrius finally decide to make their grand entrance.

Caleb strides over to me, a large maniacal grin on his face. He claps me roughly on the shoulder and I flinch under the force. "Good on ya!"

I pinch the bridge of my nose before looking at Demetrius. "What do we do now?"

Caleb's dark, demented chuckle pulls my attention back to him. He hunches down and impressively hosts Elisha up and over one of his wide shoulders, still grinning. "Things really get interesting now."

***

It really had been altogether too easy to smuggle a fully grown adult male into the inn, up the stairs, and into Caleb's chambers. Even with Asa giggling every ten paces or so. Unnervingly easy. Must remember to never get 'napped in this part of town.

Demetrius stands close to the bound, unconscious man, brow furrowed, those bottomless dark eyes trained on Eli curiously. "You suppose these ropes will hold him?" He spares a glance over his shoulder at a gleefully smirking Caleb.

Caleb's brown eyes gleam with far more excitement than the rest of us have combined. "That, boy, is a strangler knot. The most effective binding knot on the Seven Seas. Your concern should be on the blasted chair crashing beneath him." They share an unsettlingly companionable laugh, the glee on Caleb's face mirrored on my guardian's.

I sigh, shaking my head.

Getting the inn's chair up the stairs had been, shockingly, the most difficult part of all this. When the landlady caught us, Demetrius's had to go as far as using his strange nymph allure on her, a dangerous feat in public. But the landlady had wandered away in a daze, and we'd wrestled the chair into the room where Caleb had waited with the unconscious man, and young boy.

Caleb hacks loudly and wipes his mouth with the back of his hand before hooking a thumb at the still-unconscious man. "And you say I'm the brute. Pretty sure yer lass knocked him back a decade or two."

Demetrius snorts out his laugh, eyes twinkling with amusement. "Any less, and I would've wondered why I wed her." They share another laugh, and it makes my stomach twist as tightly as one of Caleb's knots.

Once Demetrius calms his laughter, he reaches to lift Elisha's still-dipping chin. He tilts his head slightly and I expect him to use his curious powers to wake him, as he had done with Asa previously…

SMACK

The echo of skin against skin has me gasping out loud, and Asa scuttling closer to me, his small hands knotting tightly into my trousers. I allo him to, needing

181

something solid to ground me, as my heart beats wildly against my ribs. I've never seen Demetrius so much as raise his voice in true malice, let alone raise his hand to anyone. What's going on with you, Father?

Elisha wakes with a start, looking around in confusion. He then looks at us all, his eyes passing over Caleb and Demetrius, and landing on me.

I watch his top lip twitch as his eyes narrow in anger. Then his gaze drops to the lad partially hiding behind me and his glare turns positively murderous. "Asa... you pathetic scrap of kelp."

Demetrius's hand connects again with the already reddened cheek, his face a stone mask. "No speaking unless we ask you a question. Nod if you understand and intend to comply."

It's that cold bottomless unfeeling look about him, all over again.

Eli scoffs, and the gash I'd given him on his lip oozes with fresh blood. "I won't be as easy to break as the cabin rat."

Asa clutches tighter at my clothes.

Demetrius chuckles, the dark sound even more threatening in the quiet room. "I didn't expect you to. I have a whole different game planned out for you, Elisha."

I suppress a shudder as gooseflesh flushes my skin at his deadly promise, and my pulse climbs higher as Demetrius pulls Elisha's own pistol from his sash and looks at it distastefully.

"Even worthless weapons like this flintlock pistol have their value." He toys with it, rotating the safety mechanism forward before pulling it back. His fingers slide down to the trigger, but instead of grasping it to shoot, he jerks it hard to the left, snapping the small steel trigger off the gun. Eli glares at Demetrius with a tightly clenched jaw. Deme smirks. "Sentimentality may be the most dangerous emotion to have in our sort of life." He snaps off the entire hammer mechanism from the pistol as if it were nothing, tossing the metal carelessly over his shoulder. "We know about your three hideouts. Might as well save everyone some time and tell us their exact locations. They're having salad with cheese at supper this eve. I'd quite like to get some, before that fiend Solomon commandeers all the cheese for himself."

Elisha tilts his head to the side. His dark, almond-shaped eyes glint, and he snorts another laugh. "The bilge rat should have told you to nab someone else. He chose the wrong man, if you're expecting an easy, friendly chat."

Beside me, Asa sticks out his tongue at Elisha and shields himself more behind my body.

Demetrius throws down the pistol so that it clatters loudly against the wooden floor. "Wrong answer." His fist connects with Elisha's jaw, the force snapping his head to the side. Impressively, the buccaneer takes the hit quietly, then turns his head and looks up at my father, inhales sharply and spits out a wad of bloody spittle that misses Caleb's boot by a breath.

"The wench hits harder than ya. You're going to have to try better than that."

Caleb's deep growl pulls my attention from the splotch of ruby staining the chestnut wood. His brown eyes glisten with barely controlled rage. "It's my turn to teach you something, lad."

Demetrius holds Caleb's stare, unwavering, before finally sighing and nodding. Leaving the broken, useless gun where it lies, he moves to my side, folding his arms tightly over his chest.

As Caleb replaces Demetrius in front of a bound man, the way Asa shifts to my right side, away from Demetrius, isn't lost on me. The boy presses his small, quaking body flush against me.

Caleb's usually aloof gaze turns deadly focused as he stares down Elisha. "Here are my rules, Indian, and ye best listen to them. Answer our questions, and you might just leave here with only a broken gun."

Elisha's wide shoulders begin to tremble, then a moment later he throws back his head and laughs loudly. "If you're gonna hit like that boy," he gestures with his head toward Deme, "I suggest you send in the wench again."

His laughter is abruptly cut short as Caleb whips the hatchet that the Chandler had foolishly traded him earlier from his leather belt and, without hesitation, brings the sharp, curved blade down upon Elisha's middle and index fingers. Both fingers, as far as the second knuckle, fall to the floor in a bloody heap.

"Hope ye aren't right-handed. That'll make shooting a gun mighty hard."

Eli clenches his jaw and, by some god or goddess, doesn't utter so much as a whimper. He grinds his teeth and shuts his eyes as the pain of his severed digits sweeps over him. But even still, he doesn't mutter a sound.

Beside me, Deme squawks a high-pitched sudden laugh. It has both Asa and I jumping simultaneously. "Well, how about that? You were right about needing that oafish hatchet."

Caleb only laughs, his eyes intently watching the slow flow of crimson dripping onto the wood. "Too tough to scream? More fun for us then. You still got eight more digits to bet in our little game."

***

5 July 1691
Île Sainte-Marie, Dauphin

I yawn, digging the heels of my palms into my dry-as-Hades eyes. We're back in Caleb's quarters again for the day, and we've yet to make any progress with our tight-lipped chum, regardless of any torture or threats placed upon him. Elisha still sits bound to the chair, his head hanging low as he rests his eyes, his now-loose ebony hair thankfully shielding his face from my view.

Asa is napping curled into the smallest circle possible not far from my side. Una and the crew are aware of Asa, and know he's staying with me. Demetrius has had to hold up his magic nearly all the time, now that the child refuses to leave my side for anything longer than the time it takes to have my meals, and bring him his. He isn't trusted enough yet to actually meet the crew face to face, though. They're also aware of Elisha, bound in Caleb's chambers. Even though she wishes nothing more than to come here herself, Una's trusted in our abilities to obtain the information that she so desperately wants. And even though she said those things, I know she feels something else entirely. Words said to bolster our spirits and raise morale, while inside she's withering in her own self-doubt and frustrations.

I sigh, my head pounding in time with my racing pulse. To add to my sullied hands and constant worry, the exhaustion and urge to fling myself into the ocean every time I pass it is becoming overwhelming. My skin painfully tingles constantly, and there's an ache that runs deeper than my bones. Waking is getting harder and harder to do, and by the start of supper I'm ready to turn in for the day.

Demetrius, in his Aurelius disguise, has his lips pursed into a hard line as he stares blankly at the wall. Yet another thing driving me completely loopy. Ever since yelling at me, Demetrius has been odd. He goes from his usually carefree, quite annoying self one moment, to not pulling punches, frightening children and drinking Ambrose under-the-table the next, despite me never seeing him drink so much as a light beer until the start of this crazy adventure. I feel disconnected from him, out of sync. It'd always been so easy to talk to him, as easy as breathing. Now, it's anything but. I don't know what he's going to do or say next. I can't gauge his reactions. Is he somehow losing himself? In his mission to save my life, has he slowly been corrupting his own? Or is this just the real him? A side I've not seen before now? This lurking unknown is the main reason I haven't told Demetrius about Atropous and the incident with his hair.

Deme sighs abruptly, arms folded tight. "Want to try his toes, Caleb? He may be more forthcoming after losing more blood."

Caleb huffs out an amused laugh, clapping Demetrius on the shoulder. "We don't want the infection to kill him before we get our answers, boy."

Demetrius's ink-pot eyes suddenly light up, a mischievous smile curling his lips. "Asa!"

The sleeping child shoots into a sitting position, his small hands immediately balling into fists. His large eyes open wide. "SIR!" His voice is a loud squeak as he pushes himself to his feet as quickly as he can.

Their loud voices rouse Elisha, who now watches with his one good eye. The other is swollen shut, the skin around it a multi-colored pattern of nauseating bruises.

That mischievous look spreads over Deme's face until a familiar twinkle appears in his eyes. "Go get our Captain. I'm sure they'll be very eager to finally get involved."

***

The sound of the knob turning has my head jerking towards the door. Asa runs in, his bare footfalls pit-pattering as he runs to my side with a wild, frightful expression, eyes full of unshed tears. He hides behind me, hands twisted tightly into the fabric of my trousers again. Elyse had been, by Asa's accounts and the scars he has to prove it, a brute of a Captain to him. Beating him, threatening him, she had traumatized the poor boy so much on her ship that seeing Una, his tormentor's twin, still has him dissolving into fear like this. I know he understands, logically, that they are not the same person, rather identical twins, but his seven-year-old emotions have a tough time remembering that. I rest my hand lightly on his head, the way Demetrius had done for me countless times over the years, hoping to provide some comfort. Asa tenses slightly, before relaxing and pressing closer.

Una enters, and I jolt, tingles weaving their way throughout my body. My heart stutters, then almost fails me as I notice she's wearing the deep-ocean-blue bandanna I'd given her two days prior when hers had come up missing. Coin well spent when I see how the bright blue of the material makes the pale blue in her stormy eyes stand out. Those brilliant eyes are partially shielded by her trifold as they land on me. I swallow and tear my gaze from her deliciously warm one and back to Elisha.

Caleb's chuckle mercifully interrupts my thoughts that have suddenly scattered themselves across the universe. "Captain," he says. "*So* nice of you to join our little jolly. We may need your certain kind of... *touch* for this bucko."

Unable to see our newest arrival, Eli snorts and rolls his one good eye. "Bringing in back up? If they're anything like you lot, I'll die of infection before you get what you're looking for."

Una kicks the door closed behind her and removes her trifold and bandanna, tossing the hat, uncaring, onto the floor, and wrapping the cloth around her wrist twice before tying it in a knot. She shakes out her now chin-length locks, a menacing smile curving her lips as she stalks closer to Elisha. The effect is just what my guardian had hoped for.

Elisha's skin pales, and for the first time since capturing him, the snarky buccaneer looks afraid. "Una... You should be rotting in Davy Jones' locker by now."

Una merrily laughs, the sound making my stomach churn and my cheeks feel feverish. "Seems my *dear* sister has spread quite the reputation for me. Look at you, you're trembling in your knickers, lad."

Eli swallows, his one good eye darting around like he's trying to figure a way out of his current situation. Beads of sweat collect on his forehead, his remaining fingers clutching the arms of the inn chair. Just what had Elyse told her crew members about Una? And why? She must suspect Una of being alive to elicit such fear in Eli, to even bother telling him about her at all.

Una slowly draws her cutlass and stretches her arm until the tip of the blade kisses the tip of Elisha's nose. "Then you also know I have a very short fuse and hate to have my time wasted." Her glistening eyes narrow. "My sibling and Kai, where are they? Tell me your hideouts, or you'll be losing more than just fingers."

Eli's eye widens. "One's about half a mile from where your crew nabbed me... another by the Smith's shop, the one with the largest sign. And the last is further away, near the bakery, off the path leading into the square. But- but it doesn't matter... they aren't going to be at any of them..."

Una lowers the blade and steps closer. "Why not?"

Elisha leans as far from the fuming blonde as he possibly can while still bound to the chair. "W– we were due to set sail the morning your crew nabbed me. They're long gone by now."

Una scowls and she grips the hilt of her weapon even tighter. "Where are they going?" The words are a barely audible hiss.

Eli doesn't hesitate to give in entirely. "Port Royal."

His hunched shoulders relax, as does her grip on her sword. I thought she'd be pleased with his answer, but the murderous look barely contained on her face tells a different tale entirely. I feel anger burning a hole through my chest with its intensity. I suddenly want to rip teeth from Eli's mouth, rip skin, draw bone and blood from flesh. My hands twitch. I think… I think this is Una's rage, hot and raw, in me. I see her act a moment before she truly seems to be aware of it; she stabs her cutlass into Elisha's abdomen. Her brain seems to catch up, and her eyes widen momentarily, but she doesn't flinch or waver. She gives the blade a rough twist before pulling it free. Eli gasps, struggling against his binds, causing his blood to pool over his belly. He coughs, tries to say something, but only blood spews over his teeth and out of his mouth.

Blank faced, Una raises her leg, wiping the blade clean on her thigh, before re-sheathing it. With one final disgusted glare back at Elisha, Una opens the door and leaves. The door slams loudly behind her, and with her, my anger departs, leaving nothing but nausea. The sharp sound of the door echoes in my ears long after her heavy footsteps fade to silence. The room is stunned; none of us, not even Caleb, have anything to say. The only sound now Elisha's ragged, bubbling breathing.

Demetrius is the first to snap out of his stupor, his gaze flicking over to me. "Go after her, Octavia. We three can finish up here."

The words are barely out of his mouth before Asa is letting go of my clothing, and I'm picking up Una's discarded and forgotten trifold. I pause a moment, glancing down at Asa, who's staring, wide eyed and fearful, up at me. I don't know why, but I bend and press a gentle kiss to his brow, the way Demetrius does to me on occasion. I don't wait for a reaction or response from any of them and head out the door.

If I were a livid Captain, where would I go? I close my eyes and focus on that ember of anger burning in my chest. Now I'm certain it wasn't mine; I was truly feeling her emotions. I follow that insistent tug, and it leads me down the staircase into the inn. I spot a smear of crimson on the railing, and know the odd connection is leading me true. How utterly bizarre. It's an odd experience, to feel another's emotions as if they are your own. Woven so tightly, it's hard not to give in to the seductive lull of her combustible anger.

As my boot touches the last step, I see a familiar flash of blonde through the window of the inn. She's so upset, she hasn't even put on the bandanna to hide her feminine features.

I run to catch her, panting, the sting of exertion in my legs making my knees tremble. "Una! Stop! Wait, please!"

Her legs lock immediately, and I'm unsure if it's the bond's effects, if Demetrius's tonic is finally losing its potency, or if she's simply shocked by my shouting of her name in public. Whatever makes her stop, when she turns, those hardened eyes shatter and soften upon seeing it's me that called her.

I hold up the trifold, giving her a timid smile. "Wanna sit on *The Revenge*? We may just make the sunset."

Her face softens, and the corners of her mouth twitch. She steps closer to accept her belongings. "I'd like that…"

I smile as she adjusts the trifold atop her head, angling it just along her thin brows, that smoldering pit in my chest lightening slightly. We fall into companionable silence as we walk along the dock together. For a moment, I let myself forget I'm disguised and sneaking around, and that Una doesn't know it's me. It's just Hanna and Una walking along the pier together. No crazed sibling or vile father, no looming hourglass over my head.

Just I, with my bonded.

Una lowers the gangplank, and we walk onto *The Revenge*. It feels strange to have the gently rolling ship beneath my boots again. She leads us onto the main deck, where we would have suppers together while we were at sea. With a heavy sigh, she leans against the rail, her eyes cast over the calm, still waters.

"Would you like to talk about it?" My voice sounds meek even to my own ears. My cheeks heat with embarrassment.

"What's to talk about?" Her voice is sharp, like a gunshot. That smoldering flame of her rage momentarily flares back to life in my chest, but as she turns her head to look at me it fizzles out. She chews the inside of her cheek before finally clucking loudly. "My apologies. You haven't done anything wrong." She looks away again, back toward the brilliant blue ocean, her sun-kissed skin flushing in the balls of her cheeks.

"Why does them going to Port Royal upset you so?"

She gazes down at her hands. "It's a fifty-eight-day journey. We'd be sailing during the most dangerous time of the season…" She growls, gripping the rail of the ship. "And that's even if we can get enough supplies and rations together to take this trek… Port Royal's the biggest pirate sanctuary in the world. Buccaneers come from every corner of the waters to indulge freely and without fear of the headsman's axe. If we get there, who's to say will actually find th–"

I lay my hand over hers still gripping the railing and Una's ramblings come to an abrupt halt. Her whole body jerks like she's been struck with lightning. Her gaze snaps to my face and I squeeze those warm fingers gently.

"So the odds seem impossible. So what? Elyse betrayed you –" I stumble to a halt, suddenly realizing Una only ever told Hanna her story, not Octavia. Think of something, quick! She's frowning at me. "Solomon…" I hurriedly add, "he told me what your sibling did to you. You should be thrice dead by now. So your plan and path didn't go as planned. So what? Carve a new, better one. Come up with a better plan. Fall into a dark place, become angry, lose hope. Just don't allow yourself to stay there. From what I've seen, you accomplish something impossible every day."

Her eyes clear and that angry flame of hers in my chest is doused completely. She squeezes my fingers back, before casually lacing them together, a playful grin curling her pink lips. "Ever been part of a raid, Octavia? I think it will change your life."

***

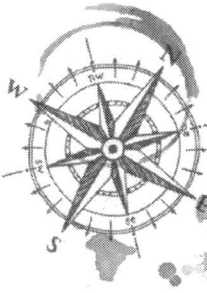

Chapter 25: Una
13 July 1691
Île Sainte-Marie, Dauphin

I smooth the rumpled, yellowing parchment against my raised knee. Once satisfied the blasted thing isn't going to curl back up over my fist again, I look up from my perch on the 'borrowed' inn chair and immediately sigh. I seem to be doing more of that every damn day.

Selina stands, arms folded, hood up as per usual, at one end of my quarters, and Caleb polishes Marigold on the other side, as far from one another as the room allows. Even after being crew mates for so long, the two are no closer than when they first met. Not that I can fault Selina for that. Caleb is a pain in my hide, and foul-mouthed to boot. Hopefully after this little outing, the tension will simmer down, or else it's going to be one hell of a voyage.

"Asa has been told, again, about keeping his lips *sealed*, Selina?"

She gives a slight bob of her hooded head. "Octavia has reminded him over two dozen times in the last three days, Captain. If that doesn't stick in his head, I'm afraid nothing will."

Caleb lets out a long huff and looks over as he re-sheathes his dirk. "Li'l bilge rat is more trouble than he's worth. Ye be just keepin' him around because he and the Indian lassie are as thick as thieves."

I narrow my eyes into a glare. "Hold onto that tongue, Caleb. You may find yourself without it. It was put to a vote. You don't want to fight the code, do ye?"

Caleb drops his gaze to the dirty, wooden floor. "This raid better prove a bounty."

It must. Ever since we learned that Elyse and Kai had set sail for Port Royal, I've been in full survival mode: tend to the ship, tend to the crew. Then, only then, can I start preparing to sail once again. Pa's words still echo in my head as loud as if he were still alive. His teachings helped me carve my path, and with those teachings, and my experiences, I'll forge a new path. One with a better, more solid plan. One that's sure to succeed. The ship's been tended, repaired, and patched to the best of our skills, and the crew healed to the best of our abilities. A fifty-eight-day voyage means supplies, and lots of them. Tonight, the final steps will be laid out; we'll strike as soon as the last sod wobbles their bleary-eyed arses to their beds from the inns and taverns.

We'll strike a few hours before the sun rises and set sail just as soon as it's fully up over the horizon, at the height of the next high tide. That'll give us plenty of time. I can read the tide clock hanging at the docks, and the tables and charts in my cabin, but I've no real knack for knowing the weather before it hits. Atropous, Selina, Jonah, and Ambrose, on the other hand, all seem to have some innate gift for weather-knowledge that makes them indispensable to me. They can, all of them, look into a calm, cloudless sky and tell me there'll be a storm three days hence. Maybe it's something in the way the air feels to them, the shape of clouds, maybe something in the swell and taste of the waves? Whatever it is, they all agree that, if we want to sail out of here with favorable winds, it has to be at tomorrow's high-tide, and so the raid must be tonight.

My stomach twists itself into thrilled knots. A good ol' raid is long past due. "Has the last round of inspections and rigging checks been done?"

Caleb nods, toying with the hilt of Marigold. "Aye, it pains me to say it's in better condition than it was, even before sailin' her here. The li'l gutter rat is giving Felix the run around."

I lean over to the mattress to retrieve my small ink pot and gray feathered quill. I dip it into the black ink a few times before marking a dark X on the yellowed parchment still held down on my knee. A list of things we need before we set sail for the waters once again:

Medisin, rashons, rum, hen or two. Cow?

"Is everyone armed?"

Selina drops her tattooed arms, the black vines crisscrossing over her pale skin holding my attention, until a *very* rare, broad grin curves her full lips. I don't need to see the rest of the odd woman's face to tell she's thrilled. She's almost vibrating with excitement. "There isn't a better-armed crew in Sainte Marie."

I snort out a laugh at her excitement and bravado. It feels good to laugh. The rage I'd felt at Elisha's news had blurred all my lines of reason. I'd felt red, I'd seen red. It had completely consumed me. I had wanted to keep on slaying and paving the cobblestone in front of me crimson...

But then Octavia had called my name.

"Una! Stop! Wait, please!"

The voice hadn't been a yell, nor a command, yet my legs had locked me in place as if she'd controlled me like a puppet master. And then her soft smile and even gaze had stunned me into silence. Not a single wisp of fear or disgust at what I'd done, just honest concern. For me. Her words had cooled that inferno in my chest and cleared my twisted thoughts. She'd smoothed out my fraying edges, and her hand in mine had grounded me, bringing a feeling of peace. Something I'd not felt since Hanna.

Caleb's yellow grin is suddenly very close, his putrid breath fanning over my face. I have to swallow and force myself to hold down last night's supper. "I see cupid's arrow has stuck yet again," he says. "Where is yer li'l turtledove?"

I begin to roll the parchment, my eyes holding his gaze. "If I didn't need ye skills, I'd gut you like I did Elisha."

Caleb's mirthful gaze dulls as it widens, and he takes a large step back.

"Octavia and Aurelius are proving their worth in Merchant's Pass, out there in the town. Ye better take your cue, before I find more worth in them than in you," I tell him. He takes another step back, now closer to Selina than to me.

Octavia and Aurelius really had thrown in their all, gathering coin, goods, favors. Whatever I seem to need, the duo are already paces ahead of me. Almost too invested in their jobs. Their actions, words, what they know, what they don't. The

193

odd weapons they carry, Octavia's actions being even more bizarre and unsettling. Could they, too, be something other than human? Nymphs or mermaids, too? Or something else entirely? Ever since meeting the strange couple, something has always been off. My head knows it, but most importantly my gut knows it. And unlike my blasted heart, my gut never leads me astray.

I try to refocus my attention on Selina. "And Solomon's mapped out all our routes?"

The grin that had slipped at Caleb's nearness blooms again radiantly. "He's prepared so well, even the routes have routes, Captain. This raid is going to be most enjoyable."

Caleb's next laugh teeters closer to a scoff. "Where'd ye find that cheese-obsessed loon, anyway? He's not like any slave I've ever met."

I glare at him, and he immediately throws his hands up in surrender.

Selina's pretty grin is cracking around the edges. "Don't call him that," she snarls, through gritted teeth.

I try to shift her enraged attention back to me. "The crew's been told the time and meeting place?"

Her hooded head angles downward and I feel her gaze on me even though I can't see those piercing amber eyes. Then she laughs, an honest-to-god laugh. "Captain, you're wound tighter than normal. This is a time for merriment. You actually aren't half a bad leader. I'm still alive. That in itself is a success."

Caleb sighs loudly but nods along. "As much as agreeing with this one makes me want to throw myself into the sea, I agree. I'll follow ye into any storm, Captain."

That small flame of hope that had begun warming me when Octavia showed her trust and faith in me sparks again. For the first time since gathering this crazy crew, I believe with my whole heart that we can, will, succeed.

***

Farewell freedom, hello gallows. I pinch the bridge of my nose wearily before looking out across my idiotic crew gathered in front of me as we stand on solid land, gathered on the docks. Asa and Felix jump around, pretending to fence with their small blades, while Aurelius and Octavia smile on blissfully. Those lads are going to stab someone's blasted eye out with their steel... and cost me more coin, no doubt.

Atropous, Jonah and Ambrose chat excitedly with unnervingly large smiles. Shite, those bastards are going to be trouble, I can just feel it. Selina has her hood down, a rare sight, her amber eyes gleaming brightly in the waning moon's light. Her excitement is as palpable as the rest. Solomon, on the other hand, looks as if he's about to lose his supper at any moment. He's standing quietly beside Selina, twisting his hands awkwardly. Lad has never been a part of a raid before... gods above... My temples flare with pain. *This* is my raiding party? A gaggle of untrained children would bear more fruitful results.

I draw in a centering breath. We've made it this far. Octavia is right, Selina as well. We can do this. I address my crew. "Ahoy! Who's ready for a raid?!"

They thrust their fists and an assortment of weapons into the air. Ambrose performs an odd jig. His hair, red as a fox's pelt, flops against his sweaty forehead. "Finally! If I had to toss one more drink to one more ungrateful patron, I was going to put my fist down his gob! If they only knew they were speaking to a survivor of Beachy Head!"

Jonah chuckles and knocks his shoulder against the ruddy-cheeked ex-Jolly. "If only our fleet commander could see you now. He'd be so bloody proud!" Jonah's cleverly hidden British accent slips out at the end of his words before he can stop it, as it sometimes does when he gets overly exuberant, or overly drunk. I still don't really understand why he tries to hide his accent. It's annoying as sin, yes, but even Ambrose, with his lilting Ulster-Irish twang, no longer bothers to conceal his arguably more-problematic accent. Being British is one thing but being Irish is another altogether. If Ambrose doesn't care, why does Jonah?

But when the pair of them dissolve into loud, echoing laughter, that dull thud behind my eyes flares with a vengeance. I grit my teeth. "Ambrose, Jonah, I'm not above telling Caleb to make sure ye two stay apart during this raid." At my words, the duo spring apart, jerking to full attention as if I'd thrown a bucket of sea water

195

over 'em, their eyes staring straight ahead. Something only trained Jollies could do with such speed and smartness. "Remember, you lot, we're here to get what we need and get the hell out. Enjoy yourselves but follow the yellow ribbons Aurelius and Octavia laid out earlier. They show where you can wander. No killing, keep the brawls to a minimum, try not to take from folks that need it more… but most importantly, follow the code." I place a hand on my cutlass as I scan the now-silent group. "Going against the code means going against me, and we all know what happens to people who cross me, now don't we?" Yells and shouts of Enoch's grisly fate fill the moon-and-star-lit sky, their voices like drum beats in my ears. Or is that the pounding of my pulse in my skull? "Don't spend longer than the count of sixty in each place. If ye can't count, find someone who can, or work faster. We set sail at the top of the high tide, as soon as the sun is up. If ye ain't on *The Revenge*, consider yourself out of the crew, and this lovely place your new home."

Selina draws her ancient-looking blade. It's not silver like steel, but a rusted gold. The weapon reminds me of a rapier melded with a fencing sword. I've never gotten more than a few good looks at it. Selina always keeps it close and guarded, like she's afraid someone will steal it. A smart move on her part.

I pull my cutlass from my sea-blue sash, the one that I'd been using previously as a bandanna, the one Octavia gave me, and raise it high into the air. "FOR THE REVENGE!"

My crew mirrors my actions and I turn, trudging up the path that leads to Merchant's Pass. The traders house themselves here, and those frilly rich bastards can afford to be lightened of some of their possessions. Houses packed tightly together, lots of shadows, too many comfortable folks thinking they're safe. This and the distance from the main square the reasons it was chosen in the first place. If the crew are careful, they won't be found. And, if by some chance, they are, by the time anyone can get to the square and sound the alarm, we'll be long gone in the wind.

The moment we cross into the quiet merchant's quarter of the island, my crew break into groups, all spreading out and eagerly jumping to their tasks, vanishing into various lodgings, stalls and shops. Most of my lot can pick locks, have armed themselves with various bits of carefully bent pins and iron hooks, but it seems these swines are lax in their security. Most of the doors are secured with only a cross bar, maybe a bolt. Street-facing ground-level windows that open with a nudge and a heave. The odd carefully broken square of glass. Nothing a handy buccaneer can't find his way around. It's almost too easy. I watch Caleb enter a modest looking home, single-story but high-ceilinged. Young Felix skips behind him, a dirk in his small grubby hand. Ambrose, Jonah and Atropous split from the group and peel off after one another, as they run as fast as they can into a tackle and bait shop. Octavia's silvery laugh has me turning to seek her out as she hoists a squirming Asa into her arms, then on to her shoulders. Aurelius walks close by, a tender smile on his face. They disappear into what appears to be a fabrics store.

"Ready, Cap?"

I nearly jump out of my skin and turn much too fast, but I'm met with Selina's glimmering amber eyes, amused in the moonlight. She stands in front of me, a troubled, timid-looking Solomon at her side.

"I'd be asking your sweetheart that question if I were you. He looks a bit green around the gills."

Solomon's cheeks quickly flush at my words.

Selina clears her throat and ignores my remark, her cheeks just as pink as his. "I believe I saw a yellow ribbon over here." She stomps off ahead of us, her shoulder-length sable hair and charcoal cloak flapping behind her.

Solomon stares wistfully after her. "We better make haste, Captain!" He scurries after and I can't help but laugh. Seems Selina can in fact get along with someone. Well shite, I owe Atropous a pint when we port next.

I follow and catch Solomon's hide entering a two-story darkened home with sprawling night-flowering jasmine trailing over its walls, the scent heady and sweet. I'm two paces behind them, about to fully step into the home, when I hear shuffling followed by a scream, sudden and sharp.

Then nothing at all.

I freeze, holding my breath, trying to make out the shadows in the dark doorway, listening for a familiar voice.

"Great form, Selina!" says Solomon. I release my held breath.

"How did you see anything? It's as dark as pitch in here?" Selina's disembodied voice soon follows his.

"I have very keen eyesight, flame of my heart."

Urgh. I roll my eyes. "Greetings. Yes, guess who? I'm still here. Mind lighting a flame, Solomon? We are in a bit of a crunch."

"Captain! R– right!" Solomon sounds mortified.

More shuffling, then a scrape of the match against flintlock. A small flame springs to life, and then a candle on a hefty brass candlestick illuminates a rosy-cheeked Solomon. Selina's head is down, her ringlets making an inky halo around her face. I follow her gaze downward to the two unconscious lumps of crumpled human on the ground.

She smirks victoriously as she holds up a small bottle filled with a honeyed liquid in one hand and a heavy looking gold chain in another. "Thirty more to go, Captain."

I chuckle lowly and follow her, a pleasant tingle setting my body a buzz, as Solomon trails close by always ready to lend his candles light. There's a desk, ledgers, and account books. I'm trying not to think of the cabin and Demetrius pouring over his texts as I trail my hands over the desk. Ink pots. Quills. No coin boxes left carelessly for me to find. Pity, though that would be too good to be true, eh? A few worthless knick-knacks. Pretty, but not worth much, and not much use on a ship.

"Is this what we're looking for?"

I turn and a loud laugh slips through my lips. Solomon has a length of good hemp rope around his shoulders, like some fancy-arse scarf, still cradling the candlestick tight in his hand.

I clap him on the shoulder as he grins broadly. "Great find, Solomon!"

"Captain!" I turn at the sound of Selina's voice, just in time to catch the small pouch she's tossed me. It hits my hand hard and an odd smell wafts into my nostrils. Nutty, kind of like the earth after a long rain.

As I open the pouch, Solomon moves closer, better-illuminating us. I stick a finger into the pouch and find its contents soft, powdery. So, I pour a little into my hand. A dark powder that looks like gunpowder in the low light. I bring my face down to the small mound in my palm and stick my tongue to it.

I sputter, dropping the bitter tasting powder back into the bag before closing it and wiping my hand over my mouth. "What in three hells is this?"

Selina grins. "Ground up dried coffee beans."

I should have known that. The word brings forth a fuzzy memory, more smell than image. White porcelain, a strong bitter smell, and even more bitter taste. I thrust the sealed pouch into my pocket. "This will sell well at the Clandestine in Port Royal."

"Sixty!" Solomon's sudden voice, urgently whispering in my ear, has my heart threatening to leap out of my chest.

"Shite, Solomon. Warn me next time you decide to suddenly speak right next to my head." My pulse is racing all over again, and that persistent pounding in my skull intensifies further.

Solomon gives me a shy smile. "Many apologies, my Captain."

My anger fizzles out at his sincerity. "Let's get going, we've dallied too long." I head back the way we'd come, out of the accounting room, through the entryway and back onto the street.

The first thing I see is Caleb heaving a cask over his large shoulder, as Felix jumps and skips around him, a big grin splitting his cracked lips, his small sword slashing worrisome designs in the air. I head in the opposite direction and turn to another home. I jimmy the window open and look over my shoulder to take the candle from Solomon, but he and Selina are nowhere in sight. I sigh and tuck myself through the opening, my feet finding a solid floor beyond. I'm immediately engulfed in darkness. That candlestick would have been marvelous right about now.

I fumble around the perimeter for a moment before sheathing my cutlass, freeing both my hands. I feel around blindly. Wood. Wood. Wood. My hand brushes metal, and I pick it up. Heavy, with the barest scent of copper. Circular with a long-ish handle. I think at first it might be a skillet, but it's got some kind of lid on it. I move it to my left hand and still can't quite make it out in the little moonlight coming in from the street. I hold it by its handle in one hand as I blindly search through the room. I brush something smooth and rectangular. I pick it up and give it a sniff. Soap?! What a find. Another reach to me left and I find what my hand recognizes as a folding razor. Handy little blade. I've seen some real damage done with one of these. I've also seen wounds cauterized and buckshot removed with one, too. I slip it, with the soap, into my trouser pocket.

"Drop whatever you got and get out of my house," says a deep gravelly voice, very close. I turn slowly on the balls of my feet and face a looming figure.

I clear my throat. "Oh, my? This isn't the brothel? Am I lost again? Silly me."

The large mass moves closer. "I won't be falling for that one again. One goose egg is well enough for me."

The thought of one of my lot, maybe Octavia, feigning naivety before striking the man has a grin turning my lips upwards. "Jig's up then? Good, I don't have to play fair." On my last syllable I swing the metal skillet-like thing I'd picked up as hard as I can at the man in front of me. A satisfying clang echoes throughout the indoor washroom – how fancy is this? A whole room to clean yourself up in?! – and the man folds up like a spyglass as he lowers to the ground, cradling his sure to be shattered kneecap. "That's going to sting a bit."

I advance on the blubbering mass, getting behind him. "Blasted pirate," he groans. "Take what you want and leave me be!"

I wrap my arm around his neck, ensuring his gulping Adam's apple is in the crook of my elbow. "Planned on it." Then I squeeze as hard as my weaker female body will allow me too, pulling the back of his skull into my chest, putting pressure on the vein that runs up the side of his neck. He claws at my arm, his blunt nails biting into the flesh of my forearm, but I ignore it. "Have an extra good sleep for me." He goes slack, and then his full weight is upon me, nearly causing me to stumble onto my arse. "Blimey! You weigh more than Caleb, and that, chum, is a feat."

I heave the unconscious body off me, so he lands on the floor with a satisfying thump. I peer past his prone form into the dark home beyond, but I don't know who else we might've disturbed. Not worth the risk, especially if one of my lot's already been in and pilfered what's worth taking. My laughter continues as I climb back out of the window into the sweet night air.

I hold the round metal thing I'd whacked that poor bastard in the knees with up into the moonlight, finally able to inspect it. It's a bed warmer. You put hot coals in the pan end and slide it under your covers to make it toasty. I'd seen one back at the inn in Sainte Marie. I consider it, hefting it backwards and forwards like a sword. A Captain with her own bed warmer, eh? Why not.

Two of my crew gleefully pass me, a tangle of brown and white nets between them. Just behind them, Ambrose and Jonah are carrying two halves of a ball that's attached to a thick metal chain. I salute them with the bed warmer. Jonah hoots into the sky. Ambrose shushes him, but laughs, their eyes alight like children getting their favorite treat or toy.

"The smith's shop around the way was hogging all the goods for themselves, just like a filibuster, hmm, Am?"

Ambrose grins at me. "Man-O-Wars, here we come!"

They cackle like gossiping fishwives as they head up the street that leads back to the port and *The Revenge*. I glance at the sky and see its coloring starting to lighten. Time for one more stop; better make it a good one.

I pass by Atropous, the muscles in his back flexing as he searches through a leather sack that rattles and clunks in front of an ironmonger's stall. Any ironmonger that leaves a sack of tools under his stall is asking to be pilfered. He's still wearing a bandanna over his hair, his pride and honor. I asked him about it, and he said Octavia had told him it keeps the sea air from 'drying out his hair.' Odd. Obviously, a lie. Not one that's any of my concern. If he wants to stop tossing his hair into people's faces at every opportunity, good for him.

I walk past a few stalls that have already been cleared and flipped of any items left out overnight. I see some bundles of cloth folded into a small woven basket sitting between two stalls that have seen better days. I place the metal bed warmer on top before I pick up the entire thing, tuck it under an arm, and continue on my way. The nervous knot in my stomach finally loosens and I take in a deep, well needed breath. A flash of light glinting off something on a torn-apart stall catches my attention. I set the basket next to me to inspect the stall, moving broken, warped wood and faded cloth aside. A vial.

I pick it up and roll the small, stoppered tube in my palm a moment, before pulling out the cork with my other hand. I bring it close to my nose and inhale. A slightly metal smell. Some kind of dye perhaps, given the faded woven cloths on the stall? I re-cork it and place the vile into the basket.

A sudden whoop draws my gaze up-and-over; Asa zips down the street back toward the port, his rounded cheeks and lips covered in a fine white powder. Octavia is close on his heels, a bulging brown sack over her shoulder, her bandanna gone and her shoulder-length chestnut strands billowing behind her. Her cheeks are flushed from exertion, her brown eyes shimmering with the exhilaration that I feel. She's grinning so widely that it makes me smile just looking at her. And right behind her, like a parasite, moving with a grace I wouldn't expect from one so stocky, is Aurelius. He runs after her, a small pouch held between his teeth. He's got a similar, slightly smaller brown pouch gripped in one hand and, under his other arm, with its head pulled downward… is that a goat?! Bless whatever god or goddess is watching over us!

The sky continues to change from soft gray to a color closer to a lilac, reminding me of a certain half-ling. I grab my basket and shake off the thought before turning and heading toward the sea. I can already see the tide is up. Shite. Running out of time. My walk turns into a trot that quickly turns into a run. Atropous is just a speck of human in front of me as he too heads back to the ship. The lingering crew begins rallying together to finish their tasks.

I peer around for any sign of Selena and Solomon. They've not shown their faces since leaving me behind at the first home. Perhaps they're already back on *The Revenge?* I take the corner that will lead directly to the pier, and to freedom. Several boot-falls pound behind me as we all touch wooden planks.

I spy my sails, already unfurled, pulling beautifully in those favorable winds the lads promised me. Her gangplank is lowered, Caleb standing on deck with his usual scowl back in place. There's a flurry of activity on the main deck. Atropous is already up in the crow's nest, his spyglass held to one of his eyes as he looks over the ocean. I leap onto my ship, my girl, and a deckhand takes my basket from me. I give *The Revenge's* taffrail a hearty slap in greeting.

"Everything by the main mast! Quartermasters'll auction the booty from the slop's chest. We'll move the rations and casks to the orlop once we're sailin' steady and free!"

"Aye, aye, Captain!"

I look over the bustling crew, two of my most important members still missing. "Caleb, where's Selina and Solomon?"

Caleb turns angry glinting eyes on me, his lips twitching as he points a grubby finger back toward the pillaged town. "Blasted blue-skin went back for the cackle fruit!"

I follow his shaking finger and burst into loud laughter. The kind that lightens your chest and makes you feel young again. Whole. Selina runs down the dock, her hair and cloak flapping wildly behind her. One small, brown satchel is tied over her shoulder and a cask of some kind is in her arms. The cask is easily twice her slight frame, yet she carries it like she has muscles like Caleb. And behind her comes Solomon, a chicken raised high above his head, a painfully large grin on his face. He holds that cackle fruit up like it's the best booty he's ever found. The crew begins to hoot and holler loudly, whistling and stomping their feet on the deck to welcome them back aboard.

Selina gives me a grin as she runs up the gangplank. "Ahoy, Captain."

I snort, clapping Solomon on the shoulder as he tries his best to hang on to the fowl. "Take the animals to the orlop now. Coxswain to the wheel, haul wind! All hands, ahoy! Weigh anchor. Gangplank up!"

Orders given, the crew divides to conquer their tasks and get *The Revenge* moving. Octavia squats in front of Asa, wiping the white flour from his face and cheeks with the bottom of her shirt. Aurelius stands close by, his back to them, eyes already trained steady on the waters.

I feel the sway as we pull away from port, hear the groan as she moves for the first time in a long while. Before we really start sailing, I stride to the edge of my ship and lean against the taffrail, reaching into a pocket and pulling out a couple pieces of eight. With a prayer to the goddess Neptune, for a safe and pleasant voyage, I toss them into the ocean. They hit the rippling water with a pleasant plop. The anticipation that had been building all night simmers as I grip the rail of my ship with both hands.

"Steady yer will, lads, our next stop be Port Royal."

***

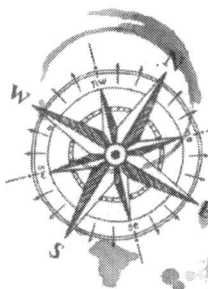

Chapter 26: Atropous
28 July 1691
Somewhere in the Indian Ocean

I press my cheek against my raised knees, relishing the pain as the starchy material catches in the scruff of my beard. I then raise my hand, fingering the secure knot of my bandanna for the fifth time since awakening in the crow's nest, checking to make sure it hadn't betrayed me in my slumber. A fluttering above has me jerking my gaze upwards, toward the sky and away from my knees.

A lone bird beats its wings harshly, doing its best to keep its robust, mostly white body in the sky. The tips of its plume feathers are black, its legs and neck are long and, if it were closer, I know I'd see a short beak and small, round beady eyes that would remind me of my trouser buttons. It's a reunion solitaire. They're birds that prefer to live alone nearly their entire lives. With the weather cooling, it's heading back to the island slowly fading behind us, where it'll forage on worms in the dirt, fruits, whatever it can find. Soon it'll be too plump to fly. Father always told me tales of the hungry seaman or pirate desperate and starving enough to hunt down the bird for food. I'd always felt bad for the unsuspecting bird, too large, too stupid to defend itself or run away. Father thought that foolish of me; animals were meant to be eaten by humans after all.

I stretch out my throbbing legs and arch my back, raising my arms high above my head. Swiveling my hips slightly, I feel some of the pain lift in my back. Sleeping in the nest... not the safest or most comfortable plan I've ever had.

The fear of my hair changing again, this time in front of the least forgiving of our crew, Caleb, is what spurred me to make the climb as soon I returned to the ship after the raid. That fear kept me from experiencing my first auction. I'll still get my rations and my dues, but I lost the opportunity to barter for the loot. I pull my aching legs back up to my chest, resting my chin once more on my knees. I keep my eyes downcast. I don't even dare look to the thrashing currents below me.

My unknown condition is throwing my entire world off kilter. The ocean had always made me feel safe. When Father would be out at sea, before I was old enough to go with him, I'd spend hours at the dock, skinny legs dangling over the pier, dreaming of all the adventures he and I would one day have. I'd been alone, but the ocean always made me feel at peace, at home. I'd never, not once, been afraid of those unbounded waters. Now?

I sigh, touch my normal-looking brown hair. Up here, dry, it's not the cool, wet, twisting mass it became when I'd been sprayed with the mist. Now I'm afraid all the time.

And atop that crippling fear is guilt; guilt for lying to Una. She's my Captain, but over these last few months she's become my friend. Giving a snot-nosed sprite like me a chance when I really had nothing of value to offer her. Not telling her is a physical ache, one I feel every time we share a flask of rum, or work side by side to plan the next move. Guilt for forcing Octavia to bear my sin along with me. I'd searched for signs that her puzzling partner knew of my oddness, but by some god above, she doesn't seem to have told him. Octavia is an honest-to-goodness kind person, a rarity in this type of life.

While Una's kindness is hidden, and only shows itself around those she deems worthy of her trust, Octavia's is freely given, to anyone who may need it, wherever they may need it, for however long they may need her. It's pure, with no hidden motives or darkness. A true friend.

A sudden strike to the top of my head has me jerking up; a bread roll from the inn on Sainte Marie tumbles down and across the floor until the side of the nest forces it to stop. What the blazes?

I touch the secure knot at the nape of my neck and pull myself to my knees. I crawl to the side of the crow's nest and, with a quick inhale, peer out. In the name of all that is holy and pure! Long legs dangling, gray scarf whipping in the wind, hanging from the ladder rigged to the side of the nest, is Solomon.

My stomach lurches so hard I'm afraid I'll up-chuck. My heart hammers hard against my ribs like a jack rabbit. For a moment, I'm tempted to scurry back to the far side and pretend I haven't seen him visibly struggling in the rigging.

"Ahoy, Atropous! I could use your assistance! My hold seems to be slipping!" He throws me a sheepish, embarrassed grin and I feel my resolve to ignore him dissolve. I reach over and grab a handful of his cotton shirt, and with a heave, pull the lad into the nest with me. It's crowded; after some twisting and adjusting, we end up sitting cross-legged facing one another, knees touching.

His alert, hazel gaze flicks over my face and chest, like he's checking me over for some sign of injury.

I clear my throat, feeling flustered under his inspection. "Does the Captain need me for somethin'?"

Solomon shakes his head and picks up the discarded bread roll he'd launched at my head. He smiles, offering it to me. "You skipped breakfast this morning. You shouldn't. The fresh food won't stay that way for long. Eat while it's not hard or perished."

I return his smile, taking the offered food, the kind act warming some of the frost from my bones. I take a large bite and succumb to its delicious softness. My stomach rumbles loudly, yelling at me for denying it sustenance.

Solomon laughs. "Why did you skip? You're obviously hungry."

I quickly finish the fist-sized roll and sigh. "Not feeling too good. Must be adjusting back to my sea legs."

Solomon's eyes widen; huge, worried things that make the skin around them draw tight. "Do you ache? Gums bleed? Has your hair begun to fall out?" He suddenly reaches out and snatches my bandanna from my head to better inspect me.

I grab for my hair, hands moving before my mind has completely formed the thought. "No, nothin' like that, I'm sure it's just the thrill of the raid wearing off. It was my first one."

The worry in his eyes melts away, replaced by a blazing inferno of excitement, a new kind of mirth in his gaze. Jealousy burns in me at the obvious hoot he had during it. My experience had been diluted by my gnawing fear, afraid the sky would open and share my secret with them all.

The Revenge suddenly jostles us from side to side, possibly passing over a berm or reef. Solomon laughs joyfully and raises one of his arms, shielding his face from a spray of water her hull has stirred up.

Water.

I look down and see spots dotting my dry clothes. No, no, no. Hair, be good, *please* be good.

I see Solomon's joy shift into shock, just as that cool, prickling sensation covers my head completely. Then his shock turns to wonder, and he leans forward, eyes glued to the crashing currents about my shoulders. I expect the lad to shoot to his feet, scream about devils or, at the very least, go to the Captain. But he does none of that.

He leans even closer, cupping a hand over his mouth, eyes darting everywhere like he's afraid someone is spying on us. "Are you a mermaid?"

"No!" The word tumbles from me, then I lower my voice. "I mean, I don't think so? I– I'm really not sure." Blast, I sound like a raving loon.

Solomon leans back, folding his hands in his lap. "You don't know? Would you like to explain?"

His reaction, like Octavia's, completely baffles me. But, never one to take kindness for granted, I decide to tell him. What choice do I have with my hair a topsy turvy disaster? "It never happened before, not until we found Elisha. Octavia saw me the first time it happened. It seems to happen when I get wet. Last time it lasted only a few moments until returning to normal."

Solomon stares on, no disgust on his face, just open curiosity. How strange. "So Octavia knows?"

I nod, bringing a hand up to my hair again. The chaotic swell of it reaches out for the fingers on my hand, and I delve them into the coolness, the familiarity of it surprising me, despite it being so unknown.

"Does that mean Aurelius knows as well?"

I shake my head, then shrug. "I don't think he does, but those two are an odd pair."

Solomon continues to stare, his hand slipping from his mouth to cup his chin, something he does when he's thinking very hard. "It may well be they're stranger than you."

I throw the strategist of questioning look. What is *that* supposed to mean?

He drops his hand and smiles at me. "So, you are going to join us for supper, yes?"

I stare at him. Does he have wax in his ears? Has he not heard anything I've said? "You... you're not going to tell Octavia that you know? Or go to the Captain?"

Solomon shakes his head. "I understand you've been hiding away from us and why it's not my business to be talking to any of them about this, whether they already know or not. It's a hard tale to tell when you don't have all the pieces yourself. But you can't let the fear of being caught stop you from fully living your life." He grins. "If I'd let my fear control me, I'd be a slave in some faraway place, or dead from starvation. Sometimes you have to ignore those fears. They may never come to pass, any who." Solomon claps me on the shoulder, that warm grin turning brighter than the sun itself. "Live your days like each new one is a grand adventure! Dive into it unafraid of what may happen." That grip on my shoulder tightens. "And know, if that time may come, you have my vote."

I swallow and fight back the sudden sting of tears. "So... supper?"

He clamps his hand on my other shoulder and that look of glee returns. "Yes! I hear from the cook; we're cracking open the cask of brandy."

***

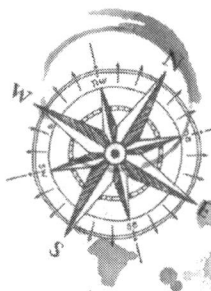

Chapter 27: Solomon
3 August 1691
Somewhere in the Indian Ocean

I clean my hands on the thighs of my trousers. A crushing heaviness settles in my stomach, like someone's dropped a heavy stone in it, a feeling that follows me as I exit the galley. The raid's thrilling energy is long spent now, with only a faint ghost remaining of the buzz that had sailed its way through my veins and left my mind reeling. I can't ever remember feeling that feeling before, the feeling of life rejuvenated… I'd never seen Selina looking so radiant, either.

Heat quickly fills my cheeks as I remember her glowing amber eyes, her untroubled, jovial smile, her laughter sudden and sharp like a raven cawing, so lighthearted. All that good, raised spirit had run through the crew for nearly a fortnight. Morale at an all-time high, food and rum freely given and often, surprisingly, shared by the most unlikely companions.

As promised, I've not told Octavia that I know of Atropous's 'condition', nor that I know she herself knows. Whenever there's the threat of rain on the horizon, he's come to me with a near crazed look in his large green eyes, a nervous twitch to his lean shoulders, his bandanna tight on his head. On those days he said he could feel the water in the clouds, said it would rain and that he needed to stay below deck. I always took the wheel those times or took his lookout post. I've learnt quickly not to doubt his new-found ability; it's yet to fail us.

But then food began to perish, and the fresh water began to stagnate. The fresh vegetables Caleb had commandeered were the first to fester and mold, and this caused the rats on board to breed almost out of control.

Illness began after that. Fevers were shared by at least seven of the crew that then progressed to vomiting. Among the sick, Octavia. She'd been spending less and less time among the waking world and a lot more time resting. Aurelius had begun taking her rations back to their shared bunk. I've not seen the Indian woman at all now in nearly four days, nor would Aurelius allow her to be moved to where the other sick people are.

Jonah, too, has fallen sick. It began with a headache that quickly moved to full body shakes two day ago, the strong, proud man reduced to a pale shivering sweaty mess.

I clasp my hands together in front of me, offering a quick prayer to the beyond. Please. Please let them all survive. If they can all just make it to Port Royal, there surely must be a doctor there that can help us… I follow the dimly lit corridor into the forecastle, the oil lamps turned low here because the light hurts the eyes of the sick. The small flames cast dancing shadows along the wooden walls.

There's dried blood caked under and around my fingernails; the goat Aurelius had so gallantly taken during the raid has finally met its end. Its meat will be put to good use. I'm almost at the stairs that would take me above deck when I hear Ambrose's quiet voice from within his bunk. Usually so carefree and jolly, now his voice is low and quivers with emotion. I pause at the foot of the stairs. I don't need to see Ambrose's face to feel his grief echo darkly in my heart.

"Ya can't go and die on me, you big gowk. You said we'd do this together…"

A loud clanging follows his words, like a metal tray clattering to the wooden floor, and I fear he's lost his senses, is flinging things around his bunk. I know he's upset but I can't help pushing into his bunk. The sight that greets me stuns me to a stop. What in the name of sweet Jesus is Ambrose thinking?! Jonah is in here with him, laid on his own cot, unconscious and stripped to his waist, doused in sweat. Ambrose is beside him on hands and knees, one hand resting on an upturned metal bowl, the water it had obviously held now spilt across the floor. Fear and angry grief twist his boyish face.

Harsh words of discipline well up in my throat; I'm fully ready to use my rank against Ambrose if that will protect him and the rest of the crew. All ill crew members have been, at Captain's orders, moved to quarantine in the bottom of the hull, as far away from the well people as possible. But the words die on my lips as I take in the scene. My concern deepens when Ambrose doesn't lift his head,

211

doesn't even acknowledge my entrance. He's so lost in his thoughts and worry that I'm a phantom to him.

I clear my throat gently. "Ambrose? Are you okay? Are you hurt?"

His head whips up to me and, startled, he blurts something that sounds like "*Eessa Creest!*" in what I know is his mother-tongue, some form of Gaelic. He grabs the metal bowl up to his chest, his pale green eyes and freckled cheeks pale with the fear that surges over his face, fear I know very well. "Jesus Christ, Solomon." With a few fast blinks, he's quickly corrected himself to English, though still with his sing-song accent. "I mean, uh, good evening. Didn't hear you approach. No, I'm not injured…" He picks up a small cloth sitting beside the cot and begins to hastily clean up the spilled water, deliberately avoiding my eyes.

I can't be angry with him. I can only find concern in my heart. I spare a glance at Jonah, who groans faintly. His usually neat dark hair is splayed messily over what looks to be Ambrose's bright green brocade coat. His chest rises and falls too fast and loud, like it pains him. The imposing man is now barely more intimidating than Felix, and somehow just as fragile looking. It unnerves and deeply troubles me that someone as seemingly untouchable as Jonah can be brought down like this.

Ambrose sits up and settles cross-legged beside Jonah, his eyes not leaving his bed-ridden friend, and I shift uncomfortably from foot to foot, feeling that I'm imposing on a private moment. "Is… he doing okay? Are you certain he should be in here?"

The edge of the cot comes just above Ambrose's chin; he looks like a child huddled beside it. His eyes flick to me for only a breath, before moving back to Jonah as he begins unwinding a knotted red bandanna from his upper arm. "I carried him here on my back last eve when everyone was too busy in their duties to notice. He couldn't bear to stay down there with the others, it reminded him of our Navy days." With the cloth now free of his arm, he dutifully mops the sweat on Jonah's head, heaving a soft sigh from somewhere deep in his worry-darkened soul. "Here will be better for him. He… I need him to be in here with me. I'm being careful as I can. Swear not to tell Captain, and I'll buy you whatever your heart desires when we port, cross my heart." His attention finally turns fully to me and he throws me his best and widest grin, as full of charm as it ever is when Jonah is awake and well. It's forced, though, I can tell, tainted from the shadow of darkness that lies in his soul.

I won't tell Captain. How can I? Another secret I will bear for a hurting friend... I hold onto that thought as I nod, steadying my will. "I won't. You have my word. If this is what Jonah needs to feel better, then I won't interfere. But what about your health?"

His grin is huge, and a ghost of his usual self shows through. For a moment, I'm sure he's going to smother me in one of his exuberant embraces, but he only readjusts himself on the hard floor, and looks back to Jonah. "I don't owe him anymore, but I do, ya know? I was just *Cairbre* when I was brought to him. Now, I'm more than I could've ever been on my own."

'Owe him'? 'Brought to him'? Was Ambrose some kind of servant? And what was a *'Cairbre'*? I open my mouth to ask, but a weak cough has my mouth snapping closed as fast as it had opened. Ambrose nearly jumps from the ground, his hand and the red bandanna falling from Jonah's face.

"You telling that old tale again, Am? Making me sound like a Saint. You always were one for flattery." Jonah's hoarse string of words has him coughing again, body trying to fold up around the hurt of it. Ambrose's focus is fully on Jonah again, hands on his shoulders as Jonah coughs. I suppose I shall have to learn about my crew mate later.

"You clod." Ambrose is trying to help him to lay back on the sweat-sodden cot. "It's 'bout time you decided to open your lazy eyes. Only been asleep half the day." The jibe is said with no real malice, as relief blooms on his face, his hand clenching the red bandanna tightly.

Jonah laughs weakly, a glimmer of his old lively humor in his tired, slightly unfocused eyes. "This sort of beauty takes a strict routine, and any routine worth its salt starts with rest, and lots of it. Look at me. Am I not the very picture of beauty right now? Do the results not speak for themselves?"

Thank goodness Ambrose laughs first, because mine comes barreling out in a surprised guffaw that might otherwise have seemed ill-timed. The three of us laugh. Jonah coughs again, but it's not as pained as the first. I'd blame the yellow fever, but he's just the same on his best days.

I relish in this light warmheartedness amongst all the sickness and gloom that's weighed so heavily on us all these last days. I let it fill my weary limbs with a renewed strength and hope. We're still chuckling when a stampede of boots rush past the bunk, with a loud clamor of jumbled voices raised in alarm.

I share a look with a worried Ambrose. "I'll go see what's happening, keep tending to Jonah."

He nods and I turn, exiting the small bunk. I'm instantly met with a human wall of resistance. Half the crew stands huddled in the hallway, shoulder to shoulder, muttering so low I can't pick out their words, more like the buzz of insects. What *is* going on?

I try to shoulder my way through the pack of men, but can't, as cold tendrils of dread begin to writhe in my stomach. Suddenly the men part in front of me, backs to the wall, all falling silent, and I see Caleb. His cruel smirk gone, replaced with an expression so unusual for him that it takes me a moment to place – lost. He looks lost. His jaw is clenched. His eyes, so often filled with anger, are sad as he stares down at a small bundle covered with a blanket in his arms.

No…

Caleb walks the corridor solemnly. He passes by me, does not look up, tucks a corner of the blanket more securely around the limp body in his arms, and his unexpected gentle show of care brings a sudden lump to my throat. He's at the foot of the stairs when small, hurried footfalls fill the silent hallway and Asa bursts around the far corner, tears tracking trails down his dirty, rounded cheeks. "He'll wake up! He will! Felix – he was just tired, Caleb! He… he was just tired…" Asa catches the tails of Caleb's sash in his small hands, and tugs. "Don't take him!"

Ambrose, drawn by the commotion, appears beside me, and his hand goes to my shoulder, gripping it. Caleb, a rude man, often cruel, a thug, a cheat at cards and a man who's made my life hell from the moment we met, turns to look down at Felix, and his face crumples. His eyes mist and his throat works to swallow his grief.

Octavia pushes her way through the gawking men. I'm shaken by the heavy circles beneath her dull brown eyes. Despite having been asleep more than awake these last weeks, she looks exhausted. Her tanned skin is washed out, hair brittle, limbs thin from the illness tearing her fragile body apart. She stumbles out of the crowd, dropping to her knees and taking Asa's hands from Caleb's sash. The boy turns his face, all saucer-eyes filled with tears and trembling lip, to her and she pulls him to her chest, hugging him tightly.

She's whispering something to him, trying to comfort him, no doubt. He buries his face into her neck, wailing, "I want to go with him! He's my friend… he… he's my friend…"

She peppers soft kisses along his brow as tears of her own fill her illness-dulled eyes, momentarily, with life.

Caleb's still hovering on the bottom step, holding Felix's lifeless body so tenderly to his chest. It surprises me that the brute's capable of such gentleness. Tears stream down his scarred cheeks, unbidden. "Ye can't follow where this one is headed lad…" Then he turns and climbs the stairs up to the main deck. Felix will get a burial fit for a buccaneer like himself. A burial at sea.

Asa sobs.

Aurelius appears beside his spouse and the bereft child, helps her to her feet and watches on silently as Octavia lifts Asa into her arms gently. He places a hand on the boy's head, and speaks his words for Asa alone, but I'm just close to them to catch it:

"You'll meet again, child. We will all see Felix again, one day." He protectively lays his arm around Octavia's shoulders as she hushes and soothes the boy, and they withdraw back to the privacy of their own bunk.

The rest of us stand silent, heads bowed in a shared moment of respect and grief for Felix. Silly little cheeky scamp. A smile whatever the time or the weather. None better with a clove hitch knot. That particular scrambling run he has whenever one of us calls on him. Had. Gone now.

Ambrose, beside me, sniffs and wipes his face, before slipping back into his bunk. I catch a quick glimpse of Jonah propped on his elbows in his cot, peering out at us as Ambrose gently closes the flap. The moment is shattered as Selina descends the steps in a brisk trot and pauses to stare at us all.

I suck in a gasp, dearly hoping no one notices. Her hood is lowered, the cloak whipping as the wind tugs at it. The sun behind her illuminates her willowy form, the tattoos on her pale skin seeming to radiate a light all their own. Her ringlets are tied back, displaying all the distinct angles of her cheeks and jaw. Her amber eyes pick me out of the crowd, hold my gaze a moment before she claps her hands. "We've all tasks to attend to. You know Captain's orders!"

The crew ripples and slowly, quietly, disperses – some to their bunks, others above deck, and some below to the orlop.

I wait until I'm sure only she and I remain before stepping closer to Selina. "You have vanquished me. I am an eternal prisoner to your ethereal beauty, Sel."

Selina's pale cheeks catch fire. "Well aren't you a sight for sore eyes. Thought I'd be stuck staring at Atropous all day."

I smile, her words warming the sadness and worry in me. She's like the first sunny day after the harsh winter frost, bathing me from head to boot in her all-consuming light.

Her warm, slender fingers slide between mine. "Are you well? You were fond of the lad were you not?"

The weight of my grief presses into me once more, trying to claw its way up my throat. I'd given him rum a few weeks back, after the raid, since we were all in such good spirits. Octavia had scolded me like I was a child, said Felix had to wait until he hit his fifteenth year to have rum. He'll never see his fifteenth year… I squeeze her hand, soaking up that silent comfort I've no right to bask in, letting her strength become mine for a moment longer. Then I release her hand. "'Tis the cycle of this life. As sad as it is, the boy was suffering. It's better this way. Now his soul can be at peace."

Selina's usually hard-as-steel gaze softens as she looks at me, and it causes my stomach to tremble. Then she smiles a small secret smile, a smile she saves just for me, as she tugs me after her towards the deck. "Come on, flame of my heart. Let me show ya how to properly tie a double hitch knot."

***

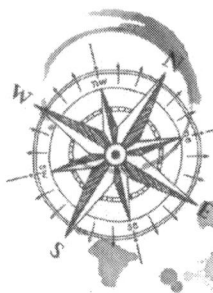

Chapter 28: Hanna
10 August 1691
Somewhere in the Indian Ocean

I clench my trousers as I hunch over my knees, unsure if I'm going to lose my first meal or faint. The latter sounds much more appealing right now. My stomach tosses and turns like the ocean outside the ship's hull and bile rises to the back of my throat, causing a sharp sting behind my eyes and a wretched taste on my tongue. My stomach gives another violent shudder. My guts feel as though they're trying to strangle themselves.

Close proximity to Una no longer seems to satisfy the bond's pull or dampen the lightning strikes of pain that make me want to tear my skin off every moment of the day. The body-numbing, logic-defying exhaustion has grown more persistent in the last few days. It's had me nearly wishing for Lady Death's seductive lull to consume me while I slept. The energy-zapping bond and the grief at young Felix's passing tightens the knot in my stomach.

The strain of Felix's death on sweet Asa has been hard to witness. The boy had begun to come into his own skin since joining Una's crew and coming under my care. He was witty, cheerful, always knowing what to do or say to brighten my day. Now, it seems I'm the one trying to get the lad to run a rig and play a caper with Demetrius and me. The boy has been so sad. He had seemed to perk up a touch over the last day or so, so I'm hopeful he'll be back to his cheerful, sweet self soon.

I finally gain control of my twisting gut and straighten, but when I do, my blasted sash comes loose, slipping down my narrow hips again. I've lost weight and keeping my sash tied tightly isn't something magic can fix. I try, and fail, to tie the knot again, my fingers refusing to quit their frustrating trembling. Fed up, I tear the cursed sash from my hips with a growl, and my weapons crash to the floor with nothing to secure them. The sound of metal clanging to the floor makes my fragile head pound. I gasp out loud and grip my throbbing temples, still holding the sash tightly.

"Do you require assistance, Octavia?" Demetrius's disguised, worried voice sounds through the false door and I lower my hands, blinking away the black spots that threaten to overtake my vision.

Feeling utterly defeated, I sigh loudly. "Please, that would be very helpful…"

Demetrius wastes no time in coming to my aid. He's disguised as Aurelius but the crease between his brows shifts his face into a familiar Deme-like expression. He doesn't utter a word, but casts me a smile before retrieving my fallen weapons. He places them on my small cot before turning to me. Those dark, infinite eyes look me over and, for a moment, it's like he's looking through me instead of at me. A chill races up my spine, followed with gooseflesh. He holds out a bronzed hand, wiggling thick fingers for me to pass him the sash now hanging limp in my grasp. I hand it over without protest. He takes it and shakes it out by his side in a dramatic flourish before looping it around my hips.

"How are you feeling, Guppy?" His voice is gentle, a tone I remember from when he first brought me to the cabin he had built by the sea, the first time he coaxed me into the ocean, the first time he encouraged me to swim alone. One full of familiarity, warmth, comfort. A tone that subdues the gnawing fear, makes me feel like I could achieve anything, do anything, be anything. He's so kind to me. Guilt at keeping secrets from him, of Atropous's discoveries, suddenly consumes me.

I swallow. "The bond is just being troublesome again. I'm sure it'll pass." He finishes tying the sash, straightening it a bit before ruffling my hair gently. He scoops up the weapons from the cot, then offers them to me with a soft smile. I shake my head, taking a step back. "Hold onto them for me. I'd just end up doing more damage than good with them at this point."

His smile slips as he thinks about it. I can almost see that strange, complicated, brain of his working out the pros and cons of him keeping hold of my weapons. After what feels like an eternity, he finally nods, tucking them into the belt under his cloak. Then his smile brightens again. "How about a turn about the deck? Some sea air will do you good."

At his words I can nearly taste the salty air, feel the cool water against my constantly hot skin. The sea's siren song, always a dull whisper in the back of my brain, is now a seductive, deadly croon. The itch, transformed into a searing pain, has tremors knocking my knees together. Cool fingers pull me from my dark thoughts. Demetrius pushes my sweaty hair from my eyes, cupping my feverish cheek gently in his palm.

"Just a pass or two? Asa's round is now. I'm sure he'd enjoy seeing you up and about." His gaze pleads with me, and squeezes my cheek, a slight pout twisting his thin lips.

I roll my eyes. "Let's just take it slow. I don't think my body can handle any more excitement."

***

Asa presses a wet kiss to my cheek before scampering off, nearly tripping over his bucket and scrub brush. I laugh as I climb to my feet, every bone in my body groaning as I straighten. I move slowly, trying to be careful with my tender body, and spy Deme trying to barter a swatch of green cloth from a slowly recovering Jonah, whose movements are still sloppy and slow from the illness that even now tries to take him from us. My guardian intends to craft the green cloth into a new bandanna, since his own is beginning to fray around the edges.

I chuckle at them wearily and lean my elbows on the cold railings of *The Revenge*, peering over at her hull disappearing below the waves. I close my eyes, inhaling the air deeply. It momentarily lights my heavy limbs with energy, but unfortunately that surge quickly passes, and I'm left feeling wobbly.

"SAIL, HO!" Atropous's shout of warning reaches my ears too late. I'm knocked hard against the railing as something large slams into the side of the ship, making the vessel shake violently.

I grab the railing, as my vision swims. I clench my eyes closed to try and clear them, my knees buckling dangerously as a wave of nausea rocks me to my core.

Another terrifying jolt against the ship, there's a tremendous sound like trees falling, cracking, around me, and a strange weightless feeling enters my stomach, causing it to flutter and roll oddly.

I pry my eyes open, blinking hard against my spinning vision, and am confronted with a view of the side *The Revenge* as it sails past me – no, as I sail past it. There's a hole in her hull, belching smoke and flames. I reach desperately for the Jacob's ladder dangling over the side of the ship. It's rough in my palms, slides through my hand, leaving friction burns. I hold tighter, but the rope bites into my skin. I'm too heavy. I'm too tired to hold myself up. I'm trying, I'm holding on with both hands now, willing myself to climb, to swing, anything… but the burn in my hands travels to my arms and I can't… it's too much. I do the only thing that's left to do. I let go.

I close my eyes again and manage to count to three before I'm hitting the icy, thrashing waters. It swallows me quickly, my impact sending painful jarring needles through my skin. The relief, the rush of energy and healing that normally accompanies my transformations is absent, only the pain and the cold as my legs are forced to fuse. My body buzzes, my senses in overdrive. My blood is rushing through my veins, pounding like a drum in my ears. As the water bubbles and thrashes above me, as the ship groans and heaves beside me, I let myself sink lower, staring into calm, deep infinity.

Once Deme had taught me to control my fin, we'd gone on long swims, testing my half-ling limits. We quickly discovered I had enhanced vision. No matter the depth of water, it was like I was standing in the sun, my sight even clearer than on land. The ocean had always felt like a friend, a home. I let it welcome me back. I drift. I unfurl. I…

The seriousness of what had just happened slams into me with a jolt. The ship's been hit! The ship's hit and I've fallen overboard and now I'm transformed! Poseidon's sacred trident!

And I know I should be focused on the ship. The fear that there are people hurt, dead, yes - it does register, but somewhere in the murky depth of my brain behind my panic and the shame that's suddenly flared brightly. I've transformed in front of them. This is somehow worse than allowing myself to consider what that hole in the hull might mean. This is worse than a kraken or scylla attack, worse than having to kill Kai. What happened nearly thirteen years ago is happening all over again, but this time far, far worse.

The sound of something – someone – plunging into the water above me has me whirling around; blond hair so pale it looks white, wide stormy eyes that quickly cycle through a range of emotions. I feel them in my chest like they're my own; swirling, thrashing like the water, they threaten to overwhelm me. She's afraid, angry, relieved, other things too vague to grasp fully.

Heat rises to my cheeks as her eyes dart all over me, her brow drawing downward as she mentally pieces it all together. Little things that hadn't connected fully before, did not make sense to her, begin to; things I can't hide about myself, not from her.

I clench my jaw. Shite, this is bad.

She rolls her eyes, glancing at the ship's hull moving away from us despite its 'injury', an annoyed look crossing her face. *Shite is an understatement. They put a cannonball through my Revenge. Bastard buccaneers owe me blood. To really make things worse, that confusing half-ling is here with her meddling gill-fish. How could I have been so damn blind? It was right in front of me the entire time! Damn siren call is what it is!*

Her thoughts ring in my head as loud and as clear as if she had said them out loud, as if they are my own.

She snaps her head round to look at me, her eyes huge, the pupils so blown I can't see the color in them. She reaches out to me, like she wants to touch me. *Hanna?*

I raise a hand, giving an odd greeting. *Una… it's been some time since we've got to speak face to face.*

She nearly flips head-over-feet in surprise, one hand gripping the side of her head, before quickly grasping her throat, her eyes are wild. *Am I breathing underwater?! Are you in my head right now?! Did I just… hear your thoughts?!*

222

My head spins from her frayed emotions and mine. I momentarily curse my mother for leaving me before she instilled some sense of what the bond could actually do. *It seems so.*

A steely resolve enters my chest at the same time I see it enter those cerulean eyes, and for a minute I'm certain she is going to try and fight me underwater. But then her loud words echo in my skull. *You.* She points at me. *Me.* She then points to herself, jabbing her thumb into her chest. Then she aggressively points above her. Without another thought, or waiting for me to respond, she begins to swim towards the surface, her strokes and kicks strong and sure.

My heart pounds as I watch her retreating form, the panic swirling in my veins nearly cripples me. I wait a moment before swimming after her, catching up after just two beats of my tail fin. I let her surface first.

I surface to the smell of smoke and gunpowder, not unlike the scene I'd awoken to that very first morning I found Una half dead in the sea beyond my cabin. The broadside of the ship is a cavernous gaping hole. Thankfully, the cannonball that tore into the ship has missed the cannon we have; I can see its muzzle poking out of its porthole, so we're not completely defenseless. But the cannonball has sparked the gunpowder stored in the hull and a bright blazing wall of flame licks the ship's walls, beginning to consume the wood. The enormity of what this all means only now hits me. *The Revenge* is going to sink.

Una's turned toward the horizon, drenched clothes clinging to her upper body, hair plastered to her head. I follow her gaze, and the sight pulls a gasp from me. A two-masted schooner is racing toward us with ease. Una's emotions swirl through my odd tether to her; shock, fear, the wisps of anger that are quickly rising to smother the weaker emotions.

Shouts from the ship draw our attention. Someone has thrown the Jacob's ladder down. Arms are waving to us. Listing though she is, *The Revenge* was sailing fast with the wind when she was hit and has sailed on past us. We'll have to swim to catch her. I can get us there in two pulses of my tail fin, but will Una let me carry her? I look at her sheepishly, but find she's already lifting her arms out of the water, annoyed, to grip my shoulders.

Fine. Just go. Her soft, fleeting thoughts are sad and angry all at once. It twists my gut. But I go. I propel us back alongside the ship, and she grabs the end of the ladder.

"Can you climb?" she asks.

Her words have mine stuck in my throat a moment. Her stare is more intense, more all-consuming than Demetrius's has ever been. My cheeks fill with fire. I'm honestly not sure if I can or not. But though she asked, her face shows she won't accept dispute. I'll climb whether I feel strong enough to or not. "Yes."

She hauls herself up, and I wait until she's a few rungs up before I reach as high as I can and take a hold of the rope. My palms still sting with the rope burns I'd gained trying to hold on when I fell overboard, but now, with a deep breath and a surge of my last reserves of strength, I pull all of my body, tail and all, from the water. The change is, thankfully, over in an instant, my mind too much of a whirlwind to focus on the shift of bones, and soon the wind is whipping against my bare legs. Gritting my teeth, I place both my feet on the rung. I let them support my weight a blessed moment before I follow Una up the short ladder, my eyes glued to the slowly burning ship as I climb.

My arms feel limp by the time she swings her legs over the railing and disappears as she re-boards the ship. I'm afraid my strength is going to give out, and I'm going to fall back into the waters of the ocean, when Selina's face pops over the side, her amber eyes wide, her jaw tense. Then I see who's beside her, hair no longer as blonde as wheat stalks, nor eyes of bottomless ink. Instead, dark haired and emerald eyed, Demetrius stares back at me, obvious shock and concern etched into his every feature. He and Selina each grab an arm and pull me onto the deck. I shiver, painfully aware of my nakedness, as a gust of wind whips my long, dark hair around my face, obscuring my vision. A heavy cloak is suddenly draped over my shoulders.

Demetrius's warm, stubbled cheek presses against mine. "Your transformation completely shattered my spell. There's no going back now, little Guppy."

I scrape my hair back and force myself to look up as Solomon runs to Selina's side, his hazel eyes wide. He looks at me only a moment before seeking her out again. "Selina, you saw the fin, did you not?! She – she's a mermaid!"

Though people are running, shouting, dealing with the wreckage and aftermath of the cannonball, a fair few stop and stare at his words. A small crowd gathers. Asa, little Asa, looks terrified of me. My heart pounds, head swims, I'm sure I'm about to faint, when a sharp crack draws all eyes away from me and onto a steely-eyed Una. She tosses her still slightly smoking pistol to the deck; it skitters until it hits the side. Even drenched, droplets still sliding down her cheeks along the gentle curve of her throat, breathing ragged, she looks every bit as deadly a Captain as she ever has.

"Atropous, get your lazy arse outta the nest. This," she gestures with an angry sweeping hand in mine and Demetrius's direction, "will be decided later with a vote. For now, I need that ship, because some bastards' put a hole in this one. Get me a new ship. Take whatever you find." Her frigid eyes, that had slowly begun to warm over the course of this journey, freeze over once again. "No prey, no pay, lads."

***

225

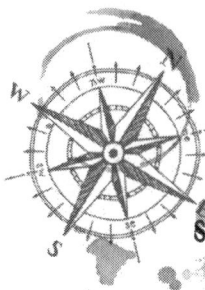

Chapter 29: Una
10 August 1691
Somewhere in the Indian Ocean

Infuriating pain-in-my arse half-ling… meddling nymph… this entire situation has gotten out of hand. I'm losing control of my crew. My ship is sinking. I've lost at least two deckhands in the blast. Several are wounded from the shrapnel. Caleb's got blood trickling down his forehead but he'll live. One of the hands has a shard of oak as long as my palm sticking out of his shoulder. Someone'll have to tend it later, else it'll go septic. Chaos swirls around me, and yet I can't take my eyes off her.

Hanna grips Demetrius's shoulder with one hand as she struggles to pull up the spare pantaloons the gill-fish had run to fetch before we'd climbed out of the sea. My gut never fails me, it *knew* something was amiss the moment the strange pair walked into that blasted tavern. *"Until then, Una."* The first mistake she'd made; the only one I should have needed, to see through the bizarre magic. They may have looked different, may have altered their behavior, but it was there, as clear as every cloud in the sky.

The moment Octavia fell overboard, the Aurelius's magic *thing* had broken and Demetrius just as I remembered, stood next to a rightfully shocked Jonah managing to look sheepish with his vividly green eyes. The pieces had begun to fit themselves into their rightful places, then the feeling of utter betrayal had hit me full force. And yet, despite the fresh sting of it, I'd jumped overboard, plunging into the icy waters intent on saving the deceitful half-ling. I hadn't thought about the consequences of me abandoning my ship and crew to save one hand. I hadn't thought of my single-minded goal of revenge. I acted without thought or reason. Something I haven't done since I was a child.

Despite the betrayal burning my veins to ash and the dark hollows beneath her startling lilac eyes, my heart soared upon seeing her, seeing the *true* her. The itch to close the short distance between us and trace those bruise-like shadows nearly blots out all reason. Hearing her voice after so long is like the first breath of sea air after being on land for far too long, and having her so near, nearly has me forgetting the approaching vessel. Tack on breathing underwater and whatever mental link this is with the half-ling and my sense of this world and what it may hold is severely off kilter.

Thankfully, my will to live above all else swells, another thing I can silently thank Pa for instilling in me at a young age. I tear my eyes from Hanna and to the schooner, out of my complicated thoughts and back to something I'm sure about. The ship is on the chase, its narrower hull making it superior in speed to *The Revenge*. Its smaller size means less space for crew, booty, and weapons, but after the yellow fever and the cannon blast, there's fewer of us, anyways It'll have to do. My ship is groaning and protesting already. The ship shudders and I can feel the heat building from below. Won't be long before the flames and the ocean claim her entirely. My girl *The Revenge* is done for. If we don't take the schooner, we shall be too. The decks of my new ship will run red with their blood. Only giving one warning shot across our bow with no chance for a surrender? Barely time to spit before they follow it with a death knell? And when we have a yellow jack flying high, too? Desperate fools! Is there no law of the sea?!

I shake the sea water from my hair and turn toward my still-stunned crew. All remaining hands are above deck now, and there are fewer than I'd hoped. All eyes dart back and forth between Demetrius, Hanna and I, the thick unspoken tension hanging in the air, swirling with the dark, thickly billowing smoke. A funeral pyre made of my ship, my *second ship*, its life rising into the sky like that night Elyse betrayed me and Pa. My stomach clenches again as my mind tries to pull me back to that night when my entire life changed.

Their quiet shock, standing around like dullards, is what snaps me back here, to this moment. "Get the barnacles outta yer ears! Gather anything not already on fire that we'll transport over to my new ship. You take it with you, you hear? We've no time for dillydallying. Once over there, any of you lot see their Captain, give no quarter. He's dug his and his crew's graves. Quartermasters to me. If there are any injured that can bear arms, then do so. Any unable to bear arms, *The Revenge* will welcome your company at the bottom of the ocean."

A quake of thunder from above vibrates through the ship. It travels the length of my body, near the pit of my stomach. My crew moves to act on my orders, darting across deck and below to salvage what they can. I turn to address Atropous and find him not at my side. I see no hide nor hair of him on the main deck. I then look up and spy a shock of blue bandanna still in the crow's nest. He's not moved so much as a finger. Bloody sod.

"Atropous! Get your arse down here, I won't be asking you a third time!"

I watch with growing annoyance as Atropous swings his leg over the lip of the nest and onto the rope ladder at a snail's pace. I feel my eyelid twitch and I grip the cool, comforting hilt of my cutlass, trying to use its presence to quell the ever-growing fire in my veins. My head pounds in earnest now. I know I'm reaching my limit.

I feel torn, pulled in two different directions. Half of me, the logical part, the part that's kept me alive this long, feels the burn of Hanna's betrayal like a knife wound. It has me wanting to do what needs to be done, then leave, never to see her again, as was originally my plan. The other half, the side the half-ling seems to coax from some buried place in me, hopes, *begs* for there to be a reason behind all the secrets and lies. This is the part of me that thrills at the prospect of Hanna and Octavia being two sides of the same mysterious, intriguing doubloon. It makes my curiosity, the draw I'd felt to the Indian girl almost right away, make more sense. That side of me wants to put everything out of my mind, never mind the ship and the crew, and speak to Hanna, hear her voice, touch her skin. Both sides fight aggressively until my brain feels like soup and I'm even more unsure than before. Since I can't seem to make up my mind, I'll just do what I'm good at. I risk a peek at Hanna and find her busy looping her espada and the gun I had given her from Enoch's useless corpse through the sash around her waist.

"Did you want to sell the gun? I can send it ahead with Felix?"

"I'll keep it."

I want to throw myself over the side of *The Revenge* again, and this time not take the ladder back up. I really over thought this entire thing. Elyse would be laughing her guts up right now if she could see me... Where in Seven Hells is Atropous? The lad is trying my patience. I look back toward the crow's nest only to find him hovering three rungs from the deck, eyeing me nervously. I place both my hands on my hips, grinding my teeth. "With a *purpose*, Atropous, if you will!"

That gets him moving, but not quickly enough, not like my ship is burning beneath our feet at this very moment and slowly, but surely, keeling as we watch. What has gotten into the lad? He finally touches down onto the deck, and turns, fingers winding tightly together in front of him as he looks over my shoulder to Demetrius and Hanna, then to Solomon, who stands close to Selina, his hazel gaze filled with unrest. I see that he's afraid, and though that needles me, I try to smooth out some of the sharp edges to my voice before I speak.

"Enough of this Atropous, if you freeze up out here, you die. You've raided before, you've been in a storm before. A fire and a busted hull are no less challenging. This is nothing you can't handle."

He huffs out a half-hearted laugh and begins to unknot the tie to the bandanna he's worn religiously for months now. "It's not the raid I'm concerned about, or the storm... or the fire..."

My hands drop from my hips, exasperated, watching him tug the blue cloth from his unruly locks. "That ship'll be upon us soon. We must board them before they try the same to us, or this one gives out beneath our feet. We've come too far together to die out here at sea."

He drops the bandanna to the wooden deck, his eyes trained on me with an almost apologetic look. Asa is running past with a bucket full of sloshing water, perhaps to throw upon the flames in our hull, for what little good that'll do, but Atropous steps suddenly into his path, causing the boy to trip. Atropous takes the small wooden bucket from the frowning boy, who scrambles back to his feet, unsure and afraid looking.

I frown, too. "Explain yourself, now."

Atropous answers me by raising the bucket above his head. "Please... don't hate me."

Then he's emptying the bucket over himself, soaking his long brown hair, making it a shade darker. The water droplets collect in his scraggly beard, trailing down his chest and soaking his shirt. Whatever words I might have said desert me as I watch his coveted hair begin to change. It morphs from normal human strands into a thrashing current of deep blues and sea greens. It's not hair anymore, but water. His head is crowned with water. It ripples, pulsates like it has a life force about his shoulders. The realization of where I've seen this kind of transformation before hits me like a lightning strike. No bloody way in Hades... two gill-fish on my ship?! *Two*?!

"Bloody hell!" It's Jonah, at my shoulder, startling me, and dropping his end of the chest he was carrying.

"Damn it, Jonah," Ambrose scolds him from the other side of the chest. "A little warnin' next time you– holy shite on a haystack!"

My two ex-Jollies have stumbled to a stop beside me, the large wooden box forgotten now between them, both their gazes wide as they take in Atropous's new appearance.

Jonah rubs his eyes with both his balled fists. "What in the Saint's holy arse cheeks are you, Art?!" His well-practiced and perfected act of covering up his plummy accent cracks completely. The color that had only just been starting to return after the yellow fever is stolen once again. Beside him, Ambrose just stares, pale green eyes huge.

The sky gives a monstrous growl above our heads and I feel a light drizzle of rain begin to fall. It's just one more thing. One more shiteing bloody thing to add to my pile of things I don't have time to deal with right now. Which, of course, makes me look at Hanna again.

Demetrius stands next to her, his hair nearly an exact copy of the one twisting about Atropous's head. Slight differences in the colors and tumbling currents mark them as individual and unique to the person.

230

"He is a half-ling of my kind, a water nymph," Demetrius tells me.

Asa falls to his arse then, and scuttles backwards on bum and hands until he knocks into another crewmate, his expressive brown eyes nearly taking up half his face as he stares up open mouthed at both Atropous and Demetrius. It's Jonah and Ambrose that make a noise first. Twin crows of surprise that start a swell of sounds from the gathered crew; gasps, swearing, shouts of shock ripple throughout my hands like a stone cast into the ocean.

Caleb's voice rises above them as he takes a step closer to me. "Three, Captain! Ye got three demons bunking up on the same ship as us normal folk!"

"Four." Selina's usually soft voice is like another cannon blast. It quickly silences the crowd. She lowers her hood.

A rushing feeling spreads throughout my body, filling my veins, making my blood feel cold. "Selina, what do you mean four?"

Selina's full lips quirk into an amused smile as she undoes the knot of her cloak, letting it flutter the deck about her feet as the ship gives another shudder and groan beneath us. "I'm sure you wondered how I found you that first night, Captain. I'm sure you didn't honestly believe the lie about me knowing you were a woman because of your gait. You walk more like a man than Jonah does."

No. No... it's not possible. Not more deceit. I can't handle it.

Selina snaps her fingers, and the change is immediate; it's like stepping onto a frozen puddle and watching it shatter into dozens of spider webs under your boot. Her seashell pink creamy skin cracks away in jagged chunks like a smashed china doll, the dark tattooed vines disappearing with it. The color underneath is a deeper, darker, warmer tone than Solomon's mellow ochre skin. She has Black skin with warm orange-red undertones, the black vines that crisscross over this new skin, her true skin, are no longer black, but a shimmery silver, like freshly smelted metal.

She shakes her shoulder length sable ringlets out, like she's flinging water from them, but instead, the hair shortens, coils into waves that stop at her chin. When it's fully changed, she wrestles it into a low ponytail with a length of string, a small poof at the base of her neck. The only thing that doesn't change about Selina is her height, her silhouette, and those vibrant, all-seeing amber eyes. Those eyes are framed by long, dark lashes in an oval face with a button nose, narrow chin, and full lips.

I close my eyes a moment, resisting every urge to run like hell in the other direction. I've had zero control of my crew from the get-go. Seems I was the idiot all along.

"Begorrah!" Ambrose mutters.

Jonah takes a defensive stance in front of him, both wide-eyed and gaping. Jonah has one hand on his weapon, the other tight around the younger lad's wrist, like he's ready to drag them both to safety if Selina so much as blinks at them in the wrong way. Can't say I blame him. I feel my legs tremble as I pull in an unsteady breath. Watching her emerge from within her magic shell has gooseflesh erupting all over my damn body.

Solomon is still close to Selina's side. He hasn't so much as twitched a step away from her. He seems frozen where he stands, both his tawny hands clasped over his mouth, those bright eyes opened as wide as they can go. He looks as if he's going to drop dead any moment. We've both ended up with egg on our face, lad. I welcome you officially to my crew. It comes with a nice tankard full of betrayal and heartache.

Caleb, blood dried on his face, the cut on his temple sticky and dark, draws Marigold in a wide arc, blade wobbling in his grasp as his fingers tremble. The fire in his brown eyes is completely snuffed out by fear. "Ye— yer a witch!"

Selina clucks her tongue folding those shimmering arms over her chest. "I am not a witch."

"What are you?" Hanna's hoarse whisper sounds behind me and it takes every bit of my self-control to not turn toward her voice. Not the false one she used under the guise of Octavia, but *hers*, slightly deeper than any other woman I've met, one that has my insides knotting around one another.

Caleb takes a step towards Selina, Marigold raised. "If not a witch, then what? A mermaid like Octavia or are ye like these water nymphs?"

232

Selina rolls her eyes skyward. "Neither. I'm a druid."

Jonah backs up, bumping into Ambrose, who now seems to be staring in awe. Jonah's hand clasps something at the base of his throat. Something I've never really paid much attention to. A small, glinting, silver cross. "How did ya do the thing with your skin?"

"An enchantment."

Caleb scoffs, his lips twitching in anger. "An enchantment! See, a witch!"

"I am *not* a witch." Selina's annoyed voice only makes the drum inside my skull beat louder and I'm rubbing at my head, closing my eyes against the wall of voices that have risen to join hers and Caleb's, all trying to speak over one another, each wanting to get a say in the matter.

The smoke is thickening. I can feel a lean in the ship now. I can hear, above the wind and the rumbles of thunder, and their shouting voices, the crackle of flames below us. I can feel heat gathering beneath the soles of my boots. God bless *The Revenge*, taking her sweet time to die. Giving me time enough to stand here watching my crew unravel.

"ENOUGH!" My voice sounds shrill and breathy even to my own ears. "Nothing changes. We're running out of time. We raid now, vote later. Who knows, maybe we'll get off light and your oddities may just shock our enemies straight to hell for us."

I see Atropous's shoulders drop, a smile starts to curve his lips. He snorts a laugh. Asa slowly rises to his feet, hesitantly looking less afraid.

Selina smirks, amber eyes glinting. "What's the plan, Captain?"

Despite everything, despite the licks of betrayal, longing, anger, fear all twisting themselves so tightly together it makes my head swim, somehow, despite the impossible, I laugh. ' We'll draw alongside them and tether ourselves. Board 'em. Go for their coxswain. We take control of the helm and we take control of the ship. Don't go easy on 'em but if any want to join us, let 'em surrender. We could do with a few more hands. Be sharp about it; we'll need to cut *The Revenge* loose before she drags the schooner down too. Ambrose, Jonah, make haste and arm your lads. Leave the cannon, I won't risk you getting caught down there in the flames. But muskets, pistols, grab any ammunition you can find, and start taking out their men at a distance. I know the gunpowder is precious, but so are… so are you…" I swallow my embarrassment; hope they don't notice my care for them. One look at Ambrose's raised eyebrows and Jonah's grin and I know they heard me. "Be off, you devils." I shoo them.

With an ease and precision I have to envy, the two ex-Jollies sweep into a practiced salute before turning on their tails and disappearing below deck, four other hands on their heels.

"Might I suggest a plan, Captain?" Demetrius is grinning and his emerald eyes are glowing with mischief that I find I hadn't missed in the slightest.

I fold my arms, holding his gaze. "What trick do you have up your sleeve?"

His grin widens. "I'd much rather show you, but I'll be needing young Atropous's aid."

Atropous stands wide-eyed, his cheeks flushing as the remaining eyes turn to him. "I– I'd like to help, but I don't see how I could be of any use to you, Mr. Demetrius. Sir."

Sir?! That flouncy shite-fer-brains is a mister now, is he? Sir, is it? I purse my lips, and Demetrius positively glows at Atropous's words. He's loving this. I can almost hear him calling the younger lad 'my dear boy'.

Demetrius cocks his head. "I felt your powers awaken on Sainte-Marie. You are a half-ling of my species. You're of more use than you think, my dear boy."

"HA!" The sound explodes out of me. I can't help it. Pompous windbag. But I'm the only one who laughed. At his side, Hanna clenches her espada until her knuckles turn white. Demetrius brushes some wet, stray hair from her face before turning to face the oncoming ship.

"Broadside correct, Urchin?"

I grind my jaw at his mocking tone. Curse him to Hades. Afraid opening my mouth would shatter what's left of my self-control, I give him a curt nod.

And then something in the belly of the ship explodes. It heaves up through the decks. Another barrel of gunpowder, somewhere in the hull. Poor girl. We stumble. The ship pitches noticeably. My mind goes instantly to the lads below deck gathering arms, and I lean down into the stairwell, where the smell of smoke is thick and choking.

"Jonah?!" I yell. "You alive down there?!"

A pause makes my chest tighten, but his voice comes back to me. "Aye, Cap'n. Alive. All's well. Can't say the same for your boat though." He appears momentarily at the foot of the steps, soot-and-sweat streaked, a rifle thrown over each shoulder, sacks of unexploded gunpowder and bullets around his neck, and waist, but grinning wildly.

"Loon," I mutter, but I'm relieved. "Mr. Demetrius," I know the mockery is dripping in my voice, and Demetrius knows it too, by the look he gives me, but I don't care, "I fear my boat isn't feeling well. Whatever you're to do, *get to it.*"

Demetrius shifts his gaze back to the sea and raises his arms high, palms to the sky. He's the very picture of calm. "Come, Atropous, copy my posture. Chest out and chin up so you can properly circulate your breathing and connect with your magical core."

With his brow furrowed, Atropous obeys, taking up the same posture as Demetrius. Both of them face the water.

"Close your eyes and breath slowly, in-and-out, in-and-out. Feel the air swirling in your lungs? It's natural, as is your connection to your magic."

Atropous's eyes slip closed, the sky gives another rumble, and the ship gives another loud groan in reply. I have to grip the railing to steady myself. He inhales slowly, the tension that had carved deep valleys on his face melting away. The rushing water about his shoulders calms to soft, gentle waves.

Demetrius smiles. "Good. Very good. Nymphs are nature, given life from her to protect her. Extend your essence into the water and it will come to your aid. Think of a wave. One large enough to interrupt and turn them side-on to us, but not to capsize them."

He better not sink my new ship, I haven't even gotten to name her yet... I'm about to voice my concerns at how little bloody time we have, and that no one seems to care in the slightest that *The Revenge* is still on fire and sinking right now, beneath us, when a wave begins to rise, taller than the others. It rises taller and taller still, crossing the small distance between us and the schooner and crashes gently into its hull, lifting and turning it. Atropous is sweating but delighted. Demetrius grins. The wave recedes back into the ocean, and the schooner is alongside us. I can see men over there scuttling away from the sides of the ship. If my brain wasn't completely mashed into oblivion, I might actually enjoy how easy they're making this for me.

"Can you hold that ship steady for us?" I ask Demetrius. He nods in response and I see the water swell around its hull like a hand gripping it. I turn my focus back to the crew still gathered "Prepare arms. Prepare to board. Retrieve the nine-hooks and ropes from the orlop, poste haste. Asa, go help them."

Asa salutes before scuttling after the men that peeled away to fetch what we need. I turn to Solomon, who's managed to lower his hands, though his mouth still hangs ajar as he continues to stare unblinking at Selina.

"Solomon, take the helm, get us as close as you're able. They'll be keen on trying to cut the ropes to our grapples, keep that from happening at all cost."

To his credit, he snaps to attention and salutes sloppily. "Captain!"

Solomon turns, about to move to the helm, when Selina calls out to him. "Wait, please Solomon!"

"Oh, for the love of Circe," I huff, throwing up my hands. "Ship's got a hole in it, got water coming in, fire in the hull, could all go up in a gunpowder fireball at any minute, but sure, take your moment." They both look at me, pleading. "Get on with it!" I flap my hands at them.

Selina offers me a small, grateful smile, then picks up her discarded cloak and removes her strange blade from her belt before offering them both to Solomon. She gives him a timid, careful smile, holding out her most sacred treasures to him. "Merry meet, Solomon?"

They hold each other's gazes and I find I'm holding my breath for what feels like an eternity – take the bloody things, you dolt! Take them! She's too good for a dunderhead like you if all you're going to do is stare at her. But… finally, he returns her timid smile with one of his own and I exhale, grinning. He nods and closes the small gap between them, accepting the offered items with a slight tremble to his hands. His fingers light on the back of her hand in a touch I pretend not to notice. He gives her one more nod before turning and striding to the helm on his long legs.

Caleb scoffs, looking Selina up and down, Marigold still tight in his grip, and I'm about ready to punch him off the deck – I might be scared of her, a bit, if I'm honest, but that doesn't mean I'll let Caleb bully her. She's been more of a reliable quartermaster than he – but he says, "Plan on scrappin' with yer bare hands? Or do you have another witch spell hiding up yer cloak?"

Selina smirks and unties a small gray pouch hanging from her belt. "I'll be finding my own way over to the other ship, Captain." She gives me a mock salute with two fingers, and I flap my hand lazily back at her, feigning indifference. She opens the pouch and dips her fingers inside, withdrawing them covered in what looks like ash. She traces along the metallic markings on both her arms, leaving ashy smears behind. Then she quickly reattaches the pouch to her belt and closes her eyes.

Caleb stares at her arms then at her face. "What spell is that?"

Selina raises one soot covered finger to her lips, and he goes to protest, but I whack him on the arm. Her silver vine tattoos begin to pulse.

"What the devil?" Before Caleb can say more, and I can hit him again, Selina begins to transform again, to shrink. The flickering of the markings quickens. I blink and squint against the brightness of it, and every time I open my eyes, Selina looks less human and more bird-like. I scrub desperately at my eyes, shaking my head quickly, sure that when I open them, Selina will be still standing there, calm and perfectly human. But when I crack one eye open, she's... she's a...

Asa almost collides with me as I lose my footing slightly on the listing deck. His eyes widen and he lets out an excited gasp, dropping the hooks and ropes he held to the deck. "What a pretty bird!"

Where Selina once stood, a small bird now sits, its green wings striped with patches of blue and yellow on the tips and bright yellow chest. It's not until the bird cocks its tiny head at me that I see Selina's intelligent amber eyes staring back at me. Girls turning into mermaids, men turning into water, sea monsters are real too. Why not have people turn into birds. Why the hell not?!

Selina spreads her wings and takes off towards the schooner that's fallen silent beside us. No more shots. No gunfire. Not a peep from them. Around me, men are throwing grappling hooks on ropes over to the other ship.

Caleb blinks at Hanna. "Can you turn into a bird too?"

Hanna's laugh is soft, the lightest sound I've ever heard. "Nothing so mesmerizing."

My heart seizes at Octavia's playful banter in Hanna's familiar voice. Then I wince, watching for any sign of being overheard by Hanna. Thank whatever entity above that I seem to be alone with my thoughts. I clear my throat, turning to face her, careful to keep my face blank. "You up for another adventure?"

She gives me a secret little half-smile and I try to ignore the way my stomach flutters when she says, "With you 'til my dying breath, Captain."

"You hold *The Revenge* steady, Solomon! And hold that schooner steady until we're all aboard, Demetrius!" I call. "Can you hear me, you gill-fish?"

One of his eyes pop open, an annoyed look crossing his face. "You need not shout. I can hear you perfectly well. Understood."

I grit my teeth against the retort I want to yell at him, as Asa hands me my own grappling hook. I take the heavy end with its iron hook and am swinging it round in my hand as I hear Demetrius tell Atropous to, "Take a break child, I can hold it alone. You'll need your strength for the battle ahead."

I release my hook, letting it sail upwards into the rigging of my own ship, yank on it, and loop the loose end around my fist. I glance at Atropous, who's dropped his hands limp to his side. He blinks slowly, a dazed look clouding his face, and I notice a soft glow emitting from eyes that fades as I look at him.

"My head spins," he mutters.

"You good?" I ask. His foggy gaze finds mine and he nods.

Jonah and Ambrose emerge back onto the sloping deck with their little gunners' crew, each of them armed to the teeth with anything they could find and easily carry. With two rifles a-piece and all the pistols they could shove into their belts, smeared in soot and sweat, grinning madly, the ex-Jollies look like some Naval nightmare. I can't help but laugh at them. They spy me standing on the railings and pump their guns at me. Across from us, on the other ship, their crew are shouting, running, a mess of disorganized, sloppy crewmanship, as Selina dives and swoops at them, pecking at exposed skin and eyes. They flail at her, frantically trying to arm themselves too, but I see mostly blades and few guns. I don't spy their Captain. He's either hiding amongst them or hiding below deck. A coward, either way.

"Steady now, lads," I say to my boys. "Take aim, and at your pleasure, FIRE!"

A cacophony of rifle and pistol shots fills the air as my men open fire on the ship that had dared to try and attack us. Ambrose, as head gunner with no cannon to fire, is shouting commands, firing and tossing his spent gun back at Jonah to refill, who tosses him a loaded one in return.

Beside us, Caleb lets his grapples fly, the three-pronged metal hooks sailing in a damn near perfect arc into the rigging of the other ship. With a grace that tells me this isn't his first go at this, he gives the rope a firm jerk, checking to make sure it's secure. He then has the gall to send me a dramatic wink and cheeky smile. "See ya on the other side, Urchin," before he hoists his body up onto the railing of *The Revenge* and leaps across.

I'll kill him... And I'll kill that damn gill-fish. I'll kill Caleb, then the nymph. Oh, even better, I'll get the nymph to kill that sack of useless meat and then I'll kill the troublesome stowaway afterwards.

In the midst of their volley of gunfire and smoke, as the gunners fire, and the others leap or swing themselves across, as we make good on our promise to board and take the ship for our own, I seek out Hanna. She stares up at me and I know the smoke and the wind are whipping at my hair and shirt, with my rope gripped in my hand. I know how I look, then. I look like a goddamned buccaneer. A dazzlingly rakish one, at that. I wrap the rope between my legs, give her my best, most dashing, smile, hoist myself up and launch myself in a hard swing over to the other ship.

Rushing wind stings my eyes, and my cheeks pull against my face so hard it feels like the skin is going to tear from my body. My stomach twists as I swing above their deck, above their heads, and see Caleb already engaged with several of them. Someone spots me and shouts of alarm sound from below. Then I let go of the rope and drop to their deck.

I stand quickly, spinning in place, draw my cutlass from my sash and come face-to-face with a grubby, unfamiliar buccaneer.

"A lass?" The dirty sack of skin and bones in soiled clothes advances on me, his cutlass poised to take my head. I block him, the sound of metal against metal filling my ears. The vibration of his sword connecting with mine makes my fingers tremble slightly.

"A lass that's going to kick yer arse!" I aim a kick at his shin and use his surprise to push back.

A loud screech has us looking up as a green blur streaks across the sky, digging talons into the man's face. Startled, he screams, dropping his cutlass in favor of flailing at the bird attached to his cheek. With him distracted, I kick his cutlass away from us, then kick his calf, sending him sprawling to the deck with a howl of pain.

"Should have had a better master." I tower over him as he flips over to gawk at me, the bird still hanging onto his cheek. "Number one rule, never turn your back on your opponent. No matter how small or nonthreatening they may seem." I thrust my cutlass into his chest, he screams, and Selina releases his cheek, landing beside me on the deck.

I place my booted foot on the man's shoulder and rip my cutlass free with a good yank. He's dead already. Wiping my blade on my thigh, I look at an already-transforming Selina, her pulsating light just as bright as before. I blink away the spots in my eyes and there Selina stands, God's work or the devils work, thank whatever it is out there that she's on my side.

"To your knees, Captain!" The seriousness in her voice has me instantly dropping to all fours, my forehead touching wood, as Selina flings a silver knife at some other assailant. I hear him scream and thud to the floor, and I climb to my feet. Her knife is embedded in his forehead and she's smirking. "Good reflexes, Sel!" I grin at her. "Where's this ship's Captain?"

Her amber eyes bore into me. "I circled the ship a few times, and saw their Captain run below deck. It's a small crew, smaller than ours even after the losses when their cannon hit us. They truly must be desperate fools."

"DEMONS!"

I whip around quickly, cutlass at the ready, and spy Caleb by the helm, Marigold tight in his grip. His sight isn't set on me, or even on the deck, but out at the sea, his eyes as large as saucers. I step closer to the railing, following Caleb's gaze, and nearly shite myself right here. Demetrius cradles Hanna to his chest as he hops from pillar to pillar of gushing seawater that rises up to meet his feet as he leaps around the schooner, Hanna taking crack shots at the would-be attacking pirates with Enoch's old pistol, her shooting arm braced across her other elbow. Behind them, on his own pillars of water, is Asa, desperately trying to stay upright whilst hurling random objects at our enemies. A candlestick, smaller items that from here I can't tell if they're rocks or lumps of stale bread.

Demetrius lands on the deck without a sound and sets Hanna down. Asa tumbles onto the deck behind them, winded but giggling. Demetrius grins at us. "Ahoy buckos! Glorious day for a sea raid!" He pulls his weapon from his sash with a flourish.

Caleb shakes his head, extending his hand out to haul another of our crew over from *The Revenge*. "Witches. I be bunking up with damned witches."

Demetrius and Selina snort in unison as Hanna helps Asa to his feet, cradling him gently into her bosom for a moment before patting him affectionately on the head. She takes a moment to reload the pistol then pulls her espada from her sash. Asa grins, and pulls his own short cutlass from his belt. Those dark bruises beneath her exotic lilac eyes have my stomach knotting tighter. Despite the determined look on her face, I don't miss the tremble in her hand, or the slight sway as she turns.

I swallow, pushing down all unnecessary thoughts and feelings, things that would get me killed. "Selina, Caleb, spread out and make sure any remaining hands are dealt with. If they attack, they perish. If they don't, round em' up and I'll decide what to do with 'em when I have a moment to think. Demetrius, Hanna, Asa, get the rest of our crew and begin pillaging, see what they have. The Captain is mine."

They all salute me, splitting to attend my orders. I turn back to *The Revenge* and see her keening sharply to one side now, straining the tethers that bind her to this schooner. Not for the first time since that lump of iron pierced her hull, I grieve her passing. She's been good to us.

"Jonah! Ambrose! Get your arses over here!" I yell, through smoke.

"Aye, Captain!" I don't see them, but I hear their calls.

Despite everything that's occurred, how things seemed to unravel for a moment there, they all still obey. I'm still their Captain. That'll do, for now. Alone now, and on a mission, I seek out and quickly descend the grimy steps down into the underbelly of the ship.

The overwhelming smell of human waste, musk and mold greets me, causing my eyes to water and my stomach to turn. Small, old, unkempt, and sputtering oil lamps dot the dark, dank space. What foul conditions to keep a ship! Does he have no honor at all?! It's silent down here compared to the gunfire, clashing of steel and shouting above. I make my way along a narrow hallway, cutlass tight in my hand, looking about and taking stock. About ten paces in, I see a small, wooden mallet, about half the length of my arm, and am immediately sucked back into a memory the moment I fully grasp its handle.

"It's not a sword, Una. Hold it more gently, like this!"

Demetrius teaching me to play pall-mall, chiding me for not holding the mallet correctly on a sun-drenched beach as Hanna laughs her silver bell laugh a million miles and a million suns from here. Me whapping the ball too high, him plucking it from the air.

The memory is so bright and warm, it seizes my body tightly, and it feels like someone holds my beating heart in their fist, squeezing it. I don't have time for such frivolous memories, nor the thoughts they conjure. Not when my heart, my entire damn soul, feels split in half.

A loud battle cry behind me has me sidestepping to the left and kicking my leg out like a donkey. I connect with something solid, and the assailant yelps. When, in all of history, has running up behind someone, while screaming, ever gone well? Had he hoped to confound and surprise me? Clod. Without hesitating, I grip the mallet tightly in my fist and bring it down hard onto the kneecap, grinning gleefully as the sound of bone snapping echoes in the small space and he sprawls to the floor. How's that for 'hold it gently', nymph?

I look down at my attacker. In that dimly lit hallway, all I can see is slimy, nasty teeth bared at me in a snarl of pain-fueled rage, and the glint of metal in his hand. "Attacking someone from behind? And here I thought your only sin was the condition you keep this ship in. I'll have to do something about that, won't I? Seeing as it's my ship now."

He scrambles backwards, his cutlass scraping along the floor. "Ye be lass?" His voice is rough and full of confusion.

I toss the mallet to the ground behind me so the imbecile can't reach it, and raise my blade higher, stepping after him. "That's Captain to you, boy. Yield and at least die with a slither of honor."

He keeps scrambling away from me and I keep stepping after him. "A lass on my ship! Ye cursed me thrice over into oblivion, ye wench!"

"Oh, you should see the others I brought over here with me," I tell him, thrusting my sword deep into the man's gut. "A mere woman is the least of your worries today." He gurgles out his surprise, his cutlass sliding from his grip. I ease him onto his back with pressure from my cutlass and my other hand on his shoulder. This close, I can see the shock, pain, fear swirling in his black eyes. He reeks of grog and sweat, each panting breath wafting putrid breath into my face. "Truthfully speaking, right now there's three lasses on your ship. One of them's a mermaid. The other's a druid. And there are two water nymphs, though they're men. Oh, and a meathead called Caleb with a chip on his shoulder. But by your reasoning, I'd say you're…" I feign counting on my fingers, "at least fifteen times cursed. I hope hell is better-kept than this place."

Blood bubbles through his rotting teeth, dribbling down his dirty chin. I jerk my sword out and he still struggles to rise. I raise my sword and slash it sideways, slicing into the flesh of his neck with an audible thwack. A crimson arc sprays across my face. I pull my cutlass back and stare distastefully at it as he blindly, awkwardly, tries to cover the wound with his hands.

"This would've been easier for both of us if my blade were sharper."

I grab his shoulder with my free hand and hack again, this time deeper, then again, until the Captain's head tumbles from his shoulders and onto the floor with a squishy thud, into a puddle of its own blood.

I drop the lifeless corpse and pick up the severed head, holding it up to peer into the dead eyes, the shock forever etched on his face. "The mouth hanging open is a nice touch," I muse aloud, "it should stop any riffraff above, carrying *this* with me. Looks like you get to be of use to me one more time, chum."

I sheathe my blade and head back the way I had come, the oil lamp flames guttering and barely alight now. The sounds of fighting, shooting and heavy boot falls are still ringing above.

As usual, Caleb's deep voice is louder than the others. "If you turn all fishy when you get wet, how come you haven't turned all wicked sea hag, yet?"

As I ascend, I spy Hanna, standing across from Caleb, a bloody sword in her hand. She has an annoyed very Octavia-like look on her face – or had it always been a Hanna expression on Octavia's face? I'm not sure of anything anymore.

She cleans the blade on her pantaloons before sheathing it. "I don't go '*all fishy*', as you so eloquently put it, because, unlike Demetrius and his kind, I need to be completely submerged in seawater."

Caleb throws up his hands huffing and grumbling like some old fisherman's wife.

Close by, Asa darts around collecting up fallen items during the scuffle and arranging them by the tattered mainmast. He's retrieved the candlestick I saw him throw earlier.

"Mind yer back, Cap!" Jonah calls, and I step aside to let him, Ambrose and two of their gunners carry the cannon from *The Revenge* past me and below deck, going the way I'd just come. How in three hells did they get that over here?! But – I cock a smirk, impressed – we shall now be a two-gun ship.

I take a moment to look about me. My crew's all here, it seems, with the remaining attacking crew sat with hands on heads around the mizzenmast. Then I look at *The Revenge*. She's cut loose, now, drifted away from us, fire lapping at her sails and mast, her bow almost below the waterline already. Eventually the sea will swallow her entirely. I grieve for my ship. The pang of loss and guilt invades my every sense, but I push through it. I can't falter in my emotions, can't be weak, cannot bend. If I bend anymore, I'll break.

I thrust the severed head high in the sky for all to see. "It's done. I've slain their Captain, and the ship is now ours! Selina, gather all hands to me. I think we have some voting to do."

***

I stand near the pile of goods piled round the main mast on my new ship. Twenty of us now, all in. Five of them are the hands from the other crew who've sworn their fealty to me. My own crew have accepted them with a vote. So, there's twenty of us. Sixteen humans and four non-humans. We're all silent. There's a final vote to be cast, and we all, human or otherwise, get to vote. Majority will take it. In the event of a tie, my final casting vote is law.

I stare across the sea, at the burning carcass of my old ship, only her bow end still visible, then let out a long sigh. "All against the four non-humans staying on the ship, say nay and raise your hand." A chorus of nays ring in my ears and I tally the total in my head. "That's ten. All in favor of keeping them on, say aye and raise your hand."

Not surprisingly Hanna, Demetrius Selina, and Atropous raise their hands. Jonah and Ambrose exchange a quick look, and both raise their hands. Asa, eyes scornfully looking at those that voted nay, lip trembling, stretches his arm as high as he can. Solomon, face neutral, holds his hand up.

"Aye."

I add them together. Then add again. Eight. Wait... With my vote, that makes nineteen. Who hasn't voted?

I look at them all and spot Caleb, his arms folded, his lips pressed into a hard line. "Caleb. You haven't voted."

That tight line of his mouth deepens into a grimace, his next words said through the corner of his mouth. "Ye haven't either, Captain."

I grind my teeth. Cocky bastard. What's his game? I straighten my posture and hold my head high, holding his gaze. "I vote they stay. Your turn."

The crew ripples and whispers. Caleb's vote will decide it. He could vote against them, bring the nays to eleven, or he could tie it and let my vote pass in favor of them staying. He breaks eye contact with me, looks down. He's going to vote them out, the coward, the bastard, the scum.

"I vote with the Captain."

The blubbering mass of... what? I stare at him.

The naysayers explode into loud shouts of protests. The air crackles with the unrest.

246

"That fire stick loaded, Am?" I ask the red-haired lad. He nods once and tosses one of his rifles to me. I point the barrel skywards and fire it, bringing silence. I'm not going to shout. Not now. Now's time for quiet resolve. "Enough. The vote's been made. They stay. My word is law. Don't test me. Jonah, Ambrose," I toss the rifle back to him, with a nod of acknowledgment, "get to fixing the cannons in place. Coxswain to the helm. The rest of you lot? Patch yer injuries and get the corpses off my ship before they start to stink. Get us Bristol-fashion and sea-worthy."

With that, I turn my back on my crew and stoop down the steps, off to find my new Captain's quarters. As I descend, I let my legs tremble, finally.

***

I bury my freshly washed face into new linens, the old ones long since stripped, and burnt, with any hope. Asa had brought rations to me at supper time, and I've been alone since. Blessed silence. My mind is a hurricane, thoughts and emotions so muddled, they all bleed into one continuous howling gale of exhaustion.

A loud rap at my door has me wearily lifting my head. "Who goes?"

"Urchin, it is I. I need to speak to you."

I barely stop a groan from leaving my lips, but I'm on my feet and crossing the small space to the warped, wooden door in an instant. I open it and the gleaming-eyed nymph stands in front of me, his lips already twisted into his usual flashy smile. I step aside to permit him entrance. "I liked your other form much better." There's no real bite to my words and they make him chuckle as I close the door again.

His eyes dart about the room as he inspects it before they finally land on me.

"What do you want, Demetrius?" I'm so tired. Soul tired.

He takes a breath, hands on his hips, studying me with a look of... is that a sneer? "Why do you hide in here and not talk to Hanna? It's odd that you lock yourself away from her."

My blood boils at his contempt. "You find it *odd* that I don't want to talk to someone who has lied to me for nearly half a year? After the day I've had?" I snort, turning my back on him before I can do something we both may regret.

He tuts at me like I'm some child. "You humans, so fickle. If I remember correctly, you stole from us. I see no difference. You are obviously titillated that she's here, so why prolong fate? Speak to her, and her reason–"

"Reason would what? Reason for her betrayal for this long, all the lying, would just be okay?"

Demetrius's eyes begin to glow the same ethereal glow Atropous's had when they raised the wave. He sucks at his teeth, balls his fist. "As if you'd allow us passage on your vessel when you found out Hanna's relation to Kai."

My twisting thoughts stall completely as I take in what he just said. Another of those missing pieces clicks into place, and my mouth goes dry. Her father. Of course, Kai's her father. My fingers begin to tremble, and I clench them, glaring at the nymph and his glowing eyes, hissing. "You came all this way to protect me from Hanna's father? That's sweet."

The nymph is suddenly very close, eyes now two pools of sizzling green. They narrow as he eyeballs me, our noses almost touching. "That vile dolt is not her father. *I* am her father. Me. I care little about your minor pitiful human life. Hanna, however, values it, and…" his eyes flare brighter still, his lips trembling before they pull back over his teeth, his sneer almost becoming a snarl, "and you cannot even go speak to her about the bond and its effects? It disgusts me."

He's scaring me a little. I step back, bring a hand up between us. "What bond? Effects? You mean the breathing underwater and the mind link thing?"

His green eyes widen, and his face slackens for a moment. He hisses in a breath and snaps his head to look away, raking his hands into his hair and rubbing his mouth. It's obvious he's said something he didn't intend to.

I try again, my heart beating against my ribs. "What bond, Demetrius?"

My words seem to strike something within the bizarre man. His shoulders are hunched, he's staring at the floor, but he lowers his hands back to his sides, and when he finally looks at me, that inhumane glow is slowly fading. "Just, please speak with her, and when you do, speak nothing of the conversation we've had." He fixes me with a stare that's half defiant and half pleading. Then he leaves, his cloak whipping about his shins, without looking at me again.

I blink, staring at the closed door. Too much, it's all too much.

I sink onto the hard cot, all my energy gone entirely. I roll onto my side, facing the wall, away from the door. I draw my knees close to my chest and do something I haven't done in eight years.

I cry.

I cry tears of anger, for the sister who betrayed me, tears of grief for the loss of the only father I'd ever known, tears of sadness for the lives lost out at sea under my watch, for my ship, my home gone again, and finally tears of heartache. For the achingly beautiful half-ling that saved my life and hasn't let go, turning my entire existence upside down, making me question everything.

***

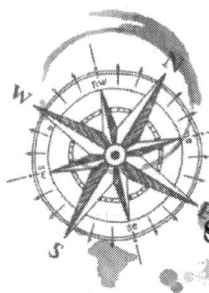

Chapter 30: Jonah
1 September 1691
Somewhere in the Indian Ocean

I pause at the bottom of the steps to the top deck, stretching my arms high, twisting from side to side slowly, feeling all the bothersome aches and kinks clicking and protesting. I'd rested for *so* long, and yet the fatigue lingers. I won't be laid out again, though. They can't make me. Too much rest can put you right in the ground before your time. I've seen it myself, more times than I'd care to admit. Honestly, for a while there, I thought I'd be joining them.

The yellow fever had flared up in me again, no doubt brought on by the shock of all those revelations, followed by the sea battle. That day was the single most shocking thing to ever happen to me, and that's including me finally plucking up the courage to get out from under my father's thumb and run away to join the Navy with Am all those years back. Creatures from Ambrose's prosperous tales in the real world? Mermaids, nymphs, druids… all surely what had rekindled the illness. I won't admit it to Ambrose, but this second bout of sickness has probably been worse than the first. Some of the others got sick again too, and back into the hull they went, again. I refused to go, again. I stayed in Ambrose's bunk, again. But this time it seemed somewhat less of a troublesome secret, what with all the other larger ones to have come to light recently.

Having caught my breath, I push my overgrown hair from my eyes and take the two little steps up to the main deck, vastly smaller than *The Revenge's*. Una has named this ship *The Protector of the Sea*. For a pirate ship, this strikes me as funny. And yet… for a band of buccaneers, this crew has more honor in its filthiest scallywag thumb than can be found in more officially reputable organizations. The bright sun and chilly air encompass me like a cool, comforting quilt, though I'm quite blind in the sunlight. Splatters of rain pelt my face. I feel haggard. Blimey, another six days of this? I'll look as bad as Caleb, by the time we port, and that is a *feat*. Loud shrieking fills my ears, and I shield my eyes, trying to see the disturbance.

"Ambrose, I can hear you running past the perimeter we laid out for the game! That makes three! We have two rules, follow them *both* or sit out with Solomon, Hanna and Caleb!" Selina's voice rises above the rest and I'm met with a peculiar sight, which is saying something, considering the things I've been subjected to thus far in my life.

The usually solemn, quiet Selina is blind folded with a bright green swatch of fabric I recognize as the cloth I'd previously traded to Aurelius, to *Demetrius,* before. Her heavy dark cloak is gone, her enchantment no longer keeping her true skin color a secret from us. Her arms are outstretched, those silvery vine tattoos visible around her exposed forearms and disappearing under her rolled-up sleeves. Her fingers wiggle as if she's seeking something, without moving the rest of her body, though the rolling of the ship has her stumble slightly. Asa dances on tiptoes around her. Demetrius and Ambrose too, creeping around her, all grinning broadly, their movements stuttering between wanting to run as fast as they can, and almost skipping, their cloaks whipping around them like tails.

Ambrose spins out of the reach of Selina's grabbing fist and laughs as he slows his pace a touch to appease the rules of the game. "I didn't mean to, Sel. I promise I won't do it again!"

Asa shrieks and ducks under Selina's arms, dropping to all fours and crawling at an impressive speed through her wide-stance legs, popping up on the other side and darting away before she can even turn around completely. "No, no! I'm gonna win!"

"Not on my life, child!" Demetrius's voice makes Selina spin so fast she almost topples over as she tries, and fails, to make contact with the chuckling nymph. He's somehow lighter on his feet than even I, his steps not making a sound. His hair is currently a slithering cyclone of deep blues and green, a life force of its own.

"You may have met your match, Deme! Asa may just be faster than you!" Octavia, *Hanna,* calls. She's wearing her waist-length hair free and it's black, so dark on a woman with such fair skin. Her eyes are just as bizarrely exotic as the rest of her, the color like the lilac blossoms in Mother's old gardens. She isn't like any lass I've ever met in my life, and I've seen a fair bit of the world. She tips her cup and drinks deeply, rounded cheeks flushed from the rum. She is most certainly the most beautiful lass I've ever seen. That beauty is dimmed by the grotesque blob sitting beside her. Caleb straddles the barrel of rum, an amused glint in those horrendous eyes, watching the game with more focus than I thought possible for the dimwitted buffoon. There's even a touch of a smile on his overgrown, bearded face, a mug of his own in his grubby fist. Solomon sits on the beauty's other side, clapping his hands as he loudly cheers Selina, who tries desperately to catch the three remaining players.

Selina gives a battle cry, but Ambrose catches my eye as he dodges her hands nearly grabbing the back of his doublet. The grin he throws me nearly too big for his face. He dances out of Selina's range and over to me, almost colliding with my chest. "Aye, Jo! Finally awake! You look loads better! Life is back in your eyes. It's good to see! You have to join us, we're playing Blind Man's Buff, remember when we played that as lads?"

I chuckle at him, folding my arms behind my back, smiling easily despite the slight daze I've been in since waking. End of the journey means less food, and far more booze. Not that I mind; the best of times happen when inhibitions are lowered because you're bloody starving and the rum's gone to your head quick.

Solomon waves a hand over his head at me, a huge grin lighting the tired shadows beneath his eyes. He had last night's shift at the helm, and it's impressive he's even able to join the tomfoolery. I figured he would be lost to his dreams by now. "Jonah, yes come join us! Have a cup with us! You can have my crate!"

"Ahoy Jonah! I may have to stay up here and keep watch, but you should have a little fun!" Atropous shouts down from the crow's nest, waving, his hair just as wild and water-like as Demetrius's.

"Yes, Jonah please, join us!" Hanna grins brilliantly and it has my smile growing. She straightens her posture, trying to look proper, raising her cup in my direction.

Caleb cuts his gaze to me and that relaxed grin turns wolfish, mocking. "Yes, boy, join us. You can be 'it' next round, show us how you and Ambrose played together."

Before I can teach him a thing or two, starting with the fact that I'm only four years younger than him and not a boy, and ending with my fist down his filthy throat, Selina whips around toward Am and I, one finger pointing directly at us.

"Ambrose, I know you wouldn't dare to stand over by Jonah, and beyond my range? Breaking the rules yet *again*, are you? Do you want me to toss you overboard?"

I grin at Ambrose. "Wouldn't be the first time you've broken rules, would it?"

Am casts me a sheepish smile, raps my shoulder with his knuckles, and returns to the game. I join the others, dropping to a crouch at Solomon's side, pressing a hand on his shoulder when he attempts to give up his seat for me and sit on the deck instead. This isn't like out there, when a man of his color and former status would be expected to give things up for the likes of me. He was sitting there first after all. Fair is fair.

Surprisingly, Caleb reaches over Hanna and Solomon's head to offer me an overflowing, frothing cup. He doesn't even look at me, eyes trained on the resumed game. "Have some, it'll keep the sickness at bay, and it tastes better than that hard tack we must have for supper again this eve."

I stare at the beverage like it's a snake ready to strike the moment I reach for it. Caleb's being oddly appeasing right now. Almost downright bearable. It's alarming. But my stomach is empty, and my mouth is watering, so I shrug off my suspicion and accept the cup. Any potential consequences aren't scary enough to stop me from consuming it. Like I'd ever turn away free flowing drink and merriment. Pfft. Only when I'm cold and dead. I sip on the ale as Selina grabs for Asa and the lad falls to his knees. Ambrose isn't quick enough to stop and has to leap-frog over the boy, straight into Selina's outstretched arms.

He groans loudly, and the jig is up. Selina shoves him away, a victorious grin on her face. "You're out, Ambrose!"

Caleb howls with laughter, stomping his feet loudly on the deck. "Out shined by a babe, lad. No wonder the Royal Navy is inept!"

I laugh and almost snort the frothy ale up my nose. I swallow hard but am reduced to the kind of laughter that hurts your ribs, makes you breathless, makes you feel light and alive. Ah it's a good feeling, even if it is provoked by that nitwit.

Ambrose plucks the cup from my hands before dropping down beside me, taking a large pull from it. He sighs, contentedly, peering into the cup. "And so, the best opponent will be revealed to us shortly. Young Asa, or the mystifying Demetrius; I'm accepting bets of any form." He ruefully holds out a hand and bless me if sweet Solomon doesn't press a few coins into it.

"No offense to Mr. Demetrius," Solomon grins, "but Asa is quite swift on his feet."

Caleb tosses a small silver throwing knife at Ambrose, his bet. "A human versus a demon? And ye call me a fool. The water sprite'll defeat a babe, easily."

"I'm a *nymph*!" Demetrius calls over his shoulder, as he leaps behind Selina.

"Show Selina what for!" Atropous yells down from his vantage point from the crow's nest. "Left! No, the other left!"

Hanna laughs happily as well, a nice reprieve from the dark cloud that's been hanging over her like an encroaching storm. The Captain's been avoiding her, we all know it. Captain only comes around to spout orders at us, spends the rest of her time holed up in her cabin. It seems the Captain and the half-ling have some history prior to our voyage. Ah well. I drink again, feeling Ambrose beside me. We all have history.

We lapse into a companionable silence as Demetrius and Asa try to outwit Selina. I don't know whether the nymph is the sort to let a child win. This is the most fun we've all had, though, since before the yellow fever struck the first time; since we lost crew, since poor Felix slipped from us.

"You never said who ye be betting on, *Gael*." Caleb's deep baritone breaks through the light laughter, his idiotic addition at the end of his words making me want to punch the smug look off his face. That word is another word for Irish, but Caleb means more by it than that. We all know Am's Irish. The lad doesn't even hide his accent these days. But we don't talk about why Am's an Irish ex-British

Naval officer. Caleb thinks, just because he's Ship's idiot, he can play it up and pretend he isn't trying to catch Ambrose out and get one of us to admit he was once an indentured servant for my father. Caleb knows exactly what he's saying. It riles me that this gargoyle seems to have guessed at something we don't talk about.

But Ambrose, as usual, takes the venom in Caleb's word in his stride, rocking from side to side like he's hearing a tune in his head. "Demetrius'll prevail. Experience always outwits youthful exuberance in the end." He plucks my cup from my hands again, pausing with it at his lips. "And, impressive, pal. You got my birthplace right, but that's not who I am anymore." He slips easily into the rich British accent he wore as a mask for so many years. "I'm a Protestant, a proper British man. Isn't that right Jonah?" His gaze flicks to me as he sips, his smirk visible around the rim. I smile back, a warmth blooming in my chest. What a silver-tongued viper.

Caleb lets out a grotesque belch before he laughs. "Quite right, Ambrose. Though I've noticed you lot took the King's coin to fight for the Crown. You do quite like to take stuff that don't belong to you. Things… places… people."

Hanna turns wide eyes to Caleb, her mouth dropping open, and Solomon flinches almost imperceptibly. Ambrose notices – he notices everything – and offers Solomon a small smile, reaching round me to clap him heartily on the knee.

Caleb just grins at me, teeth uneven. "And who do you think will win? Two votes for each of em', ye get to break the tie, how fitting, *chap*."

Ambrose's loud laugh makes me laugh too, the small ember of anger that had flared at Caleb's provoking words now snuffed. There's no use getting upset over things that once were, things we left behind, that can't be changed. Like Am said, I'm not that person anymore either. I'm me. Besides, it's not like his words aren't true, no matter how crudely spoken. There's a reason this life suits us better than the Navy did. There are things no man should ever have to endure or be forced to make others endure. I accept the cup back. "Let's back the younger lad, for once! Come on, Asa, don't make me regret betting a whole round of drinks on you!"

Solomon claps his hands and begins to cheer. "Asa! Asa! Asa!"

Caleb starts stomping his feet along with Solomon's cheering in a melodramatic manner, making us all laugh harder. "Come on, ya nymph, ya gonna let a seven-year-old beat you?!" Caleb jumps to his feet, punching the air like he's fighting an opponent himself.

I'm glad for this. This laughter, these games. Bonding. Something desperately needed to keep a ship and crew running to the best of its abilities. High morale is the goal. Low morale brings far too many liabilities and dangers. Demetrius and Asa are still whipping around Selina, dodging her.

She balls her hands into fists, exasperated. "Stop moving around so damn much, you two! Can we add in the rule where no one's allowed to move? I'm out of breath, *Cailleach* give me strength."

Ambrose, recognizing her Gaelic speech, grins and shoots to his feet. "Ayeeee! *Cailín!* Selina, do some druid magic to catch 'em!"

Solomon is now on his feet as well, his eyes sparkling like the ocean. "Yes, yes! Please, that would be marvelous to see again, we haven't seen such things since we acquired *The Protector!*"

I lean back on an elbow, feeling flushed with the grog. "You both realize, if she does that, you're both going to lose your bets."

"Since everyone's having so much fun, I'm safe to assume all tasks are complete?" Una's voice slices through our merrymaking. Hanna nearly gags on her mouthful of grog. I twist to squint over my shoulder and see the Captain standing on the top step arms crossed tightly. She's got something dark smeared over her arms and cheek – gunpowder perhaps? I'd heard sharp pops coming from below earlier and figured someone had been target practicing. Now I know who.

She's wearing that same gray cloak she wore when we first met, the bottom of it ripped and tattered. Her fair hair is hidden beneath a deep blue bandanna, and her face is set, hardened, almost as unreadable and frightening as my fathers had been. She's appraising all of us, her gaze lingering on Hanna a moment longer than the rest of us. Hanna, in turn, is pretending the contents of her mug is suddenly the most fascinating thing in the world. I try not to smirk. How very curious.

Asa still careens back and forth in front of Selina, who's frozen, who already pushed her blindfold up sheepishly the moment Una appeared, Demetrius grins. He dances over to Una, complete with a flamboyant spin on his toes, and in one fluid motion, so fast I don't really see how he's done it, swaps their cloaks. He's holding her old tattered one, stroking it like it's an old comrade. Then he pats a gaping Una on the shoulder and twirls merrily back over to Selina, dancing a little hornpipe jig around Asa without saying another word. What in all that's holy was that about?

Una's sun-tanned cheeks turn red. She scowls but says nothing, casts one last furtive glance at the mermaid sat by me, then stomps back down the stairs, her new cloak fluttering about behind her like an angry black aura. The air of fun is gone, heavy now with unspoken words. But then Demetrius laughs, a delighted chuckle that grows into a rolling, jolly belly laugh. He's bracing his hands on his knees, and his laugh is infectious. I start to giggle. Ambrose snorts, his shoulders shaking.

"I thought she was going to punch him," Solomon breathes.

"I thought she was going to shoot him," Selina adds, in a deadpan voice. Caleb hoots a barking laugh.

"What did he do? I didn't see!" Atropous yells. "Is he dancing?"

That's it. We're all done. The laughter spreads. Pretty soon, we're all wheezing and crying with laughter, even Hanna.

Demetrius twirls in a half circle, fanning his cloak out, before dipping into a very formal bow, one my father would be impressed with. "Now that I have my lucky cloak back, the fun can truly begin. Settle in, my comrades, we're in for a long eve."

Caleb whoops loudly as he refills everyone's mugs, that seed of warmth blooming again inside my weary chest. Life may be hard at times, cruel for no reason - unthinkably so, but persevere, and moments like these will unfold like sunbursts on water. These are the moments that are worth it.

***

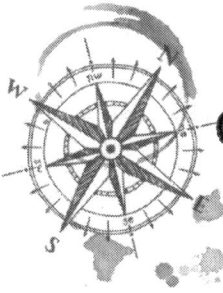

Chapter 31: Hanna
7 September 1691
Port Royal, Jamaica

I wake because someone's poking my face. The aches, pains and tremors don't waste a moment in seeping back into every bone as I surface. Poking, again, more forceful, and damp, kneading my cheeks. Soft laughter. Asa… why must his hands always be wet? He pulls his hands away, then climbs to sit on my chest, giggling still. As a knobbly small knee presses painfully under my rib cage, my eyes fly open and I grunt. His long-lashed bright eyes greet me, along with a sunny, toothy smile.

"Asa, why in the world are your hands sopping wet?"

He settles into my lap as I pull myself into a sitting position on the hard cot, my body groaning at me. I clasp my hands behind his back, steadying him as he leans back to properly look at me. "Solomon said you had a tail! You get it when you get wet, right? I wanna see it!"

Despite the soul-shaking exhaustion, and the pain from the bond that has yet to be accepted or rejected, laughter bubbles up from my chest like it has a will of its own. Asa always can coax a laugh from me. I support his body with one arm and brush some of his unruly brown hair from his eyes with the other. "We've talked about this before, my darling. I need to be submerged in the sea's waters for my transformation to occur. Merely splashing me or getting a part of me wet does nothing."

Asa twists his small mouth into a frown, puffs air into his cheeks, before falling face-first against my chest, hugging me close. The gentleness of his actions and acceptance of me lifts my heart. These last few weeks since mine and Deme's secrets had come to light, not just us but Selina and Atropous too, have been heavy, even with the occasional frivolity. But hadn't I wanted there to be no secrets? It's all in the open, now.

258

As we sit, the child and I, comforting one another, as I try to draw warmth into my cold body from him, I notice the constant rocking of the ship is now just a dull sway. "Is that why you came to wake me? We've finally docked in Port Royal?"

He doesn't move his face from my chest as he speaks. "I helped Ambrose with the riggin'... then suddenly everybody was yellin' and mad, so I ran to you."

I gently comb my fingers through his locks, about to ask him to expand on what's going on above deck, when the curtains to my bunk are flung aside, revealing an angry-looking Selina. She pushes into the room with a concerned-looking Solomon a few steps behind. Asa turns in my arms, casting a worried look at them.

"What's going on, Selina?"

"Forgive us, Hanna, but there's nowhere else quiet enough and... safe enough. My bunk's not big enough, and Solomon's sharing with Atropous, and... it's gotten very busy on deck."

That doesn't entirely answer my question. I'm still none the wiser as to what they're actually doing in here, but I appreciate that she feels like this is a safe place. She turns to Solomon and tugs a turquoise pouch from her belt. delving a hand inside. "Solomon, in light of the new information and the... *dealings* now popular around here, I think it would be best if I used my enchantment on both of us."

His nervous hands fall still. "I would look like you did before?"

Selina nods, pulling out orange-dusted fingers. "We'll pass as white folk. It won't harm you, I swear."

His brow creases as he cups his chin in his palm. I can practically see him working through all the outcomes in his head, his eyes never once leaving Selina's face. He drops his hand and nods. "What must I do?"

Her angry face falters, cracking and warming her amber eyes. "Just hold still and have faith in me." She takes her coated fingers and begins tracing her silver tattoos, as she had when she'd transformed into the bird, going back to the pouch whenever the orange powder runs out on her fingers. She repeats the process on Solomon's arms, tracing orange lines in the same patterns. Once complete, she re-ties the pouch to her belt. She holds out her orange-dusted hands to Solomon, palms up. "Lay your hands atop mine, close your eyes and remain as silent as possible, please."

Solomon lays his slightly quivering hands over hers, eclipsing her smaller hands completely. Selina's eyes fall closed and the orange markings begin to pulse, first on her own arms, then on Solomon's. The feel of it makes him tense, but he keeps his eyes shut, as instructed. Unlike Demetrius's magic, which is like ripples in an ocean current settling over a thing or a person, Selina's is like a fine mist that seems to thicken until it's a dense fog. It swirls against their skin, soon obscuring them from my sight.

Asa crawls to the end of the cot, eyes wide and mouth hanging open in wonder. His young age and limited exposure to the taint of the world means he can enjoy things that don't make sense just for how they are. I envy that in him and want to preserve it at all cost.

The twisting fog lifts, and the enchantment is apparently done. They are transformed. Solomon lifts his hands, marveling at the pale skin of his new disguise. Also unlike Demetrius's magic, Selina's seems unable to change height, stature, or eye color. Solomon's recognizable hazel eyes sit in a more oval face, narrower nose and lips, with a dimpled chin covered in brown scruff. Instead of his natural, soft, short and tightly coiled hair, now windswept straight brown hair falls across arched eyebrows.

His full lips curl, his brows shooting up. "This... is most curious."

Asa leaps off the bed in his excitement. "Curious? That's brilliant! My turn! Selina, my turn!"

I'm completely dumbfounded. Just when you think nothing could possibly compare to seeing a person turning into a bird. "Care to share what's caused this?" I ask.

Selina, looking just as she had in the days before she revealed her true form to us, narrows her eyes, with her pale skin and black tattoos, two blazing pools of amber fire. "Senior Sailors, and the main trade around here now apparently consists of slaves, sugar and timber. This is not the Port Royal I know."

Asa stops his jovial dance mid-step and slowly backs away from the livid woman and toward me.

I tilt my head; the words separately have meaning but together mean nothing. "Senior sailors?"

A frustrated, disgusted sound erupts from Selina's lips. "The walking garbage that trade in slaves. Human beings, Hanna. Being sold like objects, like cattle, wood and sugar!" She scoffs, folding her black-marked arms over her chest.

Asa inches closer, his hand finding and lacing with mine. "Royal Navy, Mum. Ambrose and Jonah were with 'em until they went and got on the account." I suppose my face must still look confused, because Asa adds, "Oh, uh, until they went pirate."

Solomon clears his throat softly and gently puts a hand on Selina's arm, looking into her face, trying to comfort and calm her. "Atropous says they've a rule in place now that makes being a pirate here a crime for the gallows."

Hadn't Selina said Port Royal was a pirate utopia? "When did they put this law in place?"

Selina aggressively tosses her head, pulling herself from Solomon's hand. "Four year ago! Those damn ex-Jollies have some talkin' to do! We've come all this way. What would Una's sibling even do in a place like this?!"

Loud boot falls and some shouts overhead interrupt Selina's livid rant. "Selina, what is going on up there?"

She huffs out another disgruntled noise before pulling her hood up over her head, hiding the venomous look in her eyes. "Demetrius is using his unnatural magic on a dock worker to gather information on the area."

"I hardly see how you can call my magic unnatural, druid." All heads turn toward Demetrius, suddenly framed in the doorway, disguised once more in his 'Aurelius' form. His obsidian eyes glare. He surveys us. When his gaze finds me, that dark anger melts, replaced with familiar warmth. "Your turn, little guppy. You and I stand out far too much in our usual forms."

Selina clucks her tongue loudly, turning away from us, though Asa pulls his small hand from mine and claps. "I've wanted to see this for ages!"

The fact that Deme thinks it's unsafe out there for us, with mostly just our strange eyes to set us apart, further reinforces Selina's worry.

Demetrius winks at the boy. "Watch and learn, child."

The room is small, already with more people in it than it's designed for, so Deme is forced to reach out to me from the doorway. Selina bristles a moment before I feel the cool sensation of Demetrius's magic travel over my body. Though my guardian is motionless and there's no twisting mist or pulsing lights, his bright eyes do glow with an otherworldly light as he accesses his abilities. Just as the cool trail of magic leaves my limbs, Asa and Solomon erupt into loud clapping.

This appeals directly to Demetrius's ego and showmanship, so he bows. "And that is how you achieve a proper transformation."

I'm about to say that Selina's spell was equally impressive to behold, but she turns rigidly to the door. "I'm going above deck. These quarters are too crowded for my liking. Hanna, join us soon." She pushes past Deme, not bothering to look back or wait for my response. Solomon bobs an awkward half bow before scurrying after her.

Demetrius shakes his head. "What an unsightly child." He curls his lips in distaste.

"I don't understand what this animosity is. You got on well before both your secret magics were revealed. And now you're always provoking her."

Demetrius says nothing, only folds his burly 'Aurelius' arms over his chest. Asa gathers my boots, my blue bandanna and weapons for me, scurrying about quickly. He's sweet, and his eagerness to help lightens the shadows that still linger in his eyes and soul after losing Felix. I smile and let him help me up. I'm weak, weary, vaguely nauseous all the time now.

"You s'pose after Captain gives us our orders and work's finished for the day, she'll let us find a doctor for you, Mum?"

I brush his hair back, chest swelling with an affection I'd never expected to feel for the young boy. "I'm sure she will, sweetness. We must remain patient until that time comes."

I knot the bandanna over my hair at the nape of my neck and tug my boots on. Though I spoke confident words to soothe the worrying child, I'm worried. Una's distance has been a strike to my gut, constantly threatening to steal the breath from me, bring tears to my eyes. It's to be expected, really… I'm no better than her sibling.

Demetrius leans close, his grin playful. "Ready, Guppy?"

I sigh and reach for my weapons. "I really wish you wouldn't call me that around others. Or call Una 'Urchin', for that matter. Last night, Ambrose called me Guppy instead of Hanna. I'd rather it not catch on."

Demetrius only laughs, straightening. "Now if I can only get others besides Caleb to call Una 'Urchin', I can perish a happy nymph."

Asa raises one of his hands. "Deme, *I'll* start calling her Urchin!" They laugh conspiratorially together as I stand straightening the gun into my sash followed by the espada.

"Come along, children, I'm sure the Captain is tired of waiting for us."

***

Even before the tip of my boot touches the top deck, I hear raised voices up there.

"You knew the entire time that their base was here and they put this confounded law in place and you *still* chose to wait this long to let your Captain in on this little development?"

Demetrius leads Asa and I into a standoff. Una stands, dressed all in black and gray, legs braced and wide-stanced, her dark, billowy too-long trousers tucked into her boots, hands on her hips as she bears down on Ambrose and Jonah. The lads wear awkward, sheepish expressions. Caleb and Atropous stand close to Una, Caleb's face twisted into an eager smile, while Atropous's brows are drawn together

263

in anxious concern, his gaze darting between everyone. Selina and Solomon are watching, too, silently.

Jonah lowers his eyes to the deck, fingering the lettering near the hilt of his blade. "Even if anyone got captured, we, *they* choose less brutish means of punishment. A trial, for a start. They wouldn't just hang us. We'd be put in front of a group of our peers, witnesses – if they could find any – would speak out against us. The Navy being here doesn't stop this being the most crooked town in the world, Captain. Where there's pirates, there's freely-flowing coin for any and all with loose pockets and looser morals."

Ambrose nods along, flicking his eyes from Jonah's face to Una's. "We've acquired some Letters of Marque just in case anyone begins to snoop. We've been safe in town already, there's been no danger. No more than usual, that is."

I bend down to Asa, whisper in his ear, "Letters of the mark?"

"Letters of Marque. Permission to pirate. 'Cept they don't call 'em pirates, then. Ones with letters get called Privateers."

I nod and stand straight again. Una's anger is like the eerie, silent calm before the impending storm. Her body is still, her face a neutral mask. But, through the bond, I can feel her turbulent emotions. So consuming, so strong my knees nearly buckle beneath me. She rages, beneath her still surface.

Caleb scoffs. "I wouldn't listen to a word that comes out of that plummy mouth of his, I'm sure he just misses havin' someone to bow to. He could be leadin' us right to our deaths! We'll all hang!"

Jonah tilts his head, takes his hand from his shiny sword hilt to his beard, unkempt from the time at sea. He calmly strokes his chin, not so much as twitching an eyelid at Caleb's vulgar words. It's a skill it must have taken Jonah years to perfect, to hide his reactions so well. "Oh," he says, airily, "the cabbage does make a habit of weeding out someone else's history besides his own, doesn't he? Why, me ol' plum, I didn't know you had the stomach for it."

"ENOUGH!" Una's voice slices the air like a pistol shot before a true argument can erupt. Her eyes are deadly and serious. "There will be no more secrets between any of us." She looks around, addressing us all, pausing on me for a breath, the first time she's looked at me in seven days. Ambrose and Jonah jump to attention, both animatedly saluting the scowling Una. She sniffs. "Caleb, you've been here before, too. Anything you think we should know?"

The beefy man puffs up his already overly stuffed chest. "Barterin' is no good here. Cold hard pieces of eight is the currency. We'll need to sell some things to make some coin. I hear blue skin sells well round here, nowadays."

I recall he's used this term before. A derogatory term for those of mixed races. Like Selina and Solomon.

A scoff comes from beneath Selina's hood. "You really want to make the witch mad?"

Caleb visibly pales, taking a step away from Selina.

"I won't tell anyone to be quiet again." Una rolls her head on her shoulders, trying to calm herself, though there's still an edge to her voice. "Caleb, lead us to the nearest corrupt merchant, we have enough non-living things to sell. Everyone grab something from below the damn deck. After so long crammed in with you lot, I'm going to need several drinks."

***

"Stay close to me, Hanna. Just because they've put that flimsy law in place in a fool's attempt at order here, does not mean there isn't debauchery a-foot. Your petals shall not be plucked on my watch."

Oh, for goodness sake. I exhale loudly and roll my eyes at Demetrius, tugging Asa closer to my side, as we weave through the busy streets of the bustling town. It's hot, the heat pressing into my already-tired body, but at the least the streets offer shade. Upon walking down the gangplank of *The Protector*, I'd been struck with how barren the beach had looked. No trees, no grasses, but I realize now what it lacks in vegetation it quite makes up for in people, buildings, and a thriving bustling industry. There are so many buildings here, far more than in Banten, or Sainte Marie, all packed into one place, with so many people, it seems miraculous to me that the island has managed to keep itself afloat at all.

In just the short time it took to sell the loot taken when we captured *The Protector*, I'd seen so many questionable corsairs that it made me wonder why the King even tried to put a stop to it in the first place, his law doesn't seem to be doing any good. The heavy pouch currently tugging Una's trousers low on her hips only makes me question it even further. Selina had been correct about seeing questionably moral dealings every ten paces, but she hadn't mentioned the surge of energy the gathered residents of the port town inspired. The sheer number of taverns and brothels I'd counted was staggering, even within the first half-mile. My legs give a painful throb at the reminder of how far we've walked already today. After so long at sea, and the added effects of the bond, my body is running on pure will alone. My vision swims dangerously as I sidestep a group of clearly inebriated men.

Jonah elbows Selina in the ribs with a grin. "See, dove. Still loads to do around here. We have your taverns, smithies, inns, gambling houses, even places to crack Jenny's teacup," he throws Caleb an exaggerated wink, "for a more… experienced taste."

Asa tugs on my hand. "What's crackin' Jenny's teacup mean?"

Caleb huffs out a loud, rib-cracking laugh. "Maybe in a few years, yer mum can explain it to you."

I glare at Caleb. I'd intended to ask Selina later, quietly, what exactly it meant myself. I don't need to, now. We follow Caleb through back streets, passing by large wooden buildings, and even taller red-brick buildings. Twenty paces and two turns later, Caleb stops at the head of a narrow street crowded with brick buildings and turns to us. He gestures over his shoulder at the biggest brick building I've seen in my life and holds his hands out. "Allow me to introduce you to The Golden Chalice. I spent many a night draggin' my half-dead carcass to my room after a long night here. We are goin' to have ourselves some real fun this night, lads."

Una adjusts her trifold over her pale locks before she shakes her head. "Not too much. I'd rather not draw attention to ourselves the first day here."

Caleb's eyes are full of dark enthrallment as he throws a beefy arm over her shoulders. "Port Royal is large and sinful. The risk that we'll hang is slim and we have the green-eyed water devil on our side. He can just put them under a spell like he did with the dock lad if we cause too much trouble."

Beside me, Demetrius tuts. "It is not a *spell*. Do not confuse my magic with that of the druid." The venom laced through his words surprises me.

Una shakes off Caleb's arm. "My pockets are lined, I'm feelin' forgiving, but touch me again, Caleb, and Demetrius and Selina won't be the only beings you'll fear."

We laugh, but it makes my head swim. Dark spots dance across my sight as I stare up at the buildings. As we move towards the tavern, each footstep brings another shock wave of pain up my legs and into my abdomen. It has my guts twisting so hard I nearly cry out. When we reach The Golden Chalice, there's a small crowd already gathered outside its doors. I'm so grateful to have stopped walking, I barely pay attention to what's going on.

"Come one, come all! Entry fee is just a drink from the pipe! Enjoy the best food, drink and entertainment in all of Jamaica!" a deep voice bellows.

I poke Ambrose in his back. "What's going on?"

Without answering me he lets out an ear deafening hoot and darts forward, weaving his way to the front of the crowd, Jonah hot on his heels.

Demetrius chuckles. "I believe we have to participate in some kind of drinking challenge to gain entry to the building. What a strange form of payment."

In front of me Atropous laughs. "Ambrose and Jonah haven't been on land a day and they're already causing trouble for the Captain."

Una seems disinterested, but I can feel, through our emotional link, amusement licking at her spine.

Asa jerks on my hand again. "Does this mean I get to try the wine too?"

Caleb pokes his fat finger into my shoulder, sneering at me. "Yeah, *Mum*. Gonna let the lad join us? Or are ye going to make him wait at the inn, all by himself?"

267

I resist the sudden urge to smack the imbecile out of him, instead turning my gaze to Asa. "Just one drink. A small one. Poseidon knows what's in that thing."

By the time we push our way to the front of the crowd, Ambrose and Jonah have disappeared inside, and the tavern's host is holding out an odd black stomach-shaped bag with a nozzle out to a wide-eyed Solomon.

"Your turn, lad, drink up!"

Caleb shoves Solomon so hard he stumbles forward. He rights himself and accepts the wine sack with a shaking hand, a mixture of shock and wonder on his face. He takes a quick drink from it, wincing harshly, and passes it to Una. She accepts it, with a glance in my direction. The moment of eye contact has my heart thumping harshly. After a quick swig, she passes it to Selina and enters the building. The moment she's out of my sight, the trickle in the back of my skull turns into a rapid flowing waterfall of urge, of desire and need to follow her. The host is holding out the flagon to me. Everyone else is already inside. Poseidon watch over me.

***

Amphitrite's sacred looking glass, someone please silence these loud buffoons. My temple pounds against my palm. Not wanting to spoil the fun, I've endured the last few hours of madness. Atropous had made me drink something that was like a clap of thunder in my head and my eyes are still swimming.

Solomon's disguise has allowed him to freely indulge in everything the pirate life has to offer on dry land with no fear of anyone shaming him for who he is. And though he's evidently enjoying himself, it saddens me that he should have to appear white to do so, here, in a land where the people born here have skin dark and rich. The timid, intelligent freed slave has one of the kindest spirits I've ever known, with one of the sharpest wits I've ever encountered, besides Demetrius. That kind spirit currently has his pallid but flushed cheek propped in his palm, elbow on the oak bench, as he watches a hooded Selina gamble with some dice and laugh with a few other crew members. There's a content, drunken smile on his lips.

Even Caleb has somehow acquired an audience, Asa among them, as he talks about the different kinds of knots and their many, many, *many* uses. This is apparently an interesting subject to a group of cupshot men and a young lad who doesn't know any better.

And now the entire tavern is singing dreadfully, that blasted song from the inn in Sainte Marie, the one about the innkeeper's wife, Jonah leading them, standing on a table and conducting with his fingers. Any attempts from him to hide his accent are long forgotten. Ambrose, four sheets to the wind, is sitting on a stool, bobbing his head along to the music, a cup of 'clap of thunder' in his hand.

An icy chill slithers up my spine and into my limbs, my vision blurs, this time not from the alcohol and I swallow back the sudden urge to empty my stomach. I turn to Demetrius, merrily swaying arm in arm with Atropous. "I'm going to wash up and turn in for the night."

He turns unfocused eyes to me. "Need me to walk you back to the inn?"

I note that, now he's drunk, he's no longer apparently concerned about my 'petals being plucked'. I shake my head. "It's less than a half mile from here, I'll be okay."

Demetrius leans forward planting a sloppy kiss on my forehead. "Keep your weapon close."

I stand slowly. "Make sure Asa gets to bed at a proper time, please."

My guardian mock-salutes me and turns his attention back to the show in front of him, Atropous drunkenly ruffling his hair. I bid my farewells and leave, feeling a heavy gaze on my back as I go.

***

I drop onto the bed. It has a real, honest-to-goodness mattress, the softest one I've ever felt, *and* the biggest. I press my face into the goose feather pillow; with my belly full, my body washed and changed into something not disgusting. A heaviness settles over me, my legs numb and feeling detached. That feeling slowly radiates up the rest of my body… and just as I'm about to slip away into blissful oblivion, a loud knock on my quarter's door has my eyes flying open.

I stand slowly, and as a nervousness that doesn't belong to me flutters in my chest, I know it's Una out there. Una is at my door… and I'm in nothing but a knee-length slip. A tremble starts in my fingers and spreads through my body. Part of me wants to fling it open, usher her in, lay eyes on her properly after she's been so distant. The other half wants to run. I'm afraid of what she could possibly want from me. Her spiraling emotions since everyone's secrets had come to light has been like a lump of coal dropped into my stomach, heavy and ready to ignite. I'm afraid of what seeing her will do to the part of me that wishes she would accept the bond, accept me.

She raps again, loudly, and I pull the door open. Una's eyes widen for a moment like she didn't think I was going to answer, then they survey my face. She tries to look nonchalant by pushing her hair from her face, then pulls herself to her full height. I've dropped my Octavia disguise, and she's taller than me. If she were to hold me, I would fit securely under her chin.

She clears her throat, her unwavering stare turning shy. "May I come in? I think it's time we talked."

I'm still trembling. Is it her nerves, or mine? I step aside and she strides in, her boots loud on the wooden floor. I close the door behind us, officially sealing the both of us alone together, both in our true forms for the first time since Sumatera Island. Both of us are raw and bruised and have no choice now but to be honest.

I chew my lips, tugging at the hem of my slip, unsure what to say or do now. "Would you like to sit?"

Una turns to me, eyes dancing along my face again. I feel them tracing every dark hollow and sharp angle. Hers has been scrubbed clean of the dirt, dust, and grime from being on the unforgiving seas for so long. Her skin glows like I remember from our days at the cabin. "Ladies first."

Her casual words make me smile slightly as I sit back down on the edge of the mattress made for royalty, curling my hands in my lap.

She hesitates a moment, contemplating me, before sitting beside me, an unreadable expression crossing her face. "I needed some time to digest what

270

happened on *The Revenge*…" I nod as she stares straight ahead, focusing on a spot on the far wall. "Once the shock of seeing you, the *real* you, in the water instead of Octavia passed, I realized I was happy to see you. Cruddy timing, absurd conditions, unbelievable, unthinkable!" She shakes her head, turning steely eyes to me. "But there was so much to take in. So much happened. I felt worn out. I needed time to think about it. All of it."

I hold her gaze as best I can, the heat in my cheeks making it difficult. "Both Demetrius and I being here… the strange abilities you have now, and the even stranger ones of your crew mates. You lost a ship, you lost some crew, had to stop it all falling apart around you. Anyone would need time to sift through all of that." I watch her unreadable gaze trace my face.

"That as well. But also, how Kai's your father, and how we have something called a bond that's somehow fated."

I feel the blood turn to ice in my veins. Damn you, Demetrius. I try to look away, ashamed, but she ducks her head to keep my gaze, leveling me with her stare. "I meant what I said aboard *The Protector*. No more secrets, no more lies. I can't handle any more betrayal, not from anyone. Not from you."

I twist my hands in my lap. "Kai had a part to play in my birth, yes. He stole me away from my mother when I was just a babe, kept me until I transformed at ten years old. As you can imagine, that caused quite the stir on his ship. He sold me to someone on land and that's where I stayed until Demetrius found me two years later." I bite my lip and will the sting of tears away. "It was my mother's dying wish that Deme find me… he was my mother's friend for nearly a hundred years." I look down at my lap. "You disappeared into the night without a word, you stole from me, my presence not needed or wanted in your plans of revenge…"

She reaches out and takes one of my hands in hers, lacing our fingers together. It makes me jump and I stare at her. She looks at our hands. "I… we barely knew each other. Yet you showed me such kindness without expecting anything in return. I can count the number of times I've been shown that on one hand." Her voice wobbles at the end and I see how hard it is for her to speak of her past, to vocalize her emotions. I lace my hand with hers more tightly, feeling the callouses on her

271

palm press into mine. I run my thumb along the top of her knuckles, hoping I'm able to send some silent comfort to her.

"You were this otherworldly beauty with a meddlesome father who, even after knowing what I was, chose to trust me. You opened your home and your lives to me. The only way I could show my gratitude was to leave before my sins soiled you, tainted that pure kindness, that pure heart. Stealing from you filled me with more guilt than I've felt stealing anything else in my life."

Her words spread the warmth in my cheeks over my face. She squeezes my hand. "And what do you think of me now? At this moment?" I ask.

Una's lips turn up into a half-smirk. "You still have a meddlesome father, and your beauty still stops me in my boots. Overlooking your God-awful luck in parentage and all the secrets, I don't think I could have made it this far without your constant companionship. Even seeing me at my lowest, my darkest, you've never wavered. I think someone as pure as you is a one-off in a life, in a world, like mine. I should've known there couldn't have been two of you."

Una's open, honest words have heat traveling down my neck and that secret longing part of me soaring to the surface like a ray of sunshine breaking through the clouds on a gray sky day. It momentarily blots out my weariness.

She squeezes my fingers again, and her face serious once more and says, "Can I ask a question?"

I nod.

"What is this bond? Does it have to do with these strange new abilities?"

I release my held breath slowly, feeling it blow over our joined hands. "Do you remember months ago, before you left the cabin? The scylla, the beast that attacked us on the beach?"

She nods, brows pulling together. "Yes... I thought it was going to tear you apart, but you ended up saving me... should've known, really. Bloody miracle I came out of that fine."

I lay my other hand over the one already tangled with mine. "You weren't fine. It nearly slayed you... I pulled you from the waters. Your body was broken. Barely breathing. A mess... I..." I falter, the image bringing with it the echoes of the panic I'd felt then. "I gave you the Gift of the Sea. It's an... *ability* my kind has. It— it healed your injuries, gave your life back. But it's also another reason I hid myself from you..." She tilts her head, those bottomless sea-storm eyes urging me to continue. "The Gift gave you life, the ability to breathe beneath the ocean, apparently grants us a mental link beneath the waves, and I an emotional tether to you. But in giving you all that, you must give something in return... Your servitude. Except for the incredibly strong-willed, those granted the Gift would find it increasingly harder to deny the whims of their mermaid, no matter the wish. You'd be drawn to me." She's trying to digest all this, her emotions flickering in my chest so rapidly I can't pick them apart. My mind is already a cyclone of its own, trying to figure out how to explain all this to her without making her think I'd ever planned to try and control her. I don't want her to think that I only saved her to get a servant in return. "Demetrius concocted a tonic that would dull all those effects for you and allow me to take them on completely. Una, your choice is the most important thing to me. I've never wanted to make you do anything against your wishes."

Her lips tremble slightly. "So... what I feel for you is just a product of this *gift?*" She spits out the last word like it's foul, her lips curling.

I turn and take our joined hands into my lap, shaking my head quickly. "To be honest, my knowledge on my mermaid half is scarce, my mother was tight lipped even to Demetrius about it and I've been slowly learning as I go, *but* what I do know is that I felt drawn to you long before I gave you the Gift, before any bond. If I didn't, I would've let you perish in the attack." Spurred on by her earnest and vulnerable expression, I keep going. "I knew the risks in giving it to you, for you and for myself, but I also knew I'd never force you to give up anything for me. You leaving so suddenly made it easier for me to handle my side-effects from the bond. I was content with my fate. But then Demetrius told me of Kai's part in your mutiny."

The tears I've been suppressing this entire time fill my eyes. "I knew what he put me through, what he must have put you through. I couldn't let you go after him and be killed by him. I didn't even know if I'd find you before you left Sumatera, or even if I'd have what it took to be in your crew, but I had to try. I couldn't let you die."

Her sun-tanned cheeks flush darker. "Your father, the nymph one, not Kai." She glances at me and I smile. "He seemed in a near panic, wanted me to speak to you the evening the truth came out. Hell bent on it, he was. Why? Does it have to do with why you've been so ill?" Sweet Amphitrite, she is observant. Damn you Deme thrice to Hades! "You never had the yellow fever, did you?" she presses. We both know it's not really a question.

I can no longer hold her gaze and drop mine to my lap. "A rejected bond means death for the mermaid. For my mother, Kai accepted their bond, but his will was stronger and he, somehow, shattered it."

The icy feeling in my body is flooded with warmth as Una's panic flickers through the bond. "You'll die?"

I chuckle, the sound holding no real joy, keeping my gaze lowered. "I *am* dying."

The hand I'm holding begins to tremble. Then she grips my fingers, crushing them. I look up and find Una turned more fully toward me, suddenly so close I see the flecks of blue in her stormy eyes. "The entire time you've been running around on my orders, raiding homes, commandeering ships at sea, and you've been *dying*? So that I can live?"

My heartbeat fills my entire body and I'm sure in the silent room she can hear it. "You do what must be done, your bravery is beyond measure. I see now why Elyse, as well as Kai, needs to be slain. Some souls are just too dangerous for this world. They've both taken so much from others, caused so much pain, when so many others are far more deserving than they."

Her lips twitch. "Me being among those others?"

I hold her gaze. If I'm going to lose everything anyway, I might as well throw it all in the pot right now. "You, above all else, deserve a happy life. Deme and I would help you achieve your revenge, I would see you survive through that meeting with them, somehow, and then I would go to rest knowing my death would ensure you get that chance to live, a chance to be truly happy."

"What about your chance to be happy?" Her gaze is intense, the emotions flashing through our link even more powerful than before, but then that's Una, a wave capable of both soft, gentle beauty and tumbling crashing, destruction.

"Una..." Her name is a whisper on my lips. I don't miss the tremble that seems to travel the length of her body. "You are my life. I've been tethered to you since the moment I pulled you from the waters next to my home... my precious person. Knowing you received what you wanted after all this time, that alone brings me happiness."

She bites her trembling lip. "What if that isn't all I desire anymore?"

It's my turn to tremble. Now we're so close, our noses brush, our hot breaths mingling. Her eyes dart down to my slightly parted lips then back up to my eyes. Her brows furrow for a moment before she untangles one of her hands, bringing it up to cup the nape of my neck. Her wind-chapped lips are on mine, barely a whisper. I lean forward, pressing my mouth to hers. The extent of my experience in this subject is only what I've read in books, seen in the streets, though this feels different than the frenzied, often transactional glimpses I'd seen. It's slow, unsure, hesitant. The hand that cups my neck slides to my cheek. She tilts my head to the side, connecting our lips more fully and I feel myself fall completely into her, everything else around me no longer matters. Only Una, and her lips against mine.

She pulls back, tears in her eyes. "I desire the bond. I accept you, Hanna. From this moment until my last dying breath."

The muddle of emotions flickering between us is suddenly clear as a bell. I can feel the pulse of her emotions like a separate heartbeat in my chest, rooting itself like it's always belonged there. I register her shock, then her wonder, and then her desire; her feelings as easily accessible to me as if they belong to me. That aching, painful weariness that's been laid over me for so long, a lead blanket, lifts, and it's like the first swim after an eternity away from sea. It fills my body with energy that I can't ever remember feeling even on my best day. My body feels like it's humming.

I know this surge of energy must've filled out my cheeks, dissolved the circles beneath my eyes, because Una brings up her other hand, holding my face like she was gazing upon a priceless treasure. "Shite, you're back to how you were when I first met you! Better!"

She blushes, her own gentleness embarrassing her, but it only endears her to me more. I touch her burning cheek, and then push the stray wisp of hair out of her face. "I quite return the sentiment. It's going to be nice being able to tell you how delightful you are. Keeping it to myself has been one of the hardest things I've ever had to keep from you."

She grins. "You are, indisputably, the most enchanting creature, human or otherwise, I've ever laid eyes on."

This time it's me closing the space between us, covering her lips with my own, praying to the gods and goddesses that I don't make a complete fool of myself. A tingle of her approval across the accepted bond gives me the courage I need to continue, deepening our first true kiss as a bonded pair. Excited, nervous tingles tighten my belly as she makes a low sound in her throat that has me holding her more solidly to my face. My heart pounds in my chest, my lungs burn, but I don't care. I'm filled with such delirious happiness that I can't think of the last time I felt so alive.

She pulls back, panting slightly, and rests her forehead against mine. "Blimey, Hanna. Where ya been hiding that this entire voyage?"

Embarrassment flares in my cheeks now. I'm ashamed of how much I want her. "Must you be so vulgar?"

She snakes her hand into the strands of hair at the nape of my neck. "No, no, don't be ashamed. It's okay…" A playful, wolfish smile curves her reddened lips. "And, vulgar you say?" She brushes her mouth against my cheek, tilting my head, dancing her curious lips along my jaw, to my ear. "I must find some way to show my apologies for my foul language…" She chuckles against my ear, vibrating lightning through me, then coils her other hand around my waist, pulling me firmly against her. It has a small gasp slipping from me. But her confident demeanor is proven a false bravado by the timid, skittish emotions coursing through the bond, and the slight tremble to her arm around me. She's just as nervous as I. She kisses my jaw softly again, and mutters, "Hanna, I… I want you. Is that okay? Can we be together?"

Euphoria. Undiluted, it rushes through my veins. I wrap my arms around her waist, the slope of her hips slimmer than mine, and pull her with me down onto the bed. Una holds herself above me, her arms braced on either side of me as she gazes down at me. I bite my lip. I'm so inexperienced, but I know what my heart and my body want. "Yes. Yes, Una. It's okay. I just… I've never… I've never done this before…"

She takes a breath and then seals her lips over mine again, her tongue darting into my mouth. It pulls a soft groan from my throat, she swallows it, pressing her body against me. She kisses me slowly, deliberately, with such purpose, her hands sliding to my hips, caressing the swell of them beneath my slip, stroking hot circles. I moan again, gripping the front of her linen shirt like she might suddenly draw away from me and leave me wanting more. In a world of things that could make grown men quiver with fear, I know as surely as I can feel Una's rapid heartbeat against my chest, that as long as she's by my side I can handle whatever this unpredictable life could possibly toss my way. My breath catches as one circling hand pushes my slip up my thighs, soon delving between them. She lifts her face to gaze at me, stroking my cheek with her other hand. It's all so overwhelming, but I'm so happy, tears slide down my face. She brushes them away with her thumb. She then blesses me with the softest, freest smile I've ever seen her allow on her face. She chuckles again, invigorated, rejuvenated, happy. She slides that thumb down my cheek, tracing the seam of my lips with the tip of it just as a tremor of pleasure courses its way down my spine, and I find myself gasping out Una's name, her hand between my legs bringing such pleasure, such freedom I almost can't breathe. I writhe beneath her. She watches my face as my eyes flutter shut and I arch against her, my vision flashing with sparks and intense, deep satisfaction.

"To our eternity, Hanna."

***

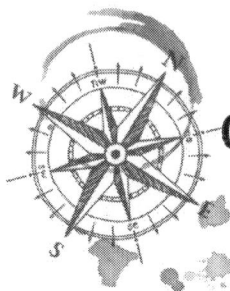

Chapter 32: Selina
30 October 1691
Port Royal, Jamaica

I swallow the overly spiced ale from my tankard as I gaze around the gathered crew. Solomon, the Captain, Hanna, Asa, Atropous, Ambrose, Jonah and I crowd around a long, freshly polished wooden bench. With Una's orders either completed or in hand, the eight of us relax at The Golden Chalice, indisputably the Captain's favorite tavern that we've visited thus far. Caleb and Demetrius have already turned in for the evening, thank the heavens. If I had to listen to one more insensitive insult from that oaf, or one more rage-inducing riddle from the nymph, it's highly likely I would've struck something. Or someone.

Una, smiling softly, pushes a towering stack of vanilla sweet cakes toward the disguised mermaid half-ling. Each dense layer of cake is separated by whipped cream and brightly colored fresh berries. Una's refused both the nymph's and my offer of disguising her as well, saying the sheer size of the island alone is plenty of cover. I can't blame her; she's done well dealing with all the oddities sprouting up around her like weeds. I would draw a line in the sand at some point as well.

The days have been blurred with constant action; Una's plan to locate her wayward sibling and the elusive Kai - whom, I was shocked to discover, is Hanna's biological father - isn't much different than when we'd been on Sainte Marie Island: locate anyone who might have information on them and squeeze them for all they're worth for it. She wanted the Captains but Ezekiel, their last living quartermaster, will do equally well.

The differences here is that Una's joined Caleb, Demetrius, and Hanna every other day when they scout. She's also made sure to spend equal time among the rest of her crew, even following Solomon, Jonah, and I into the marketplace to sell some loot. The change has been sudden; I'd just begun getting used to the cold, distant, slightly aloof woman and then she'd come to supper one day with a bright smile and sunny aura about her, a slight spring in her step.

I take another deep gulp from my tankard. The improvement in their relationship made me yearn to repair mine with Solomon. I glance at him out of the corner of my eye. His lips, disguised with my magic, are twisted into a large grin, a tankard of his own in his hand as he joyfully chats with Atropous. I barely suppress the sigh threatening to slip through my lips. Truth be told, I've had plenty of chances to talk to him about what occurred on *The Revenge*, my past, why I've done what I have done. Knowing Solomon and his ridiculously good heart, he'd listen and take everything on board as smoothly and gracefully as he always did, with that undiluted kindness that could only be rivaled by Hanna and Atropous... So why can't I do it? Blasted coward!

"Does this mean I get two mums now?"

I blink, coming back to the gathered group, and see Asa grinning a toothy smile from Hanna's side, a curious tilt to his head. Una sputters around the lip of her mug, her face flushing from forehead to chin. She coughs loudly as Ambrose and Jonah dissolve into loud laughter, and I know in this moment she's wishing Asa was back to tiptoeing around her, terrified and jumping every time she called his name. Hanna's disguised face flushes beet red, too. She shoves a forkful of fluffy cake into her mouth, looking straight down at her plate.

Una slams her mug down onto the bench, wiping the back of her hand across her mouth. "You... can call me Una, lad."

Asa nearly blinds me with the strength of his grin as he gazes happily at the still horribly blushing pair.

Jonah nudges Una with a shoulder, a huge grin of his own on his scruffy face. "I noticed the closeness. Who would've thought it was like *that* between you and the dear lamb?"

It's Hanna's turn to cough, as Una grabs her own tankard and gulps down at least half of its contents in one go. She punches him, not gently, on the shoulder.

Ambrose chuckles and slaps down a three of rapiers on the table between himself and Jonah, his pale green eyes gleaming like wet gemstones. "Lucky duck. If that dear lamb's daddy Deme heard you say that, your head would be takin' a nice trip away from those broad shoulders. I'd be careful. I swear to Mór-Ríoghain that nymph has eyes and ears everywhere. He'll hear ya, somehow." Jonah and he hold each other's gaze for a second before they both laugh raucously, knocking their closed fists together in an odd fashion.

Solomon, curious at the noise, turns from Atropous, a look of confusion drawing his eyebrows downward. "*That?* Jonah, what 'that' are you referring to?"

Una leaps into action just as Jonah's mouth pops open, a wicked smirk curling his lips. "Somthin' Jonah definitely isn't gettin' any of. I'm sure, if you asked Selina nicely, she'd be happy to tell you all about that."

Hanna and I both squawk out a strangled yelp at the same time, and she drops her fork. She recovers before I do, though, snapping her mouth closed, those soft brown eyes hardening. "What did I say about speaking that way in front of Asa?"

I'm impressed at how the half-ling uses the child as an excuse to hide her embarrassment. I have no such option and sink down into my collar. Una sends the displeased lass a smile that lightens the shadows from her face, one I've never seen on the Captain's face before. She picks up the fallen fork, nestling it back on the small dish. "The lad don't understand what we're sayin', do you Asa?"

The child responds by curling against Hanna's side, burying his face into her shoulder. "If I do, do I get in trouble?"

Ambrose, Jonah and Atropous collapse into peals of hysterics, while Hanna raises an eyebrow at a sheepishly smiling Una. The child is a lot more worldly-wise and observant than he lets on. I glance at Solomon and find him staring at me, his cheeks a pleasing shade of pink and a look of understanding now lighting his face. Oh hells. It both excites and terrifies me.

Hanna clears her throat, looking toward a still snickering Atropous. "How are your lessons with Demetrius going?"

Blessed Hanna, coming to the rescue. I owe you a drink, or *five*.

Atropous looks genuinely pleased that she's asked. There's a light to his eyes again that's been missing for months. "Great, actually. He found a deserted stretch of cove about two miles from the inn. We've started going down there to practice with the water at dawn."

Ambrose swipes up the pile of coins from the table following his winning hand. "Ya think you'll be able to change form like Deme? Or even the *draoidh* over here?" He cocks his head in my direction.

I shake my head at Ambrose's word for druid but can't help the small smile that tugs my lips upwards. Ever since discovering what I am, he's been fascinated, asking me peculiar questions every chance he gets. I quickly learned that his grandmother used to tell him tales of druid healers, traveling the lands healing people with their fantastical magics, before he went and became a Jolly. It was nice to have someone who seemed to be interested in my magic, no matter how odd it could be at times.

Atropous grins at him. "There won't be any magic that turns me into a bird, or any animal, but he does think I could be able to handle a transformation like the one he uses on himself and Hanna someday."

Asa rocks back and forth in his seat, excitement rolling off him in nearly tangible waves. "I want a tail! I want to turn into a bird!" He pouts. "I'm just... normal."

Hanna slides him the rest of her cake, pushing his overgrown hair from his forehead, smiling faintly. "There is nothing ordinary about you, my darling."

He grins back at her and I don't miss the look of adoration on the Captain's face as she watches the exchange. It has the slippery, green serpent of jealousy slithering its way under my skin again. At how easily they get along, how happy they seem. How like a family.

Jonah throws a few pieces of eight onto the table between him and Ambrose and begins dealing out cards between the two of them. "Well, aren't you three all peaches and cream? It warms my frostbitten heart."

"On that endearing, yet equally nauseating display, I'm going to turn in for the night." I rise to my feet. "Atropous, you're on deck duty with me tomorrow morn, don't be late this time."

Atropous salutes lazily with his tavern tankard, pulling a face at me.

Hanna has a smile for me as well. "Goodnight. Do be safe on your walk back to the inn."

Asa waves his cream covered fork at me. "Buh-bye dra-old-ith!" He tries and fails terribly at mimicking Ambrose's Gaelic word for my kind.

Una chuckles. "The townsfolk should be the ones kept safe from her. I pity the poor beggar who thinks she'd be an easy target."

I pull my hood over my head and turn away before they can see my smile, quickly exiting the humid tavern. Once outside, I gulp in the cool night as I dodge and weave through the still-crowded streets. If I were to speak to my past self of five year ago and tell her that we'd be a part of a pirate crew, I would have thought myself mad. I glare down at the black tattoos swirling along my arms and hands. Me ten years ago wouldn't have believed I'd have these, either. My mind then goes to Solomon, the slave turned pirate. His wit, kindness and heart are something foreign to me, baffling yet absolutely mesmerizing.

"SELINA!" As if my thoughts had conjured him, his voice slices through the night sky like a cutlass and has my legs locking, my body instinctively turning. Solomon hunches over his knees, hands on his thighs as he breathes heavily. Had he run all this way?

He straightens, smiling a gentle smile, that even in this disguise, radiates nothing but pure Solomon. "Allow me to escort you back. I know what they said back there, but I couldn't forgive myself if something harmed you."

I smile back at his sweet yet unneeded action. It warms me from my head to my toes. Doesn't he know, nothing can harm me anymore. Solomon's smile widens as he stares at me, and I feel my stomach flip. Well... maybe one thing could harm me. His smile disarms me. I swallow, my cheeks hot. "I... I'd like that."

He looks proud as a parakeet as he takes up a place on my left and we continue walking down the street, toward the inn, lapsing into a companionable silence.

Having him so close, so concerned for my wellbeing, has the thorn of guilt pressing sharply into my side again. Lying to Hanna, the closest thing I've ever had to a friend, lying to Solomon, for letting him feel things for me in this disguised white-woman form, for encouraging it, even though I knew what turmoil it put him in, what pain it caused him. How can he even stomach being near me?

"Here we are!" I'm pulled from my distressed thoughts by Solomon's chipper voice, and the large brick inn looms over us.

"So we are…"

We fall silent again, but this time it's uncomfortable. Solomon begins to fidget with the loop of his weapons sash. Say something to him, you cowardly child. Asa is braver than you, and he is seven! I open my mouth to say something, *anything*, but Solomon beats me to it.

"Could we speak? I know it's late, it's improper, but I'd like to talk about what happened aboard the ship."

Well thank Cailleach for that. Even if it makes my heart pound in my chest, so much so I'm sure it's going to beat a hole through my skin. This stagnation, this holding our breath, tiptoeing around each other, it must stop, one way or another. It's now or never. I nod my head once, giving him a forced smile. "Follow me."

***

I watch Solomon toy and fiddle with the objects scattered about the desk in my quarters. His fingers trail along the spine of a large text on herbs, then find some spare pouches, my pestle and mortar. His eyebrows pull into a frown as those strikingly intelligent eyes drag up from the desk to me.

"There's still a lot I don't know of this world, about you. I'd like to… if you'll allow me to, to get to know the true you."

Heat rushes to my cheeks as the normally shy man says such intimate words in such a forthright and earnest voice, his gaze not once straying from my face. Instead of answering, I let my eyes close, sealing off him and the world as I let the electric current travel outward from my stomach, into my limbs, filling me with so much energy it feels as if I could fly. That current turns scorching as it lights every vein, every tendon on fire. I know my markings are pulsing wildly, and by extension, the ones I'd drawn on Solomon will be, too.

I exhale slowly, willing my enchantment to shatter. Thank you for your assistance, wise ones. Your power is no longer needed, please return to your natural state. Take some of my energy with you, as payment. The energy fades as exhaustion washes over me. My knees almost buckle. The energy required to hold one enchantment is staggering, but two? It'd had my reserves nearly spent. Luckily for me the next full moon is only in a few days. I lower my hood and open my eyes to find Solomon back in his usual form, hazel eyes wide, full mouth dropped open in awe.

I clear my throat, the look on his face causing my cheeks to burn. "I've never been good at letting people get close…"

He toys with something on my desk as he continues to hold my stare. "The parts you told me of yourself, which were true, and which were false?"

Despite his gaze being open, free of any signs of hurt, that guilt presses sharply into me again. Our hours of hushed conversations on the ship, on deck at night, squirrelled under the stairs, stolen moments where we'd bared our scars and histories to one another, come rushing back to me. "It was true that I had to slay someone to gain my freedom, and it was true I witnessed my mother being slain. Eleesabeth was my guardian for six years, but she was also my mentor."

Solomon cocks his head slightly to the side, fingers continuing to blindly fiddle with things on my desk. "She was a druid as well?"

I nod. "Still is, if she lives."

His brows wrinkle. "How did you obtain your powers? I originally thought you were born as such, like the others, but the more I ponder, the more I believe the opposite."

I'm once again blown away by his intelligence. It isn't the flashy, thrown-around-to-show-off kind of intelligence like the water nymph's or the trying-far-too-hard-to-sound-smart kind, like Caleb's. Solomon just is a smart man. "I received them ten summers ago, when I was a child. It was a surprise to me and my father, and was the result of him slaying my mother for defying his whim."

Solomon gasps, his hands pausing on the desk. "He... he killed your ma?"

I nod, pursing my lips. "He intended to sell me off the next morn. You see, my father was the white master of a sugarcane plantation. My mother was one of his slaves."

Solomon's eyes grow twice their normal size as he realizes just how similar our pasts were. And now, I come to the part where my half-truths become just the truth. "I had only just met my mama, the night she was slain. I'd been brought up with children I assume were close in age with me, but that's a guess since none of us were allowed to know our parents, or age. It made it easier for them to control us." His awed expression shifts to one of intense grief. Grief for me, grief I'm unworthy of. I swallow again. "I wasn't the only one he wanted to sell off. He held us in the barn. I remember being scared, I couldn't sleep, I just stared through the cracks in the warped wood as I laid in a small pile of straw. I could see the full moon through one of those cracks. I remember closing one of my eyes so I could see it better. I remember being jealous of it, so far away from the darkness, so high in the sky, so free."

Solomon's hand has moved from the desk to grip the front of his billowing, cotton shirt, a pained look darkening his face, a mist of tears in his eyes. Sweet, sweet Solomon... who cries for the child I was, the lives we both lived, the pains we both endured.

I press on, knowing if I wait any longer, I too will succumb to my tears. "I don't know how she got the key to the barn, but it was flung open. I expected it to be my father there to sell us off early, but it was her. The moment the doors were open, she yelled at us all to flee. The others listened, running to freedom, but I was rooted to the spot, staring at this woman I'd never met, who yet somehow seemed familiar." I breathe in a quivering breath, then slowly release it, as I come to the part in my past I'd never told anyone, not even Eleesabeth. "I remember her eyes, the deepest darkest brown I'd ever seen. She shoved a small pack in my arms, exclaimed on how big I'd grown. I asked who she was, and she barely got the chance to tell me my own name and that she was my mama." My blasted lip begins to tremble, I bite it, shutting down the long-suppressed feelings. "As I stood there watching her blood soak the dirt, her words struck something within me. I knew she was telling the truth. My father was angry, he had just lost eight slaves and didn't seem to care if he lost a ninth. He re-loaded his gun as he advanced on me, and I prayed for someone, anyone to help me. I'd've given anything. I didn't want to die yet, I wanted to live." The mist in Solomon's eyes spills over, and tears silently trail down his cheeks. "My powers awakened then. I remember a surge of energy, a bright light, then he was laying on the ground, dead. These markings appeared then. The moment I fled the barn and slipped into the cover of the trees, I had my first vision."

Solomon sniffles through his tears. "Vision?"

I let his curiosity blot out my nerves, spur me forward. "Unlike my enchantments, changed forms and knowledge of herbs and tonics, things I've had to study and learn, my foresight is a natural ability. It came to me that night and gives me visions of my future – sometimes immediate, sometimes further off, but always, fated to come to pass. Flashes of land masses, images I've never seen before, smells I've never smelled before, somctimes even tastes from foods I've never eaten before. Those, along with some thinking, will power, and lots of failure, lead me to my next destination, where I'll get another vision and so on and so forth. I spent a year following these odd visions and the peculiar pull near my stomach, gaining my bearings, until it eventually led me to Eleesabeth. Upon seeing my markings and hearing how I came to her she knew that I was what she was, a druid."

His tears fall silently, both hands limp at his side. Despite his grief, a wave of relief washes over me, like a breath of fresh air finally, after so many years. I hadn't known the full weight of holding the truth to myself all this time, until telling the entire truth to someone. It's like gaining my freedom all over again.

"Did you see me with your foresight? Is it what led you to me and Una?"

I'm once again in awe at how easily he handles and accepts things as they are. "It is. Over my six years of honing all my abilities I had a vision of me being high above, overlooking an island I'd never seen before. My senses were instantly overwhelmed with the smell of brine. With the help of a map and my mentor, it started me out on my journey to this future, to help Una pull together her pirate crew. It took three years, but I eventually found my way to Sumatera Island, and to our Captain."

Solomon holds my gaze another heart catching moment before turning his attention to my desk. He scoops up a length of thin rope from one of my herb pouches and plops down onto the floor right where he stands, cross-legged. He works the length of rope over itself, working a knot, before his hands still and he looks back up at me. "Is that why you got so distant? 'Because you think you are undeserving after concealing yourself this whole time? Letting me have affection for you, not declining it, though you knew my status and what me having affection for a white woman would mean?" His large hands begin to work the length of rope again, his eyes still on my face. "You wanted to live, as did Hanna, Demetrius, Atropous. It's why they hid their true selves, and still do. Lord, it's why Una disguises her female form. Why Jonah pretends he's not British, why Ambrose pretends he is. Probably why Caleb pretends he can't read. If I damn you, I must damn them, and myself as well. And I don't think I have it in myself to do that. That's an awful lot of people to be mad at, a lot of hate to hold in my heart."

I'm utterly flabbergasted. He's taken all this in his stride as gracefully and as pure as he always has with all things. I shouldn't have expected anything less of him, but it still has my heart stuttering. "You truly feel that way?"

He nods, motioning with one of his hands for me to join him. I carefully lower myself onto the smooth wooden floor beside him. This close, I can see the flecks of green in his cool brown eyes. "I do truly feel this way, yes. It's not as if I'm without secrets. I'm sure you wonder how you and Una found me already able to read and understand maps."

My lips twitch. "The thought may have crossed my mind a time or two."

A soft, throaty chuckle leaps from between his full lips, and he looks down at the knot he's weaving. "When the pirates attacked us at the dock, I escaped. I hid and stole when I could for six months. Winter came, and food, fresh water and even beer was hard to scavenge. It had been a week since I'd had a scrap of food, and two days since liquid had passed my lips. I was surely a wisp away from death when a small, circular bottle had been tossed in the sand next to my head." He holds his knotwork up to inspect. An intricate thing, his large hands so delicate in working at it. Then he begins to work at turning the rope over itself again. "I pulled myself up and saw what I first thought was a tumbling wave, yet its presence on land made me instantly wary. That wave slowly tumbled and thrashed its way into a semi-human shape. If you saw its hair you'd instantly be reminded of Demetrius or Atropous when they become wet."

I gasp. "A water nymph saved you?"

Solomon smiles, a soft fond one that makes my stomach roll. "It was, though at the time I didn't know that's what it was. All I knew was that it saved my life. The next day I returned to the same spot, around the same time and, sure enough, the creature returned, though this time with a map and a soft pillow of bread that made me feel full and energized for two entire days. For three months, it and I did this dance. It would bring a new source to read and food or drink, and it would teach me. It had a child-like demeanor to it, kind of like Asa, even though it knew so many things!"

"Is that why you were sitting on that rock so early in the morn when we found you? You were waiting on the nymph?"

He grins. "It had actually just left me when you and Atropous arrived. You were lucky I was too full to run away." He chuckles lowly to himself and sets the length of rope in my lap, a perfectly tied clove knot in the center. "So, does knowing how I've lied to you change how you feel for me? Am I somehow less deserving now?"

I finger the knot, trying not to care that I'm blushing like a silly maiden. "That's different... I..."

Him shaking his head has me clamming up immediately. "You lied to protect yourself, just as the rest of us have. Humans, and I've since learnt, non-humans, are not without flaws. It's something that binds us all despite our many differences. While not always redeeming flaws, we come together and overlook them. We forgive. Whether it be for selfish reasons or noble. I can forgive you if you can forgive me."

288

My pulse jumps as I clench the knot in my fist. "I— I'm sorry for being so distant, also for allowing your advances and encouraging them. I should have at least waited until I told you the truth."

He gives me a grin so wide it has a slight dimple appearing in his left cheek. "I'd truly be enraptured by you no matter the form you took, and gladly take whatever pain to court you properly." The green swirls in his eyes are brighter as he leans closer.

I cover my nervousness with jests. "Have you gotten a hold of Jonah's literature again? Ya know that romantic drabble will rot your mind."

He smiles, but it's faint, distracted. His face draws closer, and the scent of citrus is on his skin, the mouthwatering smell drawing me forward. He moves at the same time I do and suddenly his lips are on mine, wind-chapped and so warm. I feel heat travel through my body. He makes a low sound of desire in his throat before one of his large hands grasp both of mine that still grip tightly to the knot in my lap.

He pulls back suddenly, his face bright red, his eyes as large as the china ware they sold on Sainte Marie island. "This is the opposite of how proper courting is done!"

I laugh then, loud and full. It's a lively energy that fills me with a warmth, different then when I was connecting and requesting fire from my ancient wise ones. I take both his hands in mine and give him the biggest smile I've ever given anyone. "We have all our lives to court properly. But for right now? Just… do that again."

***

Chapter 33: Ambrose
1 January 1692
Port Royal, Jamaica

I dig my bare heels into the cooling sands of the secluded beach. Demetrius had found this place during our first few days here. I don't know why no one else seems to ever come here. I've seen a couple of fishermen a few times, but that seems to be it. I take a deep breath, pulling the air into my lungs, and it causes me to shiver as a chill zips along my spine.

We've had some time to ourselves over Christmas and the New Year, and with all the ship's work dealt with for the day, Demetrius had asked for Caleb's help with Atropous's training. Hearing this, naturally nothing could keep me from bearing witness to whatever tricks the impish nymph is going to put the foul-mouthed ruffian through. Without much prodding, Jonah's come along as well.

I watch a shirtless Jonah deftly dodge a massive lunge from Caleb. Caleb's shirtless too, heavily panting, his brown eyes narrowed in anger as he clenches his fist and takes a swing at Jonah's jaw. Jonah, in turn, grabs the fist out of the air, stopping it a mere breath from his face, the slap of knuckles against palm loud in the quiet beach. Then Caleb balls up his other hand and tries swinging it toward Jonah's exposed ribs. Jonah reacts by roughly pulling Caleb's body toward him, then swiping Caleb's beefy legs out from underneath him with a quick swing of his booted foot. Caught off guard, Caleb tumbles to the sand, his back and then his head hitting the beach. Jonah jumps back two steps, arms already raised and poised to defend, a familiar arrogant smile curling his full lips. I can't help but chuckle out loud, remembering the massive lump I sported for a fortnight after the one and only fight Jonah and I had ever gotten into as youths.

My eyes slide from the brawling pair to the two water creatures. They stand to the side, close to the shoreline and soft waves. Their heads are tilted towards one another, their eyes focused on the fight in front of them, their mouths moving in hurried, unheard whispers. What could the *aes sidhe* be talking about?

I stretch out into the sand, letting its warmth caress my weary muscles, soothe the ache in my bones and the weariness in my heart that we have still not found any clues that would lead us to our targets. Una's sibling and Kai were proving far tougher foes than originally thought.

Caleb growls, pulling himself up from the sands, wiping the back of his hand across the blood flowing from his now-split lip. Jonah's smirk turns devilish as he watches the loud-mouthed buffoon hawk crimson spittle onto the sands.

It's truly baffling how thirteen years can change an entire life, an entire way of thinking. Yet, through all the bizarre adventures, one thing always remains the same. Steady and by my side, refusing to leave no matter what, even if it would make his life so much better. Simpler. Jonah. He casually sidesteps as Caleb hurtles at him with a bellowing battle cry, Jonah's hands folded behind his back, his posture tall, his entire form radiating superiority.

Caleb pinwheels past him, arms flailing. He begins to hop on one foot, his bad leg giving him more trouble after being struck down once already. With a mischievous grin, Jonah closes the small gap between them and pulls one of his long legs back. With a wink in my direction, he swiftly swings his leg, booted foot connecting solidly with Caleb's backside. The already-off-balance man shouts loudly in surprise before landing face first in the sand, rump up, legs twisted awkwardly underneath his large body.

"That's checkmate, old chap. Better luck next time."

Caleb wastes no time in pulling himself to his knees and turning, sputtering sand from his bloody and cracked lips. He drags his obese body to one chunky booted foot. "Fight me without all the fancy-arse pommy shite, then maybe ye can say you beat me!"

Jonah's eyes flash dangerously at Caleb's use of the derogatory term, and he takes a threatening step closer. "Would the lazy sod feel better if I bound an arm behind my back? Or perhaps if I shut one eye? Perhaps then you'd actually have half a chance against me."

The fire raging in Jonah's eyes is reflected in Caleb's, and the bigger man lays a hand on Marigold's sheath, still secured to his waist, his eyes darting to Jonah's hand slowly inching dangerously close to his own blade.

"Wanna say that to my face, ya two-bit sodomite?!"

I hiss in a breath, ready to leap to my feet and slam Caleb back to the ground, but Demetrius's clear voice cuts through the dusk sky, just as Jonah slides his glimmering Navy blade from his black sash. "Enough! Caleb, you have done your duty. Leave."

Caleb looks about ready to hurl abuse back at the nymph but sees the steel in Jonah's gaze, finds me braced to fight also, finds Demetrius and Atropous both glaring at him, and knows he's outnumbered. Halfwit. Why does he insist on saying such inflammatory things when he's always outnumbered? He grumbles nonsense as he takes a few steps from a still-simmering Jonah, hunches to pick up his discarded brocade. "What ye even need me here for?"

Demetrius clucks his tongue, his pulsating green eyes darkening with his disappointment. "It's true I'm teaching Atropous of his nymph heritage, but I'm also teaching him other things. His reading. Combat. One can learn a lot by simply observing."

Jonah scoffs, running the pad of his thumb along the dull part of his curved sword. "Even with your-arse-about face way of training, a dullard such as yourself should know at least that much."

I see the muscles constrict and ripple over Caleb's chest as he tenses, ready to lunge at Jonah, when a sudden four-foot wave comes crashing over them both, dousing the angry men in icy waters.

I inspect a glowering Demetrius, his eyes as luminous as the full moon starting to take front and center in the star filled sky. His arms are raised in front of him, his fists curled into balls towards himself. "I said you are finished. You both are."

Caleb coughs, sputtering out a mouthful of sea water as he palms his waist, making sure his precious companion Marigold didn't get swept away by the slowly receding wave. Jonah shakes out his chin length hair, swiping it back from his face, pouting childishly. It's an expression that takes me back to the day Jonah and I first met.

"I ain't gonna call you master just 'cause I have to... just 'cause you own me now."

"I don't want you too. You can call me Jonah, and I'll call you... Ambrose. It means immortal."

Jonah's deeper voice sighing overlaps with the child-like laugh ringing in my ears, and I find him sitting next to me, his fingers just finishing the last button on his shirt. Not far away, Caleb stomps up the narrow path, his burly shoulders hunched so high around his head you can no longer see his neck. I slide my gaze back to Jonah as he attempts to coif his sopping hair, the ends dripping.

I smirk. "You look worse than that time you fell into the moat."

He lets out a throaty guffaw, turning to smirk sideways at me. "I'm still too dashingly handsome for the likes of this world. And, if my memory serves me correctly, I didn't fall in, you shoved me." His hoot of loud, full laughter has some of my own bubbling in my chest and I'm once again in awe of his ability to find the good, the fun in anything. It had made being taken and sent away to a foreign place loads easier when I was a boy. I wouldn't have survived this long without him.

"DON'T!" I'm pulled back by Jonah's accent-laced yell of terror. "My knickers can only handle one wave! It's bloody cold! Do you even feel it?!"

I see Demetrius, eyes glowing, mouth set in a hard line, his hands raised halfway into the air, a threat to us for making too much noise, I suppose, while he schools his student. Beside him, Atropous looks sheepish, stuck halfway between a laugh and an expression of fear. The sun has well and truly set now, the horizon just a shade lighter than the night sky. The moon is full and huge and bright.

Demetrius rolls his eyes, dropping his arms back to his side. "If you wish to stay and watch, then settle yourselves. As to your question, no I do not feel cold, and it is my theory that the more Atropous uses his magic, the more abilities he will awaken. He soon may be immune to it as well."

"WAVE! DO IT AGAIN!" A small blur zips across the beach, flinging itself down onto the sand next to me. I look down into Asa's glittering chestnut eyes, a huge toothy grin covering his face.

When I look over my shoulder, I spy Selina, Solomon, Una, and Hanna, all undisguised and all heading down the narrow sandy path onto the secluded stretch of sand. Una and the raven-haired half-ling cross the uneven terrain of the beach, their hands clasped together, swinging slightly back and forth between them. With her free hand, Una brushes some existent, or non-existent debris, away from the exotic lass's cheek before giving a playful tug to Hanna's long hair.

Selina and Solomon are not far behind, their arms entwined casually as a soft smile passes between the two. The previous tension that caused an unnecessary rift between the two seems, thankfully, gone. I watch the draoidh's flaming amber eyes observe the beach and her surroundings, seemingly seeing everything in one sweep.

"This area is not as secluded as I thought it would be. Lucky for us I had the things I needed to put a ward on the path to this spot."

Beside me, Asa bounces, his small body thrumming with energy. "It was *so* ace! It was like the path just disappeared!"

Hanna laughs, lavender eyes gazing adoringly at the excited child. "Think, Demetrius's hypnotic allure but for an entire area. It tricks the eye into not seeing the entrance to the path. It was most fascinating."

Una drops lazily onto the sand next to Asa, reaching a hand up toward Hanna. The half-ling grabs the offered fingers with a gentle smile and lowers herself gracefully down. "Should've seen Caleb's face when he saw Selina doin' it. He's never run so fast in his life."

A ward?! A real druid ward?! I'm positively brimming with jealousy!

"What are *you* doing here?" Even before I turn my head back to Demetrius, the anger and vitriol in his voice is obvious. Despite the other people now occupying the space, the intently staring nymph only has eyes for Selina.

To her credit, she holds his impenetrable gaze, unwavering. "If it matters to you, tonight is the first full moon of the Winter Solstice cycle. I needed a place to come to meditate while my powers are rejuvenated."

Demetrius's thin eyebrows quirk, twisting his face into a sneer. "A restoration ritual, is it not? I didn't know if the myths held true. Tell me, is it also true that if you use up your powers, you become as weak as a mortal, unable to access your magic, until the next full moon can replenish you?"

I see Atropous take a cautious step in front of Demetrius, his tall, lanky frame serving as a human shield between the seething magic wielders. His eyes are filled with nervousness, the same nervousness pounding through my veins. This feels wrong. The same kind of warning like just before an attack on the battlefield, the same feeling of anticipation and gooseflesh. Jonah licks his lips, eyes carefully watching, too. Though a battle between the druid and the nymph… that would be some brawl. Wonder who would win?

Selina's jaw clenches. "I become weaker, yes. My energy diminishes every time I access my abilities. Once depleted, it becomes difficult to call on my magic, though not impossible." Those unusual eyes simmer with unsaid rage.

Hanna, blessed woman that she is, jumps in. "We've all come to watch this restoring ritual, also to keep watch over her. Please join us, Father."

That spiraling wrath all but fizzles out as Hanna addresses him, his entire body seeming to deflate. "I… suppose I could stay for a bit."

Asa cheers loudly, while Hanna gives her adoptive father a large, slightly crooked but reassuring grin.

Atropous, too, relaxes, and wanders over to sit on Jonah's other side. He smiles timidly at Selina. "Do we need to do anything to help ya?"

Her lips turn up into an amused, half-smile. "That's sweet, lad. But no, just sit back and relax. This isn't going to be as entertaining as ya think."

Demetrius settles at Hanna's right side, hooking his arm with her free one, resting his chin on her shoulder. I can't miss the look of displeasure that crosses Una's face though she quickly buries it. We all watch silently as Selina removes her dark cloak, then her shoes, and finally her weapons. She offers the bundle of items to a gently smiling Solomon.

I clear my throat, eyes darting to the warded path. "What happens if someone who knows of the pathway comes to search for it? Does your ward still trick their senses?"

Selena grins wolfishly as Solomon seats himself on Demetrius's left side, completing our line. "They *won't* see it."

The dark certainty weaved into her words has an insuppressible shudder running the length of my spine, and all my other questions fizzle out on my tongue. "Well that's the most menacing thing I've ever heard in my life."

Selina pulls several pouches from her leather belt, all of them dyed different colors, and opens them one by one, laying them on the sand at her feet. She starts with a red pouch, dipping her whole hand in and pulling out a fistful of black soot - it looks like gunpowder from this distance - and sprinkles thick, heavy lines of this powder on the pale sands. She sets the red pouch down, then picks up the green, repeating the same process.

I watch in an awed stupor as she continues to create a pattern of colored lines swirling and interconnecting in a beautiful design. As it continues to take shape in front of us, I get a feeling of familiarity. The dark markings seem to shimmer brighter under the bright moonlight.

Una leans forward from her spot between Asa and Hanna, trying to get a better look. "What's with the circle?"

Selina rolls her luminescent eyes and continues to work on her ritual. "It's not a circle, it's a spiral, a knot. It represents balance in one's life, both inside and out. It also represents water, the Sun and the heavens, and will help me center myself and make meditation easier."

Solomon raises a hand into the air a moment before speaking. "You will sit in the middle of it and... med-a-tate?" He says the last word slowly, his lack of comprehension evident.

"It's like... I go to a quiet place inside my mind, where I'll be more open, more receptive to the energy around me. The marks on my arms will help me absorb that energy faster."

"I WANT COOL MARKS THAT LET ME TALK TO THE MOON!" Asa crows. All of us laugh, even Demetrius.

With a quirk of her lips, she drops wordlessly into the center of her knot, legs folded, her balled fists resting on her knees. She sits up straight, eyes falling closed, and becomes so still it doesn't even look like she's taking a breath.

The wind picks up around us, swirling my hair in and out of my vision as Selina's marks begin to pulse like they had done when she shifted forms. Holy Dagda, this is phenomenal! Grandmum would never believe this! ...Well, actually, she probably would.

Around me, everyone reacts in varying degrees of surprise and interest to the ritual; Solomon, Asa, Atropous and Hanna are entrapped by the ethereal, almost inhuman, being in front of us. All their faces hold the same expression of wonder, awe, and shock. Una's gaze is elsewhere, not on this almost fabled creature in front of us, but on the speechless mermaid half-ling. Her gaze is clear, bright, and filled with such warmth, I scarcely believe this is my Captain. The nymph still rests his cheek against Hanna's shoulder, his head too turned away from Selina, instead turned toward the slightly thrashing waves of the ocean.

The more Selina's marks pulse, the more the air feels charged, like it does right before a lightning strike. It has all the small hairs on my arms raising, on the back of my neck too. A puff of warm breath on my cheek has me turning my head. Jonah is leant close, his breath fanning across my lips and cheek, a stark contrast to the chilled air around us.

He eyes me from the side, a slight smirk on his lips. "Ever think, when we borrowed that lifeboat, we'd end up here? Guarding a druid while she absorbs magical energy through the moon?"

I smother my laugh against my fist, not wanting to get yelled at for interrupting. "Thirteen years ago, I never would have thought I'd have been sent to work off my grandmum's debt in your stables. I definitely didn't think I'd work my way up in the ranks the way I did. And I'm not sure anyone would agree with your definition of borrowing." He grins, unabashed, as I bump my shoulder against his. "I most certainly didn't think I'd get stuck with your beastly self, but I suppose we end up where we are meant to be, in the end."

He chuckles, the sound warm, full, and happy. Far different than the dull, forced ones he tossed about when we were boys. I watch him laugh a moment longer before dragging my eyes to the endless sky and its infinite starlight. Honestly? There is nowhere else in this strange, fantastic world I would rather be.

***

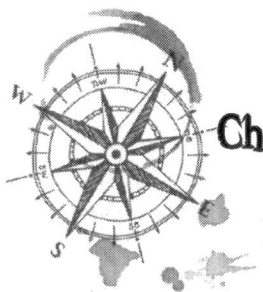

Chapter 34: Caleb

15 January 1692
Port Royal, Jamaica

"Caleb! Wait, you forgot Delilah!"

The blood surges through my veins at the smattering of laughter echoing behind me. I about-face, glaring for all I'm worth at the gathered members of the crew. A crew I'm bloody trapped in!

The mermaid that had called out to me sits on the Captain's left, an annoying smile on her face. Across from her is the he-witch Atropous, and lastly the pair of ex-Jolly tarts.

Duties done for the day, I'd somehow gotten pulled along to 'bond with the rest of the crew.' The blasted wench's words. After the last round of cards with that salt-licking Jonah cheating his perfect arse off, I have to leave before I give in to the urge to put my booted foot somewhere the sun doesn't reach.

The disguised lass holds out a decent sized, leather bound, sheathed dirk with a polished, carved wooden hilt. Delilah. A gift the half-ling had given me on Christmas. It's the nicest weapon I've ever carried on my belt, but I'll never let the she-devil know that. I snatch it from her, careful to avoid those disgustingly kind eyes and smile, and stuff it in my belt, tucking it snugly next to Marigold.

"Walk well, Caleb."

The wench's cheery words are followed by Jonah's deep rumble of a chuckle. I look to the end of the tavern bench and see him pulling a large pile of coin, folded notes, and a high-end looking gold ring on a gold chain towards himself, away from a glaring Atropous and Ambrose, who's frowning deeply.

He smirks to himself, picking up the golden chain and bringing it close to his face to inspect. "Oh, plum! Don't waste your worries on him, if his own idiocy hasn't killed him yet, I'm certain nothing will." His attention quickly shifts from the booty he'd won in his game, to another kind of booty entirely; a busty bar wench leans over him to replace the empty pitcher of ale with a full one. Her eyes immediately zero in on him, handsome devil that he is, interest clear all over her face. Lucky as sin, sure as hell doesn't deserve it! The pommy's grin turns devilish and he leans in close, whispering unheard words in her ear, eliciting loud giggles as the wench smacks his shoulder lightly.

"The only idiot here is you, Jonah." The red-cheeked, flaming-eyed Ambrose stares at his chum, disgusted. Jonah catches his tone and is torn between the jiggling wench and his friend but can't seem able to drag himself away from her plentiful assets. Ambrose, sulky, looks at me. "Aye, Caleb. Walk safe, want to have a sparring match tomorrow? My morn just opened up."

I blink at the strange lad, then snort. "Sure." Then I'm turning my back on them with a shake of my head. Weird bunch of loons.

As I push my way through the tavern toward the exit of The Golden Chalice, a chorus of their farewells ring loudly from behind me. Jonah surprises me by tossing a farewell out himself. The two of us had been nearly constantly at odds since the brawl on the beach.

Outside, I easily slip into the busy flow of townsfolk. Even though it's nearly twilight, the crooked town and its people are still bustling. I inhale a deep breath of the night air. Gods, it's good to be back here. Even if it be with unfavorable company.

I continue blindly following the river of people, with no real goal in mind, my thoughts slipping to all the tasks, missions, and dealings since the New Year. The water nymph, mermaid, Captain and I had searched from the Meat Market to Saint Paul's Church, all the way to Fort Carlisle with not a sign of her twin or Hanna's father, not even someone who had any information on them. In between scouting, Demetrius joined us, using his strange hypnotic tricks to get the merchants and stall workers to lower prices of top shelf items for us. At times, they'd hand them over, no fuss, with just one bright smile from the bizarre creature. A useful trick to keep the pockets lined, but it took the thrill out of a good haggle.

With no progress of any sort being made, the Captain's annoyance is climbing by the day. Even her little gumdrop couldn't get her to lighten up most days. Oh Lordy, what if this job never ends? I'll be stuck with these demons for the rest of my days! I shake my head quickly. No. Don't think like that, ye pathetic gutter rat. You have a pocket full of pieces and endless options. Pick somethin'! As I continue to make my way around the seemingly never-ending buildings, one sign finally draws my eyes back to it.

The sign is carved from, probably took forever, probably cost years' worth of wages! The letters that spelled out the words 'The Crimson Dagger' are also carved, also probably out of wood, painted in a deep, glossy red. With its all-brick building and high arches, it appeals to me. I pull out of the flow of people, pushing into the sizable tavern.

A low, candle-lit space with an uncountable number of dark wooden tables, stools and chairs of all sizes greet me. Musicians play a slow, rhythmic melody in one of the corners, lifted on a small platform all their own. The vibrations of the strings on their theorbos make my chest swell with the echo of it.

Patrons huddle together, heads lowered at tables, playing cards, throwing dice, or just trying the island's local food and drink. I grin as I walk to the bar lined with long legged, high backed chairs all facing toward the tavern worker diligently preparing drinks. The tall bar chairs all sport plush little plump cushions. They might be stained and torn, but by God do they look welcome. Busty wenches in loose-laced corsets scurry around the place with circular wooden trays in their hands, some piled with empty tankards, some full.

I slide on to one of those stools and nearly groan in pleasure - this is probably the softest chair I've ever sat on. An honest to God pommy pub! Where have you been all my life, beautiful? I tap my thumbs against the high counter, settling deeper into my heaven-sent seat, looking around, waiting for the busy barkeep to notice me.

Two others also sit at the high bar. The first is an older man with graying hair, clad in light brown fisherman garb. His head is turned toward the music, his weathered boot tapping the rhythm on the wooden floor. The second is a younger

301

man, closer to my age, his elbows propped on the bar, his face held in his hands, upper half hunched over a nearly empty pub tankard. A few other completely empty tankards are scattered around him. His hunched form is clothed in a deep burgundy doublet edged in expensive braiding. His pantaloons are a deep black, the ends tucked into pricey-looking leather boots. Dark straight hair is held at the base of his neck, half hidden under a deep crimson bandanna, and on his hip, barely hidden, a deadly pistol that immediately reminds me of the one the twisted Demetrius had taken from the mouthy gutted Indian Eli. So similar, in fact, that this pistol could be its twin. Could my luck truly be this good?

I finally catch the busy attendant's eye and call him over with a sharp jerk of my head. "Three peach juices, 'keep. Two for me, one for the glum fellow over there."

The barkeep dips his head in silent acknowledgment and scuttles off, as my target slowly straightens his shoulders. He then rotates in his seat so he's facing me straight on, one of his eyes hidden behind a dark black patch. This one's another Indian for sure; his sharp, angular cheekbones are flushed, his one visible nut-brown eye fogged over from the effects of his drinking. And swirling just behind that fog, is a touch of suspicion. I hold his gaze, smoothing my face into one of lazy indifference, one perfected after years that not even Demetrius's devil magic could see through.

This man that I suspect to be Elisha's older brother suddenly grins, dispersing some of the foggy suspicion from his eyes. "Well, a friendly stranger in this hell hole? Lady luck is finally shining favor on me!" He stands haphazardly, crossing the small distance between us and dropping himself messily unto the stool beside me, nearly missing the seat altogether. Only his iron grip on the back of the chair saves him from an embarrassing fall.

I watch him reach for his forgotten, nearly empty tankard, almost toppling himself over again in the process. There be no way in three hells this is that snarky Indian's older brother, this one's pathetic!

The barkeep returns with our drinks. As instructed, he sets two in front of me and the other in front of this already wickedly grinning man. I toss some pieces into the waiting palm of the barkeep and watch my seatmate guzzle down the remaining liquid in his mug before eagerly diving into the one I've just bought him.

His face contorts into one of pure bliss as he slams the now empty tankard down and throws me a sloppy grin. "Name's Ezekiel. Mighty fine tastes in drink you got there, chum."

I take a deep drink from my own mug, barely able to contain the smile that threatens to push its way on to my lips at how everything's turned so greatly in my favor. I set the mug down, clearing my throat, a final measure to make sure my grin stays where it should.

"Michael's what they call me. And ye looked to be in need of a lift." The false introduction tumbles easily from my lips. The Captain had seen a strategic use in hiding our names at the very least.

Ezekiel looks me over from head to toe with his one good eye. "How long you been ported here?"

"Just got in this morn, haven't been back here in nearly seven year." Mostly true.

Ezekiel chuckles, the noise a gruff growl. "That explains why you're still pleasant, the shine of this place hasn't worn off yet."

I slide my second, still untouched peach juice over to the loose lipped pirate. The looser the tongue, the better for me. "How long ye be ported?"

Ezekiel startles in his seat, a near euphoric look entering his eyes as he eagerly accepts the offered drink. "Feels like years. It's been months. The Captains will be here for a while to come, an' so will I."

I take a quick sip of the sweet liquid curbing my smile again. "Captains? Ye part of a crew?"

The cup shot man shoots me a lopsided, half smirk. "Thought that would be obvious, from one buccaneer to another."

Remain calm Caleb, you are in your element, you are in control. I smirk back at him. "Figured with the British law hereabouts these days, most would be a bit tighter lipped."

He shrugs one of his large shoulders. "I'm on a death mission anyway. It's just a matter of when and who is going to do the deed."

This makes it much less exciting... the bastard doesn't even care if he lives or dies. I take another hearty swig of peach juice, swallowing with a loud, exaggerated sigh. "Preachin' to the masses bucko, my number is bound to be up any day now."

Ezekiel laughs, his smirk softening slightly. "You remind me a lot of my younger brother..." That hazy fog in his one good eye is momentarily blotted out by intense anger.

"If I remind you of him, he must be a damn good man."

The inferno is put out by a sudden chill of deep seeded sadness. "Was..."

"Was? He dead?" I feign ignorance and interest, the corners of my lips twitching slightly despite my desperate struggle against it. This is just too good.

The Indian doesn't seem to notice my slip; he huffs loudly, the emotion on his face quickly shifting again as he drains the rest of his peach juice. "Might as well be! No good Captains didn't even wait for the sun to fully rise before shoving off without him. No vote, either."

Why, hello thread, I hope ye be ready to be properly pulled. I scoff, mimicking disgust. "No vote? That be grounds for mutiny."

His shoulders sag, the wind in his sails deflating. "Believe me, if I had more of the lads on my side, I'd kill the wench and sea dog where they stand, for Eli."

As I look at the ready-to-crack buccaneer I already have a plan weaving together in my head. I'd sure like to see *Jonah* pull somethin' like this off.

I lean closer to the Indian, lowering my voice, letting my eyes dart around the pub like I'm nervous someone is watching or eavesdropping. "What if I said my Captain may be willin' to lend her crew to your cause, for a price of course."

Ezekiel fixes me with an intense look, one I wouldn't think possible for someone in his condition. "You'd do that? For a stranger you just met in a pub, on an a-cursed island. Why?"

I drop my eyes to my lap, pausing a long moment, like I'm having trouble revealing my answer to him. "Ye remind me of someone too…" Also mostly true. I curl my lip. "Besides, a chance to spill dirty blood that dare go against the most basic of the code? That alone is enough payment for me."

Ezekiel's lip twitches a moment before he laughs, then just as quickly he nods his head. Got 'im

"I'll give ye three days to really think over yer choice. My Captain and I will meet you and you alone, here, to talk business." I hold out my arm to him. "Sound like a deal, Ezekiel?"

He extends his arm out, gripping my forearm in his, and shakes it once. "Deal."

I drop his hand and reach for my tankard, finishing off what's left in one long, deep drain. I slam it on the bar then rise to my feet. "Want to write down what we talked about so ye are sure to remember?"

His laugh explodes from his barrel chest and he claps me on the shoulder roughly. "Funny, too! A-hahahaha!" He removes his hand from my shoulder and wipes the corner of his patched eye. "Three days, same place. Until then, mate."

Excitement courses through my veins and pride swells in my chest as I watch the Indian stumble his way out of the busy pub, completely unaware he's just a pawn in a bigger game, Una's game.

I finally let the grin that had threatened to ruin my whole charade slide onto my lips as I finger my two dirks. Aye. Until then, *mate.*

***

Chapter 35: Hanna
29 January 1692
Port Royal, Jamaica

"Caleb, Ezekiel's leading Kai and Elyse to King's Wharf tonight at twilight, aye?" As Una says this, she moves her arm, causing Asa to squirm in turn, his bony arse digging into my pelvis as he shifts position on my lap.

There's ten of us shoved tight in Una's quarters, going over tonight's plan one final time for good measure. It's a miracle all of us fit into her room, and that no one's gotten into a fistfight or insult-slinging match yet.

Caleb nods, his brown eyes glinting with an excited spark. "Aye. They think he be leadin' us into their trap, not realisin' he be double crossin' 'em and leading them into our trap."

Jonah chuckles, shuffling his weathered deck of cards against his raised knees, nearly elbowing both Ambrose and Atropous in their faces in the process. "They were appallingly easy to deceive. They must really want you dead, Captain."

"That giant ego of hers was always my sister's biggest weakness."

I nod at Una's words, pressing my already flushed shoulder into hers in a show of support. "Kai as well. He always thinks he's the most intelligent person no matter the group. That'll be his downfall."

Across from us, long legs crossed on the floor, Ambrose pouts, one that looks rather suspiciously like the sort Demetrius would wear, as he presses one hand to his chest, the other pressed dramatically to his freckled forehead. "It's killing me that I can't join in on this. It's going to be the brawl of the century!" He feigns dying against Jonah's shoulder, knocking the cards from his hands so they fall to the wooden floor in a messy spray. Jonah rolls his eyes as he collects the spilled cards, Atropous casting him a large, sheepish grin.

Una sighs. "Ambrose, you know how important yours and Solomon's duties are at the North Docks. Best outcome, Elyse and Kai both get slain, we port the hell out of here after looting their rotten, worthless corpses, we all hit the next closest island, and you get paid back everything you've given me. I need *The Protector* ready to sail at a moment's notice, you have the sharpest eyes and quickest hands out of all of us, that's why you're my first gunner." As Ambrose flushes under Una's none-too-freely-given praise, her gaze shifts to each of us. Those thrashing eyes had come alive over the last few months. She's even dropped the 'arggh, I'm a pirate, fear me' act.

Her sharp eyes pause on a disguised Selina, who leans stiffly against the closed door. Her pale, dark vine-twined arms are folded over her chest, an undisguised Solomon the only barrier between her and Caleb.

"Worst outcome," Una continues, "they get away from us and the hunt will go on. Kai's been at this life a long time, longer than most ever manage. There's a reason for that. That chance of failure is why you won't use any magic." Her gaze narrows as it slides to a grinning Demetrius, his obsidian eyes shimmering with a familiar mirth. He's perched on the back of a stolen bar stool, his leather booted feet in the seat where his rump should be. The fact the seat doesn't tip backwards is beyond my understanding, another feat that I'm sure only he can pull off.

"*Any* of you," she emphasizes. "We can't risk them getting away from us with even a smidgen of an advantage, that's all they need to turn the tide in their favor. I learned that mistake in blood." Her eyes slide to Atropous, the other magic user in the room, hands folded in his lap, his jade eyes already lowered to his lap submissively. He's gotten quite good at using his sway over water over the last month, and despite his lowered eyes. I can see the disappointment in them that he won't get to show off those abilities in a real brawl.

Selina huffs. "If ya would only let me..." She makes a slicing motion with her hand, fingers hooked liked claws. "There'd be no chance of failure."

The life that glitters so brightly in the depths of Una's eyes turns flat like a dead sea as she glares at Selina. "I don't know what that means, but *I* hired you to help me do a job. In the end, the kills are mine." Her words are so frozen and without any of her usual, playful warmth, that any joy or excitement over tonight's excursion is sucked entirely from the room. It makes the already overcrowded, too-warm room nearly unbearable.

Selina drops that raised hand lifelessly to her side, giving one swift nod as she turns her gaze elsewhere, anywhere other than at her fuming Captain.

Una mimics her nod, satisfied. "Ambrose, lead Solomon, Atropous, Asa and the rest of the lads to the North Dock. Pristine condition, you lot. Be ready to shove off. The next time we all meet I'll finally have Kai and Elyse's heads on pikes."

***

The sun is a fiery thumb-smudge on the horizon. I try to steady my rapid breathing, focusing on Una's solid but excited emotions pulsing brightly in my chest like my very own beacon to help steady my nerves and find my way. Any moment now, I'll be face to face with Kai… sort of… I let the fact that my true face will be hidden behind my Octavia disguise sink in and hold onto that for all I'm worth. I idly trace the ribbed hilt of my cutlass.

"A proper buccaneer's cutlass for the proper buccaneer you've become." That's what Una had said when she'd given me this as my Solstice gift. Hilariously, I'd given her one almost identical in return, which seemed to surprise precisely no-one. I tighten my grasp on the hilt as I remember her warm words. It was fascinating to learn that no matter what people called that time of year, in the end it was really about the same thing – people coming together to celebrate each other, the life that came before us and the life yet to come

I let out a shaky breath. He can't hurt me anymore. I'm strong. Una's here, Demetrius is as well, everything will be okay.

Una's warm fingers covering my fidgeting ones draws my gaze from the wooden deck and into her turbulent eyes. She wears her black and gray trifold slanted, just on her brows. "I don't need an emotional tether to you to know you're afraid."

I let her pull my hand from my weapon, my heartbeat pounding as she gently laces her long fingers with mine.

"Am I truly so easy to see through?"

Una's lips curve up, like dawn itself breaking the horizon of the sky after a long, cold, dark night. Her eyes come to life once again in an instant. "Nah, I just know you that well."

I return her smile despite my tense stomach and my limbs trembling. "After nearly a year, I would hope you'd know something of me."

She laughs softly, the sound so light, yet I feel the echo of it travel through my body. Her gaze returns to the slightly rippling waters, expression serious once more, creasing lines along her forehead, around her mouth, along the corners of her eyes. "Don't be afraid. We'll get through this. Then you, me, and that blasted gill-fish of yours can go back to that perfect, vomit-inducing cottage."

The laugh that bubbles over my lips isn't forced to soothe the worried spark in her eyes, it's natural, easy. Like being with Una herself. "You would really put up with Demetrius in such close quarters? For me?"

Her smile slowly creeps back onto her lips. "I would. I meant what I told you on the turning of the New Year. It's you and me until the last breath leaves this body."

But then the warmth flooding our bond is suddenly ice in my veins. The hand holding mine slackens, before releasing it completely. Una's eyes go wide, and the icy sensation sharpens to the most intense pain I've ever felt pulsing through my body. No, not my body, through the bond, from Una. Something's wrong. I'm twisting my head to look around when I hear Jonah yell.

"AMBUSH!" His shout registers on the edges of my consciousness as pain sears every nerve in my body to ash.

Una's widened eyes fog with pain, the same pain that's currently threateningly to disarm me. She raises her hand to her shoulder, face a twisted grimace, as she turns toward the small buildings dotting the docks of King's Wharf.

That's when I see it. A glinting, bloodied tip of an arrow shines like a threatening beacon under the fading light, protruding through her shirt close to her collarbone.

The feathered end of it juts from the other side of her shoulder, a bloom of crimson already slowly staining the white cotton of her shirt.

The pain, *her* pain, pulses in my body, like the wound is physically mine. I grit my teeth and draw my new cutlass, turning to follow Una's livid stare. My stomach instantly bottoms out, my heart beating so hard I hear its increased rhythm loudly in my ears. My hands begin to tremble, then so do my knees.

Atop one of the wooden shacks that the islanders use to house various fishing baits, nets, and tackle, is a duo; one standing, the other kneeling. The one who kneels is smaller and younger than the one standing, and his bow is still poised, another arrow knocked, ready to take another shot. The older male is standing, shoulders back, held high, unafraid. Dressed in gaudy, deep-blue knee-length breeches and a flashy royal blue brocade coat with expensive trim, a collection of pendants glinting in the light, he smirks. Even at this distance, I know that smirk. Kai

"Blast it, Jacob, yer aim is off! I shouldn't've let you have that last ale!" Kai calls, his voice just as I remember it.

Laughter has me whipping around to see, right across from his bastard Captain, atop a building of his own and with an archer flanking one side, an armed pirate on his other, with a grin as bright as the moon in the sky, Ezekiel.

A near animistic growl sounds behind me, Caleb's angry roar ripping through the silent docks. "Ezekiel, you double crossin' gutter rat!"

Ezekiel bares his teeth down at us, at Caleb, looking ever the murderous pirate Una had made him out to be so long ago. "You're one to call me that, Caleb." I can see Caleb is just as surprised as me to discover Ezekiel knows his real name and who he truly is. "I *saw* you and your buckos take off with that ungrateful, snot-nosed, loud mouthed little cabin boy. Ye thought you had me fooled with your little game, chum. Looks like you are exactly as smart as you look."

The sound of Caleb drawing his weapon, the slide of metal being drawn from its sheath, has gooseflesh breaking out across my skin, and my grip tightening on the hilt of my own blade.

"Halt, boy," Kai calls to us. "One more move and the hooded one gets an arrow through the skull, and this time there won't be any missing."

Selina's amused scoffs instantly follows Kai's vicious threat, and the hairs on the back of my neck raise, the air feeling overcharged with lightning, something I've learnt to associate with Selina calling on her powers. I desperately hope she can hold herself back, and that Kai hasn't noticed the shift in energy in the air.

"You gonna shoot the arrow yourself then, old man? Seems Ezekiel didn't lie on that account – your crew's capabilities are nothing to brag about." Una pants through the pain I know she's feeling, her eyes flicking to the angered druid. "Stand down, Sel. Now isn't the time for that."

Out of the corner of my eyes I see Selina grip onto her strange blade tightly.

Kai moves first, jumping down from the low roof, taking the small drop easily, only using one of his hands to brace himself. He moves with the fluid grace I'm sad to see he hasn't lost in all the years I've been free of him. The archer follows him, while the other three remain perched opposite, still above us. Five of them to six of us. Even with Una injured, we may still have a chance…

Una holds her shoulder, cupping the arrow still buried deep in her flesh, blood now staining her fingers. Her jaw moves as she grinds her teeth, watching Kai walk closer, his archer keeping a few short paces behind, his arrow ready.

The closer they get, the more details of Kai I can see. His sun-weathered, tanned skin is as I remember, only with more dips and valleys creasing around his mouth and between his eyes. Eyes that are dark, lifeless pools of ink sparking with a malicious, cruel light, one I used to see in my dreams every night when I was a child. One I hadn't seen in many, many nights. One I *thought* I was prepared to see again. My palms begin to sweat, my grip slipping on my weapon. I try to adjust it carefully, slowly, keeping my eyes locked on the monster reappearing from every one of my childhood nightmares.

He stops in front of Una, his cruel smirk still on his lips. "Who knew we'd be seein' each other so soon, Una? I'm sure Elyse will be positively livid that she's missin' out on the li'l reunion."

Her eyes are blank and flat, becoming somehow colder and more still. She flashes a menacing smirk of her own. I know she's scared too, I can feel it, but I also know her rage is a fire inside her. "Where is my *dear* sister hiding? Or did she send her dog to do the dirty work for her? She never did like getting her own hands dirty. But I'm sure you know all about that by now. Maybe you'll actually get the job done right, this time around."

I expect his temper to snap and his anger to flare, for his voice to lash. But it doesn't. He's silent a moment before his smirk morphs into a gleeful grin, and his hand is lashing out.

But not at Una, at me.

It's so quick and sudden I don't even process it happening, even after my head whips to the side, the sting blossoms in my cheek, and the sound echoes in the empty port. No one so much as moves, not even Una, whose shock and anger I feel simmering just at the surface. She wants to kill him, even more so than before. I can feel the intent of her want, bleeding into my every nerve, my legs quiver. I try to use that anger and the thin barrier of Demetrius's disguise over me to bolster my nerves, when all I really want to do is sob and run as far as I can. As well as forbidding magic use, Una and Deme had thought it best he and I remained hidden as well, that it would do no one any good for Kai to know it was me. And yet him not knowing hasn't stopped him from hitting me.

"That," Kai says, eyes glancing at me, "is for roughing up my men the first night we were here. Stealing our jolly roger and putting them on their arses. Though I don't doubt they deserved it, I can't be letting an Indian wench be dishing it out."

I bite down on my anger and swallow the copper taste of blood in my mouth from biting my cheek hard when he slapped me.

He continues, like he hasn't just struck me across the face. "Oh lass, ye really are behind in things. Elyse has no idea this li'l outing is even happening." One of his large, scarred hands reaches under his brocade coat and draws out a gleaming silver dirk, its point the sharpest, deadliest thing I think perhaps I've ever seen. His grin twists again, becoming more malicious. "And she never will."

312

Ezekiel laughs loudly from behind us, high atop his perch. "Everything I told you? I only told Kai about. If you want to get fussbudgety about it, I didn't lie about wanting to kill the wench. I will. A lass being a Captain? Blasphemy." His unpatched eye slides over my shoulder. "And the sea dog that'll die? That'll be you, Caleb, for killin' Eli."

The pain flooding the bond is flayed wide open by Una's rage, white hot and dangerous. Even with the bond accepted, at times it's still difficult to not let her emotions flood my system, twisting her feelings and mine so tightly together that I'm sure they would never be able to untwine again. Her blistering anger kindles fire in my abdomen, pushing away the nerves that threatened to overtake me, and since the first time Kai appeared before us, my knees and hands cease their wicked trembling.

Una's smirk has that flame nearly scorching the bond between us entirely. "You better pray I kill you here. When Elyse hears of this, and she will hear of it... well, let's just say I wouldn't want to be you two idiots."

The overwhelming anger is once again doused by icy pain, but this time it eclipses the pain I felt through the bond when Una had been shot. New pain. My pain. I drag my eyes down, and spy Kai's fist flush against my abdomen.

"This one's to prove to Una I can still take everything she cares about, just..." he twists his hand, "like that. I know the Indian is precious to you, Una. Ezekiel's seen as much during his charade at betraying me. All those little secret meetings with him. Silly of you to think you can keep anything of worth. Just like your sister doesn't want you, just like you lost your pa, and your ship. You get nothing. You are nothing."

He twists his hand again, making that pain bloom and pulse anew, as my blood, flows over his tan knuckles. Some strangled sound escapes my throat. I'm faintly aware of my cutlass slipping from my fingers. The irony that he doesn't even know it's me, his own daughter by blood, is a faint, strangely calm revelation to me. He really has no real idea what he's done, what he's taken...

"No!" Una is reaching for me, the fear and panic flashing through our bond. But Kai's eyes are flying wide, and even before his mouth closes, he's dropping to

313

the deck in front of me like something had fallen on him from above. His hand falls from my torso, and I too drop to my knees. Una thuds down beside me heavily, one hand to her wounded shoulder, the other grabbing at my arm, her face a twisted mask of horror.

I feel distant from it all, not quite here. Like I'm watching it all from afar.

I press my hands around the glistening hilt of the dirk embedded in my abdomen, careful to not jostle it – removing it at this point could be the end of me. Each pulse of my heart sends another wave of pain sizzling along my body. The weapon is plunged so deep, each breath only forces blood from between my fingers.

Kai lays on his back, eyes still wide with shock, though he's very clearly dead. One leg bent beneath him at an odd angle, one arm over his chest, the other splayed above his head, and protruding from the center of his forehead, embedded down to her hilt, is Marigold. I seek Caleb, but he's holding his hands up, aghast.

"It wasn't me!" he's saying, almost frantically. "It wasn't me! It was the nymph!"

Deme? Demetrius did this?

There's sounds around me. Fighting? Yells. Una frantically talking at me, tugging at my arm. But I can't seem to look away from Kai's two huge, empty, dead eyes, the pupils blown wide, features frozen in horrified shock. The man that had caused me and so many others so much pain, finally dead.

A gunshot pierces through the spell those expired eyes hold over me. I manage to tear my eyes away from the breathless, unseeing scourge and see Jonah standing over the archer that had been protecting Kai prone now, dead at Jonah's feet. He's holding his Navy rifle, the barrel of it inches from the dead archer's chest. The bullet hole smokes faintly, and I can see powder burns on the dead man's shirt. On Jonah's arms and face too. Point blank range. Jonah looks wild and fierce, the usual playfulness wiped completely from his handsome face.

Those duel waves of pain - my own and Una's - has a whimper sticking in my throat, and I turn my head to see Una on hands and knees, a broken arrow in front of her, as small droplets of blood pool on the dock. She's ripped the arrow free from her shoulder and her hand is pressed to the wound. But her eyes are far away, trained elsewhere. I swallow, breathing through the urge to pass out, and follow Una's gaze. A gasp slips from my lips the moment I do, a chill slithers up my spine. I see a speck being flung out into the ocean by a thin, swirling whip of flowing sea water. The only clue that the flung thing is human is the frightened scream that continues until his body connects with the ocean somewhere far out of my sight. Poseidon's sacred trident, what in all Gods?!

Demetrius is no longer disguised. His hair is a thrashing current on his head, his eyes glowing the brightest, most vivid green I've ever seen. That thin whip I'd seen sling the body - presumably one of those men that had stood with Ezekiel, or perhaps even Ezekiel himself - into the ocean, is flowing from his hand, dangerously whipping from side to side. His arm is raised, his fingers curled, still poised like he'd just thrown something. His skin ripples like water, no longer pale and human-like, the surface moving like waves. He looks as he had all those years ago, when he first found me on that beach, when he'd revealed himself to me. Saved me.

"What in the devil's arse cheeks?!" Caleb stares, eyes huge, his mouth dropped open in disbelief. An arrow hovers in the air, a mere breath from piercing his chest, held back by a second thin tendril of water split from the larger, surging one flailing from Deme's hand.

My vision swims, my world filling with large black dots that return as quickly as I can blink them back. The urge to cough overwhelms me, and when it wracks its way up through my body, a mouthful of blood almost chokes me before it spews onto the wooden deck in front of me. "F– Father..."

The world spins, and I'm toppling from my knees to the floor. The sky is suddenly above me, a million dots of gleaming starlight far out of my reach, my own pain dulling until the only pain I feel is Una's.

"Selina, go to the North Dock, tell the others what's happened." Una's voice shakes. She's close by, but I can't see her. I can't seem to move my eyes.

"Captain," is the only word I hear from Selina before all is silent again, save for the rushing of my pulse in my ears.

Vivid green blocks the far away stars as Deme leans over me, his hair no longer a stormy wave, now a human mousy brown and slightly windswept. His skin, too, is back to normal, not a ripple or wave in sight. Just unmoving, human skin. His striking gaze is filled with panic.

"Y– you killed Kai…" I croak at him.

He strokes my cheek before cupping it, his fingers and palm freezing against my flushed skin. "Shh, Guppy… it'll all be all right. Everything will be okay. Everything will work out just as it is supposed to, like I told you."

Una's face pushes into view as she nudges him aside, her face ashen from worry and blood loss. "Una…" I move one of my hands away from my stomach wound, toward her, my palm slick with blood. She grasps it tightly, uncaring of the blood.

Her eyes are full of despair, the bond singing her anguish. "You'll be fine, Fishy. One down, one to go, right?" Those eyes, that always remind me to have strength, to never give up, to never give in, begin to pool with tears. "W– we… will get you all patched up, finish this, and go back to that cottage. You swore you and I would explore the ocean's depths together." She brings our joined hands to her forehead. "You can't leave me, not when you've only just become mine." She lowers our hands to her lips, pressing a kiss to my knuckles, her head lowered like she's praying, her tear-filled eyes slipping closed. "Please… Please don't go. I don't think I'll survive if you leave me…"

I feel her warm tears slide over our joined hands, and the point where her lips press against my knuckles seem to chase after that heat, until I feel it expanding, feel it in my very core. Shock blooms across the bond, smothering some of that sadness as I sense her begin to feel the same intense warmth that I'm feeling.

"Ezekiel got away, Cap… gawd blimey! Look at your hands! Ambrose'll shite bricks when he finds out he missed *this*." Jonah's astonished voice slices through the night.

The warmth has my eyelids fluttering for a moment. I fight against the urge to give in to the pleasant, comforting embrace, and see my guardian's face mirroring Una's shock. His cool thumb runs along my cheekbone in a soothing caress.

"Hanna… your wound…"

His hand drops from my cheek to my shoulder, and helps ease me into a sitting position, his other hand a solid, steady force against my lower back. Una still holds my hand, and around them is a soft, golden glow, the warm halo like a soothing embrace. The golden aura gives one more pulse before flicking out completely. I bring my free hand up and gently prod Una's stained shirt, gasping as soon as I feel the smooth, unbroken skin at her shoulder. It's entirely healed! I look down, moving my bloodied hand from my own injury. It should be an open, bleeding, angry wound. It should be. But instead, my skin is just as repaired and smooth as hers, no sign of the wound ever existing, not even a ghastly scar.

I look back up into Una's face, a stupefied, look on it, her mouth shaped into a circle of surprise. "I didn't know you could do that!"

I huff out a laugh, relief flooding me, the energy in my body giving one more dull thud, before I'm left feeling heavy. "Me either."

Demetrius strokes my hair from my sweaty forehead. "Seems you take after your mother even more than I thought." His voice is distant as he says this, like he's caught up in his memories again.

Una holds our joined hands to her chest, over her thudding pulse, fresh tears springing to her eyes. "One down, one to go?"

I clench her fingers, letting her limitless pool of courage and strength blot away the fear and worry that curls in my gut at the thought of losing Una to another wound – one I might not be able to heal. I let it blot out the extreme guilt of having Demetrius sully his hands by killing for me. I hold her tear-filled gaze and feel my own tears rise, eternally grateful that we are together and unharmed. "One down, one to go, Captain."

***

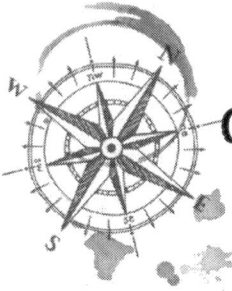

Chapter 36: Una
27 February 1692
Port Royal, Jamaica

"Straight to the inn, ya hear me, Asa? No stopping, and leave the wards *alone* this time!"

He throws me a large grin that reminds me too much of Demetrius before scampering up the narrow, sandy pathway, away from us and *hopefully* back towards the inn. That kid is going to run me ragged. I shake my head before turning away from the path and spy Hanna, undisguised, her long raven hair obscured by an oversized floppy hat that she insists is 'absolutely delightful.' An ugly thing really, something woven from straw that a fisherman might wear to keep the sun from bearing down on them as they worked, but she seems to like it, so hells if I'm going to tell her how much of an eyesore it really is.

With slippery Ezekiel getting away with knowledge of Demetrius's abilities, it's left us all wondering what he'll do with the information. He could go to my sibling and tell her the entire true tale, magical water-man bit and all. That would certainly give her an advantage against us; she'd be even harder to pin down if she went fully on the defensive, not to mention the fact that she could well send a mob of pitchfork-and-torch-wielding townsfolk after us.

But he'd made it very clear what he thought of Elyse. Caleb and Solomon seem to be in agreement that Ezekiel's going to keep most of it to himself – who's going to believe him, they said – he can keep it in his back pocket, and tell her the bare minimum. I have to agree with them. Regardless of what the snake does or doesn't do, we've killed five of her crew now. She'll see it as spit in her face; that huge ego of hers won't let her let it go. If I don't find her, she'll find me, that I am absolutely certain of.

What we'd lost in being duped by the one-eyed rat, we've made up for in coin. Lots and lots of coin. After we'd looted Kai's rotten, smelly corpse and that of the other bodies not launched into the sea by Demetrius, we'd weighed the corpses with heavy stones and dropped them off the dock, sold all their pricey gold trinkets and weapons, and made out like thieves, enough to put us up real nice for a long while.

As we'd been getting rid of the bodies, covered by the dark of night by then, a stampede of feet had sounded behind us. I'd been sure it was the Royal Navy, ready to seize us and haul us to the gallows, maybe the rest of Elyse's crew come looking for Kai already. We'd all turned, weapons drawn, but familiar shouts and cries of relief had stopped us in our tracks.

Asa, up to Hanna's chin in height now, with his long, lanky arms had nearly crushed her to him, rivers of tears running down his pale face, his cries a garble of incomprehensible words. Before I could tell him to lower his blasted voice, Atropous had gripped me in a vice so hard I'd feared my eyes would pop from my skull, my cheek pressed firmly to his rough beard, tears of his own streaming from his eyes. Tears for me. Selina and Solomon had run onto the dock, twin looks of relief blooming across their faces as they took in the scene in front of them. Selina had obviously warned them that it hadn't looked good when I'd sent her back. Ambrose had practically suffocated Jonah in a one-armed embrace, before calling him a name in Gaelic that had the ex-Jolly blanching. I wasn't sure if it was a rebuke or a term of endearment.

The rest of my crew had surrounded us, their warm words overshadowing the failure of our plan. Elyse had won again. Kai had said I should never expect to keep anything of worth to me, had nearly taken everything again... had tapped into that wild fear at the base of my spine that never really goes away. But somehow, there I was, Hanna at my side, our bond steely-strong, surrounded by a crew that seemed, against their better judgement, to actually give a shite. In the end, Kai only served to make our relationships, our friendships, stronger. It still boggles my mind. I've never, even on Pa's ship, had a crew this close. Thick as thieves. Family, almost... though that thought terrifies me a little. I've never had this many people truly care about me. The nauseating warm feelings that day had smothered the white-rage flame of my anger at not being the one to kill Kai and at Ezekiel's deception. I'd been too happy that Hanna hadn't died, that none of my lot had.

319

Soft, tinkling laughter draws me back to the present and to Hanna, who is now sitting hat-less on the blanket, bare feet curled under her, with a tender smile. The longer she stares at me, with those still-startling breath-catching eyes, the more heat floods into my cheeks. "What's got you grinning like a complete loon?" I stomp over to the blanket, plopping down next to her, folding my arms tightly, hiding my shyness, and my delight that this creature is all mine, with indignance.

My remark only has her smile turning bigger. She grabs one of my arms and tugs gently, pulling it away from the other one, and away from the cage of my chest. She slides her fingers – somehow still smooth after years of practice with her sword and her time aboard ships – down to my wrist before easily threading our fingers together.

"It's adorable how close you two have become, and how you still won't admit how much you enjoy Asa's company."

Her hand is solid and steady in mine, capable of harm and great, wondrous healing. Healing that she, when she gets the chance, has been practicing since it burst forth out of her that night. She's managed to heal a huge-arse splinter from Solomon's palm and a nasty rat bite on Caleb's ankle, much to his loud protesting.

A look of gentle – always gentle, always understanding – openness instantly quells my urge to hide how I really feel. She makes me feel like I can be all of myself, always, around her. Anything else truly feels unnecessary.

"I suppose the lad isn't bad. Definitely leagues more preferable to Caleb."

She curls into my side, leaning her head against my shoulder, her amused musical laugh filling the entire expansive length of cove. She snuggles close, turning her gaze toward the horizon and the setting sun, then peers at me from the corner of her eye, the amethyst depths swirling with amusement.

"Caleb truly is trying to do better. Need we forget the lovely gift he gave you." She snorts out a loud peel of laughter, stretches out her legs and digs the tips of her toes into the damp sand. I use the opportunity to wind my free arm around her curvy hips, tugging her closer to my side.

I sigh. I've tried to forget it, on *many* occasions. "His idea of a gift is buying me a strumpet for the evening! That certainly isn't a gift I've ever needed, or *wanted*, for that matter."

I'm once again in awe of her as she bursts into another unbound bout of laughter, tears of mirth welling in her eyes as she tries and fails to curb her mirth by pressing her face into my shoulder. One of the reasons the absurd event is forever burned into my memory has less to do with the gift itself and more to do with Hanna's reaction to it.

I remember clear as anything when she'd opened the door expecting to find Asa – sometimes he'd come to our quarters when he was in desperate need of something – but instead found a busty, cup-shot strumpet. When she had announced she was a gift from Caleb to the Captain, Hanna had nearly lost her legs erupting into hysterics. Even after I stomped over there, told the lass to return to whence she'd come, and slammed the door in her face, Hanna still continued to laugh. Anyone else would have been furious, at the very least put off, but not her.

Hanna nestles closer to my shoulder, her laugh dying into small titters. And that, in its own way, has me once again in awe of her. Will she ever not dazzle me? Despite seeing firsthand the horrendous things I've done, hearing the horrible things I've said, she's never once been afraid of me. For me, yes, but never of me. She's never pushed me away, held me at arm's length or condemned me. Even after all the secrets came to light and I pushed her away, I ignored her when all the while she was in pain, dying, to give me a chance to live. She's always selflessly embraced me, made me feel wanted, helped in every way she possibly could. Even at the expense of herself.

Even after I told her she no longer had to do the more damnable things, that's what I had Caleb and the gill-fish for after all, she still insisted that she'd keep aiding me as she always had, and keep her word. She'd said that keeping good on her promises was the only thing that made her different from Kai, which was the most foolish thing I'd ever heard her say.

"What has you thinking so deeply, Culver?" Hanna's affectionate name for me pulls me back.

"The bond lets you hear my thoughts outside the water now?"

Hanna laughs, turning her head to look more fully at me. "You didn't grumble about the sunset being over too soon."

I blink and look out across the ocean. Sure enough, the sun has set. I'd missed the whole damned thing! I sigh, my momentary slip in attentiveness finally forcing the start of a conversation I've been putting off. Even if I wanted to lie, the bond's blasted access to my emotions makes it impossible to get anything by the already clever and focused half-ling. I've got one hell of a poker face; too bad that doesn't transfer over to my emotions. It'd be a lot easier if I could turn those off at times. I know she tries her best to ignore them, but as she explained it, it's like trying to ignore the sun in the sky.

"I've been thinking about us, you, how the gill-fish killing Kai has been eating you up since. You could still be of use, keep your word, and help out another way; like tending to the ship as Solomon does, or dealing with the trades, selling to the god-awful merchants on this island, but you don't. You put yourself in the thick of things, not to separate yourself from Kai, but to punish yourself because you feel guilty over all that's happened."

Hanna tenses and I'm afraid she's going to pull away, become angry at me for being so blunt, but I just couldn't hold it in anymore. She's thrown herself even more into the dirtier dealings of this life in her search for information on my wayward sibling; even I can see it's slowly eating away at her. I see the way she watched Demetrius; her lavender eyes filled with so much guilt. But she doesn't admonish me or pull away. Her silence is an agreement of sorts. So, I continue. Why stop now that I've opened my big mouth?

"I know you think you have to help Demetrius shoulder this burden, this darkness, that it's your responsibility, but it's not. He acted how he did because the person he loves more than anything in this arse-backwards world was in danger, hurt and likely to die, because he wanted to protect you. He wanted you to live."

She tears her eyes from the ocean, where they've lingered as I've talked, and back onto me. Her cheeks are faint pink, her eyes are widened. The moon is already up and its light catches the shimmer of the faint scar that traces her right temple,

322

curving down her cheek before it stops just below her chin, making it silver against the ivory of her skin. I untangle our joined fingers to thumb that mystery scar, a mystery to me no longer as the bond provides a memory; hers. My stomach leaps as the foreign magic presses into me, slowly prodding, begging for access to my mind. I give in and am plunged in.

A run-in with a lost, wandering man during one of her early transformations had turned near fatal. The gill-fish had swooped in, dealing with the sailor, using his allure to sway the sailor's mind into forgetting the entire interaction had occurred in the first place. She'd spent weeks packed in calendula, with Demetrius worrying over her like a mother hen, making her sit under the moonlight every day while he prayed for the infection not to take her.

I open my mouth to tell her I'm sorry for the way people have treated her over the years. Seeing it so intimately, like it's my own memories makes me ache for her. Demetrius, too, I suppose. But she shakes her head, and melts into my hand, those large expressive eyes dancing all over my face, depths so warm I swear I can feel it on my skin. How had I survived so long without her? My stomach bottoms out, like the first time I grappled the side of a ship. The intense fear that the rope won't hold your weight and you'll plunge into the ocean's clutches, but at the last moment it catches and sends you swinging for a breath before, in the next, it's knocked out of you as you slam against the side of the hull. Your heart pumping your blood like a drum in your ears, so alive. It's bonkers to feel that way about someone.

"I'm sure the gill-fish would rather you choose yourself instead of participate in things that slowly kill your humanity, the thing that really matters most." I slide my hand down to cup her chin in my palm a moment, before I slide it to her chest, pressing it over her pounding heart. "If you let that happen, you dishonor the sacrifice he made for you. Honor it by living for things that make your soul sing."

Her heart-stopping eyes flick down to my lips a moment before darting up to my eyes again. "Would your father be happy about your choice, and Elyse's?"

I sigh gently. I've allowed this farce to go on too long. She'd come up with some fantastical notion that my father was some kind of daring pirate hero, a good person. "I look up to my father in some ways; his dedication to those working underneath him, how he put everything into his work, how he stuck to the code,

323

how he kept me alive. But he wasn't forced into this life like I was, he was a damn good buccaneer, a half-decent guardian, but he wasn't a good person."

Her brows furrow, her lips twisting to the side as confusion consumes her face. "Forced?"

Bet on Hanna to pinpoint the *one* thing I never wanted to think back on again.

As she looks at me, face clear of any judgment, or betrayal at me not telling her something so important sooner, I don't have that urge to just tell her the bare minimum. She never needs to use her ability to absolutely command me, to force me into doing whatever she wants. I already just want to. That's why I hate it when she blames herself when she accidentally does it. She's not mastered her control over it, and it's not like it's things that negatively affect me. She doesn't judge, and she won't force me – not on purpose. It's me that's ashamed.

But if Hanna's taught me anything with her open kindness, it's that if I judged everyone on the things they did in their past, things they'd had to do to survive, or even things that they regret, I'd not only stunt their limit to grow, to change, but my own too. How would anyone ever change if not given the chance? She truly makes me want to be a better me, for myself and for her, so I can be worthy of calling myself her bonded.

I inhale deeply, hold it a moment, then let it out. I pour it into her via our bond as she had done for me moments back. No words are needed.

The father that raised me and my sister wasn't the man who played a part in our conception. We were young, three when we were sold. My sister and I have no memories of our birth parents, just foggy, broken images and smells that I have to piece together and somehow make sense of. As I get older, that gets harder and harder to do. I'm certain one day I won't be able to recall anything at all. My first memory is of Todd, Pa, telling us when we asked him, that he in fact wasn't our father, and that he had been swindled out of his coin. I snort out a laugh. This had always reduced Elyse and I to tears every time we thought back to it. *He thought he was getting two cabin boys for the price of one. Boy was he pissed when he found out the truth. Our sniveling birth father was long gone before that ever happened.*

Curiously enters her eyes. "If he was disappointed in you, why did he keep you both? I'm certain he could have made his coin back plus interest if he'd sold you both as you were somewhere else." She raises her free hand, threading her fingers through my hand still placed over her heart, then moving our joined hands to her lap.

My stomach gives a small lurch at her touch. "That's another thing I always looked up to him about, he never left anything unfinished. He kept us on as cabin boys on his first ship. As we grew older, he taught us the ins and outs of everything there was to know about ships and buccaneer life and, as we aged, he taught us about how to clean, load and fire a gun. 'So you ain't dead weight' was a phrase I remember hearing a lot in my youth."

I try to quell the sudden pounding of my heart. My thumb works small circles on Hanna's hip. "It wasn't all cruel words and hiding. When we were ten, he started sending the coxswain away at night, only leaving us on deck. He'd let Elyse and I take turns manning the ship and practicing turns. When we were on land, he'd let us spend so much coin even Ambrose and Jonah wouldn't be able to go through it all. We got to eat whatever we wanted." I mirror the smile that's worked its way onto Hanna's face as I talked about our time ported as children, a look of wonder shimmering in her eyes. "When we matured, it became harder to shield us from prying eyes. By the time one of my father's newer crew mates made our sex known to everyone, we were fifteen, and well versed in the code and in our weapons." I smirk. "It was put to a vote of course. If Elyse and me could beat him in a sword fight, we'd get to stay, no more trouble. If we lost, we'd lose our lives. We were confident in what Todd had taught us over the years and agreed. The pitiful lad, furious at being made a fool of by two lasses, said he'd let us fight him together, to make it fairer. In the end, it was he who lost his life, Elyse and I were allowed to stay, and no one argued we shouldn't be allowed there after that." I pull Hanna close, my smirk slipping.

"Over the years, I came to see our buyer, our Captain, Todd, as a father... and, in his own way, he cared about us. He taught us to defend ourselves so we could survive. But my sister couldn't see that his thoughts on us had changed from ones of duty and ownership to ones of love, or maybe she just wanted more than Pa could give. She'd come to me a week before we set sail toward your side of the seas. She wanted me to join her in staging a mutiny against him. Said between the two of us we could pull it off. She was angry when I told her I wouldn't, *couldn't* be a part of that. Through it all, he'd never once abandoned us or tried to sell us off. He taught us how to survive, gave us a life of freedom where others would've forced us to wed and bear babes." I squeeze Hanna's fingers, letting the comforting heat seep into my palm, letting her be my courage, my anchor.

"Before we sailed, she convinced Pa to induct four new crew members; one of them was Kai and the other three others his underling. Lord knows what rock or bar stool she found them under. I, wanting to believe my sister's words were only words, didn't mention the whispers of mutiny in Pa's ear, knowing Elyse's punishment, regardless of if she followed through, would be harsh. I should've seen the attack coming a mile off. They waited until we were low on supplies, still recovering from a bad storm. I and those still loyal to Pa went down with him and the ship. I took down as many of those mutinous bastards as I could. I remember watching the last of them getting into the lifeboats through a stream of my blood."

Her eyes flick to the now-faint scar over my eye – the wound she'd healed when she rescued me. Hanna squeezes my fingers again and I feel an instant wave of cool calm rush over me. I hold her infinite gaze. "Pa would only be angered that she's gotten away with her betrayal for so long. I'll honor the blow he took for me by killing the evil that took away the only real home I ever had. She stopped being my sister the moment she decided to turn her back on the only two people that cared about her useless hide."

The sting behind my eyes threatens to overwhelm me and I blink it back, eyes darting down to the blasted bangle that even now I can't get rid of. "She isn't only a threat to *me* now, but to anyone close to me. Whatever that double-crossing Ezekiel tells Elyse, she'll want blood for retribution. She hates to lose, she despises being outdone, and now that we've thinned her crew, she'll actively be hunting me and my associates. It's only a matter of time. I'll end her, for Pa, for everyone."

I flick my gaze back to her. She stares at me like she thinks I'm a worthwhile object that might get stolen. Kai was wrong, about everything. We do, sometimes, get to keep the things that are precious to us. My heart beats so harshly I can feel it at every point our bodies touch. She tangles her free hand into the hairs at the nape of my neck. She's impossibly close. I feel her breath across my lips and cheeks with each of her exhales. We lean closer until our foreheads touch and I feel the smooth, warm expanse of hers against mine, the wisps of her hair tickling my cheek. "No matter where this crazy adventure leads us, after this is over, it'll always be home, because I'll always have you at my side, and I'll always be at yours."

A grin breaks out across her face like the dawn. "'Til the last breath leaves your body?"

She touches her lips against mine, brushing them in a feather-light kiss, one that has me humming out a sigh of approval, and knowing without a shred of doubt that I absolutely mean the next words I'm about to say with all my heart, my body, and my soul. I bump the tip of my nose against hers gently, reveling in the smile I receive as a gift. "And even after that."

The next kiss soon leads to another, and then another. Slow, warm ones that make me feel more alive than I have in my entire life, and I know I've truly found a home for my heart, for all eternity.

***

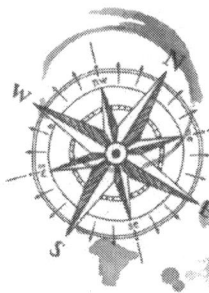

Chapter 37: Asa
13 April 1692
Port Royal, Jamaica

"Gently this time Asa. You want to hit *my* marble with *yours*. Getting all the marbles for yourself is how you win the game, 'member?"

I nod quickly and flick the small, wood ball at the one sitting in front of Atropous. It flies way past him and under the desk instead. Oops.

Mum's sat in an inn chair, her bare foot hooked up on the edge of it, a bigger-than-me book in her hands. She doesn't even look up as Atropous laughs and fetches the loose marble. I mess with the ones sitting in front of my knees and try to focus back on the game in front of me. Atropous claims two of the marbles Demetrius gave to me, and that makes me a bit sad. I liked those ones.

"When're Una, Deme and Caleb comin' back to the inn, it's been forever?" I flick my thumb and my marble shoots out, missing Atropous's by a breath. Drat!

The big navigator laughs, and leans forward, closing one of his eyes as he flicks out his thumb, shooting his marble across the floor hitting mine directly. Now I only have one left to his six. It's not fair. He's had yeeeearrrrs to practice at this. Maybe I'll do the eye thing.

"I still think you should call Una 'Mother', it's just the *sweetest* thing." Atropous's eyes flick above my head to look at Mum, who huffs out a loud sigh and snaps shut her book. The sound makes me jump and I swivel on my heels to look at her, almost falling over.

Mum holds the closed book on her lap, both feet now on the ground, her normally nice face twisted up like Elyse's used to get when she got mad. "And I think it's more respectful to obey her wishes and call her whatever she asks you to."

I try not to grin. I know, and Atropous knows too, seein' as he's winking at me, that Una would box my ears if I ever tried to call her 'Mother'. Atropous isn't afraid

328

of Mum, despite her being able to beat Jonah and Ambrose and Caleb in a fight. He shoots his marble and hits my last one, winning the round, and the game. All my lovely marbles are gone.

"NO FAIR! You were using your water nymph magic, weren't you?!" I stand and step closer, looking around him for any sign of water or glowing eyes. I only half think it's true. They both burst into loud laughter that makes my cheeks feel hot and I fold my arms over myself and turn away from them, not really upset at all, but I don't want them to know that. "You two are being such... bastards!"

"ASA!"

I peek at Mum, see her eyes wide open like something's scared her, while Atropous collapses onto his side, hair falling over his face, laughing so loud and long that I don't know if I'm allowed to giggle as well or not. It's just such a brilliant word. Jonah says it all the time.

I turn a hopefully darling smile on my new mum, my *only* mum since leaving the workhouse, and clasp my hands behind my back. "Sorry, Mum... I know you said to wait 'til I'm older."

That scary look melts away, replaced with one that says she's trying to be angry but can't really do it. She giggles a bit, too, as Atropous snorts and I grin. Mum's face shifts into that lovely smile, same as what she gave me when I first met her by that teapot stall in Sainte Marie – my very first real smile, freely given with no striking attached to it.

"Come here, treasure. Read with me. I'm looking at some of Selina's magic spells."

"That's so ace!" This might make up for the lost marbles. I cross the room to her and wait for her to move the book so I can climb onto her lap. Mum's also the first person to ever let me do that, so I try my best not to put my elbow in her face this time. I don't really need to sit like a baby. I'm not a baby no more. But it's nice. She holds the book above my head as I settle down on her lap, my legs hanging over the edge of it, one of her arms already around my waist to make sure I don't fall off.

Atropous pushes himself up on his elbows and stares at us, a big smile on his face. "Spells, you say? That's something I wouldn't mind seeing, too!"

Mum laughs behind me and settles the open book over my lap onto a page with a big circle on it and little black lines all over it, but before she can respond, the door to the room flies open, hitting the wall with a loud bang.

Una comes in with Mum's blue bandanna on her head, immediately looking for us in the room before closing the door. She doesn't scare me no more. She doesn't act like Elyse as much anymore, so it's easy to remember they're different people, even if they look the same.

She strides toward us, giving Atropous, who still lays propped on the floor, marbles all over the place, *my* marbles, a cheery wave. She ruffles my hair gently, before stooping down to press a kiss to Mum's head, something she always does now after they've been apart. Mum does it to me too, after we've been apart.

I feel Mum chuckle. "Where are Caleb and Demetrius, Culver? Didn't cast them into the sea, did you?"

This has Una laughing. "Today wasn't their day to go, love. Lucky them." She plops loudly onto the ground with a wink in our direction. "Demetrius, Caleb and the rest of the lads are waiting in the inn for ya, Atropous. Go have a pint or two on me, I'm feeling generous. The three of us'll be down a little later."

Oh? Una's got something to tell us. Only us. Atropous doesn't waste another breath at the mention of free drink, hauling himself to his feet and leaving the room. I'm kind of sad I don't get to go with him, I want a free drink. And maybe a fairy tart! Ohhhh, I wonder if Mum would know, if I snuck one out of the kitchens? Before I can ask if I can go with him, as he clumps away down the hallway outside, Una speaks again, her words sounding almost tired.

"Hanna, Asa, come sit down here with me for a bit. Read to me?" Her eyes dart up to look at us, a small smile curling her lips.

I'm being lifted up as Mum laughs again, taking me over to Una with her, and dropping me onto her lap before either of us can say anything. It's not as comfy in Una's lap. Neither of us know quite how to make it fit right. But she doesn't shove me off. Gives me a little hug. That's nice. Una's not usually a hug person. Mum sits on the floor next to us, her knees touching Una's, smashing me between them.

"I'm reading up on Selina's healing techniques, she thinks it may aid me in learning about my abilities. I'm sure it'll bore you." She opens the book, anyway, flipping open a page.

Una wraps her arms around my waist and softly pulls me against her chest, resting her chin on the top of my head. "Sounds perfect, Fishy. Right, lad?"

A warm feeling swirls inside my stomach, making my whole body feel odd, light, but not enough for me to want it to stop. It's a feeling I can't think of the name of. Like… pudding and a warm bed. Like big blue skies the day after a big storm. I nod quickly, leaning back closer against my Captain, my other *mother*, not that I would ever call her that to her face. "Right! Please, Mum, read to us."

Mum's smile is warm and she leans in closer, resting a hand on Una's knee as she begins to read to us. And now, I know the feeling. The warm pudding feeling. The feeling makes me smile so hard my face hurts. Family. This feels like family. They are my family.

***

Chapter 38: Jonah
7 June 1692
Port Royal, Jamaica

Who would've thought we'd actually get to this point after months of pure blarney? I chuckle to myself. I wouldn't have believed the peculiar, confounding nymph, since he's ever the mischievous scoundrel flourishing the truth to get a reaction from us, but with Hanna at his side, it was hard not to believe the tale they told.

They'd spotted Elyse at the smithy as Hanna, Demetrius and Atropous had been heading back to the inn from an excursion to the private beach that served as our sort of training grounds now. We practice sparring there, and Hanna practices her healing mermaid magic. Still such odd words on my tongue. They'd spied a flash of striking white-blonde hair, unusual even amongst the island's variety, peeking out from a sloppily tied bandanna. They'd trailed her from the smithy to an inn, where they watched and waited to see what Una's sibling would do. After learning her location, we scouted her out to get information, and learned her crew's routines. Asa had only recognized Elyse, Ezekiel, and one of the younger cabin boys, so she's clearly recruited a new bunch.

I remember how livid Una had been that her sister shed nearly all her old crew. Any info that we'd gathered on them previously was rendered less effective now more unknown variables had been tossed into play. We've had to carry on watching and waiting. I have to hand it to the Captain, she wants her sister's head badly, and it's impressive she has the willpower to hold off on going straight for the queen in this game. Despite having Solomon as her strategic mind, Una can put any Navy boy to shame with her sharp mind. We've watched, waited, and planned our moves down to the pinprick. Tenacious, despite dozens of sleepless nights, even more squabbles, and lots of rounds of brew.

This plan'll work out. We've worked too damn hard for this, lost too much. We will beat her this time.

332

With the Captain's words ringing in my ears, I move my gaze from the trough full of netting and tackle to the gray-blue skies. The clouds are unlike any I've seen before; they look unmoving even though a slight breeze ruffles the hair away from my cheeks. There's a glassy look to them, like the panels of colorful glass they'd put up in the churches of this gaudy island.

I shift my gaze to the figure clothed in a bright crimson brocade coat and black breeches; hair hidden under a now very familiar green bandanna. And yet, if I didn't know any better, I'd bet my left arse cheek that the twin cutting our party off from one another is the Captain.

I grind my teeth. This shouldn't be happening. It's a lucky move on Elyse's part. We've watched her endlessly; where she went, if her routines changed, who she surrounded herself with the most, no stone has been left unturned. She went to the shops just down from the meat markets, closer to the Governor's house than I would have liked, every other day, alone. We'd made sure of that.

But as that slender figure in a green bandanna securely cuts Una and Atropous off from Hanna and Asa, my stomach lurches in a way it hasn't since my father caught Ambrose staying in my chambers instead of in the servant's quarters.

Our plan was to slowly box Elyse in. She'd notice, of course, since she's just as clever as the Captain, but when she'd take her leave, she'd find herself confronted by one of us, whichever direction she might choose. Our plan was solid. Sound. We'd push her back toward this point here, surrounded, and then the Captain would finally get her wish. The problem is, I don't think Elyse has come alone today. The plan won't hold together if we're outnumbered whatever direction she and her companion choose to move in. I'm fairly certain I'm being watched.

A chill lances up the length of my spine, the tiny hairs on the nape of my neck rising, as I turn, slowly, casually. My stomach twists and my anger rises like a growing fire in my veins.

Ezekiel. He looks up, his one good winking, his lips slowly curling into a cruel, evil smirk.

As I return to my previous position, my eyes find others in the crowd, ones that are paying far too much attention to what I'm doing, smirks on their dirty, grubby faces. Three more of Elyse's crew have silently, stealthily slunk their way into most advantages positions; one cuts Ambrose off from aiding Solomon, another keeps me from defending or granting offense with Selina, and the third keeping the Captain and Atropous from making a quick escape by disappearing into the street that would head towards the mainland.

They're clearly onto us.

As I survey the early morning crowds, I spy three more: one cuts us from the road to St. Paul's church. Bloody hell. This isn't good. It's nearly noon, I skipped first meal and it looks like we're the ones getting boxed in. The only one that may be able to get away if things turn bloody is Caleb, his station closest to the Governor's mansion, a spot their side hadn't bothered to cover.

Even the nymph, stationed between Ambrose and Solomon has another 'friend' giving him a good once over from head to toe. That twisting of my empty gut has me biting the inside of my cheek, helping me quell the nerves. We are in quite the predicament…

My mind whirls with possible solutions to this crippling problem, and on my dozenth sweep of the square, my eyes catch Ambrose's bright green ones, his easy smile one I'd seen many times before, a reassuring one. I return it, fingering the hilt of my weapon, as I shift my gaze again.

A large man moves from the stall Una is at, and she shadows him stride for stride, her movements calculated. Each step and breath not wasted, her eyes are narrowed so tightly that I can't see the color of them anymore, just the cold, serious expression. Her lips curl in a feral snarl. In front of me, Elyse does the same, heading straight for Una, her eyes just as deadly, smile just as dangerous, just as void of any warmth or joy. I grip the hilt of my sword and take a step forward, ready to defend, when the ground underneath my feet gives a monstrous tremble. The strength of it causes me to stumble. The buildings begin to quiver, their foundations groaning loudly in protest as this unknown disturbance ripples over everything in the surrounding area.

The people out and about at this early hour, working, trading, buying, drinking, all stop in their tracks, looks of shock, fear, horror springing up on their faces. I'm scared too. Then a loud shriek splits through the air, quickly followed by another, and another, the cries sounding like they're coming from the northern half of the island. The ground still quakes under my feet, the vibrations resonating in my bones, like I'm shaking from the yellow fever again.

The shouts begin a panic. People start running, each more eager to move than the last, but none of us know from what. Stampedes of townsfolk divide, some running away from the sounds, and some running toward it, anxious to discover what's going on. I turn, expecting to see the lethal, traitorous Ezekiel sneaking up on me, about to take advantage of my slip in guard, but I find no one. Ezekiel's nowhere to be seen. Blast it, sniveling little worm would cower away at the first sign of trouble, wouldn't he?

I look about, careful to steady myself and plant my feet firmly despite the ground's trembling, and spy two figures chasing through the scattering masses, the pursuer wearing the Captain's familiar trifold. Virgin Mary's silk slip, this is sheer madness!

More screams and yells echo around me, more terrified, more frightful than the last. Among them is a voice I recognize, and I find Solomon standing where Ambrose had been, his hazel eyes wide, glued to the quivering earth. He doesn't budge as men, women, children run past, knocking into him. Selina, usually attached to his side, is nowhere to be seen.

"Solomon?!" I grind my teeth and break into a run, adjusting to the constant trembles under my feet. I shoulder past a large, barrel-chested man and reach out for the pale strategist. "Where's Selina? Have you seen any of the others?" I'm gripping his arm, staring about, trying to find any other familiar faces in the crowds.

Solomon's firm grip on my forearms has me turning back toward him. His entire body is shaking like a leaf on a branch in a harsh wind. "When the ground began to rock, my footing was knocked off balance. When I steadied, I saw her chasing after the pirate that had been blocking our path to the church."

Good thing I didn't bet on how well this day would turn out for us. Nervousness grows in the pit of my stomach. "Did you see Ambrose?"

He shakes his head, looking startled, dazed. I squeeze his forearm gently trying to focus his attention. "Come quickly, I have a grim feeling about this. We must move to higher ground, right this instant."

As I say this, more townsfolk surge towards us in a huge swell. I barely have time to pull Solomon out of their path. When they've passed, I finally see just what's got everyone so terrified. The ground of the street, all the streets that I can see, ripple like the currents of the ocean's surface for a moment, before the ground opens into a giant, gaping, thrashing fissure. It seems to open and close just as rapidly as I can blink my eyes, like the mouth of a beast.

A loud crack has me jerking my head. The large, bright red brick building of The Golden Chalice sinks into the earth right before my eyes, like some demon from the pits of hell itself is dragging it down.

Those dangerous, turbulent holes begin opening all over the place down there, swallowing up the slower moving islanders, their movements made weak, stunted, like they're trying to wade through mud. The constant trembles under my feet become more severe. The unfortunate souls swallowed by one of those gaping fissures are trapped up to their necks, air crushed from their lungs as the ground closes around them once more, their eyes forever frozen in horror, heads and arms like morbid trees in a tortured forest. Then the sinkholes begin to ripple out toward us at an unnatural speed, the once-solid earth now like water. The panic, the lack of comprehension, shifts, like something's kicked me swiftly in the backside.

"Solomon, we need to run now! Right this moment, run! RUN!" I run, half-dragging the strategist behind me.

My heart hammers in my ears as chaos and destruction escalates around me. Where do we go? What do I do? None of my years of training prepared me for something like this...

"Jonah, your front!" Solomon's nails bite into my skin, jerking me backwards so hard I slam into his chest, my next stride halted as a huge pillar of water shoots straight up in front of me. The plume bursts from the ground itself, flooding the street with boot-deep water. The bloody world's ending!

I suck in a breath and exhale harshly, tugging us further down the slowly flooding roads. Other eruptions of water are rising into the air, I can see them over rooftops. It's like the island is trying to rid itself of the infection of residents that live on it. "Come on, we've got to —"

Another great tremor hits, stronger than the last, knocking me to my knees, my next words knocked from my mouth as well. Solomon topples onto me, his weight suddenly bearing down on my back as the half-solid ground shifts beneath us, threatening to suck me down.

"My apologies Jonah…" He scrambles to his feet, hauling me upright but before we can fully straighten, a giant force slams into my back, sending me sailing forward to land on my stomach, all the air from my lungs forced out in a rush. I try to breathe but Solomon lands on me again, flung after me, his squawk of surprise loud in my ears.

"Get… off…" My words come out breathy, but he's already struggling to his feet, again hauling me upright by the collar of my shirt. When I look at him, I see his lower lip tremble as he stares, eyes wide and horror-struck.

"Jonah… look…"

I follow his pointed hand. The ground where we'd stood moments ago before we were launched out of the way has solidified once more, a clutch of twisted bodies trapped and crushed in it. Amongst them, caught up to his neck, face contorted in pain and lifeless eyes staring, is Caleb. His beefy, scarred arms are raised from where he'd thrown us to safety even as he sank, a gleaming silver dirk in one hand.

"Caleb…" Solomon's cry is a cracked, broken whimper as he stares into the eyes that had once caused him so much torment, were so often filled with such fiery hatred and contempt, now two glazed, lifeless pools of a corpse. A thin trickle of blood drips down the seams of his lips, from his nose and the corner of his eyes.

"He…" My mind reels. Holy shite, Caleb just saved both of us. Another burst of adrenaline kicks my gut, pulling me from the brink of completely losing my mind. "Solomon, there's no time. We must run. If not, his sacrifice will be for nothing!"

Before he can respond I'm dragging him again, along the streets, trying to find higher ground, trying to find solid ground, hopefully further from the chaos and death. But as we run, I don't find safety or refuge, only more horror. Slanted buildings melting into soggy, pulsating earth, fallen waterlogged bodies, an arm reaching from the earth. A staring face trapped in hardened mud. A dropped basket. A hole. More of the huge gushing pillars of water. Must run. Must get away. Faster. Faster! We mustn't slow!

I'm vaguely aware of Solomon's struggling to keep up with my speed. Years of training has my senses all over the place. Everything is moving too fast; things are magnified like I'm looking at them through a spyglass. My chest tightens with each deep breath, as we run, dodging pillars of water, the dangerous openings in the earth, toppling buildings, homes floating away on land turned liquid, people shouting for help, crying out in pain. If we make it to Waterman's Wharf, we may still have a fighting chance.

I turn a corner and slam into someone. A tattooed arm quickly flicks out to grab my shoulder and steady me. I look up into Selina's grim, undisguised face, her amber eyes blazing. Her cloak is in tatters around her shoulders, her hair an erratic array of dark coils. Her clothes drip like she's just swum out of the ocean.

"Oh, thank the heavens," Solomon shoots past me like a musket shot, and flings himself against her, gathering her closely in his arms, "you made it!"

"Sel? I thought you were by St. Paul's? Have you found anyone else? Ambrose?"

Selina wraps a silver-twined arm around Solomon, returning his embrace warmly. "Lost the rat when the second tremor hit and forced me to seek shelter. An entire inn was pulled beneath the earth right in front of me. The only person I've run across was the nymph and he was lookin' like quite the gill-fish, but then a rush of water separated us again."

Blast it to Hades, where are you, Am? As I ponder her words and my fear, Atropous runs through the narrow alley, gaze passing us over then darting back when he realizes it's us. His hair is all thrashing sea foam and waves, barely hidden under his soaked bandanna. He's unharmed save for a tear in his left trouser leg. He makes an incoherent sound and launches himself at me. Relief blooms in my chest as we embrace briefly. Gods but it's good to see this scoundrel. Now, if we could find Am and the others…

I clap Atropous on the shoulder. "Still alive, then?"

He grins, grasps Solomon's hand, touches Selina's shoulder as if he's not sure if we're real.

"Have you seen any of the others?" I press.

He shakes his head. "You?"

"Caleb's dead," I say, the words heavy and sticking in my throat. "He… he saved us."

Atropous's jade eyes glow bright and ethereal. He fidgets with the tear in his trouser leg. "After the first shock wave, I ran. I haven't seen anyone… the earth's being swallowed by the sea…" Grief etches deep creases into his face. He looks as if he might weep at any moment.

Selina lets out a frustrated cry, threading one of her hands with a wide-eyed Solomon. "Can't you and the nymph just make this stop? You are water nymphs, for Danu's sake!"

That near broken look on the young half-nymph's face almost cracks as he shakes his head. "I– I can't. It's nature. Demetrius said we mustn't meddle in nature, that we can't meddle with the balance of things, that it's a sacred rule of our kind."

Selina looks outraged, like she's about to punch Atropous, and I'm about to intervene, when Solomon halts her with a gentle squeeze to her hand. "We mustn't turn on one another, we're all that we have left. If we let this tragedy divide us, we'll all surely perish here."

His surprisingly calm words ripple through us and helps steel my resolve to put the plan I've been working on into action. "You three try to get to the High Street if you aren't able to find high ground. Stay away from the holes opening and closing in the earth; if you get caught in them, you're dead."

I see the darkness enter Solomon's eyes as he remembers Caleb's sacrifice.

"I'm going to scout for the others," I tell them, already taking a step back from them. "At the first chance, you get back to the ship and if she still floats, you get out of here. Steal another ship if you have to, and don't look back."

Solomon shakes his head. "We can't just leave you to this... this *hell*! Let us aid you, we are your family!" The ferocity of his words snuffs out the last embers of my nervousness.

I give Atropous's shoulder one more squeeze, flashing them all my trademark, cocky grin. "I was made for missions like these. I'm quicker than all of you. I'll have better odds finding the others alone. Now go, my bizarre endearing family, and don't stop running."

I turn my back on them, bolting down the turn I'd taken before colliding with Selina, but instead of heading toward the Merchant's Exchange, I turn left again, running as fast as I can make my aching legs move. I haven't run this much in an age.

I dodge round pockets of shifting, whirling ground, the sounds of screaming now everywhere, as more gushing towers of water burst up from the earth to tear this once-corrupt yet joyous town into a place of pure terror. I push on, desperately trying to ignore the wails for help, the bodies...

I push past people, my breath coming in quick puffs, every muscle in my legs screaming for me to stop, but I can't, I don't. I run, looking for a familiar shock of red hair. Damn it, Ambrose, where in God's name are you?

I round another corner, and it's like something out of one of the scary tales we used to tell to keep long voyages amusing. The water here is up to my shins, even more buildings slanting at odd angles. I have to dodge some obstruction every pace or two. Higher ground, that'll give me the best advantage. I look wildly around for anything still standing solidly that I can climb, until I spy a smallish building with a blue tiled roof. It looks to be sturdy

With one more look around for any sign of my four missing crew mates, and casting a thought to those I'd left behind already, I make a mad dash past a half-submerged shed, using the corner of its roof still above water to catapult myself as I jump. I aim my grasp for the sill of the second story window and use the sharp gables of the overhanging roof to pull myself higher.

I grab a skinny little chimney stack and stand up, moving to the top of the steep triangular rooftop, looking down at the streets below. All the buildings around me are in various stages of collapse, all leaning, cracked, or partially submerged, the people a flurry of frantic movements. I turn carefully to avoid losing my footing, and look out across the slowly crumbling, flooding island.

I squint as a sudden shock of long dark hair flailing in the wind catches my attention, and spot two figures, huddled close, one just barely taller than the other, clinging to a rooftop of their own. It's Hanna, with Asa! Oh, thank the Lord! I'm about to call out to them when another loud shout, close behind me, has me tensing and reaching for my Navy blade. I don't even get to fully grasp it when a flurry of kicking legs erupts around me and two wrestling bodies sail past, rolling down the other side of the sloped roof, towards the ledge and the slowly sinking town.

A flash of familiar hair, red as a fox's pelt.

"NO!"

I lunge, grabbing at him, missing, pitching myself after their thrashing bodies, sliding on my stomach, and as Ambrose's pale green eyes find mine, as he tumbles off the roof, just as he grabs blindly at thin air, I hook one arm around the metal pipe of smoke stack I'd clung to climbing up here, reach out...

And clutch at his wrist.

The strain of the weight sears into every part of my worn body, almost forcing me to release my grip, but I hold firm, somehow, by some god. I haul back on the weight, the effort forcing a grunt that's almost a yell from my lips and hook my legs around the metal chimney, until I'm sitting cross legged around the stack, sticking out of the roof at an angle. The strain is almost too much for my arm to take, but I feel a warm palm clasp tightly around my wrist. Hells, Am needs to lay off the biscuits.

I stretch my neck out from the chimney pipe, leaning to look over the edge and almost lose my grip on him. Ambrose's dangling body is caught about the waist by a now patch-less Ezekiel, who's hanging onto Ambrose desperately, and pinning his other arm to his side. All Am can do is weakly kick his legs, too afraid to jostle me harshly. Ezekiel squeezes Am's body tighter, the only thing keeping himself from falling to a watery death, and stabs at any part of Ambrose he can reach with a bloodied dirk. Ambrose screws his face up in pain but doesn't yell. I do.

"Oi! Get off him!"

They both look up at me, Ezekiel's one brown eye burning with rage as bright and as vengeful as any demon. I'm holding Ambrose's gaze, can see the blood soaking through his shirt and trousers from the stab wounds already.

"I was coming for you, nancy boy," Ezekiel snarls, flailing his knife. "Shoulda been you going over the edge!"

I realize then what must have happened. Ambrose must have spotted Ezekiel and wrestled him away from ambushing me. Stupid Ambrose. Stupid, brilliant boy saved my life again. The strain in my arm is all consuming and I pant through each breath, and Ambrose's eyes, so usually full of life, are full of pain now. My heart tightens.

"NO!" I grunt through clenched teeth. "You fucking hold on, you bastard." He smiles, then, his signature grin, totally idiotic, too bright, too big for his face, but so full of trust and warmth. The smile that makes me want to be stronger than I am, for his sake.

That's when a third tremor hits. Stronger than the other two combined. I have to press my cheek into the metal of the chimney pipe until it bites into my face, gripping Ambrose's wrist, to keep us from falling. I hear loud cracks, groans, screams, as a large building opposite us sinks straight down, down, down, into the quickly rising water. A smaller tavern melts sideways, flowing into the harbor as its

342

base gives way. The smaller buildings and people are swallowed by the unforgiving ocean, not even the peaks of their roofs visible. The water keeps rising until it's level with the second-story windows. Then there's another loud crack, like a tree coming down in a forest, and the house I'm clinging to begins to tilt.

A rushing, rumbling, thundering sound, growing louder, makes me turn my head, and immediately I wish I never had. A three-foot wave is surging in-land right for us. I tighten my grip even more, shut my eyes and yell into the void, "HOLD ON!"

I don't get time to close my mouth before the wave batters us. Cold, dark, terrifying, rushing, pulling, worse than any wave Demetrius has ever put me through. The water lifts and lightens the strain in my arm just the tiniest bit, just for a moment, and it's like heaven. Heaven that's short lived, as the wave recedes, trying to pull me from the roof, Ambrose from my grip, leaving us hanging and as heavy as we were before it hit. With a stomach-turning wrench, my shoulder dislocates. I almost pass out.

But I force my eyes open, and with a pained groan, lean over to see Ambrose hanging from my arm, now alone. Ezekiel is gone. But Am's head is lowered, his body trembling like he's shivering from the cold.

"Am?" I call, "Ambrose?!" I try to shake him, but the pain in my arm, my broken shoulder, brings sharp tears to my eyes and pain leaking from my mouth in a grunting moan. "It's going to be fine Am. Hanna'll patch you up and we'll port out of here. Anywhere you want, just like I swore."

As I say her name, I turn to seek her and Asa out on that other rooftop. I find Hanna, both her arms wrapped tightly around the pointed corner of the roof, her eyes, visibly large, horror-stricken even from here, stare out at the sea, at another wave already tumbling at us, faster than the last. Asa is no longer clinging to the roof with her. No… no, not the kid too.

I do as I'd done under the force of the first wave's assault, as the second one rolls over us, pulling parts of the roof and house away as it recedes. The house beneath me groans again, and tilts forward until all I can see is Ambrose dangling from my hand and the currents of endless, foaming muddy water below him.

I pull with all my strength, all my might, my shoulder screaming, my vision swimming, but even putting all I have left into it, I can barely lift the limp, waterlogged body. My entire body trembles, every signal, every instinct to survive ordering me to let him go. I try lifting him again, refusing to give up.

Something's going to give, I just don't know what yet. The building, my ability to stay conscious, my arm's ability to maintain the weight and grip, hell the entire island might implode on itself before anything else... even my gambling-happy arse couldn't put coin on this, even if I was able to.

Ambrose comes to with a flinch, his stringy, red-locked head lifting, his eyes meeting mine, and a sob breaks in my throat. His eyes are dull, dazed, foggy. Blood drips from his mouth down his chin, from the knife-wounds Ezekiel had left him. His hand no longer grips my wrist; my hold on his pale, cold skin is the only thing keeping him from plummeting into the abyss below us.

Those blood-slicked lips tremble before he opens his mouth. "L– let me go... you can still make it to paradise..."

I choke out a sob at the reminder of the childish promise we'd made foolishly when I'd been fourteen. One day we'd leave behind all the rules, regulations, expectations. One day we'd find our own piece of paradise, and truly be free. The Navy had just been rich men treating human lives as chess pieces and gambling coins. I hadn't seen the point in dying for something I couldn't believe in. That hadn't been our paradise, it had been a hell. So, we'd run, again. Together.

My head begins to shake even before my mouth can form the words. "Not bloody likely, you arse. Shove off and let me save you."

He gives me a dimmed version of his sunny grin. "I– I'm tryin' to shove off and save *you*... but you won't let me..."

I laugh, but it's strangled, choked with sobs I refuse to let bubble out of me. I can't... I can't save him. I watch another wave tumble towards us. This one will be the last, whether I want it to be or not. My grip begins to slowly slip. I try to force my cold, numb fingers to tighten on him, staring into his clover eyes that have been by my side longer than anyone else, as their fire, acceptance, joy, *care*, begins to burn out. I can't save him, and I can't let him go, either.

His eyes flutter a moment before slipping closed completely. "Jonah... thank you..."

Then those unforgiving currents crash upon us and I make my choice, without taking my eyes off Ambrose's face.

I let go of the chimney.

I'm sucked instantly beneath the waters, my stomach torn across tiles and brick as we're ripped from the building. Before my hold slips entirely, I reach out and fist a handful of Ambrose's clothes, dragging him to me, locking his body against mine. I close my eyes, holding my breath as the wave pinwheels us both out of control. We slam against something hard, and I suck in a lungful of seawater. I can't tell which way is up. It's murky, and cold and I can't breathe.

I look down at the long-expired Ambrose, his handsome face serene, and feel nothing but peace warming me even as the frigid water chills me to the bone. Wait for me, Am. We'll go together. Just like we promised. Just not quite the destination we'd had in mind...

At least this time I'm dying for something I believe in. A smile curls my lips, as I count the freckles that scatter across Ambrose's cheeks and nose, like stars in the night sky.

Something worth it.

***

Chapter 39: Una
7 June 1692
Port Royal, Jamaica

I press my forehead against the cement stack I'd anchored myself to, slamming my fist against the side of it. We'll meet again Jonah... Ambrose... But this world will be grimmer without you both in it.

The intense tremors seem to have settled. When they hit, sporadically now, it's like being rocked by the waves while at sea. The island, what's left of it, seems to have stopped sinking. The ground seems solid once more.

After the first giant tremor hit, Elyse had turned tail and run as the quakes caused the once proudly standing brick buildings to quiver. As I'd chased her, it had worsened, and buildings had begun to fall. People began to disappear into the ground, Hades sent pillars of water that began flooding the cobblestone streets, but still, like a twisted version of the childhood game we used to play on the ship, I'd continued to chase her. After the third and final shock, the strongest of them all, knocked me to the ground, I'd lost sight of her for good.

I'd climbed to my current position to gain a higher viewpoint but had been stunned into frozen silence as the first huge wave crashed upon the unsuspecting, unprepared island. It pulled down entire buildings, sinking them into the ocean. Call it good luck, fate, an act of God, but I'd chosen a structure on the side of the island that hadn't come close to falling into the water. My boys though, had not been so lucky. Once their building had begun sinking, plunging lower than mine, slipping piece by piece into the thrashing, gray waters, I'd seen Jonah, the bloody fool. Heroic, true to himself, true to Ambrose, to the very end.

I pull my face from the comfort of my refuge and force myself to look upon the utter destruction I know awaits. My stomach churns like the waves lapping where towering buildings once stood, lost now to the ocean's endless abyss. York Street will be my best bet. The military forts will be in shambles, the Navy lads will be

346

trying to keep order. If Elyse didn't get swept away by a wave, she'll have headed inland, started to loot for supplies, then find a ship to get off this death trap. I clench my fists. That's what I'll do too.

I slowly retrace my steps, crawling backwards and carefully descending from the roof to the second-floor balcony of this inn. My throat seizes as I find the 'better off' side of the island just as destroyed as the side that had taken my crew from me.

From the balcony, I see the once-thriving town, with all its densely packed buildings, all its trade posts and prosperity, is flooded. Wrecked by the waves that thundered across the island after the quakes. Uninjured townspeople are already looting the bodies.

I glance down at the side of the building. I reckon, if the building does hold and doesn't shake me free like a monkey from a tree, I should be able to shimmy down. If I dangle from the balcony, I think I can reach the brickwork around the window below, then just a small drop would put me back on solid ground. Praise God, or Danu, or the Morrigan, or whatever being has blessed me with this luck. I swing my leg over the railing, try not to think too much, and work my way down to the street. I land in a crouch, worried the ground might shimmer and ripple and swallow me... but it doesn't.

Ambrose and Jonah are gone. The grief of that hits me all over again as I stand, feeling lost, in the street. The rest of my crew that had hung back at the inn awaiting my orders, an inn now completely swallowed by the sea – all of them likely gone now too. Hanna's burning lavender eyes flash through my mind, followed by Selina's amber glare. Caleb, Solomon, Asa, Atropous, even Demetrius. I think of them all, those that had followed me out here on this ill-fated day. What's happened to all of them?

I think again of Hanna and it muddles my thoughts. My goal of achieving my revenge, avenging my father and my previous crew, had been the only thing giving my life a purpose. I'd thought of little else for so long it'd become an obsession, slithering through my veins like a fiery, angry serpent. Now, chasing after that fire, is the rushing, near-addictive swell of affection. It pulses in my chest the longer I think of Hanna and damn it, Asa, the brat, as well. But the longer I dally, the further

Elyse and my revenge slips from me. I make my decision. If I can't find Elyse by the time I cross into York territory, I'll find Raven, and Asa, too.

I head through the calf-deep sludgy water, the soft sand of the streets now turned into a thick, sticky mud under my boots. The smithy's supply shop sign is cracked and slanted at a dangerous angle; one more after-shock could knock the rest of it down at any moment. Looters pick through the abandoned shops; townsfolk aid their injured comrades. Women, men, children, homes, livelihoods, all gone, just like that. The island that had been overcrowded and sweltering is now nearly barren. This is truly the most hellish sight I've ever seen, and I've seen some true horrors in my lifetime.

I continue running, my feet, legs, even my hips on fire with the effort, the pit of nerves in my stomach now a vast cavern. My breath comes out quick as I press on, pushing my body long past its limits. My crew and I had been through so much this last year; the pain we've shared, the tears we shed for one another, the shenanigans. Despite how much they've tested my patience, they've become my family. Hanna most of all. My chest constricts tightly.

"LOOK OUT, SON!"

Years of parading around under the guise of a lad has me whipping around to see an avalanche roof top, tumbling at me faster than any of the waves that had hit Port Royal. I lunge sideways, landing hard on my stomach, splashing into the silty floodwaters, winding myself, covering my head and most important parts with my arms, as the structure collapses, so close to me some of its rubble hits the bottom of my boots.

My heartbeat is a drum in my ears and, as the racket around me quietens, I lower my arms and prop myself on my elbows. I peer over my shoulder, seeing just how close I'd come to becoming one with the earth. Despite my weariness, fear, and grief, I chuckle. Death by building. Not on the list of ways I want to be taken out.

It's that thought which suddenly makes me realize, hits me like that building almost had. What would my death do to them? What pain would it cause Hanna? Would she die if I died? I push myself to my feet, a new resolve settling deep into my very core. You'll get what's coming to you, Elyse… but I've finally found

348

someone, many someones actually, that make this arse-backwards world worth living for.

My life no longer belongs to just me.

That thought is a lynchpin being pulled from beneath me. My revenge is no longer the most important thing. With wobbling knees, I head towards the Meat Market where it all began. Hopefully, it's still above water. Hopefully, the others, too, will head back to the last place we were all together.

My soaked trifold flops into my eyes again and I tear it from my head, throwing it over my shoulder into the wasteland of a town, no longer caring to hide my appearance. A new determination burns a hole through my chest. It gives my once sluggish steps more energy. Filled with a new purpose, I push past a pair of bearded buccaneers hoisting a large wooden crate between them. The survivors are going to make out like kings. Better than. Someone grabs me, arms wrapping tightly around my middle, and I'm about ready to start kicking, when:

"Captain!" A familiar deep, smoky voice has hope gripping my heart so tightly that sudden tears blur my vision.

"Atropous?!"

As he embraces me, his entire body begins to shake, as loud sobs break in his throat, the force of them vibrating down my face, into my chest. This instantly has guilt twisting my insides. I've caused gentle Atropous so much pain with my single-minded goal. I lock my arms around his trembling form, crushing him to me just as tightly.

"Cap! Thank Sucellos!"

"UNA!"

Selina! Solomon! Their voices are filled with emotion as they both throw their arms around Atropous and I. Those pesky tears pool in the corner of my eyes and spill over, sliding down my cheeks, wetting Atropous's beard as my crew, my family, crushes me between their bodies. The familiarity of the embrace makes my tears fall faster. I'm no longer able to hold back the wave of them that's been building since I saw Ambrose and Jonah be taken.

We stand like that for a few more moments, soaking up the comfort before pulling away from one another. Atropous clutches at the tips of my fingers like a child instead of the twenty-year-old man he is. I squeeze his cool fingers and look from his glowing eyes and the thrashing currents of his hair to an undisguised, un-cloaked Selina, who's holding an equally undisguised Solomon's hand. They all look so tired, haggard, grief-stricken. But they're alive.

"You three don't know what a relief it is to see a face that isn't screaming bloody murder, or already feeding the fishes!" I'd meant my jest to lighten the hopeless situation and lift their spirits, but it has the opposite effect. Their faces fall, and suddenly I'm afraid. What do they know that I don't? I squeeze Atropous's finger again, swallowing past the lump in my throat, trying to keep my tone light. "Have you seen Hanna or Asa? Or that scoundrel Caleb? I was sure I would've heard him screeching demons and witchcraft from halfway across the island by now. And that nymph? I'm sure he is just loving all the water."

Their faces tell me what I fear. They look as I'd felt, watching Jonah and Ambrose tumble into that wave. Oh gods… who else?

Selina breaks the silence, her amber eyes pulling up to look at me, their usual spark barely a flickering flame. "Caleb's gone. He saved Jonah and Solomon when the earth tried to swallow them…"

The quiet sniffles from Solomon turn into sobs. He turns his body into Selina's, seeking comfort as the knees of his long legs threaten to buckle under the strength of his sorrow. Shock floods my system at her words, then overwhelming sadness. Caleb had been an utter arse, a shite of a person really, but his loyalty had been something I'd immediately noticed, despite his mouth, and admired him for. Now I know just how loyal he really is. Was…

I clear my throat. I must tell them before my courage gives out on me. My lip trembles and I bite it a moment before speaking. "Jonah and Am too. Jonah gave it his best shot, but one of those demon waves pulled them from a roof. The rest of the crew, too, back at the inn… the inn's gone. I don't think they could've escaped it. They all were honest-to-god buccaneers, through and through, to the very… to the very end." I drop my head as my throat closes in grief. My tears for my lost comrades, my lost family, slide down my face. I can't bear it. For a second time, I've failed everyone I ever cared about. Some Captain I've turned out to be. Atropous holds my fingers tightly as we take a moment to remember all our fallen.

Hanna.

It occurs to me, almost stupidly, that I've blindly assumed she's fine, that she's survived all this. Why? Because of some healing ability that she was still learning to use? As soon as that question rises, I feel a burst of incandescent fear. I'd simply not been allowing myself to consider that she might not be okay. When the silence becomes almost too much, I raise my head, my heart pounding in my chest, my ears. "Any… sightings of the others?"

Selina rubs soothing circles on a still-softly crying Solomon's shoulders, her brows drawn down in distress. "Just Demetrius earlier, but one of those great water spurts separated us."

What if she's not okay? What if she's… no. The bond. I would know, wouldn't I? If we can share memories across it, if we can find each other, be drawn to one another across it, I would know if she were dead. Wouldn't I? I try and focus on that odd pull near my chest that always seems to tug me toward Hanna. I quieten my mind, in the middle of this flooded street, and focus. I don't feel anything. Not a tingle. Not a flicker. Nothing. Panic laps at my spine. "Oh gods…" I breathe, a hand coming up to my mouth. "What if she's… I don't know if she's…"

Atropous puts his arm around me. "Selina, what about your flight form?" he asks. "You can use it to get a better view of the island. You can find the rest of them and find our way to freedom!"

I lean against him, grateful for his logic. It hadn't even occurred to me. "Can you, Sel?" I ask, too eagerly perhaps, because as the words leave my mouth, Solomon glares at us and takes a protective step in front of the druid. Selina smiles at him, rises onto her tiptoes and, in a very vulnerable display, presses a soft, lingering kiss onto his cheek. His face goes slack and whatever argument he'd been about to start is over before it's begun.

She squeezes his fingers, then looks at us. "I'm low on energy, supplies and magic, but I'll manage. We have to find them." The desperation and determination in her voice ignites my hope again.

An unfamiliar feeling swells in my chest as I look at the first crew member I recruited. My eyes, my sight, I realize how much she's truly changed, from lone wolf to one of the crew, one of the family. "Thank you, Selina. I mean it."

She smiles as she steps into the concealing shadow of the building behind us, those amber eyes softening a moment before they fall closed. "I'm not doing it 'cause my Captain ordered me to, but 'cause my friend asked me to."

I'm going to cry again, damn it. I sniff and blink hard. I can't remember shedding this many tears in my life. "I'm no one's Captain anymore, Sel, I'm just Una from here on out."

That smile on her face twists into a smirk as her markings begin to pulse. The air shifts as it charges, the hairs on the back of my neck rising as she calls on her magic. She tried explaining to me that magic is always present in the air, invisible to a non-magic wielder's senses, weaved perfectly together, waiting to be called upon. When my neck prickles like this, I can believe it.

"Hmm, Una… I don't know, I quite like 'Urchin'."

Before I can decide what feeling to unleash on Selina at her jest, her human flesh cracks like ice and is replaced by brilliant green feathers, her body bathed once again in that ethereal light that has you shielding your eyes, whether you want to or not. When the spots clear from my vision, the tiny green bird now perches on Solomon's shoulder. Selina ruffles her feathers like she's coiffing the hair on top of her head, chirrups at us, and flies high into the gray, cloudy sky.

Solomon, looking up after her departing tiny form, smiles faintly. "I admire her ability to jest in these harsh conditions."

Without Selina beside him, and with his face still grief-stricken, he looks so much smaller, so fragile.

I hold out the hand not holding onto Atropous to him. "Well, I admire your ability to make even the most dangerous killer, like Caleb, your chum."

His watery smile is replaced with a true grin, as bright as any of the sunrises we've ever watched together. He crosses the space between us in two quick strides and grips my offered hand like it's the only thing holding him together.

The three of us stand like this, me Solomon and Atropous. I bump my shoulder against Atropous's. "And I've always admired *your* constant gentleness no matter the situation, your willingness to trust." I squeeze his fingers again, and he holds my gaze. "You inspire me every damn day. I'm proud to call you my first, true bucko."

The inhuman glow in his eyes dulls slowly, returning to the human green ones I know well, and an equally familiar smile emerges on his scruffy face.

"SELINA!" Solomon's cry startles me, as a flurry of tangled limbs tumble from the sky and into the sloshing floodwaters at our feet with a splash.

Solomon's at her side, aiding the heavily panting lass to her trembling legs in an instant. He helps her pull her shirt straight. Good God, a fall like that should've killed the woman! But she seems uninjured, just exhausted. Hollow cheeked, gray, ready to collapse again, as Solomon cups her heart-shaped face between his large hands, his eyes darting all over her, checking for any sign of injury. Her chest heaves, her eyes are cloudy, her bottom lip trembles. "Hanna... she's heading this way from the north alley... but... she —"

That's all I let her say before I'm turning, shooting towards the north alley, the hope that had slowly been filling me now freezing in my veins. I keep running until I reach the alley, looking for her in the shadows between the buildings. I run into it, feet splashing, the sound echoing, and I stumble to a halt when I spy a familiar lowered head of dark hair, her bright blue brocade like a beacon in the dark. "HANNA!"

My call has her legs locking, her head raising. It's then that I notice a small bundle in her arms. I squint, trying to make it out. It's too small to be Asa. Has she found some stray cat or something?

I run closer still and see her clothes are drenched and torn. She's not wearing any boots, or trousers for that matter. Her stretched out, water-soaked shirt hangs just above her knees, the hem a dirty brown, but she doesn't seem to care. I'd expected her face to light up when she saw me, but it remains blank, her eyes red-rimmed and distant. Dark. She's been crying. I realize the bundle is her trousers wrapped around her rapier, the pistol I'd given her and Demetrius' blade glinting, dangerously.

"Hanna, what is it?" I stumble towards her and she won't speak. She's barely looking at me, staring through me as she shuffles forwards. The moment I'm within her grasp she collapses against me in a heap, her full weight pulling us both to the sodden ground. I don't need any special bond or tether to feel the agony rolling off her shaking body in waves. "I couldn't feel you, Hanna." I push the wet and matted hair from her face, stroke her cold cheeks. "I thought you'd... I thought..." I gather her into my arms, her wet body quaking, as she finally reacts to me, crushing me to her, her sobs ringing in my ears, the loudest sound of despair I've ever heard. Dread wells up in my gut, sharp. I stroke the back of her head, doing my best to calm her. "I'm so glad you're safe..." I'd not dared to let myself entertain what the enormity of losing her too might feel like.

Her body shakes even as she pulls back in my arms, her lilac eyes filled with such anguish, such agony, that I feel it as strongly as if it's my own, as if it's a part of me. Her lips tremble as fat tears slip down her cheeks, cutting through the dirt, mud, and grime polluting her skin. Before I can ask again what's happened, her hands climb up my back, fisting tightly into the fabric of my clothes and she speaks words I once would've thought as unlikely as my own sibling turning against me. All warmth leaves my body, reminding me of the intense cold I felt when jumping overboard after Hanna all those moons ago.

"Say that again," I tell her.

"Asa's dead... Demetrius as well..."

***

354

Chapter 40: Atropous

7 June 1692
Port Royal, Jamaica

It couldn't... they couldn't possibly be, no... The finality of Hanna's words punches a hole through my chest. Something in the Captain had changed. The calm level-headed cocky woman that had approached me on the fishing dock outside my home with her offer – to help her navigate her ship and see a life of adventure I couldn't even dare dream of – is gone. Replaced with a softer version of herself, a truer version. Freer with her emotions and feelings about others. When Selina told us she'd seen Hanna approaching, when Una had shot off along the street like a cannonball, she was just a terrified woman, worried that someone she held close to her heart could be hurt.

And so, I'd followed. I followed my friend because she might need me. And now, I stand up to my shins in water, in the dank alley, twenty paces from the kneeling, embracing pair, and Hanna's sorrowful howls vibrate in every bone of my body. The heartache I hear is too real to be false. I know Asa and the seemingly impenetrable Demetrius truly are dead. Tears immediately overrun my vision as I feel the loss, all the loss, pierce my heart, as damaging as any gun or knife wound, knowing this will leave just as permanent-a scar.

Since my powers had awakened, Demetrius had taken me under his wing, taught me of our shared history as well as the things that marked him different from me. He'd been a stern teacher, going over the basic knowledge all young nymphs learned when they came into existence as if I too were a child. He would never explain how nymphs came into existence, though. Apparently, it's not quite the way humans do it... but he remained tight lipped on it no matter how many of his tests and challenges I passed. He would only offer that it was a 'sacred ceremony' that only the *vanhin* – the eldest – nymphs could take part in or even witness. Despite his elusiveness on some matters, despite the arse-whippings and headaches, we'd grown close. He'd become like a second father to me. So much still to learn. So much left unanswered. And now he, too, is gone... gods, why?

Solomon and Selina appear beside me. I don't need to tell them. Hanna's uncontrolled wails is all the information they need to know.

"No…" Solomon's voice cracks into a whimper, his hazel eyes forlorn.

Selina slides down the brick wall beside us to sit in the watery mud, dark circles beneath her eyes, weariness and sadness pressing into every line of her face. She pulls her long legs up to her chest, wrapping her arms around them. Despite being undisguised by her magic, her tattoos are inky black rather than silver, showing me the true extent of how far she's pushed herself.

Even when she'd been disguised as Octavia, Hanna had never hidden her kindness. But her sadness, her pain and suffering, she'd always buried and kept from us. Now she can't do that. It pours from her like a lanced abscess, no matter how tightly Una holds her. My heart aches for her. She's lost two of the people she cares most for in the whole world. She'd spoken about the cabin by the sea, the one that Deme had built, and how they were going to go back there, Una and Asa too, as soon as we finished this mission. I'd asked, only half in jest, if we could all go there if we survived. Una had snorted and rolled her eyes, saying it was too small for all that nonsense. Hanna had chided her and said of course we could, when this was over. But, as Solomon kneels beside Selina in the mud, as Una cradles and rocks Hanna's sobbing body, I realize we're it. There's only us left. The five of us. Jonah and Am won't ever see the cabin. Asa won't ever run along the beach. Deme won't ever show me how to be what he thought I could be. Caleb won't get drunk and piss everyone off. The lads won't sing as they haul sails again. It almost buckles my knees.

The grief mixes with the constant tingling, tugging sensation near my belly button. I've come to associate it with my nymph side. It's an ability Demetrius says… said… all nymphs have; the ability to sense even the smallest drop of water around me, like how I used to be able to tell when it was going to rain before it happened. It's how I'd sensed those hellish eruptions of water before they burst up from the earth, how I'd navigated through the maze of death, destruction, and chaos.

Since fully awakening in me, it's like water and I have become one. I can feel the pull and push of the tides, the waves, when a storm is brewing. I'm in tune with nature in a way I never dreamed possible, and it's mind-boggling. Being so connected to this wild nature leaves my body buzzing with so much energy, as if I could maybe control waves as big as the ones that had destroyed this poor island and its people. All this untapped nymph magic and I couldn't do a damn thing, I couldn't help anyone. Demetrius had told me the consequences of meddling with this sort of thing would be dire. Gods forbid I might've made anything worse. It's not fair... My throat swells and I clamp my eyes closed, refusing to let my pain and sadness overwhelm me. No... we're going to get out of here.

I move over to the two women and lay a hand on Una's shoulder. She looks up at me. For the first time since meeting my head-strong, unbeatable Captain, she looks completely defeated. I squeeze her shoulder firmly, hoping to provide some strength and comfort to the lost woman.

"Una... you wanted revenge for your father, and to protect the ones that mean the most to you. Hanna, you almost died wanting to protect someone you cherished above all others from someone who should have been protecting you. Jonah and Ambrose ran away from people who dared defile what they believed in most – each other. Even Caleb, with his silver tongue and skin thick as armor, died protecting that thing we all so desperately want. Something each member of our crew searched for, dreamed of, yearned for. Some of us lost ours, some of us never had one to begin with." More tears slide down my cheeks, but this time I don't try to stop them. "A family... a home, a place to call our own. They might not all be able to physically go to your cabin by the sea, but we can still take them with us." I place my free hand over my heart. It pounds loud, alive, despite the sorrow threatening to drown me. "Because they'll always be alive in our hearts, and in our minds. We'll never forget them. But let's not fail them. Let's bring our family home."

Tears stream from Una's usually guarded stormy eyes, making them glitter like two priceless jewels. Hanna raises her head, sniffing, her otherworldly beauty no less diluted down by the deep shadows bruising the pale skin beneath her eyes.

She offers me a small watery smile on her puffy, reddened face. "You sounded just like Deme... he must have rubbed off on you."

I make a sound that's half-laugh and half-sob. "He was a fantastic teacher... and a phenomenal father. I'm going to miss him. I think we all will, despite him being a bit of a bastard..." I grin ruefully as Hanna squawks out a laugh, even as new tears pool and spill down her cheeks. Her smile is larger, though, and I'll take that as a win.

Una guffaws too, wiping the snot from her nose on her muddy sleeve, and slaps at my shin, her smile turning teasing. "It's time to turn your eyes Atropous, let us get Hanna properly dressed before you decide to give us another heartwarming speech."

Heat floods my cheeks as I notice for the first time the pale, bare legs and thighs of the half-ling. "Holy Jesus! Sorry!" I whip around so fast I almost fall, and both the girls laugh at me. Damn it if that doesn't make me blush more.

Solomon's struggling to help Selina to her trembling legs, his mouth moving quickly as he speaks unheard, hurried words to her. I rush to help but he slides an arm around her curvy hips, his lips twisted with concern.

"Is she going to be alright?"

He flicks his hazel eyes at me and ponders my words, like he's not sure. "Before Jonah and I ran into her, she'd used up a lot of her powers. That last feat to locate Miss Hanna had her dipping into the reserves she saves for later in the moon cycle. She'll be alright if she gets rest, some food, and does not use any more magic."

Selina snorts and jabs me in the chest with a finger. Her cheeks are flushed like she's had too many tankards of rum. "This 'she' is perfectly well, and aware enough of her surroundings to see that limp of yours. Are *you* okay?"

At her words, my hand goes to my left thigh, to the tear in my trousers. "Just a scuffle wound from one of Elyse's crew, it's nothing to worry over."

Solomon's eyes narrow with a shrewdness I've seen more and more frequently over the last year, a look that tells me he's about to let me know what he really thinks, and not pull his punch. "And what good will you be to us when your leg rots and falls off? We must not risk it, Atropous! Remember what Miss Hanna said about treating a wound as soon as we can to lower the risk of infection?!"

I sigh, already knowing I'm not likely to win this one.

"He's right Atropous, let Hanna heal you. We can't lose you either," Una says, and I glance back to see both she and Hanna on their feet. Hanna's got trousers and boots on again, her sash back around her waist and weighed down by two rapiers. She's shoved her feet into her boots. The half-ling's eyes, though not full of tears, are still full of the weight of the sorrow in her heart. But she nods at me.

"It's time for us to turn our eyes away, Solomon, Atropous is about to shed his trousers! Let it all be free, friend!" Selina cackles loudly, followed by a jumble of slurred words I don't quite make out. Una, watching Hanna cautiously, still has the pluck to wink at me hugely. I defiantly refuse to look away from them, though I blush again.

My embarrassment is matched only by Solomon who, red from forehead to chin, is towing a still chortling Selina backwards out of the alley. "We'll give you three some privacy... please forgive her, she doesn't know what she says..."

"Oh, she knows exactly what she says... whip 'em off, Atropous, woo woo!" She waves her hands, erupting into giggles as Solomon forcibly lifts and carries her back out into the street.

It makes the rest of us laugh. Tired and soul-bruised as the druid might be, at least she seems to be enjoying herself! I'll have to remind her of this when she's 'sober'.

Una shakes her blonde head, grinning. "Good to see that one hasn't lost her sparkle. You heard the lass, let's see you out of those braies!"

Hanna has the decency to look appalled. "Culver, please..."

The smirking Captain squeezes the frowning woman's petite hand. "Oh, it's not like he has anything we're interested in anyway."

Heat burns in my face. I know she's only trying to lighten the mood, but still, I fold my arms over my chest, turning my head away from them. "Really making me want to let you help me, Cap…"

They both laugh this time, and it has the knot of dread in my stomach uncoiling slightly. "I might not be what you two are fishing for, but I have been told I'm quite the catch, I'll have you know," I quip, diffusing my uneasiness with humor as I reluctantly tug down my damp and tattered trousers, unable to meet their gazes. Now I'm certain. Absolutely. I'd rather succumb to infection than be put through this. Smite me down now and end this embarrassment.

Once my trews are below my knees, I hitch up the hem of my undergarments, peeling the fabric from the knife wound in my thigh, and let myself look at it for the first time since it happened. Hanna's face darkens as she stares at it. It's already hot to the touch, as long as my palm, puffy and angry around the edges. Crusted blood clings to the jagged edges and it oozes.

Una's face contorts with rage. "Atropous! That's 'nothing to worry about', is it? Blimey!"

I scratch at my cheek. It's like being scolded by your mother. But she's right of course. If not for Hanna and her capabilities, this'd be a life-threatening wound.

Hanna lowers herself onto her knees; Una goes down with her, not once letting go of Hanna's hand, smiling at her, even though the half-ling's eyes are trained nervously on the cut. "It'll be okay, you can do this. Just like in practice. Just like that splinter in Caleb."

Hanna's lip wobbles and, for a moment, I'm afraid she is going to cry again, but she swallows it down. "My healing didn't work on Deme… when I needed it the most, I couldn't save my father. My magic couldn't heal his broken body. What good is it at all? What if I can't heal you either?"

I grab her free hand and give it a soft squeeze. "None of that. You are one of the most remarkable beings, human or otherwise, that I've ever met. This is child's play for you. Believe in yourself the way Una and I do. And get on with it, because it's most disconcerting having you both kneeling in front of me like this." I wink at her and grin.

Hanna squeezes my hand back before dropping it and giving me a grateful smile. She then lays her palm flat against the wound, uncaring of the grime and mess of it. From what I've got to see of her healing abilities, direct contact with the wound seems to strengthen the extent of her powers, and how easily she can call upon it. The glow is faint, just a pale wisp, but a warmth spreads over me as her magic kindles. Her eyes close before she releases a slow breath, something I've seen Selina do to center herself and focus on the task at hand rather than all the outside forces trying to steal her attention. That warm spark of her magic turns into a smolder as the glow around her hand turns from a pale ray of sunshine to a halo of gold. The throbbing pain in my leg, that had begun some time ago, starts to dull. Her magic weaves into my skin, hot now, like the sun is shining all its glory on me, warming me from the inside out. The thud of pain melts into oblivion as that near blinding glow starts to fade

Hanna's eyes open and she moves her hand. "Una, may I use your water pouch?"

Without a word, Una pulls a small pouch like the ones Navy men carried from her belt and hands it to Hanna. Hanna accepts it and releases Una's other hand to tug an awfully familiar bright green bandana from around the hilt of Demetrius's rapier. I feel the pang of loss for my father, teacher, friend, all over again as she pours water onto the bandanna, and wipes at the blood still smeared on my thigh.

Before I get a good look at the wound, a cry of relief leaves the mermaid's lips. She sits back. The nasty wound, which could have ended my life if not properly taken care of, is completely healed. Not even a scar has been left in its wake.

Una leans into her shoulder, a grin the size of *The Protector* on her face. "Knew you could do it, Fishy."

I touch the smooth skin with wonder, then turn and wrestle myself back into my trews as Una and Hanna climb to their feet.

"Are you still naked, water boy? Has it rotted and fallen off yet?" Selina, sprawled on the ground and propped against the wall facing the street, hoots over her shoulder at us. Solomon pokes his head back around the corner with a questioning look.

I give him a thumbs up. "All present and correct. It seems I shall yet live to embarrass myself another day."

Selina whoops. "That's one for us magic folk and zero for human weaponry!"

At her side, Solomon grins. "Well done, Miss Hanna! You truly are a miracle!"

The dark cloud that has been hanging heavily over us clears slightly. The crippling weight of our loss is a manageable squeeze instead of a suffocating choke.

Selina's staggering to her feet, looking grumpy. I'd say 'hungover', though this has little to do with grog. "We need to raid for supplies. My mouth is so dry I can barely swallow."

I nod my agreement. "We should head back to the docks, see if *The Protector* still floats. If she doesn't, we'll have to see if we can find some other boat or ship amongst the wreckage."

I look to Una for guidance, used to her dishing out the orders, but she's already nodding. "I agree with you both, we'll loot as we go."

Hanna leans into her, thin, arched brows drawn down. "The quicker we get out of Jamaica, the better…"

Una squeezes her fingers. "Atropous, could you help Solomon support Selina? We'll cover more ground that way."

Before the druid can protest or giggle again, I've already taken up my position on her left side, pulling her arm over my shoulder. Her skin feels feverish.

"Don't get any ideas, bucko." She forces a smile. "Solomon's still my favorite."

"Roger that." I nod, gravely, and waggle my eyebrows at Solomon around her hair. He smiles, clearly getting more of a handle on all this, and his own awkwardness.

Una's drapes Hanna's arm over her shoulder too, ready to support the half-ling, her stormy eyes now filled with a determination that had been lacking since we found her. "Let's get the hell off this island."

***

"Your *other* left, Solomon!" We almost miss the corner Una and Hanna had just taken and nearly tear poor Selina in two as we awkwardly lumber after them. But the ladies have paused, allowing us to catch up. I can't bear the thought of losing them again, of being separated again. Hanna's bent over a pile of fallen bricks and plucks up a small palm-sized pouch and a pocket-watch. She opens the pouch and sniffs at its contents. "Gunpowder. Una, can you please put this and the pocket watch into the bag? We might be able to sell this."

Una slips the offered items into the leather bag slung over her shoulder that we'd found rummaging in the silversmith's shop.

Solomon and I both carry bags as well. Mine's filled with enough light beer bottles to weigh it down and rub a raw spot on the back of my neck, as it swings back and forth against my hip with each awkward step. Solomon's is filled with gauze, ingredients for tack, and a coin pouch that'll serve us well when we get to the mainland where there'll be things to buy rather than steal. He's also got a bundle of rosemary tucked in there. Selina insisted he take it when she saw it on an up-turned shelf in a bakery.

"HALT! Wait. Don't go any further!"

Before I fully register Una's breathy warning, I've already seen what she was trying to save us all from. Actually, it's the smell that hits me first - the pungent smell of rot and death. Greenish, gray waxy skin clings to the puffy blob that remains of Caleb's head and exposed arm. His right eye is a mess; some animal's already had a go at it. The other eye oozes from the socket. The bloated skin looks blistered. Shiny bone peeks at us as the flesh dangles in grotesque tatters from the right side of his face. Yep. Definitely an animal's doing.

The other bodies trapped in the mud around him are in no better condition. The smell is sickeningly sweet, like the cheap perfume the strumpets wear in the taverns.

I can taste the sour flavor on the back of my tongue and know I'll be smelling and tasting it long after I leave this godforsaken hell hole.

My mouth waters and the urge to vomit rolls through me at a dangerous speed, nearly causing my knees to buckle. I can't let Selina fall, so I turn my head away, meeting Solomon's stricken eyes over Selina's shoulders. She's pressed her face into his neck, grimacing. Then, his expression turns to steely determination. "Can you support Selina alone for a moment?"

I nod, stunned into silence, as he helps Selina into my arms and turns toward the forest of grizzly, decaying bodies. He passes Hanna and Una, head held high, fists clenched tightly by his side. The timid Solomon who used to end every sentence with 'master', who used to bow before leaving us, is a thing of the past. The Solomon striding toward the most horrendous thing I've ever seen, with a confidence comparable to Jonah's himself, with a determination that makes Una's a fizzling flame, is a new Solomon. This Solomon has become one hell of a buccaneer.

With steady hands, he reaches out to Caleb's raised but sagging arm and grips the gleaming Marigold, still grasped in Caleb's lifeless hand. He uncurls puffy, fat fingers and takes the blade. Then he lays one large hand atop Caleb's bloodied scalp and bows his head in prayer.

My stomach lurches. Though Caleb never showed him a word of kindness in the living world, Solomon shows him dignity, respect, and kindness now. I watch, heart-sore, as Solomon tucks Caleb's most precious weapon into his sash. No matter who you are, Solomon's undiluted, endless kindness eventually whittles you down. He turns from the body and comes back to us, head still held high, but his eyes lowered like he's finally reached his limit on the amount of death and heartbreak he can handle. Hanna and Una lay a hand on each of his shoulders, silently sharing their strength with him.

"You have a good man at your side, Sel. You better treat him right," I tell the woman in my arms.

She snorts, arching an eyebrow at me, a mischievous sparkle in her honeyed eyes. "That almost sounded like a threat, water boy. I'm quaking."

I chuckle, bumping her shoulder with mine. "Careful. Pretty sure I can take you in your current condition."

She smiles wearily at me, the energy in her eyes countering her haggard, worn appearance.

Solomon takes up his position back at her side. "Many thanks, brother. Let's be off."

I steady myself under the weight of my satchel and Selina's wobbling body and we set off again. We round a few more corners, stumbling around debris and bodies, trying not to act like we notice, and come to the street that would take us to the docks and the wharf and... it's completely gone. Holy shite. I'd expected it to be underwater, but the shore is right here, the edge of the ocean at my toes, halfway down the street. Everything beyond this point is gone. The scattered remains of people, homes, boats, crates and barrels, swathes of fabric that might've been ship's sails, all jostling, and bumping against the new shoreline. The sheer destruction of what occurred once again shocks all of us into silence.

The Protector is gone, claimed by the sea. Not even a mast left jutting above the water to show where she'd once been anchored. The five of us stand facing the tremulous sea, eyes dotting the waves for any usable ship.

"There's one!" Una's sharp cry jolts me and I follow her pointing finger.

A single-masted sloop bobs against the waves, still in one piece, its anchor still dropped. Her bowsprit is almost as long as her hull. She's small, but she'll be fast. The only problem is the ship's too far out for any of us to get to.

An idea strikes me like a bolt of lightning, and I plant my legs a shoulder-width apart, finding my core. Dropping Selina's arm from around my shoulders, but keeping one around her waist, I use her to help ground me. She seems to sense what I'm about to and lord bless me if she doesn't match her breathing to mine to help me, watching me. With a quick sweep of my surroundings, making sure we're free of spying eyes, I focus on that tingling sensation in my belly that wants to connect with the water, concentrate on making the water at my toes flow backwards, causing the already-rippling surfaces to move harder, causing a current to swell against the hull of the ship.

I raise my free hand out towards the sea and turn it sideways, fingers hooked like claws, like Demetrius had shown me, and rake my hand forward. Slowly, with intent, the ship draws closer despite its dropped anchor.

"Bravo! Good show!" Solomon's shouted words have a smile coming to my lips.

Una gives me an impressed look. "Damn, lad. Once it's close enough, I'll climb the ladder and raise the anchor. Can you hold it steady while the others board?"

I nod, confident in my ability to maintain it. Of all the things Demetrius had taught me, teaching me to regulate and stabilize my magic was by far the most useful.

"Angle her Jacob's ladder to me… good, good… STOP!"

I chuckle and lock my fingers to stop the sloop's turn as it drags its hull on the silt. I watch Una splash into the shallows and scurry her way easily up the rope ladder, and I work to keep my emotions steady. Demetrius had taught me to clear all negative feelings when I use my magic. Water is healing, friendship, love, and purity. The more I feel those emotions, the more receptive the magic and the water will be, the more quickly it would come to my aid. Selina removes her arm from around me as the Captain slips over the top railing of the medium sized ship. Solomon leads her forward, letting her grasp the ladder first and watches with a worried expression as she begins to sloppily climb to the top, whistling a joyful tune as she goes. He follows, after a pause.

I notice Hanna beside me, watching them climb, as she ties up her long mane of hair into a tale at the nape of her neck. She catches me staring and smiles. "Selina's delirious and Una's close to dropping. You've helped so much, but you need to rest, too. Now it's my turn. We don't have time to waste on getting to a safe island. I know from the maps Una had on *The Protector* that there are islands north-east of here. We'll get there faster if I pull it."

I blink down at the willowy woman. "Pull it? Can you truly do that?"

366

A very Octavia-like smirk curls her pouty lips. "I never have before, but that doesn't mean I can't. I'm willing to give it a try. My mermaid half is as much of a mystery to me as your nymph half is to you, but I'll get us to safety if it's the last thing I do."

I nod, laying a hand on her shoulder, impressed at the lengths she's willing to go to, to make sure all of us are safe. "Then we'll all heal up, find a smaller boat the five of us can man, and then we'll go home."

She lays a small hand on top of mine, a bright smile lighting the dark pits in her eyes. "Home…"

But then Una's climbing back down the ladder to us, and I know what's to follow won't be for my ears. "I'll head on up and give you two a moment."

She casts me a curious look, her eyes wide. "Can you hold the wave while you climb?"

I give her a cheeky grin. "Never have before, but that doesn't mean I can't. I'll give it a try."

She laughs delightfully. "Well, I'll see you in a while then, brother."

I smile, my heart full when once I thought the hollow emptiness of it would crumble me. "Sister."

As Una touches the shallows, I pass her, reaching for the ladder with one hand and giving her a lazy two-fingered salute with the other. I'm both relieved and impressed to see that my wave continues to hold strong, that the ship doesn't start to drift. My intent is strong. I haul myself up the ladder quickly, leaving the two women to talk, and clamber over the railing onto the deck. That tingling sensation is a cold, soothing, swirling energy that now fills my entire body, making me want to run in circles until I burn it all off. I think of Asa, him clattering across the deck. Sweet boy.

Solomon's sitting cross-legged in front of Selina, who leans against the mast, her hands folded in her lap. Her black tattoos pulse a slow, steady beat, turning back to silver with each slow rise and fall of her chest.

"What's she doing?"

Solomon looks over his shoulder, his eyes shimmering with affection and excitement. "From what I understood from her explanation, this is another way for her to draw in some extra energy. She has a sprig of rosemary in her mouth to help focus on her magic and as an offering. She'll be like this until nightfall."

I blink, taken aback. Selina's endless surprises never fail to amaze me. This world is truly a mystifying, beautiful place.

"Miss Hanna has a plan, yes? That's why the Captain went back down?"

I nod. "She plans to hurry our pace by pulling the boat along."

His eyes nearly pop from his skull as they widen. "Selina's going to be so cross when she finds out she missed Hanna pulling an entire boat."

I laugh as Una vaults over the rail with ease, landing on the deck with a solid thud. Her cheeks are flushed cherry red as she clears her throat and digs around in her satchel. I smirk. They're sweet, but incredibly obvious when they've been lovey-dovey. After a moment, she pulls out a long length of rope and deposits Hanna's weapons, boots, and trousers inside.

She tosses the rope at me; I catch it and stare down at it a second before turning my gaze back up to hers. "Tie this to the bowsprit and drop the end down to the water, poste haste."

Despite her telling me she's no longer the Captain, I still salute her. It'll take a while to break that habit. I stride across the deck and, as instructed, tie the rope around the long bow and let the other end of it sail overboard. I lean over to follow the rope's journey down to the grayish-blue water and see a dark splotch down by the rope. Hanna wastes no time in tying the rope around her waist, her large purple tail fin splashing behind her as she prepares herself for a feat I wish Ambrose could be here to witness; he'd piss his trousers. I, too, get into position, my stance once again wide, and I focus on the current of ripples under the ship as Hanna begins to swim, her tail fin beating strongly behind her. I try to help, lifting the ship from the shallows, urging the water to aid in carrying us over the waves. We lurch forward. Una's sudden laugh and Solomon's squeak of surprise has me turning to grin at them. Solomon hugs Selina against his body, the sudden motion having knocked the unconscious woman sideways.

Una laughs into the wind, putting her hands on her hips. "Now *this* is sailing in style."

***

7 June 1692 (night)
Unmarked Island north-east of Port Royal, Jamaica

I plop down next to Hanna, who's splayed in the sands in her slip, her bare feet almost being brushed by the tide as it rolls in. As the sun was setting on the end of what feels like the longest day of my twenty years, we happened upon an island. It had a shallow canal to dock the ship in and, a mile up from our port, a sandy beach. We haven't found any signs of inhabitants, just trees as far as the eye can see. It's not a big island. I'm pretty sure I could walk it in a day. But it's quiet. It's safe.

Hanna's done more than her fair share of the work. Honestly, she's gotten us here with very little of my help. I'd had to sit down when my head began to spin. My training not nearly close to being completed, I was a mere novice in her presence. We'd told her to rest herself here while we set up camp. I'd fished, using my magic to pull fish from the sea, and Selina had cleaned and gutted them while Una and Solomon foraged and build a fire. Now, I'd been sent to check on her.

"Salutations, Atropous." She opens one eye to peer at me lazily. "You did well today."

I chuckle. "I think we both know I was as helpful as a wet dishrag. You did most of the hard work." We share a companionable laugh as she sinks further into the cool sands. "Do you ache?" I ask. She pulled us for half a day, after a day to end all days.

She laughs again, the lightness of it making me smile. "I honestly didn't know one's legs could hurt so badly. I can't wait to eat and turn in for the night."

I nod, understanding. My stomach's been growling since I'd pulled up the first fish. "The fire's already set and Solomon's cooking the fish as we speak. They'll do us well through the night."

Hanna tilts her head to look up at the star-dotted sky, the small lights reminding me of a thousand little torches. "We were very fortunate."

I sigh, placing a hand over my heart in a salute. "We had a lot of people watching out for us."

She doesn't move her eyes from the sky or say anything, but I see her full lips turn up into a sad smile. We share a moment of comfortable silence, the complete stillness after the seemingly endless screams and panic and rushing water and tears like a breath of fresh winter air. My eyes are just about to close when sand crunching under a heavy boot has them flying open again.

Una stomps towards us from the camp. "You two loons ready for supper? I'd be swift if I were you, Selina burnt the last fish to ash."

In the distance, where the campfire glows against the inky night sky, Selina shrieks, "Don't you listen to a word that comes out of her lyin' mouth!"

Hanna and I look at one another before succumbing to laughter so strong, it's almost delirious. It has my stomach aching. I push myself to my feet and hold out a hand to her, the stars and the campfire and Una's laugh and Hanna's smile and Selina yelling that the Captain was nothing but a scoundrel making a small flame of hope to burn away some of the grief, the doubt, and fear.

Hanna grasps my hand, still smiling. "Look forward, not behind us."

I lace our fingers together and grip her hand tight in mine, pulling her to her feet. "Towards dawn. Towards a new day; a better day."

***

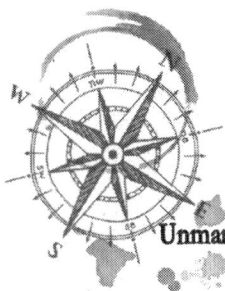

Chapter 41: Hanna

8 June 1692
Unmarked Island north-east of Port Royal, Jamaica

My hand is halfway to a bush full of reddish-blue berries when a sharp sound splits the silent, early morning sky. I'd intended to slip away from the camp before the others woke to pull together a first meal for us. My enhanced sight makes forging before the sun rises a simple task, if I can find things I recognize. The echo of the sound fades away and it looks like I've not managed to get back before the others wake. I really hope Solomon hasn't misfired my flintlock again. I wanted to save that gunpowder to trade later...

But my thoughts skitter away when I feel Una's sudden shift in emotions through the bond. My stomach twists sharply. A rush of hot rage has the satchel I've been putting the berries into slipping from my hands. Something's very, very wrong.

"Una..."

Fruit forgotten, I sprint toward the campsite as fast as my still-sore legs can carry me. Please, please let everyone still have all their fingers and toes. I don't think my heart can handle anymore misfortune...

I duck under a low swinging branch as the tether of the bond pulls me to the right of the camp, to the sandy beach I'd laid out on last night. The foliage and small bushes are loud under my boots as I dash from the cover of the canopy of trees, fully expecting to find Atropous or Solomon nursing a blown-off foot... but what I find is so much worse.

Una is down on one knee, one hand braced in the sand, the other gripping her cutlass, her hardened sea-storm gaze trained towards the shoreline. Solomon's in front of her, arms spread protectively, eyes screwed shut. Selina's standing, arms

371

raised defensively, amber eyes bright and focused. Bile rises in my throat as I follow their stares.

Elyse stands on the shore, dripping sea water, pressing a glistening, deadly dagger against Atropous's neck. Atropous is frozen, wide-eyed, Elyse's arm drapes casually over his shoulders like they're old friends despite the blade she holds to him. He, too, drips, his shoulder-length curls still a writhing thrash of sea foam. In Elyse's other hand is my own flintlock pistol, still pointed at Solomon's chest.

My stomach churns with my fear, and Una's. Though her eyes are trained on her sibling, I know she senses my presence. Elyse really is a perfect copy of my beloved, save for the jagged scar that splits her sneering face from brow to jaw. A playful smirk consumed with a twisted darkness that puts Una's deadliest look to shame. Even her blonde locks look dull and stringy compared to Una's fair spun corn-silk.

Elyse's icy eyes turn to me, so like Una's and yet so different. No glimmer of kindness burns there. It's like staring into Kai's inky black pits all over again. The only thing that keeps my trembling knees from giving out is Una's swirling coil of anger, so potent it's almost searing my flesh from my body. I feel it so strongly, I instinctively tighten my grasp on the hilt of Demetrius's rapier.

Elyse's deadly smirk cracks as she takes me in, disgusted. "I was wonderin' when you'd show your face, Hanna. Any weapons you have on you, put in the sand between me and my darling sister. One wrong move and handsome here gets a haircut. A very short one. Then go stand with the blue-skin and my foolish twin."

Without hesitation, I stride forward, pulling both my rapiers from my sash, stomach twisting around itself at how even their voices sound so similar. I hold Atropous's terrified gaze as I lay them where instructed, trying to mentally tell him it'll all be okay. Then I back up to Una and Solomon.

Solomon embraces me once I'm within range and I sag into his steady comfort, relief washing over me since that shot seems to have missed him entirely. Without taking my eyes from Elyse, I lay a hand on Una's shoulder, still knelt on the sand. She jerks at my touch and rises slowly to her feet, jaw clenched.

Elyse looks at Selina. "You too, druid. You've wasted enough of my patience. Weapons in the pile, any herbs as well, then go join your *chums*." The last word is a hissed spit.

My heart jerks into my throat. She knows of Selina's abilities! How?! Selina stomps over to the pile of weapons and delicately adds her odd antique blade to it, before obediently moving over to us and taking Solomon's large hand in hers. They hold one another's gaze as if they too share some kind of mental connection.

Elyse yawns loudly like she's bored, making Atropous startle and jump. He flinches slightly as the sharp weapon presses into the tender flesh of his neck. "Your turn, Una. All the weapons in the pile, and I do mean all of them. I remember how much you like your hiding places."

Una's rage almost singes our bond to ash as she pulls from my grasp and thrusts her cutlass into the pile. She then pulls her gun from her sash, a dirk from her sleeve, two throwing knives from the front of her brocade and tosses them into the pile as well. Just when I think she's going to rejoin us, she reaches into her leather boot and produces a small dagger, then tosses that into the ever-growing pile of weapons. With a sneer, she spits on the sand beside the weapons like she's ridding her mouth of a vile taste, and steps back to me, eyes always on her sister.

Elyse tosses my now useless flintlock over her shoulder into the ocean's clutches. It's quickly pulled out of my sight, my very first gift from my bonded now gone.

Una takes my hand, and there's a slight tremble to her fingers, her eyes a violent, worried storm. "You got what you wanted. Let him go, Elyse."

Elyse's face contorts with rage and then disgust. She scoffs before lowering the dagger from Atropous's neck and shoving him away. He stumbles forward and she kicks him hard in the rear with her boot, sending him toppling hard to the earth, his face nearly kissing the sand.

Her repulsed expression deepens, bolstered by her fury, as she watches Solomon and Selina help Atropous to his feet, though she directs her words to Una. "You've grown even more disgustingly weak in my absence." She pulls a small bracelet from her wrist and tosses in uncaringly into the sand at her feet. It's an identical bangle to the one Una wears, and has somehow managed to keep hold of since I first rescued her from the shipwreck.

Selina's mouth opens, then snaps shut again, like she's thought better about whatever she might have said, clenching her jaw and grinding her teeth instead.

Elyse smirks. "That's a good slave. You know as well as I do that one more trick like the one you pulled just now, making my shot miss your lover with the wind, and it's hello to the inside of your eyelids. Don't push yourself, little druid, you don't belong in my game anyway."

The inky vines crisscrossing Selina's arms give a weak silver pulse, as if they agree with Elyse. But how? Could she have implanted a spy among our ranks? Who... who could have it been?

Elyse plays with the dagger, running the pad of her finger along its flat side. "An entire year of following me across half the world, with endless advantages at your fingertips, and *this* is where it all gets you? You should've killed me in Port Royal when you had the chance, instead of going after this –" her hateful eyes slide to me, making my blood turn to ice *"mermaid* wench..." The vitriol in her voice makes me clench my fists as she shakes her head almost sadly, face shadowed with a darkness that makes her hardly look human. "You never were very good at thinking ahead. That gut of yours can only get you so far. Mutually beneficial alliances, coin, and people fearing you are the only things worth a damn in this life. You used to know that. This friendship you found?" She spits into the sands like Una had moments ago. "Useless."

Solomon pushes his shoulders back, lean muscled torso puffed up like Caleb used to do to make himself seem more imposing. His eyes are steel "They are not useless! They are the only things that matter in this crooked world. Not coin, or land, or the number of slaves you own, but the friendships that you make. That's something Una has that you never will."

Elyse cocks her head, mildly surprised that Solomon dared speak to her. The corners of her lips give a noticeable twitch, then another, and suddenly she's laughing. The sound is chilling. She dabs at the corners of her eyes with the back of her knuckles. "Friendship? What did *friendship* ever get me? Betrayal from my own sibling, that's what. How about Ambrose and Jonah, what did friendship get them? Or Caleb, for that matter? He saved a slave. Jonah tried to save another dirty slave, and he died in the process. But you're right. There is something my sister has that I never will. A gift for soiling everything and everyone she touches."

Una goes rigid at my side, the flame of her fury extinguished, replaced with that same desolate helplessness she'd felt at Kai's words months back now. It's a vice around my heart, squeezing until I'm sure the force is going to crush me.

My own anger licks up my spine in response. Una had only just chosen to give up on her single-minded desire to kill her sister, only just decided she wanted to come back to the cabin by the sea with me, when Elyse comes tramping from the sea and squashes her so low? Threatens this new quiet life we might have, after everything? My self-restraint snaps. "How do you know all of this?! How the hell did you get off that island and how in Poseidon's name did you find us?!"

This has another laugh spilling from her. "And he said you were the intelligent one of the group. Still can't put it all together? Perhaps you and my idiotic sister do belong together." She raises her dagger towards us, her smirk cruel, cold, evil. "Maybe I should just kill all of you now…"

Una snorts out a joyless laugh of her own, squeezing my fingers. "That'd be a bold move for you. Even without Selina's magic, you're still outnumbered. You should know that much, seeing as you seem to be all caught up on the latest gossip about everything else."

Elyse rolls her eyes. "And *you* should know outnumbered doesn't always mean immediately losing." She turns her head slightly, looking over her shoulder towards the gently lapping waters. "Why don't you come and join the game? I know you must be dying to." She waits a pause before sighing harshly. "You knew the moment we saw this many of them still alive you'd have to get your hands dirty. Come out and play with us." She sings the last words gleefully.

My temper flares again and I open my mouth to speak, when the sea begins to thrash and churn. Pushing, pulling, peaking, breaking like a violent storm is trapped within the water. It froths and foams, spilling onto the shore, swirling in a familiar way, the blob of snarled water twisting in on itself, forming itself into a human shape.

My stomach drops. Beside me, Selina gasps. Familiar, emerald eyes have a sob breaking in my throat.

"Deme?!" Seeing him whole, no longer crumpled and fragile, bloodied and broken, has tears pricking my eyes and me taking a step toward him before I can think otherwise. Elyse's dagger impaling the sand at my feet stops me.

"Did I say you could move, wench?"

I look to Demetrius, expecting him to come to my defense, but instead I meet an indifferent look, his arms causally folded over his chest. He doesn't even look at me, his eyes trained only on Elyse.

"I think your attitude may be worse than the urchin's. Our deal did not include Hanna. You would do well not to sully our alliance more than you already have, child."

Deal… alliance… The air rushes from my lungs like I've been punched squarely in the stomach. I stumble backwards into Una; her hands steady me.

"Son of a bitch…" Atropous breaths.

Demetrius finally looks at me and the darkness I see lurking in the depths of his gaze almost winds me again. He died! I saw him die! I held him as he died! My magic wouldn't work to heal him… I don't understand… this isn't right, can't be right, this uncaring thing standing there with the cruel eyes can't be him. Tears stream down my face. I can't speak. I can't breathe.

Una's grip on my fingers tighten as her anger flares. "Pathetic, lying gill-fish! I knew something felt wrong about you the moment I met you! How long?! How long have you been back-stabbing us?!"

Una's betrayal burns right alongside my own. He died… I felt him leave… He was the spy?

Atropous is shaking his head, eyes ablaze with rage. "You couldn't turn on us… what possible reason could you have for betraying your own daughter?"

376

Atropous's words seem to have an effect on my blank guardian; his pale skin ripples again, unstable, like it's lacking form. His chestnut hair darkens before flecking with graying strands. His tall stature shrinks, his thin lanky body putting on more weight. His trousers and black and blue brocade shift as well, becoming simple merchant's clothes. I'm perplexed; I've never seen this form of his before.

But Selina, Una and Atropous come alive with shock and recognition.

Selina turns wide-eyed to Una. "That's the…"

Una nods even as Selina trails off, both of them staring at Demetrius's shifted form. "The tradesman who haggled me for days and sold me *The Revenge* back in Banten…"

Solomon whimpers as if looking upon a demon and steps back. I draw back too, tugging Una with me.

Elyse laughs. "That's the form he took when he saved me from a watery death."

My stomach rolls and my body flashes hot, then ice cold. My mind is a murky fog. I'm certain only Una's hands and her rage thudding through our bond is keeping me rooted in sanity. "You… saved her? Deme, you were *dead*… I saw your body melt away. Explain this to me. I need to understand this. It's not making any sense."

Elyse snorts out another cruel laugh that makes me want to withdraw and cower. "The water spirit definitely bragged too much about you. Why'd you want to save *her,* Demetrius?"

"SILENCE!" His eyes snap shut in frustration, his voice thunderous. "Too many voices speaking at once!" His fingertips spark blue lightning and when he opens his eyes again, they pulse with a dark, ancient power. Gooseflesh breaks out across my arms. The waves behind him crash against one another, reacting to his distress. Elyse's sinister smirk falls away as she, too, takes a hesitant step from him. Her expression is one I recognize from Una – she's afraid.

Demetrius brings his hands to his head, wincing like he's in extreme pain. His skin surges yet again, changing form, this time to one I recognize. Long, straight raven hair tied at the nape of his neck, one almond-shaped nut-brown eye, the other covered by a thick black patch, high cheekbones, golden sun-tanned skin. Ezekiel?!

The form doesn't stay solid for long, he shifts and ripples like he's having trouble holding his form. His body slims out again, chestnut hair flowing over black, the length shortens. His skin bubbles again before smoothing out to the flawless, pale, Demetrius I've known all my life.

He lowers his arms, presenting himself to us with a little flourish, like he's performed a parlor trick. "I was the merchant you haggled with for your ship. You were gathering your crew far too quickly, I needed to slow your progress until Hanna was feeling well enough to meet you in that inn. If I had not intervened, Hanna would have surely perished from the unaccepted bond."

My heart leaps, my chest feeling with joy, with relief. All just a misunderstanding! He's done all of this to save me… and yet… no… why did he save Elyse and strike some kind of deal with her?

His handsome, ever-youthful face is a snarl, eyes full of nothing but malice, and I find myself, for the first time in my life, questioning everything he's ever told me, questioning everything I know about him.

Una grips my fingers, her anger warming my chilled core slightly. "Cut the shite, Demetrius! What blasted deal did you make with my sister?! Say it, you coward, you turn-coat!"

His eyes surge with a hate I've never seen in him before. "If I saved Elyse and led her here to you, she would ensure you were slain."

Solomon gasps loudly, clapping one hand over his mouth, the other clinging to both of Selina's for dear life. Selina's face is now void of shock or hurt, but undiluted rage lights her honey-colored eyes, her face shadowed with the potency of it. Atropous's anger is gone now, though. His eyes hold no hate or anger, just sorrow, and tears. He turns his head away, face ashen, as the depth of the realization hits us all. *He made a deal to have Una slain.*

"Why…" My voice cracks. I clear my throat and try again. "Why, Deme? You know what Una means to me, what she *is* to me. Why would you want her dead?"

The lightning that sparked from his fingertips earlier moves to the sky behind him in a flash. The air crackles with his energy. "When I saw you swim out to that burning pirate ship, I should have stopped you, but my curiosity gave me pause. I wanted to see what you, someone who hated pirates so venomously, would do. So I watched. Watched you save the urchin, risking your safety, *our* safety, for someone you didn't even know."

The waves churn behind him, curling against his calves. Elyse tugs nervously at the empty sash around her hips.

"You saw me save Una? You said you'd heard of the pirate ship and its burning from someone in the market! You said —"

He clicks his tongue, cutting me off, and rolls his gaze to the sky. "I saw the entire event; the ship being set ablaze by Kai himself, just as vile as I remembered him, the murder of the crew, the fight, everything. Then I watched you save her."

Una snarls beside me. "Others were dying. If you were spying the entire time, why didn't you help? You could have stopped the whole thing."

Demetrius's eyes flash with glowing fury. "Do you not listen? My kind does not meddle in human affairs, it is not our way."

Atropous shakes his head sadly, refusing to look up. "Isn't that what you're doing now? Have been doing all along? Meddling?"

Demetrius ignores the question entirely, his gaze locked on Una. He purses his lips, contemplating, the most Deme-like expression he's shown since rolling onto the shore in an angry wave. "I saw the natural bond, the attraction, forming between you both. I should have put a stop to it then, but I saw how happy the human made you…" His glowing eyes settle, soften, and finally, I'm looking into the eyes of the Demetrius I'd known my entire life. But, just as quickly, his gaze hardens on Una. "The scylla attack should have been the end of it all, but *once again,* Hanna's pure heart surprised me and she saved you, bestowed the Gift of the Sea on you, linking her to your inadequate mortal being forever." He begins to pace across the beach, hands braced behind his back like he's giving a lecture. His skin begins to bubble,

379

his whole body shuttering, rippling, shimmering in and out of solid focus, his green eyes ablaze.

"YOU!" Una roars, finger raised, accusingly. "You sent the scylla to attack?!"

No. There's no way. He wouldn't… couldn't… I'm going to vomit any moment, or faint, or possibly some combination of them both.

Demetrius shrugs with a great sigh; answering the question seems to put a great strain on him. "I truly did not mean to. I didn't think my allure would work on a beast so large. I wondered, though. You know what my curiosity's like. It started as an accident, but my allure stuck. When you struck it, the pain broke my hold on it, and it ran away."

Then I really do vomit, right into the sands at my feet, nothing but a burning liquid leaving my empty stomach, streaking out of my nose and mouth.

He continues pacing, ignoring me as Una lays a hand on my shoulder, the only thing grounding me right now. "I gave you and your idiotic crew far too much credit and we wasted precious moments bumbling around on Île Sainte-Marie. So, while you and half the crew were drinking yourselves into oblivion, I was searching and gathering information on my own."

He smirks as he paces, and it turns my stomach again. As he strides past Elyse, he ruffles her hair roughly and it makes me want to cry. Howl. Bury my face in his chest and demand he give me back my Deme.

"Remember those brutes of Elyse's we ran into upon getting there? They really were too easy to track down. It's a wonder what you can achieve when not drinking yourself silly and don't require sleep." His smirk turns taunting, the way it had when he'd pressed Elisha for information. "It's also a good thing this one here chose to enlist such a weak-willed and weak-minded crew."

Elyse's glare is murderous, her jaw working as she grinds her teeth, but she doesn't so much as mutter a word under her breath.

Demetrius turns on his heels with another flourish. "It was also *embarrassingly* easy for me to convince those fools that I was one of theirs under one of my transformations. They gave me all the information I needed to make you believe you'd gotten a lead from one of the druid's contacts."

Selina frowns deeply, thinking, then looks up, aghast. "You were my secret admirer? The one who gave us the locations on where to find Asa? How...?"

Beside her, Solomon's brows furrow. "When he went to the outhouse to relieve himself, he returned moments before we received the missive."

Demetrius points at Solomon with a grin, like he's just won a prize. "Correct! I had hoped that would be the last time I'd have to do your work for you. I was honestly relieved when we were forced into the open. Hanna's life would no longer be at risk, and she'd be healthy once more." His eyes turn deadly and my heart skips a beat in response. "*Then*, Una, you proved once again how unworthy you are to even stand in her presence. Instead of speaking to her about it, you acted like a spoiled child and risked her life. She was mere *days* from perishing."

Embarrassment and guilt fester the bond like a putrid, old wound. I seek out Una's gaze. She squares her jaw, her hand tightening on mine, but I know she's afraid I'm going to pull away.

"That's why you want me dead so badly?"

He sighs, those crazed eyes softening for just a breath. "The bond was finally accepted, and you were back to your usual self, better even, and I was glad..." Then his eyes cloud again. "Then everyone became placid, content, so much so that interest in finding Elyse and Kai waned. Near half a year and not a single shred of information. So, I, once again, had to do your work for you." He glances at Elyse. "Clever move replacing your crew upon arriving in Port Royal. It took me some time to find a way in." He pokes the tip of her nose in a playful manner. "But keeping the anger-filled weak-willed Ezekiel sealed my victory in that move of the game." His focus shifts to me once more. "Your neglect, your sweet honeymoon period, made it easy for me to search without fear of being caught. I disguised myself as Ezekiel and let Caleb find me in that pub. The fat oaf truly thought he'd put the nail in your coffin, Elyse. Ezekiel's mind was all too easy to manipulate, extract his memories, implant everything Caleb and I discussed. After that, Ezekiel did everything exactly as I wanted him to, thinking it his ideas the entire time. A simple extension of my allure."

"You made a puppet of him," Atropous mutters.

Solomon gasps aloud again. Selina swears hotly in her foreign tongue, her face hardening. I feel like I've been struck several times then dropped into the ocean during the middle of winter. I don't recognize this person. He's a stranger to me now.

Una wrenches her hand free of mine. "BASTARD! Hanna almost died that night, was that part of your game as well?!"

Tendrils of spiraling water twist around him like they had that night he killed Kai. "I meant for you to be the one to taste Kai's blade. Hanna being injured was an unfortunate miscalculation on my part… but, like most things in this world, the outcome was a double-edged blade. Her healing powers awoke to save her own life, but she saved you again." He stops his endless pacing, turning his glare to my bond-mate. "You've proven, time and time again, annoyingly resilient. Found yourself a sense of honor in there somewhere, too. Too late, since your crew were all dead by then."

I shake my head slowly, bringing my arm to wipe away my tears. My sorrow shakes my body, seeping into every crevice of my soul, tearing through me like I'm nothing more than parchment. "You were losing me to Una. That terrified you. You kept trying, and failing, to get rid of her… and in the end, you knew I'd never forgive you if I found out you harmed her in any way. You had to make sure Elyse survived so she could finish what nothing else could." I slide my eyes away from him, my heart cold, dead, unfeeling in my chest. A part of me has been stolen.

"Won't Miss Hanna die if Una dies?" Solomon's voice is barely above a whisper.

I shake my head sadly, looking deeply into the sands wishing nothing more than for them to open and swallow me up. The feeling intensifies as Deme speaks, his voice emotionless, like he's reading out of one of his huge books. "Once bonded, the mermaid's life is out of danger. If Una dies, it bears no ill on Hanna. There are rare occurrences when, if the will of the bonded is strong enough, the magic of the bond will snap, and the mermaid will perish. But I could see plain enough that Una wasn't strong enough to do that."

"Deme, did you really feel Kai's lingering energy on me, or… or did you…?" I press a hand to my mouth and swallow the bile that rises again. "Demetrius, what did you do to my mother?"

Guilt enters his eyes for the first time since his appearance on the beach, a flash of the old Demetrius of my youth, of the one who always told me he loved me, would care for me. "I did sense Kai's energy threads, yes. And your– your mother was always so secretive about her mermaid upbringing. I didn't know Kai leaving permanently would shatter their bond and kill her. I just wanted my friend back…"

Demetrius had somehow convinced Kai to leave my mother. He'd used his allure, or mind control, or similar. He was the reason I lost the only parent that ever really loved me and was tossed into hell. He'd been the cause of her bond shattering, of her death, all of it. And he wanted to kill Una too… all out of jealousy? My knees give way, and only Una and Atropous on either side of me keep me from falling.

"It wasn't a lie that she came back to me in the end and with her final breaths asked me to find you…"

My sadness flares into rage once again at his words. "You never truly cared for me at all! I was just a way for you to atone? To make yourself feel less guilty for killing your best friend?"

The glow fades from his eyes, and they fill with tears.

The sky groans with thunder, the clouds grow darker, the lightning flashes, illuminating his tall, lanky, frame, suddenly frail-looking. "At first, yes. I cared for you in hopes that one day my sins could be forgiven. But sometime in your fifteenth year, I found you crying in your room, that same unquenchable loneliness *I* felt in *your* eyes, and I found myself wanting to ease your pain. You truly became my daughter that day, not out of obligation, or guilt, but out of love."

My throat burns and that lump that had been choking me dissolves as my tears once again begin to stream down my face. I hang my head. No… no, no…

"I only wanted it to go back to how it used to be," he pleads. "I didn't want to be alone."

I can't bring myself to look at him. My heart is broken.

Una is livid; the heat rushing through the bond makes me lightheaded. Before I can collect myself, Una explodes. "And now that Hanna knows every dark, dirty thing you've ever done, what's your plan now? Huh?! Let's say you two do manage to kill Selina, Solomon, Atropous and I? Then what? Do you really think she's going to go with you after unearthing all this? Are you going to force her? Get inside her head? Are you willing to hurt your daughter, Demetrius?"

He physically stumbles back toward the sea as if she's landed a punch squarely on his jaw. The wind around us picks up. The waves crash against the shore. He grips one side of his head, like he's trying to hold himself together. "I…" He's shaking his head, face contorted. "No, I… I do not want this! You… you're all so loud! I want it how it was! I… don't know…" He brings up his other hand, his skin no longer looking human or solid. He ripples and shimmers, his hair a writhing mass of water thrashing around his shoulders like it has a will of its own.

Una, watching him with eyes narrowed, seizes his distracted uncertainty, and darts towards the pile of weapons. Elyse has the same thought, lunging forward, each of them drawing a weapon. Elyse grabs Selina's antique blade, Una has her cutlass. They straighten at the same time, blades pointed at one another. Demetrius remains frozen to the shoreline, pressing the heels of his palms into his eyes, his body trembling like the last leaf about to drop in a storm. The twins surge towards one another, screaming into the wind. Their blades clash, steel against iron, again and again as they thrust, parry, dancing back and forth in the sand, grunting, shoving, striving, each desperate to draw the other's blood. I can't move, my legs can't support me. Atropous is trying to hold me up and I look at him, pleading.

"Do something! Help Una!"

He shakes his head, shame flushing his cheeks. "Something stung my heel as I was coming up from a swim. Then Elyse had a dagger to my throat. I haven't been able to feel connected to the water since. I kept trying to throw a wave at them all that while… it's not working. My legs and upper arms have gone numb. I've lost my power… forgive me…"

Selina grabs him. "Show me the sting. Precisely where the pain comes from."

Atropous blinks at her and raises his bare foot so she can inspect it, keeping one hand under my elbow to stop either of us from falling.

Selina peers at it a moment before curling her lip in distaste. "Jellyfish venom and patchouli. A dampening tonic… it cuts you off from the magic around you, but it's not permanent. Strong, though. I'm surprised only your legs and arms are numb. The nymph has utterly lost it. He's crossed a line. That tonic is forbidden, dark magic."

No, he can't be lost… he's ill. Something is very wrong with him. We must help him somehow. Poor, poor Demetrius.

Deme's lower half seems to have disintegrated into mist while his upper half shifts between holding a solid human form and a swelling breaking wave. His hands are still clenched at his face and head. In front of him, back and forth, the sisters duel, like one image flipped in a mirror. Despite drastically different weapons, they match each other move for move. As Elyse goes high, Una's already there to block her. If Una moves right, Elyse's stepping to match it. They move with a deadly fluid grace that takes years to hone, hours of practice. Just when I think neither of them will make any headway, Elyse ducks under Una's horizontal slash, grabs a handful of sand as she spins, and hurls it into Una's face. Elyse sweeps her leg and Una comes crashing down to the sand, her cutlass skittering away from her.

"UNA!" I scream.

"Not today, wench! Aileen, to me!" Selina's command cuts through the crackling air like a fresh bolt of lightning, her hand thrust out in front of her. The ancient sword, which Elyse has raised high ready to deliver the final blow to a blind and fumbling Una, trembles. It makes a high-pitched trilling noise, like a bird, before wrenching itself free from her grasp and flying toward Selina's outreached hand, hilt first. Selina grips her weapon, Aileen, her black tattoos pulsing with silver light.

385

As Elyse stares, dumbfounded, Una recovers and wastes no time in tackling her gasping sister to the sand. She balls her left hand and grips the front of Elyse's shirt with her right, before delivering a swift punch to Elyse's face. The satisfying sound of Elyse's nose crunching echoes along the beach. Una hauls her dazed sibling to her feet, spinning her and pressing a forearm across her throat, holding her tight.

Elyse flails, tries to bring a fist up to punch her, but Una squeezes her throat tighter. "I wouldn't do that if I were you." She digs her free hand up under her voluminous shift and pulls out a gleaming, thin, silver shiv. "Since you know I like hiding places so much, you should have seen this coming."

Elyse seethes in Una's hold, dropping her arms lifelessly to her sides. Her lips are curled in rage, blood coating her teeth from her split lip and busted nose.

Una looks over at us, me on my knees, Atropous still holding one of my elbows, Solomon, and Selina on either side of us. "Ya couldn't have done the magic trick with the sword *before* I got a mouthful of sand? I'll be tasting this shite forever."

Selina's honeyed eyes glint with mischief as she loops the now-lifeless sword through her weathered sash. "Had to get my strength back. Besides, everyone needs a trump card up their sleeve, Captain, and I figured you needed the exercise."

Una snorts a laugh even as Elyse splutters, struggling to breathe in her stranglehold. My relief that Una's unharmed, let alone able to exchange quips now, makes me giggle out a strange choking sob.

"It's alright, my raven," Una reassures me.

Elyse raises a pitiful hand towards the still-out-of-commission Demetrius.

Selina laughs. "No use asking him for help, filth. He won't be helping anyone anymore. You lose, Elyse."

Elyse gnashes her blood-stained teeth at us, her eyes full of hate as she struggles to break free.

Una only shakes her head. "Even you aren't fool enough to try something while completely pinned down, lose with digni—"

"DIVE down! NOW!" Atropous's shout of alarm instantly has me dropping flat to my stomach, arms coming up to cover my head and neck. Sounds above me and sounds of the others dropping down around me fills my ears, my heart thudding right along. What is it? What now?!

I force myself to count to thirty before daring to raise my head, and nearly inhale a lung-full of sand as I gasp at what I see. We'd all of us heeded Atropous's warning, Una even abandoning her sibling to take shelter on her belly, except Elyse. Elyse had stayed on her feet, and now two thick stakes of swirling water pierce through her torso: one between her breasts and one in her abdomen. Her eyes are huge, staring down at the sharp points of surging water spearing her, blood already dribbling thickly from her mouth and onto the sand.

I follow those spears of water to their origin and find them emanating from Demetrius. What used to be Demetrius. He's completely unrecognizable, that vapor now consuming him up to his chest. The spears of water piercing Elyse are what were his arms. The waters of Demetrius's hair surge, the glowing pits of his eyes stare ahead, unseeing, as he begins to pull the water spikes back into himself, drawing Elyse towards him, flinging her free of the spikes in in one quick jerk. She sails through the air, over Demetrius's shoulder, like she weighs nothing, and hits the ocean, disappearing beneath the waves.

Una's astonishment thumps through the bond, only amplifying mine. I dig my fingers into the cool sands, my breaths quick, my heartbeat loud in my ears. Elyse... is dead...

Atropous is first to push himself to his knees, eyes wide with fear. He slowly stands to his feet, legs visibly shaking as he faces the thing that was Demetrius. "We... we have to get away. We can't..." His voice cracks as he turns his forlorn gaze on us.

I understand his fear, the need to run away. My own fear threatens to undo me, along with all the grief and anger. Part of me hates Demetrius now, despises him for what he did to my mother, to Una, to all of us. The creature thrashing in front of me is not my father.

And yet, he is.

Thirteen years, he took care of me, taught me, raised me, loved me in his own way.

"Over here, Guppy. You did it!"

"I am so proud of you, Hanna, I knew you could."

"Do not fear crying, for it shows how much you truly care."

"I'm here for you."

"I love you."

"I am your father, regardless of where we started. I chose to love you when I didn't have to. That, that is what makes us family."

My heart shatters all over again as I push myself up from the sand. All around me, the rest of the remaining crew, my family, are rising to their feet, varying degrees of panic on their faces. Solomon rushes forward, quickly gathering our discarded weapons, nervously watching the unraveling nymph the entire time.

A hand on my shoulder jerks my attention to a serious-faced Una. Her other hand cups my cheek, her gaze the only thing holding me to this earth as my entire world is turned upside down. She fixes me with her steadying gaze, nods once at me. She only drops her hand when Solomon hands her weapons to her. He holds out my two rapiers, my heart stuttering as I slide Demetrius's silver sword through the loop in my belt. As Solomon hands Atropous his gun and sword, Demetrius's spiked arms slowly begin to drip, melting away to reveal semi-liquid human arms underneath.

"Atropous, how are you feeling?"

Atropous looks down. "Still numb, but truthfully, even if I were at my full power and not almost pissing myself in fear, I don't think I could subdue him. He's too strong."

Una laces her fingers into mine. "You have to talk to him." She's calm, her rage spent now. "He'll listen to you. The only thing he really cares about in this world is you."

The last shards of my heart crumble to dust and, like Atropous's arms, my body feels numb. I turn to look into Demetrius's blazing whirlpool eyes, so crazed and unseeing I'm unsure if even this will get through to him. Shakily, I step towards him. His legs are still a sea mist. His skin is still fluid. "Deme, please... cease this. You can end this. You're unwell. I understand why you were so upset. You thought I was going to leave you like my mother did. You didn't want to be alone or forgotten. You were afraid. Come back to me, and let's go home, all of us. Please, Father..."

The wind around us calms, the dark clouds begin to lighten, the surging surf begins to settle. The ethereal inhuman glow in the flaming abys of his eyes dies down. Am I getting through to him? Hope surges in me; I reach out a hand to him... but he begins to laugh.

The sound is sharp, a twisted cackle that slowly grows higher, more maniacal. His body begins to rock with the force of it. His spine extends, his shoulders flex, as he turns his head upwards. That spark of hope is snuffed out as quickly as it was lit.

"Understand?" His voice is the wind over the ocean at night, the thundering of waves, the roar of the tide in the caves. "I used to think you understood. That we could stay together by the ocean forever, but it is clear to me now that the human has tainted you... like Kai tainted your mother..."

I shake my head, trying to take his face in my hands. "Father, no... please..."

He jerks away from me, that unnatural glow bursting back to life in his eyes. The vapor that had started as his legs has nearly consumed him now, up to his chin, and he's more of a ghostly figure than solid form. "The humans have been tipping the balance slowly in their favor for centuries..." Those bottomless eyes are chasms that stare straight through me. "It is time it was finally tipped in favor of nature."

My stomach bottoms out again; dread consumes me. I try again. "Deme, please, reconsider this."

His face is gone. His voice is disembodied. He is a sea mist, formless. He begins to recede out over the ocean. "The time for talking is over, child, the next step is action." His glowing eyes fizzle out until just a thin wisp of him remains, then the bodiless voice speaks again, and I feel the vibrations, the finality of it, reverberate through my entire essence. "The next time we cross paths, I will not show mercy to any of you. You are either on the side of nature or against it, against me."

And just like that, the cloud of mist disperses across the ocean, into the sky.

The air is sucked from me. My cry breaks in my throat and my legs give out. Una is beside me, catching me, cradling me, pulling me to her chest before I can fall, and then three other pairs of arms are tightening around me too, the only things holding me upright, holding me together. My tears soak the front of Una's clothes as I sob out my heartbreak, my grief.

We're all crying.

All crying for different reasons; Atropous for a lost teacher, Solomon for a lost friend, Una for the betrayal and her lost sibling, Selina for the family she never thought she would have, and I for the only father I've ever known, who betrayed me and has broken me, possibly beyond repair. His ominous words ring loud in my ears and I know he meant every word of it. He'd given in to his primal elemental nature. He was never human. He was a thing of emotion, of extremes, and now humanity is in grave danger.

I gulp down my tears and find Una already looking down at me, her cheeks pink from crying and for a moment, feel the silent strength from the people surrounding me. "I have to stop him. There is light in Deme, still. I know I can bring him home…"

Selina lays her cheek on my shoulder, tears clinging to her dark lashes like stars in the night sky. "What if talking doesn't get through to him? What will you do?"

I tighten my arms around Una's waist, grasping onto the tether, ever my saving grace, ever my constant comfort. "I will stop him and make sure the order of things stays in balance, no matter the cost."

Una presses a kiss onto my head, her gleaming eyes full of pride and love. "We will stop him. Like we're going to let you do this alone."

One by one, each of them nod, laying a hand on a part of me. Solomon on my left shoulder, Selina on my right, Atropous's large hand on the top of my head.

Tears blur my vision again. "You will?"

Solomon squeezes my shoulder, his dawn-breaking smile lighting the balls of his cheeks. "Of course. We're family, and like Atropous said at Port Royal, we're going to bring all of us home. Demetrius counts too."

My chest constricts and I choke out a sob.

Atropous ruffles my hair like Deme used to do, his eyes glistening. "You aren't alone, Hanna. You have us, and you will always have us, until your last breath. You can't get rid of us that easily."

Selina nods too, my unlikely sister. "Another grand adventure then? Sounds like we have much raiding to do."

I snort out a laugh, somehow, despite the tears still slipping down my cheeks, and the cavern in my chest where my heart used to be.

Surrounded by my found family, I know no matter where this next journey leads us, we will succeed.

We will find Demetrius, stop this war from starting, and then, all of us will go home.

The End

For Now...

With Demetrius's vow to put nature on top, what lines will Hanna have to cross to make sure he doesn't destroy everything she holds dear? What truths will she discover about her father, mother, and herself? Will Una and Hanna's bond be strong enough to withstand this storm? Or will their journey meet its end long before the war even begins?

To be continued in book 2 of The Harmony Series: *The Truth of the Sea*

Coming soon.

About the Author

Tabatha Bishop lives in too-humid Texas, with her younger sister, mother and bratty husky named Nakita. A long time dreamer with the goal of publishing her very own book, but always too shy to even attempt, now breaking out of her comfort zone to bring you stories that, hopefully, stay with you, bring a smile to your face, or heck, even tears to your eyes - she's not picky.

When not writing, which isn't often, you can find her reading (both books and manga), taking pretty photos, watching anime, and trying out new recipes in her kitchen. Continue following her writing and life journeys at @t_bishop_writes and see her latest book-related inspiration by following Tabatha Bishop on Pinterest and Spotify, updated daily.

Made in the USA
Las Vegas, NV
26 December 2021

39477752R00231